MR FINCHLEY TAKES THE ROAD

MR FINCHLEY, BOOK 3

Victor Canning

This edition published in 2019 by Farrago,
an imprint of Prelude Books Ltd
13 Carrington Road, Richmond, TW10 5AA, United Kingdom

www.farragobooks.com

By arrangement with the Beneficiaries of the
Literary Estate of Victor Canning

First published by Hodder and Stoughton in 1940

ISBN: 978-1-78842-163-8

With grateful acknowledgment to John Higgins

Printed and bound in Great Britain by Clays Ltd, Elcograf S.p.A.

Have you read them all?

Treat yourself again to all three Mr Finchley novels –

Mr Finchley Discovers His England
A middle-aged solicitor's clerk takes a holiday for the first time and finds himself in all sorts of unexpected adventure.

Mr Finchley Goes to Paris
On the point of proposing marriage, Mr Finchley is unexpectedly sent to Paris, and gets into a fine tangle.

Mr Finchley Takes the Road
Finchley marries and explores the countryside in a horse-drawn caravan, attracting more interest than he bargained for.

Turn to the end of this book for a full list of Victor Canning's humorous works, plus – on the last page – the chance to receive **further background material**.

For my daughter
Lindel

'…they saw a gipsy caravan, shining with newness, painted a canary yellow picked out with green and red wheels. "There you are!" cried Toad, straddling and expanding himself. "There's real life for you, embodied in a little cart. The open road, the dusty highway, the heath, the common, the hedgerows, the rolling downs! Camps, villages, towns, cities! Here today, up and off somewhere else tomorrow! Travel, change, interest, excitement! The whole world before you, and a horizon that's always changing!"'

Kenneth Grahame, *The Wind in the Willows*

Contents

I
In which Mr. Finchley retires

IT IS unlikely that many people noticed Mr. Finchley that morning. Not because Mr. Finchley was the sort of man you wouldn't notice, but because it was the sort of morning when people's thoughts had little place for other men and women. It was a summer morning, a bright, slightly metallic morning with the air full of the warmth of dusty gutters and hot roof tiles. It was a pleasant, stirring warmth that invited the mind to thoughts of the country and lazy scenes that lay so close in the summer's future.

It was a morning for walking to the tube station or bus point with a stare of mild preoccupation and the beginnings of a self-satisfied smile about the lips. Girl typists and shop assistants thought of hot beaches and coloured bathing costumes, and their nostrils caught the phantom odour of dead seaweed and the alien smell of boarding houses; young clerks and students twitched their shoulders to the imagined weight of rucksacks and remembered dark little bar parlours in country villages where their long thirsts caused no comment; family men recalled drowsy days in deck chairs and the squeal of excited children around a stranded starfish ... In the stretch of road that is Haverstock Hill, Mr. Finchley, had he any reason to concern himself with the thoughts of his fellows that morning, would have been surprised at the exuberance of summer thoughts that the warm morning sun had drawn out. The road was crammed with enough memories of summer and holidays to stock a seaside town and crowd the beaches of Devon to unpleasantness.

Mr. Finchley was only aware of his fellows as part of the general movement about him. For more years than he liked to recall he had moved down the hill each morning surrounded by a city-going crowd. He, like the hundreds about him, was part of the great morning routine. There had been mornings when he had resented the inflexibility of the economic system which had kept him moving each morning between his home and his office, like a tide pulled and moved about by the moon, and there had been times when he had longed to face about and walk away from the tube station, right out into the blue of forbidden delights.

This morning things were quite different. For him this was no ordinary morning. In himself he showed no signs of the change which was close upon him. He walked soberly along, his umbrella hooked over one arm, his morning paper tucked into place under his shoulder and his bowler hat pushed back, not enough to disturb his dignity but just enough to indicate that the morning was better than usual. His black coat, his grey-striped trousers and his brilliantly polished black shoes were just as they always were, the neat, orderly symbols of his clerkly profession. He walked with the faintly important step of a man who is short and inclined to plumpness and who has borne nearly fifty years of life without losing much of his optimism or faith in the ultimate decency of everyday people and things. And the face which looked out under the bowler hat reflected much of this philosophy. It was a large, round face, genial but losing no firmness to mere unconsidered good humour. It was the pleasant, controlled face of a man who knew how to laugh, when to be stern and how to fly the signals that proclaimed, through the subtle evidence of crease and line, that here was one who had a natural sympathy for his fellows without inviting exploitation of his good nature.

It was this sympathy which was swaying Mr. Finchley that morning. It gave him a sense of guilt that he was so close to escaping for ever from the habits of a lifetime, from the habits which would still hold firmly the rest of the people around him. He was escaping. This was the last morning he would ever go down to the office. Already some of the last things were done. He had already come out of his house on the corner of Nassington Avenue and walked quietly into Haverstock Hill, dropping into the newsagent's shop for his paper and pipe tobacco.

"Morning, Mr. Finchley," the tobacconist had called. "Nice morning."

He had handed Mr. Finchley his paper and tobacco and for a moment Mr. Finchley had hesitated. He felt he ought to tell the man that this was the last time he would come in of a morning. For years he had been handing him his "usual" and for years he had never strayed beyond the strict conversational limits of "nice," "cold" or "wet morning."

He had gone out, telling the man nothing. It would have been wrong to trample down the habit of years by starting a conversation on his last morning.

All the way to the tube station he had been watching out for "last" things, taking a queer pleasure in recognising them and trying to still that faint awakening of shame because he was looking for them. It was the last time he would walk by the cab rank regularly at eight fifty-two and see the drivers lounging round the counter of their shelter, drinking tea and reading folded copies of the racing sheets. It was the last time he would knock out his breakfast pipe opposite the post office and a few yards from the station entrance. In the years he had knocked his pipe out there the accumulated ash would have amounted to quite a spectacular pile ...

He entered the station entrance, gave himself up to the urge of work-bound folk and became one, for the last time, of that quiet, paper-reading, patient crowd. The gates of the lift clanged home like the grill of a prison and the floor dropped away.

He was on his way to the office for the last time. The young men about him had years of work before them, and the older men had many of them to go on working much longer than he had worked. He had earned the right to retire but, for all that, he could not rid himself of the sense of desertion which was growing with every moment that brought him nearer the office and closer to other workers. Last night, this morning had seemed a happy prospect, and now the morning was proving to be a changeable pleasure. The habit of work could not be easily broken. There was pain in parting from a routine which had once roused thoughts of revolt.

Mr. Finchley tried to forget that this was his last morning. He tried to act as though this were one morning out of many more to come, but the sight of a young girl opposite him in the train reading her library book, her attaché case balanced on her lap, took his thoughts away from the paper. The girl would be there tomorrow morning, reading her book. Many of the people would be there in the same compartment, all being carried to their offices and shops—and he would be at home. They would not miss him. He realised now that he would miss them.

He must have been staring at the young girl unconsciously, for she suddenly raised her head a little and over the top of the book gave him a faint smile.

Mr. Finchley returned the smile. It was part of the freemasonry of travel. As her eyes went back to her book, Mr. Finchley felt a little happier. He was not yet an outcast.

At nine-twenty exactly Mr. Finchley entered the offices of Sprake and Bardwell, Solicitors. The office boy gave him a bright and undistinguished good morning, as though he were determined not to make any special fuss about the retirement of a managing clerk who had addressed occasional hard words to him.

Within ten minutes Mr. Finchley was at work. It was a busy morning and he was glad of it, and he was glad too that no one made any mention to him of the special occasion. There was only one thing to mark the day, and that was the quiet deference with which people asked his advice and put their work before him. By lunchtime he felt as though he were a patient for whom absolute quiet had been prescribed, with the warning that any refusal of his desires would bring about an immediate relapse. His typist spoke to him in a quiet voice as though the shock of normal conversational tones would be too much for him; the other clerks addressed him with a subdued, vaguely conciliatory suggestion in their speech which made him feel like an old man. Only the office boy was unaffected. He whistled down the corridor and banged the mailing-room door. Mr. Finchley welcomed the sounds where before he had frowned at them.

He went out for lunch with a friend from a neighbouring office. They had lunched together for years.

"So this is your last day," said his friend. He was a dry-humoured, thin man, a bachelor.

"It is."

"And are you glad or sorry?"

Mr. Finchley hesitated and played with the salt cellar. "I really don't know. It's difficult to ..."

"Course you don't know. It's a bit of both, I suppose. Glad because you've finished with work and sorry because the mere fact of finishing with work indicates that you're no longer young. You've changed, you know, Finchley. Two years ago and I should have said you were heading for the same fate as myself—a crusty old bachelordom. Then you go and surprise us all by marrying and adopting a boy. It was a brave thing to do."

"It was the wisest thing I ever did," asserted Mr. Finchley sincerely. "You've no idea how it changed my life."

"Nonsense. I've every idea. Wish I could do the same myself. Well, well—don't let's get sentimental. This is the last time we shall lunch together like this." He stirred his coffee noisily and then leaned back and slipped his hand into his coat pocket. "I've got something for you. Here, take it."

Mr. Finchley found himself holding a long, round paper parcel.

"What is it?"

"Open it and see."

Mr. Finchley opened the parcel. It held a long bottle made of green-tinted glass. Inside the bottle was a ship model. Mr. Finchley's face brightened with pleasure at the beauty of the model. It was a three-masted sailing ship, all sails set, leaning strongly into a cotton-wool sea.

"Isn't she a beauty?" asked his friend. "Every detail perfect. You feel that if you once broke the seal on the mouth of the bottle and let the wind get to her she'd sail away from you."

"It's lovely," said Mr. Finchley quietly. "But I can't take it from you. You couldn't want to give it away."

"Quite right. I don't want to, but I'm going to. You're going to have it. I've had that model since I was a boy. I bought it in Plymouth at the end of the last century, saved up my pocket money for months. Every piece of sail, every block and spar on that boat was carved from bone. I believe it was made by French prisoners of war at Princetown in Boney's day. It has a history, a ship like that would have. You take it, Finchley—I want you to have it. You take her. She's out of place in my lodgings. It's time she set some youngster dreaming again. Your boy'll love her …"

Mr. Finchley looked at his friend. Their friendship had been long, but it had seldom gone further than the confidences and conversations over their daily lunch. For a moment he was permitted to see more of the man's real nature and he wondered that he had never suspected this hidden love before. It was true that only at the end of their acquaintance had they come any closer …

"Robert will love her," he said, and he thought of his son, who was away at school. "*Le Bon Accord*," he read the ship's name from the gilded prow.

"Yes, *Le Bon Accord*," mused his friend. "How many years ago was it that I saw her in a shop window in Plymouth? Since then, I've sailed with her all over the world and she's a reliable ship—she always gets me back to Camden Town in time to walk into the office at nine every morning. Ha, well, must be getting along. Let me know how you are from time to time."

He was gone before Mr. Finchley could stop him. Mr. Finchley went soberly back to the office, hugging his parcel. At four o'clock he was conscious of a growing stir in the office. His typist disappeared, the corridor was full of quiet footsteps and whispers and once or twice he heard a giggle or two.

Unheralded by whistle or slamming door, the office boy came in to him and with deliberate unconcern said "Mr. Sprake would like to see you, sir."

Mr. Finchley nodded and rose. He could guess what was coming, and he found his stomach revisited by those gnawing, hopeless fears which had possessed him as a boy before examinations or after disastrous misdeeds.

Of the firm of Sprake and Bardwell, there was left only Mr. Sprake. Mr. Sprake was a jolly, sporty man, fond of good living and company. He looked like a wealthy butcher and he had the strange power, which fortunately few men possess, of welding to themselves a half-gale of wind, like some harnessed genie, so that when he entered any room loose papers flapped and robust draughts went racing round the walls lifting the pictures. He was also an astute and scrupulous solicitor.

Mr. Finchley opened the door of Sprake's room and stepped inside. The whole of the office staff was crowded into the little room, leaving a free space before the fire.

Here, legs straddled, thumbs tucked into the armpits of his waistcoat, stood Sprake. At the sight of Mr. Finchley he let out a lusty bellow of welcome and stepped forward.

The staff began to clap, timidly at first, as though they were anxious not to impair the authoritative aura of the head of the firm's room, and then more vigorously, taking courage from one another. Mr. Finchley was possessed by a strong desire to turn and run. He hesitated. Sprake seized him by the arm and drew him to the fireplace.

"Come on, my dear Finchley! There's no escape from this!" Sprake half-guessed what was in Mr. Finchley's mind.

"Good old Finchley!" A thin voice piped from the back of the staff and Mr. Finchley saw a conveyancing clerk turn and frown at the office boy.

"Ladies and gentlemen!" Sprake held up a hand for silence and his voice boomed confidently around the room. "Ladies and gentlemen, fellow-members of the staff—" he let his eye roam over the men and women and finished with a broad smile for Mr. Finchley. "We all know the reason for this occasion, and we all know what Mr. Finchley's feelings must be today. For that reason I do not feel it would be right for us to cause him more embarrassment than we can help. But there are some things we must say and do. Mr. Finchley is retiring after thirty years' service in this office, thirty years of loyalty and honest application to the interests of this firm, thirty years in which he has won and maintained the affection of all of us here and many more who have passed through this office. His is a record of which any man might be proud. We shall miss him, we cannot deny that, and some of us may jealously feel that he might have stopped a little longer with us. But there is not one of us who does not sincerely wish him every happiness in the years of his retirement. He is retiring early because—lucky man—he can afford it and because—wise man—he knows that if you leave your retirement too late the habit of work is so strongly ingrained in your system that it becomes almost impossible to make a new life. However, what Mr. Finchley intends to do in his new life, I don't know. Perhaps he'll tell us himself in a minute. But whatever it is, I feel I have your absolute good will when I say that each one of us here wishes him the best of luck and the greatest of happiness, and it is because we feel so that we ask him now to accept, as only a small and inadequate indication of our affection for him, this watch and cheque—"

He turned to Mr. Finchley and held out to him a small leather case and an envelope.

"Go on," he cried, amid laughter. "Take them, they're for you."

Mr. Finchley took the gifts and held them. In all his pictures of this moment he had never imagined the weight of sentiment and feeling which would close upon him. For a moment he was seeing each member of the staff in a new light. They were his friends, they were smiling at him now, calling pleasantly to him to open his gifts, and for a second or two he was superbly conscious of the ties that grow between men and women when they work together for years.

He snapped back the lid of the leather case and took out the watch. It was of gold and was inscribed on the back, *Affectionately Presented to Edgar Finchley, Esquire, by the Staff of Messrs. Sprake and Bardwell, Solicitors, on the Occasion of his Retirement and in Recognition of his many years' loyal Service.* Under the inscription was that day's date. In the envelope was a cheque for thirty pounds.

"Speech, speech!" cried someone and the cry was taken up. Mr. Finchley turned to them.

"Thank you," he said, his voice catching a little and then strengthening as he went on. "Thank you for these magnificent gifts. I don't deserve them, nor the nice things which Mr. Sprake has said about me. While I've been in this office I've only done what any other man would have done, and there have been times when I have been irritable and short-tempered. Because a man is retiring it doesn't make him an angel. Still, I do think we've been as happy here as in any office. You ask me what I am going to do when I have retired, and all I can tell you is that I wish I knew exactly. I'm going to leave London and go and live in the country. What I shall do there I don't know, but whatever it is and wherever I am, I shall always be reminded of this office when I look at this watch, and of your generosity and affection …"

He could not go on. He was aware that the words he had spoken were only the conventional response to what was a common situation. Suddenly he was bereft of words and the real emotion engulfed him and held him prisoner. He could only feel.

And the people in the room shared his feeling. They seemed to know what was happening. For a moment an awkward silence settled on the room. Sprake's red face turned towards the window, a girl typist frittered at her handkerchief and the clerks hawked in their throats with little sounds of nervous embarrassment, and then from the back of the room an adolescent, piping voice sang out, off key, and wavering—"For he's a jolly good fellow …"

This time there was no frown and in a second the whole room was singing heartily, glad to find an escape from its hesitancy.

Mr. Finchley went home, carrying his gifts and a few personal possessions. The evening was dusty and hot, the newsboys loafed at the street corners and sparrows in the gutters seemed too tired to quarrel and the whole eventide movement of workers was sensibly slower and more leisurely. For the first time, Mr. Finchley realised that it had been a blazing hot day.

He walked down Nassington Avenue until he reached his house, which was on the corner. It was a neat little house, modest, well-kept and with a space at the side for a garage. The agent had told him that he could sell it for twelve hundred pounds almost any day. Mr. Finchley wondered when that day would be.

He went in and was greeted by his wife. Mrs. Finchley was a small, dark-haired woman with humorous, restless eyes and a gentle, birdlike habit of moving her head as though her interest in things around her could never be satisfied. Her voice was quiet, but with a firm inflexion that told of a strong faith in her own convictions. Mr. Finchley had known her as a widow for some years before they had married and adopted a small boy, Robert. Their marriage had been a success chiefly because they both appreciated that there is much in late marriages which can wreck them. They made allowances for one another's personalities and they understood that it was hard to break cleanly from the habits of bachelor life or the indulgent comforts of a comfortable widowhood. To hold them together more firmly was their love for the small Robert.

"So it's all over, dear?" She spoke gently.

"Yes, it's over. I'm a free man," said Mr. Finchley, as he moved towards the dining-room.

"I'm glad. Were they nice to you?"

"They gave me a watch and a cheque. It was far more than I expected, and they were all splendid. I was quite sorry to go."

Mrs. Finchley looked at the watch, turning it over in her hand. She glanced up anxiously at her husband. It was very largely her idea that he should retire. She had a comfortable income and he himself was moderately well off. It was she who had persuaded him to leave the office some years before he would normally have done so. She watched him anxiously to see whether this mood of sadness was more than the gentle melancholy which must attend all separations.

"It's a beautiful watch. They must have been very fond of you. But that's no reason why you should go on working any longer. You have been with the firm ever since you were a boy, you've given them the best part of your life. Now you deserve a chance to do what you want to do. We can go and live in the country. Both you and Robert have talked about that for months, and you know that I want to go …"

"You're right, dear. It's no good letting myself get too sentimental. Still, I can't help feeling a little sad."

"Let's have supper. We can talk afterwards. It's been such a hot day, I thought you'd like cold salmon and a salad. Look—" she indicated the table.

It was spread with cool cutlery and shining glass and reflected in the table lights were the green of salad and the pinky flesh of fish. Standing at the side of the table in an ice-pail was a bottle.

"Champagne?" Mr. Finchley turned and smiled at her.

"Yes, champagne. This is an occasion! We are going to celebrate your freedom."

In a moment the spirit of Mr. Finchley's mood had changed. He understood the anxiety which must have lived with his wife that day, understood the eager love which had set her planning for him and the fear which she had carried with her that she might have made him unhappy instead of opening for him a new prospect of freedom and pleasure. He leaned forward and kissed her.

Mrs. Finchley knew then that everything was all right. The champagne cork popped, the glasses were filled and, as the heady bubbles streamed upwards, they, too, seeking freedom, a swift came streaking down the narrow canyon of houses, screaming with abandoned pleasure, striking at the gnats that danced above the shabby plane trees.

Mr. Finchley raised his glass. "To the future," he cried. And Mrs. Finchley echoed him. "To the future!"

II

Of a canary-coloured caravan

MR. FINCHLEY'S first day of freedom from the imperious demands of a clerkly life began inauspiciously. For ordinary mortals Nature seldom makes any special show of her artillery or her graces to mark the climacterics of their life. Such signals of thunder or banners of blue and white are kept for conquerors and the bright-starred characters of tragedy.

It was a dull day with that dullness which justifies the optimist in saying it means heat and persuades the pessimist that it foretells rain, and which confounds them both by staying dull all day without sign of heat or rain.

At breakfast Mr. Finchley took up the conversation which had been started the previous evening.

"We mustn't dither," he said firmly. "We must have a proper plan of campaign. If we don't, we might easily spend the rest of my days discussing what we should do and never do anything."

Mrs. Finchley nodded her head in agreement.

"Now, let's see where we are at the moment. One can think better in the morning." Mr. Finchley cracked his egg smartly on the head. "We're going to settle down in Kent. Why?"

"Because, dear, we both happen to come from Kent. Your grandfather and his family before him were from Kent, and my people came from Sevenoaks. Robert's at school in Kent, and it would be nice to be near him, and we both happen to like the county very much and it's not too far from London if I want to come up shopping."

"I'm not sure," said Mr. Finchley, "whether I should describe my grandfather as being a man of Kent or a Kentish man."

"Is there a difference"

"Of course. If you were born east of the Medway you're one and if you were born west you are the other, but I can never remember which is which—"

"As though it matters".

"It matters very much in Kent. However—" Mr. Finchley dismissed the subject with the air of implying that the question involves loyalties and traditional feeling which a woman could not properly be expected to understand.

"The question is—where in Kent?" Mrs. Finchley turned the piece of bread on the electric toaster and looked shrewdly at Mr. Finchley.

Mr. Finchley put one elbow on the table and stared happily over his wife's head and through the window far away to the blue hummocks of the Kent weald. "A nice little house," he murmured, "a few acres of land, just enough for a pony for Robert and maybe a piece of woodland, a stream or a pond with fish—carp, fat carp and roach. My father used to talk about that. Maybe we could have more land and do some farming. I could learn to milk a cow—"

"The point is," Mrs. Finchley called him back, "where in Kent?"

"Ha, yes. Where? Well, that shouldn't be difficult. We've got enough lists of properties from the agents."

They had written, when they had decided upon Kent, to the principal estate agents of that county asking for lists of properties. That had been two weeks ago and, since then, scarcely a morning had passed without the postman dropping through their door envelope after envelope containing lists of properties. On Mr. Finchley's desk there was at that moment a neat stack containing well over three hundred lists of particulars of properties which might suit them and some which, at a glance, were obviously no good to them at all. The agents' response to their requests for a modest country property with anything up to ten acres of land had revealed an amazing and apparently common faculty for distorting facts. Judged by ducal or plutocratic standards some of the properties were "modest," but Mr. Finchley found it impossible to follow the subtle reasoning which led an agent, on a request for a modest property with no more than four bedrooms and a few acres, to convince himself that here was a chance to get rid of a fine old Jacobean residence with a wealth of old timbers, twelve bedrooms, stables and grooms' apartments and well-kept grounds comprising walled garden, ornamental shrubbery, Italian grotto, small lake and decorative wildfowl at the very low price of seven thousand pounds or offer. And he was even more mystified at the vinous abandon with which he was sent lists of well-found licensed premises, free-houses and tobacconists' and newsagents' shops and going concerns. He might, had he been a man easily tempted by the prospect of a country pub, have quickly been the landlord of any house from the Albert Royal Arms to the Seven Tuns. He had come to the conclusion that on receipt of a request for a property all agents sent out immediately a list of everything on their books, thereby allowing for any change in their customers' minds and assuring themselves that they had done all they could. Mr. Finchley's great objection to this comprehensive method was that it threw upon him a lot of unnecessary reading and selection.

"I'm getting," said Mrs. Finchley, "a little tired of reading those lists as they come in."

"Sometime today I'll go through them and weed them out. We'll keep the ones that look to be what we want and then we'll go and see them. I've been thinking, perhaps we might buy a little car and make a sort of holiday of it, going from one to another. After all we're in no hurry to decide. In fact, we mustn't decide in a hurry. The place we take must be the place. I can see it in every detail in my own eye. It's old-looking but it's comfortable inside; there's a wistaria growing up the porchway—yes, there must be wistaria. I could never get it to grow in this garden. And maybe, somewhere a walnut tree. Pickled walnuts, we could make our own ..." Mr. Finchley forgot his toast in his reverie and Mrs. Finchley smiled covertly as she watched him.

"You're an innocent," she said at last. "It's easy to see you've never done much house-hunting. It's the most nerve-wracking, disappointing business. You go miles, full of hope, to see places which are hopeless. And generally you finish up by taking some quite inadequate place out of sheer desperation and you are full of wonder that house-agents don't frankly become fiction writers and make people pay to read their stuff."

Mr. Finchley laughed her aside easily.

"We shall find a place," he said. "Leave it to me. We've got plenty of time. The great thing is to have method. We know what we want, all we have to do is to find it." He looked at his watch. "Nine-thirty. All the fellows are in the office now. They're working and I'm sitting here as idle as a lord. It seems funny, doesn't it?"

Mrs. Finchley turned from the doorway.

"If you want some work to do, my dear, why don't you begin your methodical search for a house by sorting out the lists of likely properties from that batch of particulars on your desk?"

"Hum, yes, I must do that." Mr. Finchley got up and felt in his pocket for his pipe. The cold roundness of the bowl as he handled it gave him a little thrill of delight, a pleasure which he could only ascribe to the leisure and freedom which were before him. "Yes, I'll do that. But I think I'll have a pipe first and take a stroll on the Heath before I begin."

"I should, my dear." Mrs. Finchley left him, smiling.

Mr. Finchley took his hat and umbrella and went out, making his way towards Hampstead Heath. Although it was a dull day there was a quick stir of morning activity everywhere. Errand boys swerved around corners on their bicycles, whistling and calling, the red trolley buses bounced and jolted along the roadway like jolly top-heavy barges, fleets of tradesmen's vans slipped in and out of the traffic, their bright colours moving like shuttles in a busy loom, and along the gutters the corporation men pushed their thick brooms, seriously pursuing their Augean labour. For a while Mr. Finchley felt a little lost in this steady stir of ordained business and affairs. He was out of it, and his mind took in, with a quick cast, memories of oldish men sitting talking on park benches, hunched below the shield of a newspaper in club chairs, of men who moved in narrow, dull orbits of life, little, faded fragments thrown off from the whirling, speeding ball of life and work.

It was to escape that fate that he had retired early, early enough to make something out of the life which remained. He must, he told himself, have a system. He must know what he was going to do. His faith in the invulnerableness of a system was simple and pathetic, but it was nonetheless less a faith, and that was enough. If a man had the courage to analyse his position, to add up his assets and liabilities, and to see clearly what he must do, then that was half the battle towards doing.

Mr. Finchley turned on to the Heath. He wanted to find somewhere to sit down and think.

Mr. Finchley was not the first person to take his thoughts on to the Heath and then forget them. It was a trick which the Heath often played. To it, from all parts of London, came men and women oppressed by sadness or indecision, and to them it offered the balm of its green walks and shining ponds. Beneath its pines and great trees they found their troubles sliding away into the remote, grey-touched distance of London below, and they were left in the happy isolation of this oasis of country life. The grass on its hills, thin and worn by many feet, claimed a more ancient lineage than any of the traffic-filled streets of London. It was old and wise with the confidences of many generations, and from its hollows and walks there seemed to arise a spirit which possessed those who passed, working in their thoughts with an odd alchemy so that they found themselves eased of their thoughts and aware only of the small things around them - the cry of a tit from the elms, the button-eyed stare of a squirrel and the crisp sound of sheep cropping over the grass. It was a little contemptuous of the murky London that washed around the foot of its hills like a dirty tide, it was out of sympathy for the men and women who passed their days in the narrow streets and whose eyes seldom saw the beauty of a night sky or the silver-bellied run of a tree-creeper going up an oak trunk. But when they came to its wide spaces, it took them forgivingly into its secrets and made them forget their cares for a while.

Mr. Finchley spent more than an hour on the Heath and he did very little thinking. He just walked and watched and forgot that he was a retired man, and eventually he found himself on the far side of the Heath and close to a little public-house where, during a Sunday morning stroll, he often called for a glass of shandy before returning home. It was a tidy little inn, tucked away in a cul-de-sac and pressed between the bullying shoulders of two high walls that shielded private gardens. This pressure seemed to have made it shoot upwards, elongating it into a lanky growth that reached for the sun.

Mr. Finchley went into the bar and was surprised to find it empty. On Sundays it was always full. He stood for a moment, undecided, wondering whether he had come in before opening time. A grunt from under the bar counter, the appearance of a thin face topped by a grey cloth cap and the final slow emergence of a very long body revealed the landlord.

"Morning, sir," he said, and then, to explain his business under the bar counter, "There was a mouse in the potato-crisp tin. I missed it. We ought to keep a cat, but the missus don't like 'em."

He served Mr. Finchley his shandy.

"You're not very busy," said Mr. Finchley.

"Not in the mornings. Evening and weekend trade, this house is. Select and prosperous clientele, two bars, easy to run and small overheads."

"That," said Mr. Finchley, "sounds like a property agent's description of the place."

The man nodded. "It is. I've been here over a year now and whenever I get fed up with the dull mornings I repeat that to myself—just to prove that I knew what I was coming into. Don't think," he insisted quickly, "that I'm grumbling about the house. Very nice little place. But I do miss the morning trade. It's a big difference to me. I come here from Trowbridge. There was a morning trade there all right. Farmers, cattle dealers and the cloth buyers. But the missus wanted to come to London. Always 'ankerin' after the metropolis, she was, and I didn't blame her. She's London by birth. We was married during the war while I was in barracks at Enfield. So we come and if it weren't for missing the morning trade—I wouldn't say I was sorry. Some of them farmers could drink, too. They knew how to take their beer. There was no sipping of it or drinking these new drinks. Still, change and decay is all around us."

"Change, yes, but surely not decay?" Mr. Finchley, as a Londoner, felt bound to defend his kind and his life against this charge.

"Yes, decay. Nothing wrong with decay, as you would know if you're a gardener. Got to have it. Things have got to die and rot, otherwise there'd be no crops, no manure, no heart in the land. Are you a gardener, sir?"

"In a way." Mr. Finchley took a prodigious gulp at his shandy to avoid any suspicion of sipping and nearly choked himself.

"So am I. Haven't got much. Just a little piece in the yard at the back, twenty feet by thirty."

"What do you grow, flowers or vegetables?"

"Vegetables. No use for flowers much. If you're interested, perhaps you'd like to come round the back and see my piece?"

"I'd like to very much."

"Come on then. The bar'll look after itself." The man lifted up a flap in the counter and let Mr. Finchley through. He then conducted him out of a little doorway, down a narrow passage and into a large courtyard at the back of the inn. The courtyard was flanked by the house and a long stable building, and in the far wall was a pair of double doors. Half of the yard was still cobbled. The other half had been turned into a small vegetable plot that ran up to one of the walls that protected the neighbouring garden.

Mr. Finchley was quite unprepared for the vegetable plot. It was a miracle of neatness and precision. The soil was rich and dark. It had the well-fed, prosperous air of a pet pony which gets only just enough exercise. No weeds spoiled its beauty, no untidy edges marred the correctness of the plot. Across its surface with geometrical precision ran lines of young vegetables. There was a row of young onions, each one the same size, each onion the same distance from its neighbour and each bearing the same length of green flag; there were two rows of lettuces, one of cos and the other of cabbage, and the rows ran in perfect succession of size from one end to the other; there was a line of peas, no plant more than eighteen inches up the methodical entanglement of sticks; then beetroots, their coppery leaves dropping daintily towards the fat earth, feathery fronds of carrots and a line of luxuriant spinach. It was a perfect plot. No slug, Mr. Finchley was sure, would ever dare to invade its well-defined frontiers, no wire-worm lurked in that healthy soil, no sparrow would ever be given the chance to peck off the flowers of the peas and no hand, he was equally sure as he watched the pride move across the landlord's thin face, but that of the owner ever tended to its needs.

"What do you think of it?" The question was asked with that slight breathlessness which demands and deserves an enthusiastic, reverent reply.

"It's incredible," said Mr. Finchley. "It's … it's beautiful."

"Ay, it is. It's beautiful. No flowers ever looked as well as those onions, and the lettuces… you can keep all your roses so long as I can have those."

"You must put in a lot of work on it."

"Half an hour a day, the rest is done by nature. The sun, rain and manure, our old friend decay. Of course, the yard being enclosed shelters it, and the sun comes down over the stable in the mornings. Yet we get plenty of shade during the afternoon." He jerked his hand towards the lightening in the dull sky above the stable where the sun rode behind layers of cloud and, in following the line of his hand, Mr. Finchley's eyes were caught by a splash of colour, of yellow, red and green.

Across the yard the stable doors were open and he saw that the stable had been turned into a garage. There was a small two-seater car in the stable and close beside it a caravan. It was this which had caught his eye. Instinctively he moved towards it and the landlord, realising his interest, laughed and went forward to the stable.

"It's a colourful affair, ain't it?" He stood with one hand on the door-post and nodded to the caravan. "You don't see many of them about these days, more's the pity. All motor cars, no horses to drop manure, only stinkin' petrol fumes and speed-limit signs instead of drinking troughs."

Mr. Finchley said nothing, but he moved closer. It was a horse-drawn caravan, its body painted a bright canary yellow, its wheels painted red and the spokes and hubs picked out with thin green lines. Along its sides and over the projecting pieces of woodwork were fanciful scrolls done in red and green paint. The doorway at the front of the caravan was overhung by the curved roof which had been scalloped and carved. From each side a little window looked out and at the back dropped a set of steps that led up to a half-glass doorway whose lower and wooden panels were painted with two country scenes, one a castle rising above a wood with cows in a meadow in the foreground, and the other a lake upon which two sailing boats tilted dangerously and a swan moved from the cover of a bank of bulrushes. The whole creation, against the dull red brick of the stable and the hard, matter-of-fact precision of the two-seater car, was charming and detached from the world of petrol. It stood there like a young girl lost in a crowd of strange people, hesitant, aware of its fresh beauty, and yet a little ashamed because it had no relation with the life around it.

"Is it yours?" asked Mr. Finchley.

The man paused before replying, then rubbing his chin doubtfully, he said, "Well, yes and no".

"What do you mean?"

"Well, it was here when I took the place. The previous landlord had garaged it for the owner. He paid his dues for the first two months and then he disappeared. He hasn't been heard from since. That must be over two years ago. The previous landlord had the man's address, the one he left when he brought the van here, but when he went round to see him about the rent he wasn't there. He'd gone and they didn't know where he was or anything about him. He'd only stopped there a couple of weeks. He hasn't been heard of since and he owes a tidy bit for dues by now. I don't reckon he'll ever turn up. In fact, I'm sure he won't though why not I can't think. I've even advertised. You know—'if the owner don't turn up within so many days then the van'll be sold to defray garage expenses'. It's properly legal. I suppose now I shall sell it, if I can find anyone to buy it. But people don't want that kind of thing these days. They like a trailer they can stick on the back of a car. Funny he should go off and leave it like that, ain't it?"

"It is," said Mr. Finchley reflectively, his eyes on the caravan. "It looks to be in good condition."

"It is. I've given it a rub down occasionally to keep the paintwork fresh and the woodwork's sound right through. Would you like to look inside it?"

He opened the doorway at the top of the stairs and led the way into the caravan. The interior reminded Mr. Finchley of a boat. Everything was shipshape and designed to take up as little space as possible. The caravan was divided into two compartments by a partition which had a curtained opening in it. Forward of the partition were the sleeping quarters, two bunks set on each side above storage lockers and lighted by a little window in the front driving door which was shut at night. In the living compartment was a little table screwed to the floor and which folded in the daytime to a narrow strip. There were shelves, cupboards, two long upholstered seats that could also serve as bunks, close to the door, a little galley, lined with zinc for cooking on a primus stove. From the centre of the roof hung an oil-lamp.

Mr. Finchley stood in the living compartment and looked around him with pleasure. Inside the caravan was another world, a world of miniature completeness. This was how, Mr. Finchley mused, a snail felt when it retracted its horns and withdrew into the seclusion of its shell. You shut out everything except yourself, and like the snail you could travel with this completely personal world. It was not anchored to the earth with foundations nor doomed all its life to face in one direction. You could turn it to catch the dying sunlight, you could take it from wood to meadow, from town to town as you willed. With it you could follow the idle promptings of a summer's wanderings or fasten close the doors and sit tight and snug against the battering of any winter gale. It called to the nomad in every man. Beside the black and steel two-seater it was an argosy of colour and adventure. Its wheels were made by craftsmen, its spokes chamfered and fitted with a skill that was dying, every piece of carved panelling, each board and strut spoke of men who were the last of their kind. Beside the car it was an arraignment of an age that failed to recognise the folly of its mad lust for progress, and by itself it was a glorious vindication of the love for beauty and the respect for wood and iron which men once had with an intensity which was near to religion.

They went back to the bar and Mr. Finchley had another drink and treated the landlord, whose name, he discovered, was Sydney Harricot, to a beer.

"I wonder," said Mr. Finchley slowly, "that you haven't sold it before this."

Mr. Harricot looked at Mr. Finchley and his thin face seemed to draw itself out even longer, the wrinkles stretched finely over the pale skin. His eyes were large and deep-set and they were full of an understanding which would have surprised Mr. Finchley. Mr. Harricot had not stood behind a public bar for the greater part of his lifetime without coming to know something about human nature.

"I ain't tried very hard for one thing. 'Tisn't many people get into the courtyard to see it for another. I don't care to have folk wandering around too near my little patch of vegetables. And the few that have seen it, well, they haven't all been as interested as you."

"Perhaps you were asking too much for it." Mr. Finchley drained his glass at a gulp. "How much, for instance, did you ask?"

Mr. Harricot did not answer at once. He polished a glass industriously and breathed hard upon it as though unsatisfied by the first sheen.

"Well," he said, "there's just over two years' garage dues. That would come to about fifteen pounds. There's the time I've spent keeping it clean once a month for a year, that's another pound. There's the cost of advertising for the owner, another two pounds. Eighteen pounds in all, and then of course there's the value of the caravan itself. If I was to sell it for the eighteen pounds and the owner did come back, he might be annoyed because I'd let it go too cheap and then there'd be trouble. I don't want any trouble. Twenty-five pounds is a fair price, I think. In another twenty years it'll fetch a hundred pounds as a museum piece. That is if this crazy old world ain't blown itself and the museums in it to red hell before then."

"Twenty-five pounds." Mr. Finchley nodded agreeably. "That seems a fair price. I wonder you haven't sold it before."

"No market for it. Nobody wants a caravan these days. Too slow."

"But it's the slowness that makes it so attractive," cried Mr. Finchley.

"I agree. But you and me, sir, we're either ahead or behind of the times, I'm not sure which. You and me believe in slowness and let's-have-a-look-at-what-we're-passingness, but there's not many others that do. No, sir, this world is full of bouncing, speeding, shouting, do-it-before-you've-started demons whose eyes are so full of road-dust they never see what passes 'em. They want to do everything in a hurry. That's why most of 'em haven't the patience to grow vegetables." Mr. Harricot spat deliberately into the spittoon below the bar. It was his final and most effective comment on the twentieth century in which he had the ill fortune to be living.

"I think you're right," said Mr. Finchley.

"I know I'm right, sir," said Mr. Harricot, as he watched Mr. Finchley rise, ready to go. "Do you want to buy it?"

The suggestion was a shock to Mr. Finchley. He had fallen in love with the caravan immediately. Anyone with an ounce of feeling would have done so. It called out to all the wayward, half-forgotten dreams that have possessed men and women since men and women constrained themselves to a life whose only solace sometimes is those dreams. But he had never gone so far in his thoughts as imagining himself the owner of the caravan.

"Good Lord, no !" he said hastily.

Mr. Harricot smiled. Mr. Finchley saw the smile, and he was always to remember it. Sometimes, long afterwards, he was to wonder whether it was not Mr. Harricot smiling at him from behind the bar, but some spirit which had temporarily possessed itself of Mr. Harricot's body. The smile was long and vaguely mocking, it was intelligent and suggestive, as though the mind behind the smile was saying "Go on, don't kid yourself you haven't thought of buying it. What do you take me for?"

"Pity," said Mr. Harricot. "Still, if you change your mind it'll be there. No one else is likely to buy it. Twenty-five pounds and you can leave it in the garage until you're ready to take it away. You can leave it there while you fit it up ready for the road, and any little repairs or additions I'll help you with. Something to do in the mornings."

"It sounds attractive ..." Mr. Finchley had his hand on the door.

"It is attractive. If I'd been a single man, not tied to a bar, I'd have been off in that before now. Know what I'd do? I'd wander off, down West somewhere, looking for the right kind of country pub. A tight little place in a market town, about twenty thousand inhabitants, a twice-weekly market and a busy morning trade, and I wouldn't say 'Whoa!' until I'd found it, and when I'd found it—" his voice dropped, and he looked over his shoulder to see his wife was not around, "I'd marry a plump little country-woman who wouldn't be for ever 'ankering after the delights of the metropolis."

Mr. Finchley went home very thoughtfully, the sound of Mr. Harricot's "Whoa!" persisting in his ears.

He was unusually silent during lunch. Mrs. Finchley made no comment on his reserve. She was an understanding woman and she realised that the first day of a man's retirement from active work must necessarily be quite unlike any other day and must impose upon him moods with which it was wiser for a woman, even his wife, not to concern herself.

After lunch Mr. Finchley went to his desk and got out the pile of agents' lists. He spent the whole afternoon going through them. He attacked the job systematically and was rewarded by seeing the pile sort itself out. In the end he had a respectable pile of lists of properties which might suit him. The others he consigned to the waste-paper basket. He then took the pile of possible properties and arranged them geographically. With the help of a map of Kent he sorted them out, allocating them to various districts, the districts being determined by the neighbourhood of the various large towns in the county, so that there was a Maidstone district, a Canterbury district, an Ashford district and so on. It was with considerable pleasure that he came to the end of his task.

"I've finished," he announced gladly to his wife at tea-time. "There are about seventy places we ought to look at."

"That's a lot," said his wife, "since more than half of them will be quite hopeless, despite the agents' descriptions." She went on, holding a letter in her hand which had come by the afternoon post. "I've had a letter from David. He says now that you've retired, why don't we go and stay with him for a few weeks before we begin looking around for a place?"

David was David White, Mrs. Finchley's bachelor brother, a retired mining engineer who had settled down in the north of England. Mr. Finchley frankly did not like David, and David, who was ten years older than he, did not care for Mr. Finchley, and so far Mr. Finchley had skilfully avoided visiting him.

"That's kind of him," he said. "But do you think this would be a wise moment? I want to get this business settled. We've argued the dangers of postponing it." He paused for a moment, eyeing Mrs. Finchley sagaciously over the lid of the hot-water jug. "I suppose you wouldn't like to go up by yourself to him. You see," he went on hurriedly, "if you did that, I could go down into Kent and look at these properties and weed out the unsuitable ones. If I boiled them down to about a dozen or so places which were something like what we wanted, it would be far less fatiguing for you."

Now Mrs. Finchley knew how her husband felt about her brother and she did not resent it. Because David was her brother she entertained no delusions about the peculiarities of his temperament. And she was not excited by the prospect of a long and exhausting house hunt. She had hunted houses before and knew what trials the chase pressed upon the hunter. Twelve houses she could face cheerfully, seventy houses made her grow cold with a quick withdrawal of courage and hope.

"It's an idea," she said gently. "David would understand. But do you want to do it by yourself? Won't you be lonely?"

Mr. Finchley shook his head. "I shall enjoy it."

"How will you go to Kent? Buy a car, as you suggested this morning?"

"Yes, I suppose so. Yes." Mr. Finchley became firmer. "I could buy a car, or something like that."

It was then that Mrs. Finchley looked up suddenly and caught sight of his face, blandly innocent, yet written boldly with the symbols of guile, and it was then that she smilingly assured herself that Edgar would never have any secrets from her. His nature was too generous to allow him to keep a secret.

"And what do you mean by 'or something like that'? A car is a car, isn't it?"

"Of course, dear, of course. I was just speaking figuratively. After all ... yes, I suppose you're right, we must buy a car. It would help a lot."

"And what might we buy if we didn't buy a car? Is there anything else which would do?" Mrs. Finchley, sensing that she had much to discover, pressed her advantage home.

For a while Mr. Finchley tried to avoid giving her an answer, for a few moments he regretted his irresponsible bachelor days when there was no woman to insist upon a reply to a question, when he had been his own master. He had to give way.

"We might," he said at last, haltingly, "buy a caravan. It would do the job as well, if more slowly, and it would save hotel expenses."

"A caravan!" There was no doubt of Mrs. Finchley's surprise.

"Yes, a caravan, a canary-coloured caravan with red-and-green wheels!" Mr. Finchley cried enthusiastically. "I saw one this morning, and it was only twenty-five pounds. All we'd have to do is to drive it off. If you didn't want to come, I could go myself while you're with David. It would be splendid fun, and afterwards we could keep it in the garden of the house we buy and use it as a summer lodge. Robert would love it. It's the most perfect caravan, my dear. Inside it's all fitted up with shelves and bunks. When I saw it I felt that it had been waiting for me ..."

Mrs. Finchley sat back and let this gush of words overwhelm her. She listened and knew as she listened that she was glad that it was Edgar Finchley she had married, Edgar Finchley who could fall in love with a canary-coloured caravan.

III
In which Mr. Finchley, like Cinderella, is helped to a horse by a fairy

MR. HARRICOT was not surprised to see Mr. Finchley the next day. In fact, it would almost be true to say that he had expected him. When he saw Mr. Finchley's round face come through the bar door and observed the excitement that sparkled in his eyes, Mr. Harricot experienced a moment or two of sorrow. He knew what Mr. Finchley was after. He knew that very soon the caravan would belong to Mr. Finchley, and in the months during which it had rested in his stable Mr. Harricot had become very attached to it. He had never been able to use it himself, but there had been many an evening, after the bar was closed, that he had gone out and sat on the back steps of the caravan, smoking his pipe and looking up at the star-stippled wedge of sky above the courtyard, imagining himself far away. Now all those pleasures would be taken from him and he could only feel sorry.

Yet, if Mr. Harricot was a romantic, he was a generous romantic, and, almost immediately, he began to feel happy that someone else was going to have the joys which had been his only in dreams. He could not escape himself, but he was no mean-souled obstructionist of other men's desires.

He looked at Mr. Finchley as he approached the bar. He had on a light grey suit, a new Panama and carried a yellow stick. He looked fresh and eager. He looked a little too neat, thought Mr. Harricot. He looked, in fact, just the sort of man whom the possession of a caravan would benefit. It would take the edge off his neatness and put experience behind his eager happiness. Some men are born to spend their enthusiasm on dogs, some on horses, and some on gardens, some give their love to books and some devote their spare hours to the cult of their body, raising their muscles and hardening their wind; each man has his love, the joy which is beyond his ordinary life, and to Mr. Finchley had been opened the love of a caravan. He approached the new altar timidly.

"Morning, sir! Shandy?" Mr. Harricot beamed at him.

"Please," Mr. Finchley nodded, and there was the sound of the beer being drawn into the glass and the faint hiss of the troubled lemonade.

Mr. Harricot handed him the drink and stared at him. "I know what you've come for," he said at last. "You want that caravan."

Mr. Finchley nodded and then sipped his drink.

"Yes," he said, a little breathlessly. "I've made up my mind. If it's still for sale I'd like to buy it."

"Twenty-five pounds," said Mr. Harricot, keeping his voice hard and commercial with an effort. It was better to be brisk and businesslike because it made the parting easier. "Twenty-five pounds, and dirt cheap at the price."

"I'll give you a cheque," Mr. Finchley drew out his cheque-book as he spoke.

The cheque was written. Mr. Finchley finished his shandy and the deal was sealed with a glass of sherry each. The caravan belonged to Mr. Finchley.

When the bar was closed they went out into the courtyard to the caravan.

"How," said Mr. Harricot, as they stood looking at the caravan, "did you put it to your wife?" He had gathered in their conversation that Mr. Finchley was married, and he took a distinctly practical interest in the method which Mr. Finchley had employed.

Mr. Finchley explained fully to him. His wife was a reasonable woman, he said, and she had made no pretence of the fact that she did not want to go jaunting around the country in a caravan. She was neither indolent nor luxury-loving, but she just did not wish to go caravanning, and he, Mr. Finchley, had appreciated her point of view. But she had no objection to his going, especially as he was going to look at properties for them. She would take her holiday in the north with her brother, and he would combine his business and holiday in the south with the caravan.

"Marriage, you know," explained Mr. Finchley, a little pontifically, "isn't always a question of finding a middle course acceptable to both of you. Men and women are different creatures and want to run different courses. If you recognise that fact and acknowledge the personality of your partner it makes for a lot more harmony. For instance," he expanded the idea, "it would have been silly for me to have said I wouldn't go caravanning unless she came, and equally silly for her to have come out of a feeling of loyalty to me. We should have both been uncomfortable."

"You're lucky in havin' a reasonable wife. They ain't all like that."

Mr. Finchley spent that afternoon in and around the caravan. For the most time he had Mr. Harricot's company. After a while, indeed, it became obvious that Mr. Harricot looked upon the setting up of the caravan for a journey as as being as much his problem as Mr. Finchley's. Mr. Finchley accepted his assistance willingly.

They sat inside the caravan and made a list of all the things which would be needed. They detailed the stores which could be packed away into the little cupboards. They decided upon the odd repairs which must be done and the colour of the curtains to hang against the windows. They jumped up and down on the floor to test the springs of the undercarriage, and finally, with the help of a stepladder, Mr. Finchley climbed on to the roof to see that it was well-caulked and that none of the seams was open against the weather.

Mr. Finchley went home happy and tired.

"Tomorrow," he told his wife, "you must come up and see it. I'm sure you will have plenty of suggestions to make about fitting it up."

Mrs. Finchley did not tell him so, but she had spent the better part of the day fitting it up in her mind, listing stores and deciding upon crockery and cutlery. Although Edgar was going off on his own, she was determined that he should go off backed by the wisdom and foresight of a woman's competent victualling.

Later that evening he sat down to write his weekly letter to his son, Robert, who was at a preparatory school near Goudhurst in Kent. He knew that Robert with his violent enthusiasms for anything pertaining to the country would have to be handled carefully when it came to telling him about the caravan. He filled the first part of his letter with the description of the presentation to him at the office and how he felt now that he was a man of leisure. When he came to the caravan episode, he hesitated, but only for a moment. They were thinking, he explained, of buying a caravan—it would never do to say that it had been already bought—with the idea of using it to go around Kent looking for a house. And when the house was found they might still keep it and use it in the holidays to go wandering away into the country, all three of them (for he was sure that by then Mrs. Finchley would have been converted) without a care in the world.

Mr. Finchley, who had been guarding against the stirring of too much enthusiasm in Robert, found himself swept away by his own enthusiasm. The letter drew out in length. He was away in his dreams, jogging along behind the horse, smoking his pipe, with Robert's head sticking out of the doorway above him and his wife somewhere at the end of the caravan seeing to a meal …

"We'll pull up at night in the shade of some coppice," he wrote, "ready for an enormous meal. We shall all have our separate duties. I shall fetch the water and firewood—because we shall cook over an open fire as much as possible, in true gipsy fashion; mother will look after the cooking, and you?—well, you can always have the job of unharnessing the horse, rubbing him down and giving him a good feed of oats—"

It was at this point that Mr. Finchley stopped suddenly and looked up with an expression of alarm on his face.

"Good Lord!" he exclaimed. "I'd never even given it a thought!"

"Given what a thought?" questioned his wife from her chair.

"The horse! We shall have to get a horse for the caravan. It never occurred to me!"

"But I thought there was a horse with the caravan," queried his wife. "Didn't you buy a horse with the caravan? A caravan isn't any good without a horse. They go together, don't they?"

"A horse and a caravan for twenty-five pounds! My dear!"

"Well, why not? It never occurred to me that anyone would sell a caravan without a horse. It's like buying a ..." she searched for a proper parallel and could not find one. "Well, it's incomplete. You talked about the caravan being in a stable. I naturally assumed there was a horse."

"No, there isn't a horse, my dear. You don't necessarily buy the two together. We shall have to get a horse."

For a moment Mr. Finchley was appalled at the thought of the horse. The caravan had no terrors for him. It was inanimate and understandable, but a horse was a very different problem. A horse was alive, it had likes and dislikes and it had to be handled. It had to be harnessed and fed and looked after ... it was a wonder, he thought bitterly, that Mr. Harricot had not presented that aspect to him. It was unlike Mr. Harricot not to have thought of the horse.

"And how much does a horse cost?"

"I haven't the faintest idea," admitted Mr. Finchley.

"And where do you buy one in London?" His wife was relentless.

"I wish I knew," said Mr. Finchley. "Bless my soul—how could I have come to overlook such an obvious thing!" He was inclined to be irritated with himself for his stupidity.

"I should finish your letter and not bother about the horse tonight," advised Mrs. Finchley. "You can worry with that tomorrow."

Mr. Finchley finished his letter, but he went on wondering about the horse. That night he dreamt of horses, of racehorses, carthorses, shire horses, seahorses and horses of every conceivable size, villainy and phantasy. He was glad to wake up and find it was morning. He looked out of the window and was greeted by warm sunshine, a burst of sparrow chatter and the cheerful clatter of a United Dairies cart coming up the road. It was drawn by a brown horse with a white star on its forehead and, like a cool balm after the night's horrors of equine malignancy, it looked docile, contented and manageable. The dairyman called to it and it moved on, stopping and starting with a sweet obedience that gave Mr. Finchley a new confidence.

It was not until after breakfast, when he was walking out to post the letter to Robert, that Mr. Finchley remembered Mr. Queen. It was the letter in his hand and the sight of a large black cat rubbing itself against the pillar box which brought Mr. Queen to his mind. Mr. Queen was a cats'-meat man and he had a stall in the Queen's Crescent market off Malden Road. Mr. Finchley did not know him very well, but he was very friendly with Robert. Robert had no social inhibitions and, when he was at home, he often visited Mr. Queen, whom he had pronounced to be an interesting man. There was nothing Mr. Queen, so Robert said, did not know, nothing, that was, which could be of any interest. A vision of Mr. Queen arose in Mr. Finchley's eye. He was an enormously fat man, dressed always in a straw boater, a navy blue suit tied round with a greasy red apron, his throat wrapped about with a white scarf and in his right hand he held the long, shiny, sharp knife with which he cut strips of meat from the horrid joints and carcasses which adorned his stall. Every other stallholder called him "Fairy" for obvious reason, and Fairy, unabashed by his ignominious trade, stood like a colossus before his stall, his voice louder than any other, his good-humour unquenchable by bad weather or poor business. He was a London street trader, had been all his life, and desired no other occupation. For him a stall-lined, crowded thoroughfare was the world. He suffered from rheumatism caught from the cold pavements, his voice was crusted with the fog of winters, his stature, his manners, his whole being and existence was Hogarthian and there was not a small boy within two miles of his stall who did not know him and regard him with the delicious awe of one who is at once mysterious and amusing.

Mr. Finchley went to see Fairy.

It was Saturday morning and the Crescent was crowded.

It was hot, too, and the air was heavy with the smell of fruit and vegetables and meat and fish. Mr. Finchley edged his way through the crowd towards Fairy's stall. Fairy was standing at one side of the stall, flourishing his knife and bellowing happily:

"H'yar, then! H'yar then, ripe and rich!" And he thumped with his free hand on a pile of old newspapers on the counter, newspapers in which he wrapped his penn'orths of meat.

"Lervly ripe tomatoes! Lervly! Fawpince a pahnd, lidy!"

"Who says fish? Who says fish? Juicy cod!"

Fairy had plenty of competition, but his hoarse voice rang out above them all, raucous, shearing its way through all opposition. His red face worked as though it were

India-rubber and, almost without seeming to stop his shouting, he would bend forward to catch the request of a customer and slice his meat, sometimes tossing a titbit to the group of pariah dogs that sat against the wall and watched him.

Mr. Finchley came closer, trying not to look at the obscene slabs of meat which decorated the stall. Fairy saw him, recognised him as Robert's father, and gave him the faintest nod of the head. The friendly overture encouraged Mr. Finchley. He went closer and cleared his throat, struggling to avert his eyes from the glittering, evil skirmishes of the bluebottles about the meat.

"Mr. Queen—"

"Come on! Don't forget your old mogger! Don't forget your furred and feathered friends at home. Meat, meat, lovely meat for pussy!"

The sally burst over Mr. Finchley's head and drove him back a pace, and a customer slipped in, muttered something to Fairy and was rewarded with three deft slashes of the knife, a quick whirl of paper and the handing over of a packet of meat.

"What is it, me old china?" The question came to Mr. Finchley in a penetrating rasp. Fairy was looking at him.

"I was wondering," said Mr. Finchley, "if you could help me—"

"Help anybody! Help you all! Help you all for the love of your fat and friendly faces! Meat, lovely meat, cheap and savoury!" The roar sailed away into the market, like the salvo of a battery, and then, huskily on its heels, as the knife weaved to serve another customer, came the words:

"What do you want to know? Something wrong with your cat?" Fairy had a certain reputation as a cat doctor.

"No, not that. I was wondering if you could tell me where I might buy a horse—"

"A horse!" Fairy broadcast the words wide. "A horse," he sang like a crow, like a monstrous, megaphone-mouthed crow. "My kingdom for a horse and here's the best horse meat in London. Buy, buy!"

Mr. Finchley, unaccustomed to this type of conversation, stepped back, but was trapped by the wheezy aside. "You want a horse? Dead or alive, racehorse, or battle horse?" He laughed at his own sally and it was like the complaint of leaky boilers groaning under high pressure.

Mr. Finchley laughed, too. It seemed polite.

"I want a horse to pull a caravan," he explained, and added, "a good, strong horse. But I don't know where to go to buy one."

"Easy! Easy!" sang Fairy. "A live horse—don't forget your tabby, lady—a horse for hauling a caravan. Easy—Jimmy Rivers, good ole Jimmy, Macintyre Mews, Canal Street, Camden Town. He'll sell you one. Tell 'im you come from me, tell 'im—the old horse-thief—not to overcharge you or I'll never do any more knackerin' jobs for him. Come on, there! Who'll buy, who'll buy, a pig's head and a sheep's eye! Juicy titbits for domestic pets ..." he roared with vaporous laughter.

"Thank you. I'm very grateful." Mr. Finchley thanked him. Fairy waved the whole business aside with a flourish of his knife and Mr. Finchley retired.

Jimmy Rivers of the Macintyre Mews, Camden Town, was hard to find. Mr. Finchley took the bus to Camden Town. He knew where the canal was and he soon found Canal Street. It was a dingy row that ran alongside the canal, separated from it by a tall wall. This wall was covered from one end to another with the most varied collection of chalk inscriptions that Mr. Finchley had ever seen. It was as though some member of every sect, religious and political, and a great many individuals labouring under repressions and fixations, had found their way there, chalk in hand, and had been spurred by the great expanse of brick into violent and emphatic declarations. No aspect of human relationships was missing; politics, religion, sport, sex, art and literature ... somewhere on that wall they were represented. For the people living in the houses opposite it must have been an absorbing and ever-changing study, a rude palimpsest for ever revealing new treasures.

Canal Street was a cul-de-sac and crowded with children playing their games safely in its traffic-free road. Mr. Finchley went up the street looking for Macintyre Mews and found it, a tall, double pair of green doors, firmly shut, with no wicket and no bell. He stood outside of them undecided. From the other side of the doors he could catch the faint, ammoniacal smell of horses and the occasional snap of a hoof on hard cobbles as a horse stirred in its stall. He knocked with his fist loudly on the door.

The action brought the street children around him at once. They made a ring about him and surveyed him with an eager, but silent curiosity.

There was no reply to his knock. He knocked again. No one came.

"Whatcher knockin' for, guv'nor?" A small boy edged forward and asked the question.

"I want to see Mr. Rivers." Mr. Finchley spoke kindly, he felt suspicious of the children and preferred to have their goodwill.

"Give us a penny, mister!" The cry came shrilly from the edge of the crowd.

"Got any fagcards, mister? Flags of the British Army."

Mr. Finchley found himself besieged by a mob of children. They pressed closely about him.

"No, I haven't any cards or any pennies. How do I find Mr. Rivers?" He shook off a pair of grubby hands that were supplicating at his coat sleeve. "Here you," he caught hold of the small boy who had first spoken, "I'll give you a penny if you find Mr. Rivers for me."

"Sixpence," said the boy firmly.

Mr. Finchley had to agree. "All right."

The small boy laughed and then withdrew into the roadway. "He don't take no notice of knocks, guv'nor. He always thinks it's us playing on the door. This is what you do!" He turned and charged towards the double doors and threw himself against them. They swung inwards at once. Mr. Finchley found himself standing at the entrance of a small cobbled yard and across the yard he saw a row of loose-boxes. He paid off the small boy and went in. The doors were pulled to behind him by the children, who apparently knew enough of Mr. Jimmy Rivers to keep off his premises.

Mr. Rivers was sitting on a small stool against the wall of the stables. He was smoking and reading a newspaper, and it was not until Mr. Finchley was within a few feet of him that the paper dropped and he found himself being scrutinised by the bluest pair of eyes he had ever seen. They were as blue as a hedge-sparrow's egg and as hard as diamonds and they looked out from a thin, wedge-shaped face that was more an angular caricature of a face than an actual flesh-and-blood com position.

Jimmy Rivers was a small, middle-aged man without an ounce of spare flesh on him, his legs were bowed and clad in tight breeches, he wore a yellow jumper over a black shirt and his head was covered with a cap which he wore at a jaunty angle. He looked like a jockey, an old and very dusty jockey whose body had lost the trick of growing long before he had become a man, and whose whole life was circumscribed, contained and epitomised in the word—horse. And that happened to be the whole truth about Jimmy Rivers.

"Good morning," said Mr. Finchley. "Are you Mr. Rivers?"

"That's me." Mr. Rivers stood up, spitting out of the corner of his mouth.

Mr. Finchley explained what he wanted and that Mr. Queen had recommended him to come to Mr. Rivers. Mr. Rivers received this news without any show of emotion. It seemed to be no surprise to him that Mr. Finchley should want a horse for pulling a caravan.

"You'd better see what I've got. There's only three for sale—all the rest belong to the canal company. They stable 'em 'ere." He led Mr. Finchley along the stalls. "There you are," he said, stopping before one of the stalls; "there's a nice little mare, ten years old and reaching about fifteen hands. Only had her in last week. She's had a thin time of it somewhere, but with a month's proper feeding she'd pull you and the caravan to the moon and back."

The mare turned in her stall at the sound of their voices and from the gloom Mr. Finchley caught the red glint of an eye and the white flicker of teeth where her lips curled back as she whinnied. It was a warning, unfriendly sound.

Jimmy Rivers saw that Mr. Finchley was not very keen about the mare. He led him to the next stall.

"What about this one? Used to be owned by a Swiss Cottage baker—gone bankrupt. Been pulling a van all his life. Gelding, comes of good stock. A nice creature. Look at them legs. You don't often see legs like that on a baker's nag. Good bit of Yorkshire coach horse in him somewhere. Twenty pounds. What do you say?"

Mr. Finchley looked at the shining quarters of the black gelding and frowned.

"Isn't that a lot of money?"

"Horse is worth it. Like to see its action? I'll take it up and down the yard for you?"

"What about the other horse? You said you had three." Mr. Finchley felt that Jimmy Rivers was trying to rush him into buying the gelding.

"You wouldn't want that," said Jimmy. "It's a fool of a horse."

"Do you mean it wouldn't pull a van?"

"Oh, no! It'll pull a van all right, but it's more a patchwork quilt than a horse. Come and look at it, then you'll understand."

He led the way across the yard to a separate stable. He pushed open the top half of the door and leaned across it.

"There you are. Take a look at it."

Mr. Finchley looked and saw a horse, a grey and white horse with rather a long tail, a thick head on a very short neck and a curve in the back as though the beast had eaten too much and could not support the weight of its stomach.

The horse turned and moved slowly towards the door. A pair of black, gentle eyes settled on Mr. Finchley, an ear flicked forward and then a warm muzzle came up and nosed towards him in an unmistakeably friendly gesture.

"He wants sugar," said Jimmy contemptuously. "He thinks the whole world goes about with its pockets full of sugar for him. What a horse—he's got a tail like an Arab, a colour like a percheron, a neck like a Suffolk punch, the tricks of a Shetland and—I'll give him his due—he'll work like a trojan so long as he feels like it. That there horse, sir, is an enigma. That's the only word for it. How old he is I can only guess— fifteen years, I'd say. What he's been is nobody's business, but, from the way he takes on when he hears a brass band, I'd say he's been in the army or a circus sometime, and from the way he's always after sugar he must 'ave been somebody's pet. But as far as points go—he ain't a horse. He's an unorthodoxy. If you're goin' in for museum pieces, you can have him and a set of harness for your caravan for fifteen pounds. And that's dirt cheap, 'cos I could sell him to Bostock and Wombwell's for fifty pounds any day."

As Mr. Rivers finished speaking the horse blew through its nostrils, a good-matured sniff at the jibes. Mr. Finchley found that, despite Mr. Rivers' chronicle of defects, he liked the horse. Points meant nothing to him so long as he had the assurance that the horse could pull the caravan, and it was comforting to have the feeling that the horse was of a friendly disposition. Mr. Finchley felt that here was a creature he could handle.

"What's his name?"

"Well," —Mr. Rivers hesitated—"the man who sold him to me—actually I took him as part payment of a debt— said he was called Churchwarden, but I could never get round to calling him that. I just call him Albert. But you can take your choice. Some days he seems to answer to Albert and other days he wants to be Churchwarden. Do you want him?"

Mr. Finchley felt that this was an historic moment. He was buying a horse. It meant the completion of his plans to go caravanning, and there could be no drawing back once Albert Churchwarden became his.

He looked at Mr. Rivers and nodded, drawing out his cheque-book.

Within a few moments the horse was his and he had arranged for Mr. Rivers to deliver it at Mr. Harricot's yard the following Monday morning at ten o'clock. Mr. Rivers had promised to show him how to adjust the harness and to give him an hour's tuition in driving.

Mr. Finchley walked home proudly. He was the owner of a horse and a caravan. He watched the splendid private cars roll by him along the road with a feeling of extreme contempt.

IV
How Mr. Finchley
takes the reins

THE memory of some joys lives for ever in our minds, no detail dimmed, no moment's breathless pleasure forgotten. We close our eyes in reflection and are back at that moment of delight, lost to the present, completely immersed in the past. That morning, in some quiet side street, or down some dew-bathed lane, when a father's hand held the saddle of a bicycle and we mounted, our legs just able to tip the pedals, our hands fast around the cork handle-grips and we moved off, wavering, full of a strange determination to master this mystery of easy balance and speed; that fraction of delirious time when we turned and saw that father was a good four yards away, and we had moved alone, unaided and ignorantly master of the mystery, and then the swift debacle as charging human fear swayed us from the seat into the receiving lap of nettlebed or box-hedge …

There are other joys; the proud sobriety of emotion that marked the end of the first week of real work, work for which we were paid and so accorded an adult title; that first and distant love, when the glory of some pantomime beauty shone upon a young world like the northern lights; the incense of sausages frizzled upon a green stick before a wood fire, and the following, world-stirring fragment of time as we saw our first dawn, after a night in the open, sweeping over the lip of the land, turning black shapes to gold-rimmed silhouettes of beasts and farmsteads. If men and women have ever known these they do not forget them, and if they have never known them they touch our pity.

Mr. Finchley had known his share of such moments, but at precisely ten-thirty on a Monday morning that summer he added another joy to his happy experiences, another golden memory to the rich store which his years had accumulated.

He drove a horse and caravan. A slight drizzle was falling, just enough to smear the roads with a faint perspiration and fill the cups of the flowers with tiny pools. He held the reins in his hands, oblivious of the drizzle, and on either side of him on the ample driving seat sat Mr. Harricot and Mr. Rivers. Mr. Harricot's long body leaned forward, his thin face suffused with colour at his excitement, and he kept making clicking noises with his tongue at the horse as though, denied the pleasure of handling the reins, he must contribute something to their progress.

Jimmy Rivers, a little embarrassed by the obvious excitement of two middle-aged men about a horse, sat jauntily alongside Mr. Finchley, the skip of his cap well down over one eye, giving instructions and advice.

"These roads is 'ell for horses. Simply 'ell. You want to be careful, sir, 'ow you pull 'im up. And remember the right-hand side of his mouth is as 'ard as leather and the left as tender and soft as a baby's whatchermacallit. So pull hard for right and easy for left."

Mr. Finchley could say nothing. He could only sit holding the reins, full of a rich and royal pleasure. Through the long straps he could feel the pull of the horse's head and the motion seared through his hands and up into his body like an electric current.

The cause of all the excitement, Albert Churchwarden, moved comfortably along Hampstead Lane and showed no interest in anything except the square of tarmacadam immediately below his nose.

"He seems a nice sensible kind of horse," commented Mr. Harricot.

"He is," agreed Jimmy. "He ain't such a bad old stick when you get to know him and 'e's got a heart like an elephant."

A motor car flashed by them, very closely. Mr. Finchley frowned after it.

"Don't you worry about them abominations, sir," Jimmy cautioned him. "Horses is used to them these days. Now, then, we'll go off to the right here. Don't forget—hard for the right. That's it."

Mr. Finchley put a strong pressure on the right rein and Churchwarden swung round obediently.

"You see," exclaimed Jimmy, "he knows the master 'and. But don't you be too pleased yet, sir. All horses, like women, is individualists and sets themselves up against man's authority sometime or other. But if you keep firm and let him see you're the master you don't have to worry. Don't never give in to the 'oss. It's like learnin' to ride one. Never give in. People do, of course. You've only got to look at 'em in Rotten Row of a morning to see that half of 'em are going where the 'oss wants to go."

"What if I want him to stop?" questioned Mr. Finchley, aware suddenly that he could not go on indefinitely.

"Just lean back on the reins a bit and say 'Whoa, there!' "

Jimmy's cry was so authoritative that Churchwarden stopped.

Mr. Harricot laughed. "He thought you meant it."

"A good thing, too! Always give your order as though you meant it. Go on, sir. Make him start, like what I told you."

Mr. Finchley flicked the reins and cried, "Get up, there!" as loudly as he felt was compatible with the prosperous street they were in. He did not want to make himself conspicuous by bellowing at Churchwarden.

Churchwarden leaned forward in the shafts and the caravan rolled on and Mr. Finchley's heart sang in triumph.

For two hours they drove about the quiet roads and lanes. Mr. Finchley learned to turn the caravan round, to get down and back Churchwarden and the caravan into a narrow gateway, how to tap the horse commandingly on the leg to make him raise it so that his hoof could be examined, and while they drove Jimmy expounded upon horses. Mr. Finchley had no idea that the subject was so vast or interesting. Jimmy spoke of the feeding of horses, the diseases of horses, the queer tricks some horses indulged in—illustrated by stories of horses he had owned or managed—the care of horses, the ignorance of most folk about horses and the superiority of horses as friends, workers and entertainers over anyone or anything.

Although the caravan kept to the quiet streets it caused plenty of comment. Through the drizzle that gradually put a sheen upon its canary-yellow sides, it moved like a bright argosy demanding attention. Small boys followed it for a while, like jackdaws fascinated by the colour, policemen on their beats stopped, hitched up their belts and pursed their lips in legal pouts as though they felt there was something which perhaps ought to be done about it, housewives dusting their front parlours were drawn to the windows, as fish swim from the weedy shadows of aquarium depths, to press their faces against the cold glass and watch the movement and strangeness of the outer world, an insurance collector, in love, stopped on a doorstep and followed it with his eyes down the road, dreaming of himself and his love travelling far away into a bucolic paradise where man's expectation of life was an idyllic infinity, and a nursemaid quietened her charge by holding him up to see "the bright yellow cart with the funny man driving it'.

On the way back, Mr. Finchley generously allowed Mr. Harricot to take the reins for a while. Back at the courtyard Churchwarden was taken out of the shafts, the details of the harnessing were rehearsed again by Mr. Finchley, and then the horse was put into the stable with a feed of oats. The wheels of the caravan were washed down, and then the three moved to the bar, empty of customers, and presided over during Mr. Harricot's absence by his wife, a laconic, fluffy-haired creature with a recurrent and deprecatory sniff.

Mr. Harricot dismissed his wife and then drew them drinks. They drank one another's health like men who meet to part upon the dark paths of a great adventure.

"When do you reckon to move off?" asked Mr. Harricot.

Mr. Finchley considered this point, staring into his glass as though some mirage would arise from it to give his answer.

"By the end of this week. It'll take until then to get all the stores and things in and it'll give me time to have a few more mornings getting used to driving Churchwarden."

"That's right, sir. Don't be in a hurry." Jimmy tapped an empty glass on the bar and Mr. Finchley had it filled for him. "Take your time. You can't 'ussle an 'oss. I'll come up once more to go with you and then you'll be ready for the road. And if you'll take my tip, if you're going to Kent, you'll start ripe and early in the morning before there's much about. Get across London before all the traffic begins. 'Osses is like anybody else. After a time traffic begins to get on their nerves and they may get awkward. But you'll be all right. Blimey, I wish I was cumin' wiv you. I ain't seen the country since Derby Day two years ago."

Mr. Harricot said nothing, but a liquid glint in his eye seemed to express the dream which flitted through his head that moment of a nice little public-house in a distant country town with a good morning trade.

Mr. Finchley was aware very keenly of the momentary longings of the two men, and for a while he was sorry that it was only he who was going off in search of a home, into the blue expectancy of the future.

"Life's hard," said Mr. Harricot slowly, "but it's healthier that way. If you get what you wants too soon and too easy it only makes you dissatisfied with it."

They all three nodded gravely. It had been a good morning, a morning they would remember, even the hard-bitten unemotional Jimmy, and they felt that they had a right to that deep melancholy, sweet and heavy, which follows all joys.

V

Which proves that not all churchwardens are to be trusted with forbidden fruit

THE great date was heralded in for Mr. Finchley by his alarm clock. It burst into noise angrily and buzzed like an impetuous dictator. It woke Mr. Finchley with a start. He put out his hand and shut it off and sat up in bed, rubbing his eyes. Slowly he made contact with the world around him and the significance of this particular day. His eyes turned to the window with the same eagerness which, as a child, he had shown on the morning of birthday and other treats. Was the weather fine? It was.

After that, there was little time for reflection. He had to get away. At six o'clock he was breakfasting with his wife, the edge taken off his appetite by his excitement.

Everything had been most carefully planned by Mrs. Finchley so that he could get away early. The previous day they had taken up his luggage and stowed it away in the lockers of the caravan. All the food supplies were aboard, the water tank was full, the primus stove was filled, and a supply of oil stored in the little cupboard under the galley sink. Cutlery, washing cloths, soap flakes, condiments, first-aid outfit, boot-cleaning gear, tin-opener, tub of frying fat … there was nothing Mrs. Finchley had forgotten. There was even a bottle of brandy in case Mr. Finchley got wet and took a cold.

Inside the caravan looked neat and clean. There were bright covers on the cushions of the seats, the bookshelf was tight and trim with volumes of books which Mr. Finchley hoped to have time to read, and the woodwork was polished and shining. Above the curtained archway that led to the forward sleeping compartment, the model of *Le Bon Accord* rested securely on a little shelf.

Mrs. Finchley accompanied her husband to Mr. Harricot's yard to watch the start. They walked up through the early morning beauty of the quiet streets, both filled with a gentle excitement. Mr. Finchley wore his dark blue blazer with its brass buttons, a pair of grey flannel trousers and a soft blue shirt. At the moment he wore a trilby hat and a tie, but the moment he was clear of London he meant to replace the trilby with an old and favourite Panama and to take off the tie and open his shirt neck to the sun. In his hand he carried a small attaché case, which held the particulars of the properties he was to see and a neatly drafted itinerary.

"I almost wish," said Mrs. Finchley, as they entered the yard, "that I were going with you."

"I wish you were," said Mr. Finchley. "I'm sure you'd enjoy it."

Mrs. Finchley shook her head wisely. "No, I shouldn't. It's always as well to know yourself, my dear. I should enjoy it for a week and then be uncomfortable. I'll join you for a week when I've finished my stay with David. That'll be enough for me."

Mr. Finchley said nothing. He congratulated himself upon having married a woman who knew her own mind. Mr. Harricot, as nervous and excited as they, let them into the yard.

"The great day!" he cried, his long face working with excitement. "Not a moment to spare if you want to get away before the traffic gets thick."

But despite their anxiety to be away quickly, things did not go so smoothly as they could have wished. It was the first time that Mr. Finchley had harnessed Churchwarden without the overlooking eye of Jim Rivers, and Churchwarden seemed conscious of the absence of the horse-dealer.

When he was backed towards the shafts of the caravan he insisted on stepping over them, and it was not until Mrs. Finchley and Mr. Harricot each put their weight against his quarters to keep him straight that Mr. Finchley got him squarely between the shafts. Once there Church-warden accepted the inevitable, but he shook his head and snorted through his nostrils as though he were hinting that three to one were not fair odds.

Mr. Finchley put the harness on, Mr. Harricot hoisted up the little steps at the back of the caravan and, locking the door, brought the key to Mr. Finchley. Mrs. Finchley took a last look in the corn-bin under the caravan to see that it had been filled, and then went to the yard gates and opened them wide. Mrs. Harricot stuck her fluffy head out of a top-floor window and was glad that the caravan was going off. Perhaps her husband would be less restless with it gone.

Mr. Finchley kissed his wife. He shook hands with Mr. Harricot, and then climbed to the driving seat, taking up the reins.

"Goodbye and be careful, dear!" called Mrs. Finchley.

"Good luck, and send us a postcard now and then," cried Mr. Harricot.

Mr. Finchley braced his feet against the footboards and shook the reins over Churchwarden's back.

"Git up, Churchwarden!" he shouted, his voice a little thin with nervousness. Churchwarden leaned forward in the shafts. The caravan jolted and then rolled across the cobbled yard with a lively rumble of thunder.

"Goodbye all! Goodbye!" shouted Mr. Finchley. A flock of sparrows chirped madly at him from the stable roof, a cat stretched itself lithesomely along the yard wall, the sun smiled down at him from a sky that was soon to be brazen with heat and Churchwarden turned out into the road, and the thunder of the wheels died as they met the smooth surface of the tarmacadam.

Mr. Finchley was off.

He went soberly down the road, keeping well into the left, and behind him his wife and Mr. Harricot stood in the yard gate waving and watching until he was out of sight around the corner.

Mr. Finchley was never to forget that day. It was one of those days which mark all men's lives, a day when they learn much, when they are treated to a view of life and the people around them which is entirely foreign and, at first, a little frightening.

From the top of a bus, from the inside of a cab or from a pavement, Mr. Finchley knew his London and its people, but from the driving seat of a caravan he was afforded a very different aspect of familiar things. And, before the day was out, he had cause to remember many of Jimmy Rivers's remarks about horses. In cunning, in obtuseness, in devilry Machiavelli and a whole trunkful of European dictators had a childlike, charming innocence compared with the labyrinthine workings of Churchwarden's mind.

It was not, Mr. Finchley decided afterwards, that Churchwarden was bad or good. Horses, Mr. Finchley found, were neither good nor bad, they merely reflected the qualities of their masters, and in order to reflect those qualities they had to discover them, and to discover what a master's qualities were they started by giving an exhibition of evil qualities, ready at the first lash of adamant authority to change their manners or at the first sign of apathy or encouragement to increase their wickedness.

For the first twenty minutes Churchwarden was placid, obedient and no trouble. Mr. Finchley had planned to go by the back of King's Cross Station into Gray's Inn Road and so by Holborn down to Blackfriars Bridge. Once over the river he was on the road to Kent.

The trouble began at Tufnell Park Station. On the wall outside the station was a large poster advertising the delights of London which might be reached by use of the Underground. The poster was of a circus ring, filled with galloping, gaily-trapped horses and spangled dancers riding tiptoe upon their backs.

As he came abreast of the poster its bright colours caught Churchwarden's eye. His head turned slowly towards it and, as slowly, the caravan came to a halt. Churchwarden stood eyeing the poster, champing leisurely upon his bit.

"Git up, Churchwarden!" Mr. Finchley cried, flapping the reins.

But Churchwarden did not get up. He continued to stare at the poster as though it reminded him of old circus days. Mr. Finchley called to him again, but he took no notice. Mr. Finchley looked around. It was still early, but there were a few people about, and those few were watching him. A street-cleaner, a policeman and two or three workmen waiting for their mates at the entrance to the station, they all eyed him curiously, aware of the conflict.

"Perhaps he'd rather go by tube, guv'nor?" suggested one of the workmen. The policeman smiled widely at this witticism and said heavily, "You can't park there. Bus stop. Move along, please."

"Didn't oughter allow 'osses in London," said the street-cleaner with feeling. "Mikes more wuk fer the likes o' me, and it ain't fair on the 'osses neither."

Despairingly Mr. Finchley raised his voice into an angry yell and cried: "Git up, Churchwarden!" and at the same time he gave the reins a vicious tug. The jolt and the cry, revealing new depths to Mr. Finchley's character, moved Churchwarden. He started forward and Mr. Finchley sighed with relief. All that it wanted, he told himself, was a firm hand. He had to show Churchwarden who was master. But he was annoyed that the horse had not forced the battle last week when he had Jimmy at his side to help.

After that Mr. Finchley kept a sharp lookout for posters and whenever he saw one coming he would stir Churchwarden to a faster gait and keep a tight hold on the reins, ready to jerk his head away from the luring colours.

He had no time to observe the way people turned and stared at the sight of the yellow caravan swaying along the grey, drab streets. His whole attention was on Churchwarden.

Near the Caledonian Market he had an anxious moment. A magnificent poster stretched for nearly twenty yards along a wall advertising a film of the Charge of the Light Brigade. It was a glorious spectacle of leaping, battle-maddened horses charging into the mouths of cannons, blue tunics, bright swords, lancers' caps, bloody carnage … a furious riot of colour.

Mr. Finchley saw it coming, remembered the poster, for he had passed it a few days before, and knew that Church-warden would never resist its appeal. Fortunately the road was empty, and as they came to the poster he was able to draw the horse away at an angle and they tacked across the road to the far side so that Churchwarden's blinker hid the poster from him. It was a trying moment and it was not improved by the sudden squealing of brakes as a private car came tearing up the road, taking advantage of the quiet to speed, saw the caravan slewed across its path and swerved violently to avoid it.

The car drew up beyond him. Mr. Finchley heard a man's voice crying shrill imprecations, but he drove on. He had no time for argument or explanation.

That was only the beginning of his troubles. A lesser man would have been discouraged. But not Mr. Finchley. He was filled with an obstinate determination. Ahead of him lay Kent, lay weeks of pleasant ambling through country lanes to find the house which somewhere wait-ed for him. No horse was going to destroy that prospect or hold him back from the reality that lived behind his dreams.

There was more traffic in Gray's Inn Road. But Church-warden gave no trouble. Mr. Finchley's confidence began to revive. He even had time to look about him.

It was a Monday morning and the world was going back to work, relinquishing the gay weekend, turning its thoughts to desk and counter. Not a few people were made happy at the sight of the canary-coloured caravan, for it reminded them of the country they had recently left, of the leisure which was gone for another week.

Mr. Finchley was aware of their interest in him. He expanded under their curious looks and glances. He cocked his hat just a trifle more to the side, sucked more vigorously at his pipe and tried to achieve an air of nonchalance.

Ahead of him rose the black-and-white frame of the face of Staple Inn and the swirling movement of Holborn. He drew up before the traffic lights as they flashed red and found himself at the head of a waiting column of traffic. He and Churchwarden waited for the lights, Mr. Finchley pleased that Churchwarden showed no signs of restlessness at the noise and dash of traffic before him, and Churchwarden showing no emotion, his head slightly down, his mouth churning slowly as he chewed.

Mr. Finchley glanced round the side of the caravan and saw behind him a railway delivery van, a taxi-cab, several private cars and tradesmen's vans. The traffic lights flitted through amber to green and Mr. Finchley flipped the reins and cried, "Come up!"

Churchwarden shook his ears gently as though flies were bothering him and went on studying the peculiar composition of the road surface beneath his nose.

"Churchwarden!" Mr. Finchley bellowed angrily at the horse, tugging on the reins.

Churchwarden took no notice. He just stood where he was, wrapped in the deepest of philosophical studies. Because of the road island to their right they completely blocked the way into Holborn. Churchwarden slowly fanned the tresses of his long tail and behind the caravan there broke out a cacophony of klaxons, bells, electric hooters, whistles, cries and shouts.

Mr. Finchley went red with embarrassment. A flood of nervousness surged through his body and for a moment he was flustered, not knowing what to do. He leant around the side of the caravan and waved one hand to mollify the waiting traffic.

"It's all right," he cried haltingly. "It's all right. I'll be gone …"

He was aware only of the ferocious scowl of the driver of the railway van. The man had a face like a prize fighter and he seemed in a bad temper. He twisted his head round the side of his cab like a jack-in-the-box and yelled sharply, "Hurry up and get that yellow peril out of the way, buddy!"

Mr. Finchley shouted at Churchwarden and jerked the reins. He shouted and tugged, but Churchwarden was stone. He was aware of a crowd watching him from the pavements, a happy, amused, working crowd glad of a diversion on their way to work. He was aware also of angry individuals swarming around the side of the caravan and away in the distance a policeman approaching with unhurried steps.

"Hey! Wake up that crocodile and tell it to clear out of the way," shouted a taxi-driver. "It's keepin' 'arf o' London waitin'!"

"Whoa! 'In my gipsy caravan …' " sang a newsboy in a reedy falsetto and the crowd roared at the discomfiture of Mr. Finchley and the waiting line of traffic.

"Churchwarden!" Mr. Finchley shouted at the horse like a captain bellowing to a helmsman through a gale. It was a mistake. The horse took no notice, but the crowd seized upon the name.

"Churchwarden! He ain't no churchwarden. He's a sexton. He thinks he's at a funeral. Wake up, Sexton!"

Behind rose the protesting hoot of horns. Before him were the angry faces of cab-drivers, railway-van drivers and private drivers, all anxious to get somewhere, all resentful of this stoppage.

"Can't you control that ox! Get him out of the way or I'll push into the back of you and shove you out of the way!"

The newsboy, eager for public plaudits, broke into 'Jogging along behind the old grey mare.'

"Call a policeman—"

"Tain't a policeman you want, mate. It's a demolition gang. They'll 'ave to tike that Methuselah to pieces to move it!"

Mr. Finchley flung profuse apologies around him. "I'm sorry, gentlemen. I'm sorry, but—"

"Come on, father! Get that covered wagon out of the way. You can't camp there!"

Mr. Finchley made one last effort to stir Churchwarden with the reins. The horse was completely oblivious of him and the ribald crowd. It was immobile, unaware of mundane disturbances, wrapped in a splendid isolation of contrariness.

Mr. Finchley lost his temper completely. He slipped out of the driving seat to the ground, muttering to himself words which would have shocked his wife, and boiling with a fury that was completely out of place in his mild nature.

He went to Churchwarden's head, caught the rein close to the mouth and jerked the horse's head forward. It was a jerk that had all his strength behind it, and behind his strength all his ire.

Churchwarden moved forward as obediently as a child, started as smoothly as though all he had wanted was this touch on the reins and the reassurance of his master beside him.

A lusty cheer went up from the crowd. Mr. Finchley's face cleared with relief and then a heavy finger tapped him on the shoulder.

"Now then, now then, mister. Where d'you think you're going? Can't you see the light's against you?" Mr. Finchley looked up to see a policeman and the warning glow of red light. He stopped Churchwarden and stood, bereft of words.

The policeman smiled at him paternally. The drivers got back into their cars, the morning crowd slowly moved away, and Mr. Finchley prayed that Churchwarden would move off the next time. Churchwarden did. He remembered the jerk.

Mr. Finchley led him a little way down Holborn and then got back to the driving seat. Churchwarden went away without any trouble. But it was not the last time that day that Churchwarden was to give trouble.

Once or twice he still showed his strange disinclination to pass traffic lights and Mr. Finchley had to hop down and lead him, and once he refused to start after Mr. Finchley had led him a little way and then wanted to remount the driving seat. Churchwarden, as though protesting that Mr. Finchley should ride all the time, would not move unless Mr. Finchley walked at his head. Mr. Finchley had to go a mile on foot before Churchwarden's sense of fairness was fully assuaged.

Once he stopped dead in the Old Kent Road, refusing to pass a mechanical concrete mixer. No coaxing could get him by the shaking, rattling cauldron, and at last Mr. Finchley had to request the workmen, amidst much banter at the delicate state of his horse's nerves, to stop the engine to let him pass. It was with some amazement that a mile farther on he watched Churchwarden draw him unconcernedly by another concrete mixer, not even taking any notice of the tug on the reins which Mr. Finchley gave him so that he might get down and make a similar request to the navvies. It was then that Mr. Finchley decided that all horses were evil.

It was not until an hour later that he discovered the real key to mastery over Churchwarden, the solution which Solomon had propounded long before him. It was nearly lunchtime and Mr. Finchley was still within the circle of villas and suburbs which ring London, and he was beginning to tire of the endless trek through streets, harassed by tramcars and buses.

At a road junction a policeman held him up. He pulled Churchwarden to a halt and sat, waiting for the signal to proceed. And as he sat there a hawker came up alongside of him, pushing his narrow barrow full of pyramids of oranges, apples and bananas. The man stopped abreast of Mr. Finchley and looked up at him with a friendly nod. The end of the barrow came abreast of Churchwarden's head.

Mr. Finchley, looking ahead, saw Churchwarden's neck swing round slowly towards the fruit on the barrow and then his head smoothly dipped down towards the topmost apple of a pyramid. A pair of eager lips curled back over large teeth.

For a second Mr. Finchley watched, horrified. There was no doubt of Churchwarden's intentions. To the scrupulously honest Mr. Finchley all his evils that morning were nothing compared with this crime. Instinctively Mr. Finchley's hand went out to the short switch in the whip-holder at his side. He was scarcely aware that the switch was there until now. He brought the switch down across Churchwarden's rump with a smart cut just as the horse was about to take the apple. The effect was startling.

Churchwarden's head jerked back from the fruit and then, slowly, he turned and regarded Mr. Finchley from one eye. It was a curious look, a look that held reproach and also a new respect.

" 'E's got takin' ways, ain't 'e, mate?" observed the hawker humorously.

Mr. Finchley grinned. "Spare the rod and spoil the child," he said slowly and he felt that he had found the key to mastery over Churchwarden. The horse disliked the touch of the switch. To avoid it he was prepared to behave himself. And so it proved. Once or twice more in the course of that day Churchwarden made tentative movements towards disobedience, disobedience which consisted chiefly of passive resistance to distinct commands. The switch immediately broke his determination until, finally, all Mr. Finchley had to do was to rattle the switch in the holder. That was enough for Churchwarden. He had met his master and he acknowledged him.

After that, Mr. Finchley was happier. The crowded tangle of houses began to fall away. London's net dropped behind him, until in the late afternoon Mr. Finchley found himself well on the road to Sevenoaks and beginning to be almost unaware of the flicker of swift cars passing him along the main road. A great contentment rose within him until the hum of traffic was no more than the gentle murmur of summer insects.

When the evening came and the swallows were hawking low, he turned off from the main road and found a quiet by-lane. Not far down it there was the long line of a brick wall enclosing private grounds and, opposite the wall, a green space backed by a tiny copse of thin ash trees.

Mr. Finchley pulled off the road on to the grass. For a time he was busy. He unharnessed Churchwarden, who muzzled into his shoulder as though asking forgiveness for his sins, gave him a rub down and then put his feedbag on. Mr. Finchley felt that there was a well-established tradition that one always saw to one's horse first. When Churchwarden was tied safely to an ash pole, munching contentedly, Mr. Finchley went into the caravan and, lighting the primus, began to prepare his evening meal.

As the blue light of the evening moved slowly between the slender tree trunks a delicious smell of bacon and eggs floated from the caravan and the yellow light of the oil-lamp winked through the dimity curtains.

AND as Mr. Finchley sat at his table, eating heartily and full of a sense of conquest that came from his successful negotiation of his first day of caravanning, Mr. Harricot stood behind his bar surveying the crowded room. His evening custom was good. There was no doubt about that. The door of the bar was open, for the night was warm and the air was full of tobacco smoke and pleasant chatter.

"Bottle of light ale, please," the order came from a young man who had just threaded his way to the bar.

Mr. Harricot poured the drink and, as he did so, he eyed the young man. He had not seen him before and he was always interested in newcomers. On second thoughts he decided that the man was not so young. He had that youthful appearance which many men seemed to preserve into middle-age. His grey flannel suit was well-cut and close-fitting. His shirt was expensive and the dark hair was crisp and brushed back from the forehead with just a hint of a wave, a slight shade of feminism which was curiously in contrast with the face. It was a lean, eager face. His eyes, watching Mr. Harricot closely, were full of a hidden movement and life. Mr. Harricot decided that he did not like the man and something of his feeling must have become known to the man, for his thin lips curled gently as though the man relished the antipathy he had provoked. Mr. Harricot noticed that the back of the man's right hand as he raised his glass to drink was marked with a large star-shaped scar as though at some time it had been cut deeply, perhaps by glass, and had healed clumsily.

"Hot evening," said the man.

Mr. Harricot nodded.

"Been hot all day," said the man, untouched by Mr. Harricot's reserve. "Kind of day that makes you think about the country, bathing and all that."

"I suppose so," said Mr. Harricot, remembering that his profession demanded some hospitality towards all customers.

"A friend of mine was telling me the other evening that he'd heard that you had a caravan up here for sale. Don't know whether it's true, but if it is I'm rather interested. I've been thinking of taking a caravanning holiday this year."

"Did you want to buy it?" asked Mr. Harricot quietly.

"That I do—if it's for sale!" As the man replied Mr. Harricot got the impression that the long, elegant body was strung with a quick excitement.

"That's a pity, then—for you," said Mr. Harricot unperturbed. "I sold it last week to a gent, and he only went off in it today—holidaying, same as you want to do."

"Oh," the tone was casual. "Don't know where he's gone, do you? Where he would be?"

"Kent," said Mr. Harricot laconically, and then moved to a volubility which was prompted by his illogical dislike of the man, a triumph which he could not resist; "somewhere in Kent, and right at this moment I should think he was sitting on the steps at the back of that caravan, smokin' his pipe, listening to the stamp of his old horse and watchin' the moon come up over the trees. Yes, that's what he'd be doin'—that's what anybody would be doin' who'd gone off in a caravan today."

Mr. Harricot was quite right. Mr. Finchley was doing exactly what he described.

VI
Of kippers

MR. FINCHLEY was washing himself. He had a bowl of water perched on top of a box at the back of the caravan. He had shaved—Mr. Finchley was one of those people who shave before washing—and was now stripped to the buff and wallowing in the bowl, plunging his head into it and snorting and puffing like a dog with earth up its nose. He straightened up and began to rub himself vigorously with a hard towel. Faint pink and white lines rose and fell upon his soft skin as he scrubbed at himself, and from the depths of the towel as he pummelled his scalp and the scanty tonsure which ringed his head came the muffled sounds of song. He was enjoying himself.

There was no reason why he should not have been singing and enjoying himself, as all those who have washed in the open on a morning in summer know well. The water was cold and biting on his skin—it came from the well of a cottage two hundred yards down the road and as he worked the towel he could feel the cool touch of the morning air upon his chest and the warming hand of the sun pressed upon the small of his back. The wind from his flaying towel moved the tall spikes of yellow rattle in the ditch at his side, and a goldfinch, black, scarlet and gold, hovered over a blown thistle head and sent an unmusical twittering to join his song.

Churchwarden, munching at his morning feed, switched his tail at the flies. It was a summer morning, a morning when you wake and find the world free of mist, the air clear as a jewel and the colour of each leaf and flower, the movement of tree-tops in the meek breeze and the smell of flowering beans and cottage fires vivid and sharp on the senses as though for years you had lived with dulled eyes and nostrils and now for the first time enjoyed the richness and true reality of things.

Mr. Finchley's head came out of the towel to hear a sharp click and he saw, standing in the roadway, a man holding a camera which was pointed at him. Before he could say anything the man came across to him.

"I hope you don't mind, sir," he said anxiously. "No offence, but I just couldn't resist it. A lovely snapshot. Hobby of mine." He tapped the camera and then folded it.

"That's all right."

Mr. Finchley studied him. He was a small, plump man with a bubbly appearance. His round body, his fat face and red, plump cheeks, eager eyes and the tubby legs and arms were like a collection of fat bubbles held together by a dancing, restless stir of muscles. Mr. Finchley got the impression that the man was for ever trying to raise himself upon tiptoes and never quite succeeding. He was dressed in a white linen suit, canvas shoes and a cap and he was about Mr. Finchley's own age.

"Might send it to one of the holiday competitions in the newspapers. How about 'Morning Ablutions'? Good title, do you think? Or 'Caravanner Cleans Up'?"

"I think—"

"Of course you do. You don't think much of them. Don't be afraid to say. Never take offence at genuine criticism, that's what I try to live up to. Caravanner—ugly word, isn't it? My, but it's a nice little job, that caravan. You know, caravans had never occurred to me ..." This last was said with a sort of slow subsidence of tone as though all the bubbles were deflating a little and sinking into a more compact formation. "Never even been inside a caravan."

"Would you like to look over this one, Mr ...?"

"Blain's the name. Horace Blain—I live in the house over there." He tipped his head towards the brick wall. "I'd like to, very much. Caravan. Ship of the desert—no, that's camels. Get mixed up sometimes."

He hopped up the little ladder and was inside the caravan before Mr. Finchley could move.

"Have a good look round," Mr. Finchley called as he drew on his shirt. He was proud of his caravan and not at all loath to let it be admired.

From inside the caravan a series of admiring cries and comments began to rise. Mr. Finchley made himself presentable and went in to explain the finer points of the caravan.

Horace Blain's enthusiasm for the caravan rose. Each new device, each fresh locker tucked away neatly under a seat or bunk brought a mounting pleasure to him. Before he was through he was volatile with joy and, Mr. Finchley felt, in danger of soaring clean off the floor and through the domed roof.

"It's the neatest thing I ever saw!" he cried happily. Mr. Finchley beamed with the pleasure any man takes in hearing praise of his possessions. He moved to the little cooking galley and began to light the stove. Mr. Blain watched him with wide and shining eyes.

"And that's where you cook?"

Mr. Finchley nodded and, as the primus began to hiss comfortingly, he put on a frying pan. A thought struck him.

"Would you care to stop and have some breakfast with me?" he asked casually. He had taken a fancy to the bouncing, admiring Horace Blain, and also he was curious about the man. It was hard to place him.

Horace Blain accepted the invitation with such an accession of joy that Mr. Finchley held himself in readiness to grab his ankles at the first sign of his shooting into the air.

Mr. Finchley prepared the breakfast while Horace talked. The sizzle of bacon fat and spluttering eggs made a pleasant accompaniment to the talk. Never had Mr. Finchley heard a man talk so much. It was as though within Horace Blain there rested, compressed, repressed, bottled-down and held tight, waiting until this moment, a vast store of words and thoughts, a bubbling reservoir of talk. Mr. Finchley, who prided himself on the way he could fry eggs with their eyes shut, splashed fat over the yolks gently and watched a white film creep across them.

"Yes, Mr. Finchley," said Horace, "I can't think why I never thought of a caravan. And all the things I have thought of, but never a caravan. I've been here for four years and never thought of a caravan."

"Do you mean you've lived in that house over there for four years?" Mr. Finchley nodded through the open doorway to where, above the red wall, and between the trunks of a grove of firs, he could see the white walls of a house.

"Four years, yes. And before that—what do you think?" Horace posed the question with the first sign of hesitancy he had so far shown. "What do you think, Mr. Finchley?" It was a challenge, almost pathetic, a challenge that somehow implied a sense of guilt.

Mr. Finchley looked at him as he set the table and put the coffee pot to boil. "I haven't the faintest idea."

"Hairdresser," said Horace with a swoop into doleful tones.

"Hairdresser?" Mr. Finchley did not understand.

"Yes, hairdresser. Nice little business off St. Paul's Churchyard. Always plenty doing, always plenty of talk and people coming and going. Ten years of it and not a moment that I didn't enjoy. The heads that have gone through my hands, Mr. Finchley!" Horace shut his eyes as though the vision of that line of customers' heads, stretching away into infinity, a phalanx of heads, some close-cropped, others crisp with curls, bald heads, grey heads, red heads and knobbly heads, was a sight that stunned hire.

"What happened to the business, then?" enquired Mr. Finchley, seeing that Horace needed help.

"It's there still. But I'm not. It was that ticket, that damned ticket, that tiny, crinkling little ticket that did it! Sometimes I wish I'd never bought the thing." He paused and added, with a faint mounting of pride. "I won a prize in the Irish Sweepstake. My share was sixty thousand pounds. It's a horrible lot of money ..."

Mr. Finchley pushed a fragrant plate of eggs and bacon before him, and as they ate, he heard the story. The money had changed Horace's life. His wife had insisted upon their selling the business and retiring to a house in the country. At first Horace had been as enthusiastic as his wife. They had come to the house across the way, and his wife had been happy. But not Horace. They made friends, but they were nothing like enough to compensate Horace for the daily flow of conversation which had once been his joy. Talk to him was food, the smell of unguents and vaporisers the only smell, and the click of clippers and the rasp of razors sweeter than birdsong.

"If it wasn't for the wife," said Horace, "I'd be back at the old business, like a shot. But she won't hear of it. Says I've earned the right to enjoy myself, and when I tell her that I'd just as soon work she says it would be wrong to be keeping another man who wanted it out of a business. She likes the country—and so do I—but it's quiet. That's the trouble."

"You ought to have a hobby," said Mr. Finchley, sensing the other's dejection and wishing to be helpful.

"Hobbies!" The word was pronounced scornfully. "I've had hundreds of 'em. Angoras, beekeeping, pig-keeping, photography, Cook's tours, helping with the local Boy Scouts, crosswords ... there isn't anything that really does any good. The only time I forget the dullness is when I do the gardener's hair—once a fortnight in the greenhouse. The wife doesn't know about that." He waved an imaginary pair of clippers in the air above Mr. Finchley's head and smiled, saying, his mind far away, "Nice to see your face again, sir. Been on holiday? Lucky with the weather, weren't you? Yes, it's been a good summer. I see where it says in the paper that the seasons are getting later and later. Something to do with the spots on the sun ..." His words tailed away and his eyes travelled towards Mr. Finchley's bald head; they were the eyes of a visionary greeting the goal which has sustained his struggles and road-weariness.

Mr. Finchley coughed, a little embarrassed, and poured him some coffee. Horace Blain suddenly grinned, a wide, cheerful grin, and his spirits swept back again.

"I'll get over it. Question of adjusting myself to a new life. A period of transition my wife calls it." He paused and looked around the caravan and then continued reflectively, "But I'd never thought of a caravan. It's an idea. The wife wouldn't want to come, of course. But she wouldn't mind me going off. Very fair-minded that way. And I should meet people. I suppose, Mr. Finchley, you weren't thinking of selling your caravan, were you? I'd give you a very good price."

Mr. Finchley shook his head.

"Not for a hundred pounds?"

"No. I don't want to sell it. I've only just started out in it."

Horace took the refusal pleasantly and returned to his eggs and bacon. In a few moments he was pouring out a flood of talk. Mr. Finchley had never heard anything like it. It swept over him, around him, filled the caravan and spilled into the outside world so that Churchwarden's ears stood up, tickled by the sound, and occasionally a question would be put to Mr. Finchley about his caravan and his plans. By the time breakfast was over, and Horace had insisted upon helping with the washing up and harnessing Churchwarden, there was quite a lot which he knew of Mr. Finchley's plans for house-hunting.

He took three or four photographs of the caravan, with Mr. Finchley at the reins, to have as souvenirs and then Mr. Finchley had to be off. His first house to be inspected lay five miles down the road and he was anxious to be away.

He clicked his tongue at Churchwarden and the yellow caravan moved forward.

"Goodbye!" shouted Horace, waving his white cap. "And thanks for the breakfast. If you come back this way, call and see me. And don't wear a hat more than you can help on this trip. It'll keep your hair healthy. Goodbye!" His calls floated after Mr. Finchley down the road.

"Goodbye!" answered Mr. Finchley and then Horace had gone from his sight.

After a time, as Mr. Finchley jogged along, Churchwarden behaving himself, he pulled out from his pocket the list of particulars of the house he was to visit that morning. It sounded attractive. Mr. Finchley read the agent's general note of the property … "A red-bricked country house of character and comfort, set in the midst of ten acres of pasture and woodland possessing fine views, a productive walled kitchen garden and a small but pleasant flower garden with lily pool …" The picture was complete in Mr. Finchley's eye. He saw the house, a typical Kentish country home, standing square in its little domain of field and wood, looking out to the distant hills. He saw the productive walled garden with peaches and pears trained up the red walls, he could almost feel the heat of the sun striking back at him from those walls, smell the scent of rosemary and pinks in the pleasant garden, and see gay flowers whose colours would be reflected in the dark mirror of the lily pool. Robert would love the pool. They would put goldfish in it. Maybe even widen it enough to bathe … His mind flighted on. Even the name of the property was quaint and rich with romantic suggestions … Froghole Farm.

In the village, which was a mile from the farm, he stopped and was directed to Mr. Saunders of Rose Cottage who held the keys of the farm, which was empty. Rose Cottage was one of a row at the far side of the village. There were no roses growing near it to suggest its name, and its garden was a bare patch, trodden clean of grass and littered with children's toys, a red train without wheels, a very battered toy pram loaded with stones and two dolls lying, dispossessed, on the ground, their arms outflung, their eyes staring to heaven, casualties of some child's battle. Mr. Finchley knocked at the door, was greeted with a burst of wailing from inside and, after a little while, by the appearance of Mrs. Saunders, a thin-faced woman who thrust her face from the door rather like a cuckoo jerking itself out at the sounding of the hour, and cried, "Well, what do you want?"

Mr. Finchley explained his business, was informed that Mr. Saunders was not home, that Mrs. Saunders was extremely busy with washing day and children and that if he wanted to look over Froghole Farm, he would have to go unattended, or come back later when Mr. Saunders would have returned.

Mr. Finchley decided to go alone and was given directions.

"You go up the road about half a mile and you can't miss it. A green gate on the left. You'll return the key afterwards?"

It was some time before Mr. Finchley found his way. The half a mile was a mile and the green gate was green, but with age not paint. Across its top bar were, in faded white, the words—Froghole Farm, and beyond it a grass-crested road ran into a clump of trees which hid the rest of the property.

Mr. Finchley ran the caravan inside the gateway, and, as it was lunchtime, he put Churchwarden's nosebag on, tied him to a tree so that he could not move about and tip the caravan, and then set out to inspect Froghole Farm.

He was not dismayed by the decrepit gate or grass-grown road. A new gate, fresh paint and busy feet would change all that. He went through the clump of trees, was scolded by a tit who was nesting in one of them and found himself looking at Froghole Farm.

The house stood on a little rise. It was fronted by its flower garden, and beyond the garden a large field ran away to a dark line of trees that marked its edge. There was another field behind the house, and they were both prolific with thistles and covered with an infection of warts, warts that Mr. Finchley found were ant-hills. Where there were no thistles or ant-hummocks the new grass had pushed up between a matted layer of old bents and last year's hay crop. No scythe or mower had touched the fields for years and in one or two places young thorns, bird-sown, were standing three and four feet high. It was a waste land and even Mr. Finchley's untrained eye found it distressing. He did not know it then, but he was to recognise it later, that there were many such fields in England, even in the well-farmed counties like Kent. Waste land, fertile land, going back to the wild profusion of Nature, thick with nettles, thistle, burdock and hog-weed and pitted with rabbit stabs and burrows... the house was surrounded with it, surrounded with ten acres that had not enough keep for five sheep. All over England there were such fields, such farms; land which should have felt the plough long ago, land which could have been producing food and feeding cattle, land which could have been keeping men at work and hardening the muscles of youth by its demands. Instead it was derelict, derelict for many reasons, because farmers could not make the land pay, because they could not get a fair return for their work, because they could not afford the cost of the labour necessary to keep hedges trimmed, ditches cleared, thistles spudded down and crops cleared of weeds. Where the fault lay not even the farmer could be sure, but there was no man, not even the town-bred, uninstructed Mr. Finchley, who did not appreciate the irony of the paradox that men should line up before Unemployment Exchanges in the towns, idle, and thousands of acres should stand, slowly being swamped by weeds and mole casts, idle, too.

Mr. Finchley went across to the house. He knew at a glance that he had not found the place he was looking for. The agent had not lied. It was a red-bricked house and it commanded a pleasant view over the countryside, but he had not mentioned that it was roofed with ugly blue slates, that its shape was square and as forbidding as a barracks, that the pleasant garden was completely overgrown and marked only as a garden by the presence of a rusted iron railing, a relic from Victorian days. The walled kitchen garden was overgrown and the wall in places bulging where its foundations had moved with the slip of the undrained land.

Its only fruit trees were a pair of lichen-encrusted apple trees from the top of which two blackbirds, happy in the wilderness, shouted at one another. And the lily pond. Mr. Finchley found it at the side of the house, a green-coated pool, overhung with a barrier of suckers from a tottering damson tree, its scummy surface marked with the channels cut by swimming rats and moorfowl, its only sign of lilies the pathetic flourish of a few broad leaves in one corner. As Mr. Finchley moved away through the long grass, a frog hopped away before him and jumped into the water, and he knew why the farm was named Froghole.

He did not want to go into the house. He had seen enough. But as he stood there, he recalled his wife's comments about house-hunting. He was new to this experience, but she had known it. He smiled to himself. There were other houses and it was wrong to be discouraged.

And as he stood there, looking over the garden where the last outposts of old flowers, lanky hollyhocks and dwarfed pads of aubrietia and violas struggled against the lusty onslaught of convolvulus and reaching mulleins, a strong, pungent odour came sweeping from the house to his nostrils.

He sniffed, puzzled, and then sniffed again. The smell was familiar and not unpleasant. He took a long breath and suddenly knew what it was. Close at hand kippers were being cooked. He could smell them.

He walked towards the house, following the smell upwind like a setter, and he arrived at the front door. There was no need for the key. It stood ajar and, he noticed, there was a drift of old leaves just inside the passageway as though the door had been ajar for a long time. Mr. Saunders, he guessed, did not strain himself with his caretaking duties.

Mr. Finchley went inside and was greeted, from the room on his left, by a strong smell of kippers and the sound of a fire crackling. He moved up the passage and found himself looking into the room. He made no attempt to soften his footsteps, and, as he reached the open doorway, he found himself facing a man who had come out to see who was approaching.

He was a tall, massively built man whose body seemed ill at ease within the blue serge suit he wore. He gave the impression that years ago his clothes had fitted him well, but that he had long grown out of them. A dark blue seaman's jersey came close about his neck, his face shining above it like a beacon. It was a large, rugged, red face, spotted with freckles and spread with merry, weather-beaten folds and curves. His hair was a pale, sandy colour, settling tractably over his head as though it had been scrubbed into limp paleness. From one corner of his mouth stuck out a pipe with so short a stem that the smoke from the bowl rose into one eye, making him half-wink as he looked at Mr. Finchley.

He grinned at Mr. Finchley, jerked his head affably, and then said, "Come in, shipmate. It's funny how the smell of a kipper draws people."

He went back to the fireplace in which a heap of box wood crackled and flamed and dropped on his hunkers. "Come in," he called again to Mr. Finchley, who had hesitated in the doorway. "You've got as much right here as me, more, in fact, as I can see." He nodded towards the sheet of agent's particulars which Mr. Finchley held in his hand. "I ain't even thinkin' of buying the place."

He held his kipper, which was skewered on to a pointed piece of box wood, up to the fire and turned it slowly before the heat.

"If you're not looking over the doing here?" Mr. Finchley asked as he came into the room.

"I'm cookin' my kipper. A man has to eat, shipmate. Do you like kippers?"

"I'm very fond of them ... at times," admitted Mr. Finchley.

"I hope this ain't one of the times you're fond of 'em, then," the man laughed, rocking on his heels. " 'Cause I've only got this one, and I don't mean to share it. Been on the road since seven and I'm hungry. What do you think of the place—you goin' to buy it?"

"No, I'm not," Mr. Finchley decided, shifting on his feet and wondering why he had not thought of buying kippers. The smell was tantalising and he had not had lunch.

"I shouldn't think so. Hell of a place. Owner ought to be thankful to me for coming along and building a fire in here. It must give the room quite a lift up. Funny thing about kippers, you'd think that you could get tired of 'em if you had too many. But I lived on 'em and nothing else for a month once. Making the New Zealand trip we was and the ruddy boilers blew one night. Next thing I knew I was lying on a bit of beach, sort of atoll place, all by myself and surrounded by boxes and boxes of kippers we'd been carrying what had drifted ashore. I was there a month, a month of nothing but kippers and water. Kippers fried, kippers boiled, kippers baked in co-conut leaves, kippers grilled, and even kippers raw, but I never got tired of 'em, and when I got taken off by a small trading schooner the captain he was Dutch had a native girl on board as wife and cook and she dished me up with kippers for me first meal. And I ate 'em. Never troubled me—except that from that day I've always had a most tremendous thirst, never got rid of it since." He turned the kipper and reached to the side of the fireplace where a bottle of beer was standing.

Mr. Finchley watched, wonderingly, as his long throat heaved with convulsive movements.

"Haaa! That's a little better. Well, shipmate, I wish I was generous enough to share this one with you. But I'm hungry. Docked at Gravesend day before yesterday. *Lady Leaf,* just home from a Black Sea cruise. Twelve pounds fifteen I come ashore with and my thirst. You don't know how that thirst keeps on at me, shipmate. Two pounds fifteen now and about forty miles to go before I see my brother. Always spend a few days with him when I get home. Then off again. Can't afford to keep ashore long, it aggravates my thirst."

"Isn't water any good for it?" asked Mr. Finchley, rubbing his mouth with his hand to hide a smile.

The man looked up at him, pained. "Not a bit of good," he said earnestly. "I thought I'd explained. This ain't no ordinary thirst. It's a kipper thirst. Water's no good for that. If it was I'd think about takin' a shore job."

"Well, I'll leave you to your meal," said Mr. Finchley, moving towards the door.

"Sorry I couldn't ask you to join me. But you see how it is."

"Don't mention it. You must be hungry after your walk. And I must be getting along. Goodbye." Mr. Finchley left him, wondering what it was about the man which had struck him as being odd. There was something which signalled unconsciously to Mr. Finchley and set him wondering, but he could not place the source of his uneasiness.

He drove back to Rose Cottage and surrendered the key.

That afternoon Mr. Finchley passed through Sevenoaks and turned eastwards. He saw two more houses in the district, neither of which was suitable. His next project lay a good ten miles ahead and he knew that it would not be reached that day.

The sky had dulled with cloud and he jogged along, happy with his pipe and the smell of harness and horse in his nostrils. It was pleasant to be perched up high enough to look over the hedges into the fields he passed. From a car, he thought, the hedges hid nearly all the fields.

Slowly into the train of his thoughts a queer noise worked its way, a noise that recurred regularly, like the slap, slap of a train wheel going over the joins in the line.

Slip, slap! Slip, slap!

Mr. Finchley came out of his reverie to find that the noise was coming from Churchwarden. It had a metallic tone, and Mr. Finchley was suddenly aware of its origin.

He pulled up and jumped down, going to Churchwarden.

"Get up!" he cried, tapping the horse's knees one after another. Obediently Churchwarden lifted his leg. The plate on the hind near hoof was loose.

That, thought Mr. Finchley, means a blacksmith and no more travelling for Churchwarden today. He looked ahead of him and was gratified by the sight of a slipway at the side of the road. It was a place used by road contractors to park their steamrollers, but now it was empty, its gravelled space green with lusty growths of fat hen and silverweed. It was not an ideal resting-spot, but it would have to do. Mr. Finchley pulled in. It was nearly six o'clock. In the morning he would set about finding a blacksmith.

VII
How Mr. Finchley finds a shipmate and loses a ship

AT eight o'clock that evening it began to rain, a steady downpour. Mr. Finchley darted out of the caravan and fixed a waterproof sheet over Churchwarden's back, saw that he had enough rope to move into the lee of the caravan and then scurried inside again. Horses, he supposed, and hoped, could not feel the discomfort of rain as humans did. After a while Churchwarden would bed down in the long grass under the hedge and in the morning, after a combing, he would be fresh and ready for work.

The rain had darkened the evening and he lit the swinging oil-lamp. The storm spattered against the dome of the caravan in a miniature cannonade and the tiny roof ridges which acted as gutters began to pipe out a feeble strain as the water cascaded from them. It was pleasant to sit within and listen to the rain, felt Mr. Finchley, pleasant to contrast his warm, sheltered little world with the wet, rain-sleeked universe outside.

He was glad, too, to find that the roof was tight and weatherproof.

He settled down on the long upholstered seat, propped his head with a couple of cushions and reached above him to the bookshelf for a book he had been longing to begin. It was a book which Mrs. Finchley had picked up for him in Charing Cross Road for threepence, an old book, printed in 1909, and called the *Book of the Caravan*. Mr. Finchley hoped that it would furnish him with useful hints. Instead, as he lay there, puffing contentedly at his pipe, his round, placid face shining in the oil-light, the white circle of his baldness standing out against the green of his supporting cushions, he found that he was being transported into another world and age, the spacious world of Edwardian days, the wealthy, daring yet circumspect days of new freedoms. He read of caravans that were owned by dukes and carried their private wine cellars under the floor boards, of caravans so large and luxurious that they had to be hauled by a team of four horses or sent by rail. He read on, taken back to the distant days before the Great War:

> "The dangers of the road for caravannists practically begin and end with the absurd word 'automobile.' ... If you are in charge of a horse, however, as you will be when caravanning, you may exercise the privilege conferred upon you by law ... under the Motor Cars Acts, 1869 and 1903, Art. IV, sec. 6, of compelling drivers of motor cars to pull up while you pass them. If you see some 'road-hog' approaching you at thirty-five or forty miles an

hour, leaving a trail which you will have to pass … I do not hesitate to say exercise your privilege, and compel him to pull up until the dust behind him shall have subsided … If you keep the crown of the road he can do nothing save halt, and if he delays too long to obey your signal will not improbably come to grief in the adjacent ditch or bank."

A car whizzed up the road outside, its tyres screaming over the wet surface. It was gone in a flash, its exhaust note burbling upon the night with a fat, contented roar. Thirty-five miles an hour, thought Mr. Finchley! Those days were gone. What, he wondered, would happen to him today if he stuck to the crown of the road? It would be himself who would "not improbably come to grief." He chuckled. He himself had lived from that age to this, seen the horse go down and the hated automobile come up, seen the world change its habits and quicken its pace … But there was still much in it that was unchanged, much that was worthwhile.

A burst of frenzied rain swirled down upon the caravan, slashing at the painted sides, rattling on the tight windows, and as it subsided there was a loud knock on the rear door.

Mr. Finchley sat up. The knock came again, impatiently.

He slipped from his seat and went to the door. As he opened it a gust of rain blew in at him and a voice cried from the darkness, "Evening, shipmate. Would you give me some shelter till this rain has passed?" The voice and the tone were familiar. In the doorway stood a bulky figure, balanced lightly on the top step of the narrow ladder.

"Come in," said Mr. Finchley.

The man entered, shut the door behind him and jerked off his cap.

"Phew!" He blew raindrops from the end of his nose, and laughed. "It's wet enough for a mermaid's picnic! Why strike me—" he eyed Mr. Finchley in surprise. "It's you!"

"Yes, it's me," answered Mr. Finchley. He was looking at the sailor he had met in Froghole Farm. "How did you get here?"

The sailor sat down, chuckling. "Trilby's the name, Bob Trilby, and I walked here, but I seem to have got lost or something. Then this rain come on before I could find shelter. Saw your riding light and over I came. Any port in a storm, though I must say you've got a snug little berth here. Well, fancy it being you! Funny how you run into some people all the time. Reminds me of a sailor I knew once. Pineapple he was called on account of his hair growing upwards. He was the skinniest, meanest man I ever met, and I was always meeting him. Run into him at Cardiff first of all. Month later found him drunk in Barcelona. Shipped with him that same year to Boston. Lost him there. Met him in Vancouver three months later, and then we bumped one another halfway round the globe for a year, Georgetown, Sydney, Penang, Cape Town. He was like a bloomin' shadow. Last I ever saw of him was in Barcelona again. During the Spanish War—we'd run a cargo there. Zooomp!" Bob Trilby's hands swooped over the little table in imitation of a bombing plane.

"Franco's boys came over one evening. Boom! Boom! Bombs all over the harbour. Saw one hit the deck of a freighter alongside. Ten men on deck." He snapped his fingers. "Up they went. Next minute something landed on the quay at my feet—five hundred yards away—and bless me if it wasn't old Pineapple, top-knot unruffled, but he was unlucky that time because he'd forgotten to bring his body with him!"

"Well, I hope our acquaintance doesn't end so tragical-ly," Mr. Finchley said.

"Don't worry. I ain't no Jonah."

"I was just going to make myself some cocoa and have a bread-and-cheese supper. Would you care to join me?"

Mr. Finchley was glad of company. In his London life he had not made a wide circle of friends, although there was no time at which he ever refused the chance to make fresh contacts. Men, especially men like Bob Trilby, who seemed to have filled their lives with so much excitement, fascinated him. His own life had been sober and steady. To talk to men like Bob gave him a pleasure that was rare in his life.

"That's real friendly of you—after the way I cut you out of my kipper."

"You're welcome. Take your jacket off. It's wet."

Mr. Finchley lit the stove and put the milk on for the cocoa and Bob, without more invitation, took off his jack-et, hung it up and, getting out his pipe, made himself comfortable. And as he settled himself down he chatted, punctuating his talk with gusts of laughter that rattled around the inside of the caravan.

He was very curious to know what Mr. Finchley was doing with a caravan and when he was told he was noisy with admiration.

"Good idea!" he cried. "You're an original! Always did like originals. I'm an original myself—that's why I'm a rolling stone. Never content, never settle down—the sea's the only life for men like me. I wonder you ain't never felt the pull yourself. But maybe you have. What's that?" His head jerked towards the model of the *Le Bon Accord* which stood above the alcove holding the sleeping berths.

Mr. Finchley told him, and he rose to examine the model.

"She's a beauty, ain't she? Reminds me of my first ship. She was sail, too. Built at Riga, owned by a Dutchman and manned by the scummiest, rummiest crew ever. But they were all sailors, real men with Stockholm tar for blood. I was a boy—run away to sea and been at sea on and off ever since." He took down the model and lay back against the seat, examining it.

He had it on the table between them as they had their supper and he went over its points to Mr. Finchley, giving him a lesson on the rigging and running gear. Before supper was through Mr. Finchley's head rang with technicalities ... main topgallant staysail, mizzen yard goosenecks, spanker gaff lift, futtock shrouds ... Bob talked on, lost in his own delight at the beauty and intricacy of the little model, and while he talked, although Mr. Finchley did not for one moment doubt his enthusiasm, he could not help feel that somewhere something was wrong. He stared at the limp pale hair straggling over the broad, sunburnt brow and wondered what it was about Bob Trilby that was wrong, for something was wrong, some infallible instinct within Mr. Finchley cried out in warning, but beyond the cry there was no definition of the trouble.

"Would you have reached your brother's place tonight?" asked Mr. Finchley in a pause.

Bob looked up. "No - not tonight. Tomorrow evening maybe. I was just on the lookout for a dossing place when the rain came on. It'll stop soon and then I'll have another try. Always a barn or a rick that you can use as a kippin' place. I can sleep anywhere. Could sleep on the fore-top yard arm in a Horn snorter. Been round the Horn five times and never seen it once. That's a hell on earth if there ever was. Storm and mist, fog and ice if you make too much southing. Queerest thing that ever happened to me started at the Horn. In twenty-nine it was. I was cook on a guano boat coming round from the Galapagos—I'm a fine cook when it comes to boilin' potatoes," he laughed and rattled on with his story. "Two damned slammed, weather-jammed weeks we sweated round and about the Horn, trying to make our eastward passage and not an inch did we move but run south and then north over our tracks like a spider trying to get out of a wet puddin' basin. Two weeks—and then we saw the packin'-case. I saw it first as I come up out of the galley. There it was dead amidships and not a soul but me had seen it. A big packin'-case it was. Looked like a buoy floating out there, and sitting square atop of it, large as life, but pretty nearly being washed off by every wave, was a woman."

"What?" Mr. Finchley could not repress his astonishment.

"So you can say! A woman, a thousand miles from nowhere, dressed in a sopping wet red gown sittin' atop of a packin'-case. We came round, lay to and got her aboard and, with a lot of cursin', hoisted the case aboard too. That was the queerest drift I've ever seen come aboard. The packin'-case was full of a grand piano, lovely thing, all white with sort of gold fal-lals along the legs and edges, and beautifully packed in waterproofing. It weren't a bit soiled. And the woman—she was young and good-looking, kind of Spanish, I suppose. But she was as dumb as the statue of Nelson. Not a word could we get from her. She was half-dead with cold, so we put her to bed and fatted her up with soup and stuff, and we went round the Horn quicker than a mosquito making for a fat man from that moment. She must have come off some ship, I suppose, but whether the packin'-case came with her or she picked up company with it in the water I don't know. But when she recovered we found she could play. Like a blessed angel she played and that was not all. She was dumb but her eyes could say things better than words. In a week she had every man on board daffy over her. That's bad on shipboard. At the end of a couple of weeks there was almost mutiny because of her, the less civilised lads took to knifin' one another on account of arguing which had been looked at more favourably by her, and the captain and officers was too polite about her to each other to be healthy. By the time we touched land on the American coast we'd lost four men on her account one way and another and there weren't a civil friendship left between men who had known each other for years."

"And what happened to her?" enquired Mr. Finchley, his mind flighting to that strange vision, a dark-haired woman, floating on a packing-case.

"She went ashore and we never saw her again. Just slipped us all one night—"

"But there must be some explanation," insisted Mr. Finchley.

"Not a human one. It's my belief she weren't human, and if I was to ship aboard anything that sighted a large packin'-case with a woman atop of it around the Horn, I'd say leave it alone or cut your throat first. I wouldn't believe it had ever happened if I didn't know I could go to French Street, Seven Dials, tomorrow and walk into the old captain's sitting-room there and see that white piano with its gold fal-lals and him for ever telling everybody that don't know how it was given to him by a South American grandee." Bob laughed suddenly, shaking his head. "It's an impossible story, ain't it? I don't ask you to believe it. Only a man what knows the sea and her ways could believe it and know that I ain't no pink liar. Well, thanks for the supper, Mr. Finchley. I must be on my way—"

"But you can't go out in this rain," objected Mr. Finchley as Bob rose.

"Why not? This ain't rain, this is a gentle dew compared with real rain. Anyway, I've got to find somewhere to sleep."

"There's a spare bunk here, if you'd like to take it," said Mr. Finchley warmly. The thought of the man going out into the rain to find a wet lodging under a rick was too much for him to contemplate.

"But you don't know me. I might cut your throat in the night and go off with all your money."

Mr. Finchley chuckled and passed his hand over his bald head. "You wouldn't go off with much and I'll risk the cut throat."

Bob said no more about it. He just looked at Mr. Finchley and his eyes were full of a warm friendliness towards him.

Mr. Finchley never forgot that night. When they were rolled down in their bunks and the light was out, they talked, or Bob talked. Lying on his narrow bunk, listening to the rain slanting against the caravan, sometimes catching the jingle of Churchwarden's halter strap as he stirred restlessly, Mr. Finchley was introduced to another world. He went with Bob to the uttermost places of the earth and shared with him the most fantastic adventures. Half the time, despite Bob's repeated protests that only a seaman could be expected to believe him, he was sure that the man was lying. But fact or fiction, the vigour of the stories could not be denied. There were moments when the recital flighted into the poetic. Bob Trilby, what a hundred Bob Trilbys there had been in the last thirty years! Bob Trilby living on a small island, feeding on flying-fish and bêche-de-mer, ministered to by a dusky wife and amused by the antics of tame paroquets; Bob Trilby awed by the confusion of Antarctic colours over the ice-fields, Bob Trilby gunrunning, Bob Trilby overboard, Bob Trilby drunk and fighting in Suoi Hopang or other ports with impossible names, Bob Trilby and the sea, the restless, wreck-littered, storm-fretted, gull-greeted, ship-scored sea, his first, his last, his only love.

Mr. Finchley went to sleep with his voice still booming in his ears, his laughter shaking the timbers and shelves of the caravan, and when he woke in the morning it was to be greeted by the smell of frying bacon, the hiss of the stove and the sight of the caravan, spick and span, and Bob leaning back from the galley shouting in to him, "I told you I was a good sea-cook, didn't I? Rouse up, you lubber, and get your head into a bucket of water. Breakfast in five minutes!" He laughed and the sound mixed with the splutter of fat and went circling out of the doorway into the rain-freshened air of the morning.

During breakfast, Mr. Finchley told Bob about Churchwarden's loose shoe and Bob, who seemed to know the district well through having walked up and down it on his visits to his brother, informed him that there was a smithy in the village back along the road.

It was decided, as Bob was in no hurry, that Mr. Finchley should walk the horse back to the village and that Bob should stay with the caravan. Mr. Finchley was going very close to the village where Bob's brother lived that day and he had offered to give Bob a lift.

He left Bob singing and washing up the breakfast dishes. The lusty voice followed him down the road. Even Churchwarden seemed aware of its robust, merry quality, for he pricked up his ears and shook the night's stiffness from him by shying and throwing up his head with a great snort.

The smithy faced the open space behind the village inn. It was an immense black cavern, brightened at its innermost depth by a red glow of coals from the forge. It was the first time since he was a boy that Mr. Finchley had been into a smithy. The floor was gritty with black dust and littered with odd lengths of iron, and boxes full of rusty nails, and twisted fragments of metal. Long coils of iron wire hung from the walls and soot-encrusted spiders' webs draped themselves between the beams of the low roof. The bellows, as an assistant worked them, wheezed like a giant with asthma and from the fire blue flecks of flame leaped away.

The smith himself was a silent man, his face and arms creased with black lines where soot seemed to have settled in his young days and had remained ever since. His head was bald and had a curiously brown and unhuman look. As he bent over Churchwarden's hoof, the hard skull bobbed about like a croquet ball and Mr. Finchley felt that if it were tapped with a mallet it would go scuttling off into the dark tangle of the smithy, causing no surprise to the smith or his mate.

"It's these modern roads," said Mr. Finchley as the man straightened up and felt in the pocket of his leather apron for a tool. "No good for horses." It was pleasant to be able to talk like that, even though he had owned a horse for only a few days.

"P'raps," said the smith.

"All these motor cars ..." said Mr. Finchley with a faint hint of scorn. "Can't be doing you much good."

"Maybe not."

"I expect you'd like to see the good old days back again."

"P'raps and p'raps not." He nodded towards the jumble of agricultural machinery outside his door. "I'm busy enough to suit me."

"But in the old days, you were busier then and happier, maybe?"

The smith straightened up. He had nearly finished his job and for the first time a pin-point of animation shone in his eyes.

"You don't know about the good old days, mister. Not the good old days that we knew. They weren't so good. I

111

started work when I was eight year old. Carter's boy, hardly big enough to reach the horse's mouth. Two shillings a week I got for that. There was nine in our family and it weren't often we had butcher's meat. Rabbits belonged to the squire and we had to go gleaning if we wanted bread. Children don't work from six until eight these days, mister, and I ain't seen no gleanin' done since the war. There was a lot of things about the good old days that some people don't know or forget about. I'm all right as I am. My children get somethin' more than just potatoes or turnips for dinner and they haven't gone to work at eight. The squire and the gentry might like the good old days back, mister, but not the farm labourer and the likes o' me."

Mr. Finchley was silenced for a while. In his cheerful desire to be friendly he seemed to have wakened the man's strongest feelings.

"Maybe you're right," he said after a moment.

"P'raps," said the smith, lapsing into his old mood and hammering at the plate.

Mr. Finchley watched him, watched the adroit movement of his hands as they manoeuvred plate and hammer. The smell of burnt horn was strong in his nostrils.

"But what about craftsmanship?" he said, undaunted, and feeling that his true point had not been made. "Your kind is dying out. In fifty years will there be a man left who can make a pair of hand-wrought iron gates or a good inn-sign bracket?"

The smith cocked an eye up at him, and a slow smile moved over his grimy face.

"All these bloody machines. People get what they want. If there's any call for handmade stuff there'll be men to make it. I'm not worrying."

Mr. Finchley gave him up. It seemed hard to find in the man, a man who was one of the last survivors of his kind, a direct animosity or resentment against an age which was impatient of his slow art. It was only as he was leading Churchwarden back to the caravan that he began to appreciate the sense of the man's attitude. He was not worrying because there was nothing he could do. He stood, a solid, dependable figure in a crowd of hurrying changes and minor industrial revolutions, knowing that when men wanted good work they would find craftsmen of his kind to do it, and over his obstinate optimism seemed to hang the conviction that one day men would want his kind again. Mr. Finchley wondered if they ever would.

There was no sound of singing as he approached the caravan. He had been away almost two hours. He tied the horse to the hedge, expecting Bob's long face to jerk round the side of the door in greeting. But Bob was nowhere around.

"Bob!" Mr. Finchley called to him. There was no answer. He went into the caravan. Everything was tidy, but there was no Bob. He shouted again without any result. Then he sat down, wondering what had happened to the seaman. As he dropped on to the seat his eye was tantalised for a few seconds by some strangeness in the place which he could not explain. He saw what it was.

The bottle which held the model of *Le Bon Accord* was missing from its little shelf.

Mr. Finchley jumped up anxiously. Nowhere in the caravan could he find the model, and it was then that he understood Bob's disappearance. He had gone off with the model.

Mr. Finchley was upset. He was hurt by this treachery. "Well, I'm damned," he exclaimed. "The scoundrel!"

And into his mind came the impression which he had received before about Bob. The man was odd. Something about him was wrong. He had not been able to define it, but here was proof of his peculiarity. Only very unusual men accepted one's hospitality and then went off with one's cherished possessions.

Mr. Finchley went out and harnessed Churchwarden in a mood of frowning anger. He was angry at Bob for being so wicked. And he was annoyed at the loss of the model. It had meant quite a lot to him.

VIII
Of detection

FOR two days after Bob had left him, Mr. Finchley was angry every time he thought of the man. He had been so shocked at first that he had driven on to the village where Bob's brother lived in order that he might find Bob. He had not expected to be met, on enquiry, with the information that no one named Trilby lived in or near the village. So far as the village policeman, postman and publican knew, there was no man in or near the village who had a brother, a seaman, who answered to Bob's description.

"John Dolens up at Scagware Farm—he's got a brother in the Royal Air Force. Rare handful 'e be when 'e comes home!"

That was the nearest he got to Bob.

In those two days Mr. Finchley saw five houses and a great deal of Kent. What he saw of Kent pleased him more than any of the houses.

It was hilly country he was passing through as he made towards Maidstone. On the slopes of the hills were strawberry fields, dotted with blue-and-white aproned women in thick boots, picking the crop. Along the hedges of the fields were perambulators and little groups of children, playing while their mothers worked. In the hot sun the piles of chip baskets blazed like white pyramids and the warm, almost fleshy smell of the fruit hung lightly in the air.

Up and down the hills went Mr. Finchley in his yellow caravan. Going up the hills he got down and walked to ease Churchwarden's load and, going downhill, he put the shoe on the back wheel to help brake the caravan. He was alone and he was happy. It seemed years ago that he had retired from his office and first seen the caravan in Mr. Harricot's yard, and he seemed to have slipped back years in thought and habit. He found himself watching the hedges for birds' nests and wishing that he had some means of identifying the summer flowers which lined the ditches. When he got to Maidstone, he told himself, he would buy a couple of books on wild flowers and birds. But although he did not know their names, their beauty was not lost on him. In the evening, when he stopped and began his cooking, blue and coal tits swung down from the surrounding trees and fed off the bacon scraps he hung on the branches for them and the chiffchaff called incessantly to him from the heart of the woods as he walked by Churchwarden up the hills. In the ditches and hedges the red flags of the ragged robins and the swollen cheeks of white bladder campions signalled to him, and the great spikes of foxglove, mullein and agrimony swayed companionably in the wind. And always, just ahead but never seen, a cuckoo called and called until the whole countryside rang and Mr. Finchley began to wish the bird had never been hatched. Its call woke him in the morning, it heralded him all day and sent him to sleep at night.

It was on the afternoon of his third day after Bob's departure that Mr. Finchley realised that the cuckoo was not the only recurrent companion he had. He had another, less noisy, but almost equally obvious companion. It was a man on a bicycle. The bicycle made itself known before the man. One of the spokes in the rear wheel was loose and clicked as it turned. Just as Captain Hook had his tick for warning, so this bicycle had its click.

The first time Mr. Finchley heard the click approaching him from behind he noted it with the thought that the rider ought to have the spoke seen to. The second time he heard it—the same day—coming back towards him, he noticed the rider. He was a middle-aged man of slim build and moderate height, wearing a grey suit, a trilby and a pair of pince-nez, and he rode as though he had little familiarity with bicycles. His knees and elbows were stuck well out and he frowned gently as though he neither trusted nor hoped that his present stable equilibrium could continue for long. Strapped to the back of the bicycle was a little rucksack.

On the first day he passed Mr. Finchley twice, once overtaking him and once, a few hours later, returning past him. Mr. Finchley would have forgotten him and his clicking bicycle altogether, except that the next day he had been on the road scarcely an hour before he heard the click, click, click behind him and the man overtook him. This time he wore a cap and horn-rimmed spectacles, but his knees and elbows stuck out as before.

After that Mr. Finchley was curious. The man went by him four times that day, at intervals, and once as he reached the top of a hill he found him lying under a gorse bush, the bicycle beside him, watching the slow climb of the caravan.

But it was not the fact of this constant meeting which aroused Mr. Finchley's curiosity. It was the man's peculiar behaviour. He seemed to be indulging in some form of mild disguise. He came by in a cap and horn-rimmed spectacles. Then with sunglasses, a bowler and a little black moustache. Again he appeared in steel-rimmed glasses, smoking a pipe that jutted from a wealth of luxuriant beard. In two days it was amazing how often he rung the changes between various hats, spectacles, pipes and moustaches. But Mr. Finchley never had any doubt of the man, for there were always the jutting elbows and knees and the gentle, insistent click, click of the bicycle wheel.

It was on the evening of the third day that Mr. Finchley came to grips with the man. He had stopped for the night on a little gorse- and broom-studded common, under the shelter of three tall birches. Behind the birches was a maze of gorse, threaded with sheep runs.

Mr. Finchley was tending a wood fire before the caravan. He was baking potatoes in the hot embers. Churchwarden suddenly gave a snort and a stamp. Mr. Finchley looked round and saw, staring at the fire from the shelter of the gorse thicket, a face, clean-shaven, with a red, rather long nose that supported a pair of pince-nez. In the dimming evening light Mr. Finchley almost thought he could see that nose twitching sensitively like a dog's questing game. Tired of the comedy, Mr. Finchley decided that he must do something.

He dropped a piece of stick on the fire and then sauntered idly around the caravan. Keeping the caravan between himself and the man he circled away into the lee of the gorse bushes and began to make his way round behind the man.

He moved, he congratulated himself, with the stealth of a Sioux or a Crowfoot. Not a twig snapped beneath his feet and he took advantage of every piece of cover with an instinctive judgment which convinced him that he would have been no inconsiderable pioneer.

He came up behind the man. When he was within twenty feet of him, he saw that he was writing industriously in a little notebook, taking furtive peeps at the fire and the caravan as he did so, as though he feared to miss any movement and was anxious about Mr. Finchley's disappearance. Mr. Finchley saw that he was wearing a trilby and decided that trilby, pince-nez and clean-shaven face must be his normal appearance.

Mr. Finchley coughed gently and said, "Good evening, were you looking for me?" As he spoke his heart began to thump nervously, but he was pleased with the calm tones of his speech.

The man jumped round like a startled cat, slid his notebook into his pocket and then smiled. The effect of the smile was to make Mr. Finchley forget entirely that first moment of surprise. It warmed the rather thin features like firelight and the pince-nez seemed to catch its ruddy reflection.

"Good evening, Mr. Finchley!" The man came towards him, holding out his hand, and his voice was rich with a casual, disarming frankness. He greeted Mr. Finchley as though he had known him all his life.

"How on earth do you know my name, and what are you doing, spying on me?" Mr. Finchley was surprised into the rather brusque demand.

"Oh, Mr. Finchley …" The stranger held up a long, knuckly hand much as a preacher raises his hand to ward off imaginary evil. "Please, there is no need for that … not between us."

"Perhaps you'll explain, sir, what all this means. Dodging my footsteps, disguises, spying on me …" Mr. Finchley was rather surprised to hear himself talking a little angrily.

"Anselm is the name, Mr. Finchley. Oliver Watt Anselm," the man said lightly in answer to no question, but as though he expected Mr. Finchley to be interested, which Mr. Finchley was. "Watt was from my father. He was fond of tea and an amateur inventor. My card—" He handed Mr. Finchley a card and went on. "Shall we go out to the fire? We can talk better there. These gorse bushes become too intimate after a while." He grunted as he pushed his way through the narrow gap into the circle of grass by the fire.

Mr. Finchley followed him, oblivious to the pricks of the gorse bushes as his eyes read the card. It said:

OLIVER WATT ANSELM
Private Enquiries—Strictest Secrecy
Figg Mansions, Holborn,
E.C.I. TEL. HOL 3569.

Mr. Anselm stood by the fire and brushed his clothes free of clinging gorse spikes. Mr. Finchley sat down on the little back ladder of the caravan and looked up at him, his brow huddled in a wrinkle of curiosity.

"Private enquiries?" he asked. "What's that, and what—"

Anselm's hand went up again. "In turn, in turn," he cried gently. "Everything in turn, Mr. Finchley."

"How the devil do you know my name?"

"Easy. Edgar Finchley, Nassington Avenue, Hampstead, London. It's written inside most of your books."

"My books? What books?" Mr. Finchley was beginning to feel helpless.

"The books in your caravan, of course …"

"Do you mean"—Mr Finchley gulped with anger and amazement—"that you've been inside my caravan?"

"Of course, yesterday afternoon when you stopped for lunch at the Harp. But it wasn't from the books that I learnt your name and address—"

Mr. Finchley lost his temper. At least, he let go of it as much as ever let go. He stood up, snapped his fingers angrily, and glared at Mr. Oliver Watt Anselm.

"Well, sir, I should be very glad if you would kindly explain yourself quickly. Otherwise I shall have to call the police. Entering my caravan, shadowing me for the last two days … I never heard of such impudence. You're a public nuisance and—"

"Please, please, Mr. Finchley." Anselm's eyes blinked behind his glasses and his face fell into sorrowing lines. "Don't take it like that. I'll explain, but let us talk in an atmosphere of reasonableness. Yes, with reason and frankness. I'm a great believer in frankness—and also I have my living to make, Mr. Finchley. You wouldn't deny me the right to make my living, would you?"

Mr. Finchley calmed down a little. "That depends," he said, subsiding to his ladder.

"Of course." Anselm paused and then drew himself up a little more stiffly and said slowly, "I'm a private investigator, Mr. Finchley; one of the best private investigators in London. I am—I say it with modest but firm conviction—competent, courteous and discreet—"

"A child could have seen through your disguises," said Mr. Finchley quickly, unable to resist the impulse to prick his swelling bubble of pride.

Anselm frowned for a second. Then his face cleared.

"It was the bicycle. I don't know much about bicycles, and I thought they all clicked. I thought it was something to do with the three-speed mechanism. It was only pointed out to me today by a garage man …"

The swiftness with which he defended himself and a sudden hint of pique in his voice suddenly made Mr. Finchley lose his anger. He guessed that Mr. Oliver Watt Anselm was not all that he would have liked to have been as an investigator.

"You don't look a bit like a private detective. Sherlock Holmes, Father Brown, Nelson Lee and Sexton Blake— they were all distinctive."

Anselm dismissed the quibble with a wave of his hand.

"Exhibitionists, the whole bunch. No investigator can afford to be an exhibitionist. He must be able to mix, and the only man who can mix is the one who is undistinguished from his fellows. Anyway, I have my own line— frankness is the great secret of success."

"Then I suggest you become frank with me and tell me what all this nonsense means," urged Mr. Finchley, realising that he was not getting any nearer an explanation by digressing into the reasons for success in sleuthing.

"I will. I had always intended to be, but it was necessary first of all to examine the ground. That is, I had to get to know you a little before I could come into the open and be frank. Not everyone appreciates frankness."

"What is it all about?"

"My client instructed me to find out all I could about you and what you were doing with this caravan. All he would tell me was that a certain Mr. Finchley had bought a caravan from a certain Mr. Harricot, of Hampstead, and he wanted to know all about you and where you were and where you were going. That was last week. I traced your whereabouts in less than four days, and I also know a considerable amount about you, from one source and other. My client—"

"Who is this client of yours? And why on earth does he take such an interest in me?" asked Mr. Finchley, hardly knowing whether to be angry or amused. It was absurd that anyone should send a private detective after him.

"I don't know his name," said Anselm slowly. "He wouldn't give it. If I did know, you'd appreciate that the ethics of my profession would not allow me to divulge it. What he wants the information for I can't think. I was hoping that when I began to investigate you it would become obvious—it often does. But it didn't this time. If you'll pardon me, Mr. Finchley, for saying so, but all my information leads me to believe that you are a perfectly respectable citizen who is taking a caravanning holiday and also looking at country properties as he goes. No doubt you have some idea of settling in the country. But what my client can want with that I do not know."

"That's true. That's exactly what I am, and I'm dashed if I can understand why anyone should be taking an interest in me. The man must be mad."

Anselm was silent for a moment. Then he said quietly, "I've thought of that, too. It wouldn't be the first time I've been employed by a crank. He doesn't look mad, but that's no sign that he isn't. However," Anselm brightened up a bit, "I'm glad to have been able to have this chat with you, Mr. Finchley. We've been candid with one another. I find that helps in my work a lot. I always come out into the open if I can. You get more from people that way."

"What," said Mr. Finchley slowly, probing with a stick in the embers for the baked potatoes, "would you advise me to do?"

The dusk had settled evenly over the little common and the bright core of red embers washed a pale light over the sharp contours of the gorse bushes. Around the dome of the caravan a pair of bats chased one another, the flip of their wings making brittle sounds against the calm of the night.

Mr. Finchley handed Anselm a hot potato as he finished speaking. Anselm juggled with it until he found his handkerchief and wrapped it about the potato.

"Nothing," he said definitely. "Do nothing. The man—while appearing perfectly normal—is obviously insane. None but an imbecile would have you watched. Salt and butter would improve them." He nodded towards the potatoes they were eating.

Mr. Finchley went into the caravan for the salt and the butter. He handed them to Anselm, who dug a neat cavity in the heart of his potato and solemnly filled it with salt and butter. He took a bite and, with a full mouth, looked up at the sky. He swallowed vigorously, his pince-nez trembling, and then said: "This is the life. Haven't tasted a baked potato like this in fifteen years. How long are you going to be travelling around enjoying yourself?"

Mr. Finchley, glad that his potatoes were appreciated, told him how he was searching for a home, and he sketched out his itinerary so far as he knew it. After his first shock and anger at Anselm's mission, he was finding that he quite liked the thin man. There was a trusting, almost pathetic, quality about the man which made the heart warm towards him. Mr. Finchley felt that, as a private investigator, Anselm had a hard time to make a success of things. It was only right, he felt, that the man should be helped. Mr. Finchley shared deeply that spontaneous sympathy which most people have towards optimistic and persistent failures. He would have told Anselm anything about himself, not simply because he had a clear conscience and knew that he had nothing to fear from any man, but also because he wanted to help Anselm, who thought that all bicycles clicked.

"I've enjoyed this commission, too," said Anselm. " 'Tisn't often I get into the country. Most of the time I spend acting as a sort of unofficial time-keeper outside flats. A enters B's flat at nine-thirty. Left two-thirty. Divorce cases. It doesn't give you a very high opinion of your fellow-creatures, and there's no real need for disguises in London. No one ever notices you there. You just follow a man a yard or two behind and he never turns to look back. Not in London. In London people look in front or at the pavement below their noses. That's why I've enjoyed these few days with you. You looked all around and were a very difficult subject. If it hadn't been for that clicking bicycle, you might still not know about me—isn't that so?"

"Yes," said Mr. Finchley, hiding a smile. "Perhaps that's true."

Anselm sighed, finished the last of his potato and then lit himself a cigarette. "Been smoking a pipe these last days—for your benefit, but I can't really stand them. I was sick three times. But all in the line of duty."

When he went Mr. Finchley walked with him to the edge of the common to see him on the road for the village where he was staying. He watched the tail-light of the bicycle bob off into the darkness. He had quite forgotten about Anselm's strange client. He was more interested in Anselm. It was only as he lay in bed, his mind stirring with those meditative thoughts which herald sleep, that it occurred to him that Anselm might have been very much cleverer than he thought. After all, the man by his helpless front had got every scrap of information from him that he wished ... Still, even that thought did not worry Mr. Finchley. Anselm, astute or incompetent, made no difference to the fact that he, Mr. Finchley, need fear no trouble from peculiar clients in London. That was what Mr. Finchley thought.

IX
In which Mr. Finchley
is caught with his
own snare

MR. FINCHLEY came to Maidstone late in the morning, and he decided that he liked it. It put on no airs, displayed few beauties, but it was an honest, plain market town, a town which seemed to know that for all its industries, for all the canning factories, breweries and leatherworks, its real function was to serve the farmers and country people of the surrounding Kent fields and gardens. It had a history yet made no ostentatious show of it. It was content to be what it was, a market town, a modern market town with cinemas and cafés, cheap stores and large car-parks, the weekly Mecca of many a farm-wife and cottage woman. If it had a personality which could be expressed in human terms, it was that of one of the farmers who knew its streets so well. It seemed to stand beside the brown Medway and say to all comers, "Here I am, just a plain, ordinary sort of fellow, a bit careless about my appearance maybe, a bit rough in places, but I know my own business and I stick to it."

Mr. Finchley could tell it was a sensible sort of town by the way it treated his caravan. In London, along the Old Kent Road, he had been an object of curiosity. But in Maidstone the people gave him a look, for no eye could resist the pull of the canary-coloured caravan and its bright wheel spokes and painted windows, and then forgot him. A caravan was a caravan—no one got excited about it because it wasn't the first or last caravan they would ever see, not in a county which grew the finest hops in the world and yearly drew bands of gypsies and other rovers to its high-grown hop-garths.

Mr. Finchley had quite a lot of shopping to do in Maidstone. He wanted to replenish his stores and he hoped that there would be some letters waiting for him at the post office. He put the caravan into a yard at the back of an inn down a side street, tied Churchwarden's nosebag on, and left the horse to feed while he did his shopping.

For an hour Mr. Finchley enjoyed himself. Fresh air and the country life had given him quite a new interest in food, and he found that he was not one of those men who, being alone, can tolerate monotony. He liked eggs and bacon because they were a simple dish, but he had no desire to live on them entirely.

He entered a butcher's, a grocer's and a cold-meat shop with quite a new zest. He bought himself a ham, sausages, vegetables, a jar of pickled onions … The shopkeepers seemed to realise that here was someone who could take a delight in buying and they were full of suggestions and he came out laden with tinned crab and other delicacies which he had not originally dreamt of buying. He bought himself a small joint of mutton. He was not sure about this, but his mind was eager for the experiment. He had a little oven which fitted on to his primus stove and he was anxious to test his powers as a cook. When Sunday came he meant to have a roast dinner.

Before going to the post office for his letters, he stopped at a bookshop and bought a couple of books to help him identify the flowers and birds he saw. Then he went on for his letters full of a stirring, simmering excitement.

There were three letters for him, two from his wife and one from Robert. He read them as he took his lunch in a restaurant. His wife's letters were written from Cumberland and were full of those things which every wife writes to a husband who is by himself and forced to do his own cooking and washing. Had he remembered to change his underwear? He was not to forget the effect tinned salmon had on him if he took it too liberally. She hoped he wasn't continually making himself cups of tea. Was he warm at nights? And when he wrote again she would like to know something of what he was doing and less about Church-warden. Had he found a house yet? And finally a hint that she had been terse with her brother David because he had suggested that the caravan idea was the first sign of sec-ond-childhood in Mr. Finchley.

Robert's letter was longer. He wanted his father to write to him twice, instead of once, a week, and tell him all that happened and where he went because he was drawing a map of the journey and was thinking of starting a caravan club amongst the other boys ... "It will be for the encour-agement of caravans and I shall make the subscription two shillings a term. I haven't decided what to do with the money, but we shall encourage caravans because they are such a good idea, especially in the hols now that everyone has a car. Rawlinson minor won't join because he says caravans are low, like gypsies. So I have blackballed him, which is what you do in clubs. Anstey, who's pater is a bishop, says he will join if you write to say that calling the horse Churchwarden was not intended as any disrespect to the Church which, he says, is an honourable calling. It took three of us to blackball Rawlinson mi. because he is such a big brute, but we did it behind the cricket pav. at the place which, I think I have told you before, is called the arena. I have now got a wart on my thumb from the gardener's boy. It cost sixpence and a lot of rubbing. Anstey says it is silly and womanlike of the matron to be upset about it because it is all in the interests of science because now we can try the liver cure. You know about that ..." The letter wandered on into a description of the cure of warts by burying a piece of liver with a Victoria penny and leaving it for two weeks. It ended with an exhortation that if he came anywhere near Goudhurst, where was Robert's school, before the end of term, he must let Robert know so that he could come and see him and bring the other members of the club.

It was on the way back to his caravan that Mr. Finchley saw the wire snares. There was a bunch of them hanging outside the doorway of a saddler's shop, a neat arrangement of wire loops and lengths of brown cord ending in tiny wooden pegs. The sight of them made Mr. Finchley think of rabbits, of the holes in the hedges which faced him almost every night, and he thought also of rabbit stew. It would be easier to make a rabbit stew than it would to roast mutton. Rabbits were a pest and there would be a triumph in "living off the country." Never in his life had he snared a rabbit. To do so, he felt, would be to mark completely his renunciation of town life. He went into the shop and bought six of the snares for a shilling.

It was late that afternoon before he was finally clear of the town and breasting his way up the climb to the crest of the North Downs on his way towards Sittingbourne and Faversham, which was the next area he intended to visit in his search for a house.

He camped that night in a small hollow that lay back from the road on the scarp of the downs. It was a tiny chalk quarry, disused now and overgrown with brambles and young birch trees. In its centre was a patch of close turf just big enough to take the caravan and give Church-warden some grazing.

Mr. Finchley decided that, as the next day was Sunday, he would rest there for a day. He did not feel himself equal to cooking roast mutton and moving along the road.

After his evening meal Mr. Finchley explored the quarry. It was an education to him. With his flower book in hand he made many discoveries. Man had cut the raw, white gash in the hillside, but in a few years nature had reclaimed it and, as though touched by pity to a greater prodigality, had populated the little dell with a rich variety of flowers. There were the heraldic forms of centaury, the stiff purple heads of self-heal and bugle, fragile, powder-dusted scabious blooms, the trailing profusion of white and yellow bedstraws, banks of aromatic gorse bushes and the familiar overcrowding of cinquefoils, tormentils and silverweeds. And, over brambles and the dwarfed elders that lined the hollow, straggled the yellow and purple flowers of bittersweet.

Mr. Finchley, pipe lit, book in hand, wandered slowly about the place, stooping to the ground at each new find, working at the index and identification table of the book industriously.

Gradually, in search of new specimens, he wandered away from the hollow on to the down. Sheep moved slowly across the short grass and below him he could catch the glimpse of a red roof and grey walls between the trunks of a plantation of tall firs and spreading chestnuts. The evening was still and every field and distant farmstead in the valley below stood out with the clear, miniature distinction of bright toys placed in position by a discerning hand. He was standing on the ridge by way of which the old pilgrims had made their way to Canterbury. In places the trace of their old road still survived and along this road had once come the great company which Chaucer knew. They had probably looked down upon the flat valley as he now looked, their feet upon the close turf, their eyes then, as his were now, caught away from the wide view by the flutter of a trio of magpies in a nearby clump of dogwood.

But today, thought Mr. Finchley as he sat down on a large tummock near a low, rabbit-burrowed hedge that cut the down, the pilgrims to Canterbury no longer took the old road. They hurried in cars along the main road in the valley. Their eyes saw only the tarmac and the speeding traffic. He wondered if the spiritual benefits and the regeneration of old and simple faiths that came from such pilgrimages depended upon the way you went to the shrine, rather than on the shrine itself. The old pilgrims walked their way along the downs, with all England below them, their eyes constantly filled with the beauty of the land and the peace which came from good husbandry and honest humours. Before they ever reached Canterbury those miles of downland, those deep settled valleys and the sense of man's dependence upon the great forces beyond his control, the favour of the seasons, the swelling of bud and fruit and the miracle of good and bad fortune, must have cleared their minds of much that was gross and confusing. But today … Mr. Finchley shook his head over the motor cars. Man had forgotten the virtue in simple faiths and simple living.

He sat for some time, smoking peacefully, letting his eyes rove over the scene and shaking his head at the surge of slightly melancholy thoughts which inhabited it. Mr. Finchley was no different from most men. The contemplation of an expansive view produces in all of us a gentle melancholy, and we are a little ashamed of ourselves and our fellows. And this is no bad thing. It would be for our own good if more men had the opportunity to sit on the crest of downlands and eye the wide acres of the valleys.

As Mr. Finchley sat there, he suddenly heard a quick thudding sound come from the hedge at his side. He turned and stood up. In the grass at the foot of the hedge, some twenty feet away, something brown was twisting and jerking. He ran towards it and, as he reached the spot, the jerking ceased. He found himself looking down at a rabbit which had got into a snare laid across a run at the foot of the hedge. He bent down and freed the tight wire from its neck. But the rabbit was dead. As he stood there, holding the warm body in his hand, Mr. Finchley knew that he would never himself have the heart to use any of the snares which he carried in his own pocket. The limp body, the white scut of a tail, had a pathetic appeal. He knew it was being sentimental to feel as he did. Rabbits were a pest. They did an enormous amount of damage to the country in a year. But there was a friendly, familiar association of ideas between Mr. Finchley and rabbits that would make him feel like a murderer if he ever put down his own snares.

As he stood there, holding the rabbit, he heard a shout from the down above him. He looked round and saw two men climb over the hedge and hurry down towards him. They wore breeches and cloth caps; both had red, country faces and they waved to him as they ran. He waited for them.

"Got him!" cried the first man as he came up, and he grabbed Mr. Finchley by the collar.

"Got him in the act!" panted the other and he took hold of Mr. Finchley's arm, snatching the rabbit away from him.

"Hey, what is this?" cried Mr. Finchley angrily and he tried to shake himself free. The two men clung on to him, holding his arms down.

"Showin' fight, ain't he, Garge?"

"Dangerous customer, Ernie. Better hold him tight!"

Mr. Finchley ceased his efforts to escape and cried out, "What is all this about? Let go of me. I didn't know it was your rabbit. I was only …"

Garge laughed and Ernie joined him.

"That's a good 'un. He didn't know it was our rabbit."

"Will you please explain—" began Mr. Finchley, struggling to recover his dignity. Ernie interrupted him.

"What's this, eh?" he shouted as he snatched at a length of wire that was showing from Mr. Finchley's jacket pocket. He pulled out the snares which he had bought in Maidstone.

"Ho, ho!" Garge shook his head sadly. "And he didn't know it was our rabbit. But you come well prepared, didn't you? Ho, the Colonel'll have something to say to you. Come on!"

Without more argument or talk they started off down the bill, forcing Mr. Finchley between them. At first he tried to impede their progress by struggling and attempting to explain. But they were strong men and carried him along without any trouble. Mr. Finchley gave in.

They went down the hill, through a field of young mangolds and then into a small wood. Beyond the wood they struck a gravelled driveway. The driveway led through a long shrubbery to a big, straggling house built of red-brick in the style of Queen Anne. Mr. Finchley could see that it was the house of someone of wealth. The men took him up the wide steps to the doorway and one of them tugged at the wrought-iron bell-pull. A butler, bald-headed, long-nosed and looking rather like a penguin which had been rudely disturbed from a nap, answered the door. He frowned at the group.

"What's this?" he asked.

"Got another of 'em, Mr. Hawker. Caught him red-handed. Is the Colonel in?"

The butler disappeared. He came back after a while.

"Come in," he said.

The two hustled Mr. Finchley into the house. They went across the wide hall, which was littered with animal pelts, its walls hung with guns, spears and sporting trophies, and into a library.

Mr. Finchley, still held securely by the men, found himself in a pleasant, lofty room which looked out on to a small lawn. The walls were lined with books and, standing by a low desk near the fireplace, in which a small fire burned, was the Colonel. The Colonel was very much like a colonel. He was tall, his hair a white-grey, his face very red and shiny and his nose, a more hooked edition of the butler's, curved above a fine white, fish-tailed moustache. The ends of the moustache quivered as he raised his head and glared at Mr. Finchley. It was the kind of look which, almost unaided by arms, could have put down any native revolt.

"So you've caught another of 'em, eh? By Victoria, what is the country coming to? Well, sir," he barked at Mr. Finchley, "what have you to say for yourself?" His breast stirred with anger under the gleaming correctness of his white shirt front.

Mr. Finchley cleared his throat. He was not going to be intimidated by any fire-eating colonel, and he had plenty to say.

"I should like to know, sir, whether you're responsible for these men's actions? I have been brutally assaulted by them and dragged down here against my will. This is a free country and I resent the way I have been treated—"

Mr. Finchley was interrupted by a burst of laughter from the two men.

"Why, us caught un red-handed, sir. Rabbit still warm in one hand and a pocket full of snares in the other. That's true, ain't it, Garge?"

The Colonel jerked the ends of his moustache with such ferocity that Mr. Finchley, had he not been worried by his own predicament, might have wondered why they weren't jerked right off.

"Hear that, sir!" thundered the Colonel. "Don't want any high-falutin' talk from you about rights. Damn me, even the poachers are gettin' educated these days. But, by Victoria, educated or uneducated, I know how to deal with poachers—"

"I'm not a poacher!" cried Mr. Finchley. "I found the rabbit in the snare—"

"How about the snares in your pocket?"

"Well, I …" It was an awkward point to overcome with a man of the Colonel's temperament.

"Speak up, sir. Don't stutter. Are they yours?"

"Yes, they are. But—"

"But—don't give me any buts. You can but your way from here to nowhere but that won't do you any good. Damn it, the man's as obvious a poacher as I ever saw. Stealin' my rabbits, eh? Steal my pheasants, too, if you got the chance. And a man who'll steal other people's pheasants would just as soon come into your house, cut the throats of everyone there and make off with the silver …"

Mr. Finchley listened in amazement. It was obvious to him that nothing could persuade the Colonel at the moment that he was not a poacher.

"You're making a great mistake," said Mr. Finchley, trying to keep calm, but the Colonel's choler was infectious. "If you'll only listen to me I can explain—"

"Explain!" exploded the Colonel. "Explain nothing. Plain as a pikestaff—you're a poacher and you can't talk your way out of that. Not with me. By Victoria, even the poachers have changed these days! Instead of ownin' up like men they're full of explanations and standin' on their rights. I'd like to have had you in my regiment for a while. I'd have driven all that nonsense from your head. Do you good, army life would. Knock off some of that

137

fat, straighten up your shoulders and make a man of you. Look at me, not an ounce of spare flesh anywhere. Sound as a bell and a match for anyone. Sixty-two and feel like twenty-two and you try to explain away being a poacher. Do you think I was born yesterday?"

Now Mr. Finchley was not fat. He was just comfortably plump as any man had a right to be at his age. And his shoulders were straight and well-set, and also he had done his spell of army life during 1914-18, so that he felt all the Colonel's comments to be insulting and unnecessary. He was suddenly filled with a great impatience towards this man and it was more than he could do to hold it back—even though he knew he was being unwise to let himself go.

"For goodness' sake," said Mr. Finchley vehemently, "stop acting like an overgrown schoolboy, like a spoilt child. I've a perfectly reasonable and clear explanation of what I was doing with that rabbit and the snares and yet you refuse to listen to me. The trouble with you is that you've been given too much authority and too much respect all your life. You should be in the ranks yourself and have a sergeant kick you around for a while. It might make a man of you then. You may be able to bluster your men here into obedience, but you can't bluster me. There's too many of your type in the world, and it's time you realised that your proper place is in a comic opera. Now, I'm not going to say any more because I shall probably lose my temper and be led away to say more than I should. One person with a fiery temper is enough already in this room. All I ask is that you either release me at once, making a proper apology, or that you call a policeman." Mr. Finchley finished up panting.

All the time he had been speaking he had been staring at the Colonel, fascinated. The change which came over the man as he spoke was almost inhuman. His face was charged with a violent wave of colour, his eyes seemed to enlarge and spin like great marbles and his mouth opened and shut with silent motions of extreme rage. Instead of a man, he had become a monstrous, quivering, boiling, swelling, flushing aggregation of dumbfoundedness and fury.

"Whaaaaat!" he roared, and the cry came booming across the room, rising in tone like the call of a siren in a fog.

Behind him Mr. Finchley heard Ernie whisper to his companion: "By Gor, that's the first time I ever heard anyone say the likes of that to the Colonel!"

"Love us," was Garge's only comment.

Then the storm broke.

"Take him away!" screamed the Colonel, dancing up and down in his agony of offended pride and dignity. "Take him away and shut him up with the other." He strode towards Mr. Finchley, one lean finger pointing into his face. "You'll have a policeman! You'll have a policeman. I'll have you before the Bench tomorrow. Until then you can cool your heels and that tongue of yours in my store-shed. You! You! Take him away before I run him through!" he cried, his eyes sweeping to a great sabre that hung above the fireplace.

Ernie and Garge saw the look and, knowing the Colonel better than Mr. Finchley did, they grabbed him and hustled him from the room.

It was not until he was being led across a stable-yard at the back of the house that Mr. Finchley recovered enough to protest.

"But he can't lock me up like this—it's against the law of the land! I'll sue him for false imprisonment—"

"Not Colonel Greatorex, you won't," said Ernie sympathetically. He had felt a warm place widen in his heart for Mr. Finchley. "The village constable will do as he says, and the Colonel often uses his shed as a lockup because there ain't one in the village, and it's too far to take a drunk or a poacher to Maidstone. He'll say he was doing his duty and, as he's a member of the Bench himself, it'll be all right. In you go!"

As Ernie had been talking they had stopped before a low, slate-roofed building, timber-framed and windowless. The door, of heavy oak, was opened and Mr. Finchley was pushed into the gloom. The door shut behind him. He heard a bolt pulled and then the retreating sound of footsteps.

Mr. Finchley dashed at the door and beat upon it with fists.

"You can't do this to me!" he shouted furiously. "You can't do this. It … it … it isn't legal!"

He thumped and kicked at the door. Then he stopped suddenly, aware that he was behaving without thought. He stood perfectly still and forced himself to count ten slowly. At five his respiration was easier, at eight he felt his impatience sliding away and at ten he was as calm as he knew he would be for a while.

As he stood there in the darkness, from before him there came a low chuckle and a pleasant, cultured voice said softly, "Welcome, my friend, to the Black Hole of Calcutta."

X
Of confinement and cauliflowers and liberty and leeks

MOST of us have been locked up at some time in our lives. Some of us, full-bloodedly in expiation of weighty transgressions, have been locked in jails, others in bedrooms to prevent our invalid despair of bed and its boredoms from forcing us into the treacherous fresh-air of the streets and lanes, some stranded in the gloom of an apple loft because an unfaithful accomplice deserted with the barn ladder, and many more in blanket cupboards, garages and various dark and confined spaces which are served by doors with spring locks. It is a common and salutary experience. To be held against our will in one place, and that a dark or unpleasant place, is to have demonstrated to us that the human spirit could not live for ever within a cage, that the human mind suffers with the body and that any restraint upon the one is a restraint upon the other. Only men of the highest fortitude and stoutest philosophy can ignore prison bars and stone walls, and there are few such men.

Mr. Finchley was not one. Those few seconds of darkness and isolation in the shed had filled him with a sense of frustration. He felt the loss of his freedom at once, and he knew, although he was too wise after the first moment of panic, why a wild bird will dash itself to exhaustion against its cage bars. The sound of that slow, pleasant voice coming to him from the darkness was like music. It was company, and company at that moment was Mr. Finchley's great need.

"Welcome," said the voice again. "Here is another who has been unfortunate enough to anger the local Suraja Dawlah. Were you poaching Colonel Greatorex's rabbits, too?"

"I was supposed to have been. Where are you?"

"Five paces forward, two to the left and there's a large truss of straw on the floor against the wall. I've found it very comfortable and there's room for two."

Mr. Finchley followed the instructions and heard someone move on the straw as he sat down.

"Isn't there a light?" he asked.

"I've found an old candle stump. We shall want that later, so we'll save it. It's not ten o'clock yet, is it?"

"Good heavens, no. It's light outside still."

"What do you mean, supposed to have been poaching? Weren't you?"

"No, I wasn't. It was all a mistake." Mr. Finchley took some pleasure and found a great deal of relief in explaining the circumstances of his capture.

He heard the unknown chuckle over the interview with the Colonel.

"You were unfortunate," he said, when Mr. Finchley finished. "You didn't know, of course, about me. But I said almost the same thing to the old boy. Told him not to be so mean with his rabbits, the damned old feudal relict. And I had been poaching them. No doubt of that. It must have given him a shock to find two such poachers in one day. Probably thought you were an accomplice of mine. Do you think he refers to the queen or the station? It worried me all the time he was talking and raving at me."

"Queen?" Mr. Finchley was puzzled.

"By Victoria …" The shed echoed to the man's low laugh and Mr. Finchley chuckled too. There was no sense in being depressed now that there was someone to share his bad luck.

"I should think," the man went on, "that he's a little tin god around here. Lots of men like that in England. Retired, wealthy old buffers who play the squire. One of these days his kind will have a nasty shock. Greedy, intolerant, obstinate old curs. The only way to get decent ideas into their heads is by cracking them wide open. No damned right to shove us in here at all. Absolutely illegal, as you must know. But he'll get away with it. The sympathy and power of the law will be all on his side. Only he won't get away with it—not this time."

"What do you mean?" Mr. Finchley was curious at the change in the man's voice.

"That we'll get away. If this place is used as the local jug it hasn't had anyone of intelligence in it before. When it gets dark enough I'll break out of here in no time. We'll be miles away before dawn comes up."

"What's your name? Mine's Finchley."

"Marshall, Tom Marshall. History? This and that and not much ballast. Thought I was going to be an architect but never really got going. Finchley, eh? Sounds a solid sort of name. Wonder what you look like—no, no, don't strike a match yet. It's interesting to sit in the dark and wonder what your next-door neighbour looks like. We'll know how good our guesses were when we start work. Just now we're a couple of voices. Did you ever think much about cauliflowers?"

"Cauliflowers?"

"Yes, the things you eat. Ever since I've been in here I've been thinking about cauliflowers. It's just come to me that it's ages since I tasted cauliflower. I often think about food. It's a pleasant thing to think about when you're bored."

"Are you often bored?"

"Often. I'm on a sort of walking tour. Well, you know, I'm walking around waiting for something to turn up—like Micawber. And I find walking is boring. So I think about food most of the time. Which do you like best with roast mutton, onion sauce or redcurrant jelly?"

"Onion sauce, I think," said Mr. Finchley after a pause.

"So do I. I've invented a recipe since I've been in here. Like to hear about it? I've called it Poorman's Pie, or Pudding. Never got to the bottom of that 'Is it pie or pudding?' business, have you?"

Mr. Finchley agreed that it was one of those things he was not sure about and then listened to the recipe for Poorman's Pie. You sliced up potatoes, onions, carrots, turnips, and any other vegetables you could lay hands on, put them into a buttered dish, covered them with a piecrust and baked the pie.

"No meat, but that's why it's called Poorman's Pie, and all the essential juices of the vegetables are retained. It takes a long time to cook and must be done slowly. I could eat one now. I'm very particular about food. I wouldn't give a tuppenny toss for fancy stuff. You know, soufflés and exotic wines and the mucked-up dishes that Frenchmen make. No, what I like is simple fare, properly prepared and presented. Roast pork now. That's simple enough. Roast pork, apple sauce, brussel sprouts, and baked potatoes— properly cooked, I defy any French chef to produce a dish to equal it in satisfaction. Have you ever thought much about baked parsnips?"

"I can't say that I have," admitted Mr. Finchley, a little disconcerted by Tom Marshall's eager interest in food.

"You should do. If they're very well baked they're almost like sweetmeats. They change completely. Yes, the simple things I like. If I was a poet, which I'm not— though if being hungry is one of the qualifications I'm qualified that far—I wouldn't waste my genius on singing the beauties of flowers and fair women. No, sir! God gave us other gifts. I'd sing about cabbages and cauliflowers, about sprouting broccoli and even the humble turnip top. And leeks—"

Marshall was silent for a moment as he contemplated leeks.

"There's a majesty about leeks, a dignity when they're growing and a glory when they're cooked. Green and white, green passing into white like night sliding into day … Ha, leeks. I could eat a plateful now, braised in butter and with just a touch of cayenne …" He was silent for a while, but Mr. Finchley could guess that his thoughts were full of food.

This man who sat by him in the darkness and talked of food sounded a little unusual, but Mr. Finchley had the wisdom to see that he was no better or worse than other men who have their daydreams. Some men think only of adding to their wealth, others in dreams travel the world, some cheer their dull days with thoughts of backing a winner at a fine price and some of unexpected inheritances. These are all dreams and longings which help to exclude the present, the nagging, unpleasant present. Tom Marshall thought of food, good and plentiful food, probably because he seldom had anything like as much food as he wanted.

"It's Sunday tomorrow," said Mr. Finchley suddenly. "Back in my caravan I've got a leg of mutton and fresh vegetables—I was going to cook them and have a real Sunday lunch. I don't know what'll happen now. This colonel business has upset things. I'm worried about the horse and caravan, too."

Marshall stirred on the hay. "Roast mutton, hey? Tell you what. If I get you out of here within the next hour, will you let me share that meal?"

"What about the colonel?"

"To hell with the colonel. You don't think that addle-brained brass hat can get between me and roast mutton, do you? I'd like to see Hercules himself try it. For the sake of a dish of roast mutton and all the trimmings I could lift the world on my shoulders to give the celestial forces a rest. We can get out of here and, with your caravan, be ten miles away by morning. The colonel won't worry us then, because he won't know where to look and, anyway, he knows nothing about your caravan. And if he does find us, you can threaten to sue him for false imprisonment."

"And how do you propose to get out?"

146

"Like this."

Mr. Finchley heard Marshall fumble in his pockets. A few seconds later a match was struck and then the yellow, growing light of a candle began to force back the darkness of the shed.

For the first time Mr. Finchley saw what Tom Marshall looked like. It was a surprise. Tom Marshall was a big man. As he stood up Mr. Finchley sensed the easy play of his muscles and the splendid balance of the well-proportioned body. He was a giant, a tall, dark skinned colossus with crisp, black hair. He wore stained flannel trousers, a suede and very old golf jacket and from one corner of his mouth hung a cherry-wood pipe. Here was no emaciated, hungry man, but an athletic figure. His eyes were under-marked with lazy, good-humoured wrinkles.

He pulled a large jack knife from his pocket and flicked the blade open.

"I told you I was almost an architect once, didn't I? Well, that makes this job easier." He nodded round the shed. "This place is built in an old style, timber-framework filled up with lath-and-plaster work." He went to the wall opposite the door. "See this plaster. It's on a lath frame-work. Then there's a small cavity, and beyond that we have the outer plasterwork. Stand back!"

As he spoke he drove the knife into the plaster and worked it vigorously. A large piece of the plaster fell, re-vealing the slats of the laths. In a few minutes Marshall had ripped off an area of plaster about three feet square. The air of the shed was filled with the dust motes from the falling plaster and Mr. Finchley coughed gently as he held the candle.

Marshall removed the laths by the simple process of pulling them off with his hands. Mr. Finchley saw the laths of the outer plasterwork facing them.

"Now," said Marshall, "we must be ready to get out quickly because this will make some noise." He looked about him and picked up from the floor of the shed an odd length of ashpole which had been left over from a store of logs.

"Ready?"

He poised the log and rammed it at the plasterwork. In a very little while he had knocked a hole in the outer wall. A current of cool night air was sucked into the shed and the candle went out in the draught.

"Come on!" Marshall gripped Mr. Finchley by the arm and pushed him into the gap which he had made. Twisting and wriggling, scratching his hands and face on the rough, splintery ends of laths, Mr. Finchley wormed his way through into freedom. Marshall followed him.

No one seemed to have heard their demolition. They stood for a moment under the pale canopy of night sky, looking about them. Then they made for the cover of the shrubbery. Not long afterwards they were out on the little road which climbed the scarp of the downs to the hollow where the caravan was parked.

When they reached it Mr. Finchley found that no one had disturbed it. Churchwarden was lying down on the little patch of grass, and he rose obediently to his feet as Mr. Finchley caught at his cheek-strap.

Marshall watched him as he harnessed the horse. Then he took his place alongside Mr. Finchley on the driving seat. They did not speak.

The caravan jolted and swayed out of the dell on to the road and then they were off, followed only by the call of a brown owl hunting over the downs. For three hours they drove under the polished blaze of stars. It was a lovely night, free of mists and cloud. Neither of them spoke, for speech seemed unnecessary. They smoked and listened to the clatter of Churchwarden's hoofs and the creak and quiet rub of the caravan timbers.

Mr. Finchley was to remember that night for a long time. To him it was a new experience, to be abroad so late and in such a strange manner. At first he was preoccupied with thoughts of a possible chase by the colonel's men, but gradually those fears dropped from his mind and he began to be aware of the night around him. They moved through a world that was suddenly and completely devoid of all human life except their own. The farms and cottages were dark shells that showed no light or life, the fields, grey and silver in the starlight, were peopled by massed groups of sheep or the whispering gentle stir of reaching corn. The road was a white impersonal streak that stretched ahead, offering no human friendliness, lined by tall masses of trees and the dark mysteries of hedges and ditches. Sometimes a sheep with worm coughed in the night, like an old man disturbed in his sleep, and now and then came the cry of a night-bird, light on the wind and full of a dark menace to all those creatures which moved in the grasses and weeds.

It was almost dawn when they drew off the road down a by-lane and stopped the caravan in the lee of a small copse that sheltered a dark patch of water. As Mr. Finchley unharnessed Churchwarden he heard the cluck of disturbed moor-fowl on the reeds at the edge of the road.

"Bed," said Marshall when the horse had been seen to. "I think we've earned it."

"So do I," answered Mr. Finchley. He went into the caravan and lit the swinging lamp. He fitted up the spare bunk with blankets for Marshall.

"This," said his companion as he sat on the edge of the bunk and began to undress, "is what I call comfortable travelling. Comfort is a great thing. Human beings are brought into the world expecting comfort, and it goes hard with them when they are denied it."

"I suppose so," said Mr. Finchley, yawning, for he was tired. As he raised his head his eyes met a strange sight. Over the archway of the sleeping compartment, on its little wooden shelf, stood the green glass bottle with its model of *Le Bon Accord*. He stared at it in amazement. It had not been there when he had left the caravan that evening to hunt for flowers. He stared at it so long that Marshall was aware of his surprise.

"Anything the matter?" he asked as he rolled into his blankets.

Mr. Finchley covered his surprise at once. "No, nothing," he said. "I was just thinking about something."

"Then don't," said Marshall. Sleeping not thinking is the order. Turn in."

Mr. Finchley did turn in, but he went on thinking. Sometime that evening Bob Trilby, still wandering, must have come across the caravan again and he had returned the model. Mr. Finchley was made happy. Bob had not been able to keep up his meanness. He had returned *Le Bon Accord*.

There were times, thought Mr. Finchley, as he dropped to sleep, when all of us made mistakes. Bob had made a mistake, and he was glad that the wandering seaman had found in himself enough courage and good sense to regret his mistake. Bob was all right. Even the best of men had to slip up occasionally.

XI
How Mr. Finchley
wins a prize

WHEN Mr. Finchley woke it was broad daylight and, far away, a church bell was ringing. It was another fine, bright day. Outside, he could see through the small caravan window, the sky was powder blue and strung with fluffy clouds, almost artificial in their resemblance to teased wood. A willow wren was calling frantically somewhere by the pond and the bells went on, ringing and dancing as though the ringers were full of the morning brightness and were imparting their gladness to the swinging bells.

"Damn the bells," said a voice from the other bunk. Mr. Finchley twisted over and was greeted with the dark face of Tom Marshall. He was smoking, blue clouds coiling up to the roof, and from the smell Mr. Finchley recognised his own tobacco. Marshall must have guessed his thoughts.

"Ran out of my own tobacco, so I borrowed some of yours, hope you don't mind."

"Not at all."

"Thought you wouldn't. What a morning, eh? Kind of morning that makes old men think of their youth. Damn those bells! Ever thought about bells?" Marshall did not wait for an answer. "The man who invented 'em should have been tortured. Bells. Oh, this life is full of bells! They ring them for deaths and for marriages. They ring 'em in prisons at food times and at alarm times. You ring a bell to go into a house, you ring a bell to call a fire engine. You get 'em rung at you in the streets by bicyclists, by hawkers and by carol singers. You can't escape 'em. They put them on your rattle before you can speak, and they ring 'em over your grave when you can't speak. And I dislike the sound of them. What about that roast mutton, eh?"

Mr. Finchley laughed. "I haven't forgotten it."

"Neither have I. Dreamed about it. It's late. What do you say if we call breakfast off and begin right away with lunch?"

Mr. Finchley had no objection. He got out of bed and, after shaving himself, began to make the preparations for lunch. Marshall lay in his bunk and watched him and talked and smoked.

"I'm not sure what kind of a fist I shall make at cooking it," said Mr. Finchley as he put the meat in the little oven.

"Don't worry," came the answer. "You're the kind of man who is instinctively a good cook. I can tell."

While Mr. Finchley was cooking, Marshall made no attempt to move. He just lay in his bunk and talked. At first Mr. Finchley was a little inclined to resent his laziness. Then he reasoned with himself that Marshall had probably been on the road without much comfort for some time and he was reluctant to relinquish the joys of warm blankets and a comfortable berth.

"How is it that a man of your type comes to be moving about in a caravan?" asked Marshall after a while.

Mr. Finchley told him. Marshall considered the information, then said slowly, "Remember I told you I was good as an architect?"

"You said you meant to be one, but never were."

"No, what I meant was that I was trained but never practised. Well, you could do with an architect when you're looking at houses. It's awfully easy to buy a pig in a poke. Professional advice is what you want before you commit yourself. What do you say if we join forces? I'm going as far as Canterbury. Got a friend there. We could travel together and, in return for shelter and food, I'll give you the benefit of my advice on any and all houses you look at on the way. Ever think of the things that can be wrong with a house without your knowing about it? Roof beams can be all gone with dry rot, or eaten by beetle. You wouldn't notice whether there was a damp course or not. Drainage may be inadequate. Woodwork, roofing, pointing—they may all be bad, but people'll go and buy a house because it has a wistaria over it, or an apple tree on the lawn. But you've got to live in a house, not look at it. Houses can look fine and be damned inconvenient. You'd better take me along with you."

Mr. Finchley, who was busy preparing the potatoes for lunch, did not reply for a moment. He considered this proposition. He was grateful to Marshall for getting him out of the Colonel's shed and he quite liked the man, but he was not sure whether he wanted to have his company until he reached Canterbury.

Marshall, blowing a long whiff of smoke at the roof, took his silence for assent.

"That's fixed then. You'll not regret it. Ever think about beds? We spend over a third of our life in bed, in oblivion. Warm, comfortable oblivion. If I was a poet I'd write about beds. Some scope there. Marriage beds, natal beds, sick beds and death beds, and just ordinary, everyday household beds that get made or don't get made."

"I suggest you leave the one you're in and make ready for this meal," Mr. Finchley commented.

"You're right. Never eat in bed. Spoils the food and disturbs the bed. Here we go!"

With a heave Marshall came out of the bed and stood up, clad only in his shirt. It was a green shirt, crumpled and dirty and torn across the arm so that the loose material flapped like a broken wing. He stripped the shirt from himself and walked past Mr. Finchley out of the caravan. He went down the steps and across to the small pool in the trees. He turned to where Mr. Finchley was watching him from the steps.

"Here we go!" he cried again. "Nothing like a dip to rouse the appetite!"

He drew back and then jumped into the water. There was a mighty splash, a spout of spray and the alarmed flutter of moor fowl.

He came back to Mr. Finchley, blowing and grinning. Mr. Finchley handed him a towel and he danced around on the grass while he dried himself. In between his towelling he said, "I suppose you haven't got a shirt you could lend me until I can wash and mend my own?"

Mr. Finchley found him a shirt. He accepted it without any undue expression of thanks, and a few moments later they were sitting down to lunch.

It was a good lunch. Either, Mr. Finchley decided, he was as Marshall had said, instinctively a good cook, or he had been lucky. The roast was done to a turn, the potatoes browned and crisp and the mint sauce was such as only the English relish, and they both did justice to the excellences of the meal. They ate like good trenchermen, with silent, vigorous appetites.

When they were finished, Marshall leaned back and filled his pipe from Mr. Finchley's pouch. His eyes were bright with a happy mood, his face was bland with the substantial joy that comes from good eating.

"Not for a very, very long time," said he, "have I eaten such delicious, such fragrant, such wholesome, such well-prepared food. If I were a Persian shah I should now have the wonders of my treasure-house brought before you and bid you take your pick ..."

"Is it so long since you have had such a good meal, then?" asked Mr. Finchley quietly.

Marshall looked at him shrewdly. Then he smiled faintly.

"It is. Various circumstances made such meals remote and dreamlike. This is a hard, sordid, material world. It deals only in its own material currencies and I have never been well supplied with such tokens. However, don't let us spoil the effect of this repast with talk like that ... I think I shall now go and lie in the sun and sleep. It's some time since I slept on a really full stomach. I don't want to miss the pleasure."

He got up and left Mr. Finchley to clear the lunch away and wash up the dishes. When the water was hot on the primus and ready for washing up the plates, Mr. Finchley, determined that he should take his full share of the work, called to him to come and help. But Marshall was deep in sleep, so deep that no call of Mr. Finchley's seemed to reach him, and Mr. Finchley, kind-hearted, had no wish to go and shake him into wakefulness.

That was where Mr. Finchley made his mistake with Tom Marshall. Had he roughly wakened him from his sleep and shown that he was expected to take his share of the work of the caravan, the seal of a certain order would have been put upon their relationship. But he let him lie, and in doing so, he established a custom, a tradition, which Tom Marshall maintained from that day. He never did anything that he could possibly avoid. He was all laziness. He was more than lazy. He had a grand capacity for lassitude and doing nothing which swamped all his other virtues and vices. He was too lazy to be good or bad.

His waking thoughts were mostly of sleep or food. He borrowed Mr. Finchley's shirts and socks, he smoked his tobacco and used his pipe cleaners. He ate the food Mr. Finchley prepared and he drove Mr. Finchley by skilful, good-humoured propaganda and talk into preparing meals which he liked and with which Mr. Finchley would seldom have bothered.

They spent a week together on the way to Canterbury. They examined houses, and over each one Marshall spent a great deal of time. He examined them critically and lingeringly so that the journey to Canterbury would spin out. He jumped up and down on floor boards, and when they sagged a little under his great weight, as any board was entitled to sag, he shook his head gravely. He pounded the roof beams in attics with his great fist until wood dust and plaster fell all around them, and an occasional tile slid off the roof. And when they got back to the caravan, he would sink on the long seat and, looking up at Mr. Finchley, say, "Well, what about a spot of grub, old fellow? Cheer you up after that disappointment. But you're wise not to be interested in the place. Something will turn up. What about those steaks we bought? There's something solid now and calculated not to disappoint any man of sense. A fine steak and fried tomatoes. Pity we haven't got a bottle of beer to go with it. We must remember to buy some beer at the next pub we pass. Well, that examination of mine saved you five guineas professional fee, didn't it? I tell you, you were lucky to meet up with me. Ever think about strange meetings? Like ships in the night, most people miss one another, but now and then two people meet and somewhere in the sky a star begins to shine ..."

And he would talk while Mr. Finchley would begin to prepare the meal. At first Mr. Finchley had tried to struggle, but Marshall's personality bore him down. He seemed deaf to any suggestion that he should help. He ignored it altogether as something unworthy of his consideration, and an obvious lapse of good taste on Mr. Finchley's part. Gradually Mr. Finchley succumbed. There was nothing else to do. Marshall had come to stay. He could be told to go, or to stay and help, but he would hear nothing. The only way to get rid of him was to throw him out and, when it came to that, Mr. Finchley knew that it was impossible. How Marshall's body remained fit and strong was a mystery to him. But there was no doubting his strength. He inhabited the caravan like the old man of the sea. And he talked, as though he knew that the moment he stopped talking his barriers would be down and Mr. Finchley could get through to him and tell him to go. Mr. Finchley began to long for Canterbury to heave in sight. Even when it did, he feared that Marshall, having found a comfortable berth, might be unwilling to leave him. That thought filled him with desperation.

He began to understand some of Marshall's trouble in life. The real trouble was that he was a parasite, a parasite which was well prepared to cling and fight for its rights. Having little property of his own he had no respect for other people's property, and, telling himself that if he had possessions he would be generous, he looked for wide generosity in those who had the power to give. Mr. Finchley began to know real alarm when, after the third day, Marshall started to refer to the caravan as "our little home on wheels" and to apply the plural possessive to the things around him. It was, "Have you seen our tobacco?" "Isn't it time you washed some of our shirts?" and once "Don't worry, in time we shall find the perfect house. Our house, the one we dream about."

At that, Mr. Finchley decided he must, by some means, get rid of Marshall. He was sorry for the man in many ways, but he was not going to be saddled with him for the rest of his trip or for the rest of his life. Mr. Finchley started to do some hard thinking.

It took him some time to evolve a scheme, two days in fact, and before it had developed in his mind he had become the proud owner of Ella. It was Ella, in fact, who precipitated matters.

They were going along a quiet country road, after having visited a farmhouse which Marshall had sworn would probably fall down before they left it, when they came to a village. It was the kind of village which American film producers, Christmas-card and calendar publishers and the designers of chocolate boxes swear is typically English. It was the apotheosis of English villages, a freakish, pleasant survival. It had a little village green and a duck pond with hanging willows and ducks. A grey-stoned church sat at one end of the green and quaint, dark-timbered houses fronted the open space. There was an inn with a dove-cote and a red-and-yellow signboard, and a village store with tall, bottle-glassed eighteenth-century windows. Mr. Finchley could never remember its name except that it ended in bourne or mere or perhaps ham, but he never forgot the village because of Ella. If it had not been for Ella he might have remembered it for its other virtues, because, for instance, there were no barrel hoops or tins floating or wrecked in the duck pond, because the green itself was not worn patchy with the games of footballers and made untidy with the litter of cigarette cartons and toffee wrappers, because the store did not festoon itself with iron placards advertising lamp oils, non-irritant tobaccos and soft drinks, because the whole place had not suffered the scabby disease of modern assertiveness and untidiness.

As they drove down the main street into the village a white banner floated over their heads, stretched from one house to another. Churchwarden shied a little at the bright flutter and Mr. Finchley just caught the red announcement of "Village Fête."

Marshall, who was sitting beside him, nodded towards a crowd which had gathered on the village green. Around the edge of the green were stalls with gay coverings.

"Shall we stop and have a look?"

"Perhaps we should," said Mr. Finchley. He drove the caravan on to the piece of ground before the inn, where a number of cars was parked. They tied Churchwarden to the inn fence and made their way into the crowd.

All fêtes are a polite form of piracy, and it is no less piracy because the proceeds go to the upkeep of the village church, the repair of the bell tower or the local hospital. No one minds the piracy and polite blackmail. The technique is interesting, and has been well tried through the years. The stalls are manned by voluntary helpers, gentlefolk and village folk mingling in the happiest and most proper manner. For weeks before the fête the preparations go on. Sweets are bought from the market town and put into fancy bottles and jars. The jars are painted or decorated with ribbon, and two pennyworth of acid drops, lifted from the ignominy of a paper bag, become worth sixpence. There are homemade sweets, too. Fudge and toffee - made by the vicar's children and the doctor's daughter - sticky and often not well-formed (the sweets not the children and daughter, though they were sticky enough while the making was going on), they cannot be constrained by jar or carton but are spread on wide trays and handed to you in screws of coloured paper for immediate consumption if you wish to avoid the unpleasantness which follows the disintegration of fudge in a screw of paper. There is the bookstall. For weeks the Boy Scouts go from house to house with their troop cart collecting those dusty, unwanted volumes which collect in attics and cupboards. They come out into the light of day at the fête, faded red volumes of pre-war vintage, crammed with the heroes and heroines, the villains and excitements which titillated the palates of a past generation, and over these presides always the grey-haired, curiously dressed, rather formidable lady who represents literature in the community. Each community has one such person. She once saw George Moore leaving the Café Royal and is smilingly tolerant of the doctor's love of Anthony Hope and the squire's respect for Dean Hole. At a penny for ten the books would be cheap, but she sells you a dirty copy of *Monsieur Beaucaire* with four pages missing for sixpence and, as make-weight, enquires with a tolerant smile whether you have read the latest Aldous Huxley and doesn't bother to listen to your reply because she is certain that you have not.

The sweet stall, the book stall, the arts-and-crafts stall, the vegetable and fruit stall, the mystery packet stall where you pay sixpence and take what is given to you wrapped in paper, the scent and soap stall and all the other stalls with their smiling crews of gaily dressed, chattering cutpurses and, wandering in and out of the crowd, the lighter craft, the cut-in-and-kill-quickly host of corsairs who sell you tickets in raffles, force you to pay threepence for the pleasure of guessing the number of buttons in a bottle or to buy the lucky programme ... they were all on this village green as Mr. Finchley and Marshall pressed their way into the throng.

A young woman in a flowing summer dress and a wide-brimmed hat came sailing up to them. She was pretty, pink and white and bright with flowers, flowers on her hat and flowers rambling all over the design of her dress. Behind her staggered a small village boy, his stockings around his ankles, his scrubbed face shining with loathing and heat. He carried in his arms a large glass almost as big as himself. Mr. Finchley was reminded of a gracious sailing ship being followed by a tubby clumsy barge.

"Oh, won't you take a chance at the button guessing?" cried the young lady. "It's so exciting. You pay sixpence and guess the number and then—if you're right, of course—there's a mystery prize."

Marshall smiled at her and thought how lucky it was that he had borrowed Mr. Finchley's razor that morning and shaved.

"Of course we will," he cried affably. "Won't we, Mr. Finchley?"

"Yes, yes, of course. I suppose—"

"We'll both have a go. Give me that bottle, son."

Marshall took the bottle. It was crammed with an assortment of buttons. He shook it, placed his ear against it as it rattled and then tossed it lightly in his hands.

"What do you say?" enquired the young lady and she made it sound like music, her eyes bewitching them both.

Marshall was silent. Then he announced deliberately, "One thousand six hundred and seven—"

"Nonsense," said Mr. Finchley at once. "That's far too many."

"We'll see, we'll see," said Marshall, unperturbed. "Pay the young lady the shilling and then have your guess."

Mr. Finchley felt in his pocket for the money. Then he had his guess.

"Nine hundred and eighty-seven," he announced and added for Marshall's benefit, "Didn't you notice that most of the buttons are very large?"

"We'll see," said Marshall.

The young lady wrote their guesses down in her little book under their names and said, "The correct number will be announced by the vicar at five o'clock."

The small boy took up his burden and she sailed off with no more than a dim smile in parting. She had played her part and got their money. Now they were of no interest to her.

Marshall watched her go, a tender look in his eyes. He turned to Mr. Finchley.

"Have you ever thought about women?" he enquired. "About the various kinds of women and how much we men—"

163

Mr. Finchley thanked the village band for blaring into music at that moment. It saved him from Marshall's dissertation.

Before the afternoon was over Mr. Finchley found that he had bought two cakes of soap, a box of liquorice all-sorts, a leather bookmark with an Indian's face on it and had taken shares in six raffles of different kinds.

At five o'clock the band played a few martial chords, a bell was rung for attention and the vicar took his place on a small box in the centre of the green and began to make his announcements. He thanked them all for coming, thanked them all for spending so liberally and said that the total profit from the fair would be made known in the notices to be read in church on Sunday morning. He then proceeded to read out the names of the winners of the various competitions.

Mr. Finchley and Marshall stood in the crowd listening and clapping as the various winners came up and took their prizes.

"The button-guessing competition," the vicar read richly. "There was a record entry for this. No one got the right number. There were three people who were within five of the correct number and one who guessed to within two of the correct number. The total number of buttons was nine hundred and eighty-five and the mysterious prize goes to the gentleman, a Mr. Finchley, who estimated nine hundred and eighty-seven. Will Mr. Finchley please step forward?"

There was a pause. Everyone looked around for Mr. Finchley, wondering who he was. Mr. Finchley, himself, was overcome with a swift attack of embarrassment. He might never have made himself known had not Marshall, at that moment, given him a jab in the back and sent him forward into the open ring before the vicar. "There he is!" he cried.

A cheer greeted his appearance and the vicar beamed down at him.

"Mr. Finchley? Good. My congratulations, sir. Here is your prize." The vicar turned and beckoned to someone at the back of him. The crowd opened up and through it came a large man in gaiters, checked coat and hard black hat. From a string in his hand he was leading a pig.

"Here y'are, sir," said the man, holding the string towards Mr. Finchley. "Feed un and he'll grow, though he ain't more'n a little un now."

A roar of laughter rose from the crowd and the pig, alarmed at the noise, made a dart towards the maze of legs before him. The tug pulled Mr. Finchley forward and the crowd opened to let them through. It was some yards before he could pull the pig up. He found Marshall at his side.

"Well, that's a fine prize," he said, with a faint touch of bitterness in his voice.

The bitterness roused Mr. Finchley curiously. It made him anxious to defend the merits of his prize.

"I don't know," he said, and added, "I told you your estimate was too high. It was a pretty good guess of mine."

"Luck," said Marshall. "Sheer luck."

Mr. Finchley scarcely heard him. He was looking at the pig. It was not a large pig. In fact, it was scarcely more than a piglet, but it was an engaging animal. It was pure white except for a saddle of black on its back and two dark lines of black over its eyes that made it look a little like George Robey. It had dark eyes and a pink nose and it sat now on its hindquarters looking around it at the ring of small boys and curious people who had gathered. Occasionally it shook its head in irritation with the rope collar about its neck. It was, Mr. Finchley decided, as pleasant a young pig as he had ever seen. Robert would be delighted with it.

"Come on," said Marshall urgently. "We're beginning to look ridiculous." He tugged Mr. Finchley along. They moved off the green towards the caravan and the pig, dragging a little at the lead, followed them.

"What do we do with her?" asked Marshall when they reached the caravan.

"Why, keep her, of course," said Mr. Finchley. "We can't just leave her here. I won her."

"I know, but you can't carry a pig around with you all the time."

"She's got to come with us for the time being. Here, give me a hand." Mr. Finchley opened the back door of the caravan and then took hold of the pig. "Come on," he cried to Marshall, "help me lift her in."

Marshall had to help. They lifted the pig into the caravan and shut the door on her. Then they went round to the driving seat and started off. Neither of them spoke. After a time, Mr. Finchley said slowly, "I shall call her Ella."

"In Pete's name, why?" Marshall made no attempt to hide his irritation.

"For no reason. It just sounds the right kind of name for her."

"You won't be so pleased about her after a day. Pigs aren't house-trained and they want feeding. I suggest we stop at the next farm and sell her."

"Certainly not. We haven't even tried to see whether she'll take to caravan life." Mr. Finchley paused and looked across at Marshall, then went on, his voice edging on a bantering note, "Ever think about pigs? Large pigs and little pigs, the pigs you see made of gingerbread and the pigs that go to market and the ones that stay at home …"

It was to Marshall's credit that he saw the joke was against himself and he laughed.

Mr. Finchley laughed too. But they both held back from unreserved laughter because they both felt that the real issue was yet to be decided.

XII
In which Mr. Finchley feels that the more he sees of some people, the more he loves his pig

ELLA was, for a pig, fastidious, but she was not house-trained. That much was obvious that evening when they halted the caravan and made camp for the night. When they opened the door at the back they found her lying, comfortably and at full length, on the upholstered seat which Marshall usually took. The evidence of her lack of training was on the floor but, evidence of her fastidiousness and regard for others, it was close to the door and easily disposed of.

They tied her to the caravan wheel and Mr. Finchley fed her some of Churchwarden's corn and gathered armfuls of long grass and old bracken stems to make her bed under the caravan.

When they had finished supper, Marshall suggested that they should walk back along the road to an inn they had passed and have a drink. At Mr. Finchley's suggestion that he should go by himself he refused, as though a sudden suspicion had slid into his mind that he might go only to return later and find Mr. Finchley and the caravan gone off. Mr. Finchley read the suspicion in his eyes and, since he really did feel like a drink, decided that he would come after all.

It was such a mild evening that they sat at a wooden bench in the garden of the inn. Over them hung an apple tree, green fruit thick in its foliage, and from a flower border came the rich scent of tobacco flowers.

For a time they drank without much talk. But after a few glasses Marshall's tongue loosened up and he began to reason with Mr. Finchley. It was extraordinary how much he had come to dislike Ella. The real reason, Mr. Finchley thought, might be of vanity that he had not guessed the number correctly.

"It's no good, old boy," he told Mr. Finchley. "You haven't considered all the aspects of this pig question. I like animals, so do you, but you can't keep them in a caravan. Our caravan isn't big enough. And it can't trot behind us like a dog—its legs would never stand it. You've got to get rid of it."

"But I'd like to keep it. I might soon find the house I'm looking for and then I could have it in a sty in the orchard. My boy would love it."

"But it might be ages before we found our house. No, it must go. It's impracticable."

"I won't sell it!" said Mr. Finchley stubbornly. He hoped that Ella, if he persisted, would help him to drive off Marshall. But he was quite unprepared for Marshall's next move.

"No need to sell it, old boy. No need. Look!" He took his jack knife from his pocket and jerked the large, sharp blade open. "Ever think of knives? Ever think of their uses? They sharpen pencils, they cut switches to beat bad boys, they carve initials on tree trunks and they opened a way for us to escape from the old Colonel, didn't they?" He was getting a little mixed from drink. "Well, it'll help us to escape from Ella. Tell you what. Tomorrow morning we'll have a sacrifice. I'll cut her throat—" He made a horrid sound with his mouth and drew the knife across an imaginary throat. "No longer pig, no longer a problem—but just pork. Pork ain't no problem. Ever think of roast pork and apple sauce, of crisp brown crackling ..." He rambled on while Mr. Finchley stared at him open-eyed and dismayed. He was really frightened at the ferocity of Marshall's words, and he had no doubt that the man meant all he said. He could see that, if he kept Ella, Marshall, who did not mean to be driven from his comfortable caravan berth, would one day kill her. Whatever happened, Mr. Finchley did not mean to allow that.

He had won Ella fairly and, although he knew he could not carry her around with him indefinitely, he had no intention of playing such a treachery upon her. In his despair he found an idea. Marshall had to go, and like all apparently invincible men, he had his Achilles heel. As Mr. Finchley drank his beer and Marshall caressed his knife and talked of butcheries, an idea grew.

The next morning Marshall did not wake until eleven o'clock. Long before that Mr. Finchley was up and active. He knew Marshall's capacity for sleep. When Marshall woke it was to see Mr. Finchley sitting on the doorstep, smoking his pipe and peeling potatoes.

"Blimey, it's late," said Marshall. "Must have taken a little too much last night."

Mr. Finchley smiled at him. It was an expansive, friendly smile.

"I didn't disturb you. I've been busy. Been thinking over this pig business. I think, Marshall, you were right. While you were asleep this morning I walked back to the village we passed yesterday after we had won the pig. I saw the butcher there and he's coming out this afternoon to take the pig from me. I couldn't kill her myself and eat her as you suggested—"

"Of course not, old boy. Damned indelicate suggestion of mine," said Marshall nobly and happily. "I'm glad you're seeing the right thing to do. What are you doing now?"

"Preparing lunch. I thought that, as the butcher wouldn't be here until this afternoon and we shall have to stay here, we'd take the opportunity of having a good meal. I made a few purchases while I was in the village. What do you say?"

"Excellent. You're a genius."

Marshall was so pleased at the way things had turned out that he even offered to groom Churchwarden while Mr. Finchley was getting the lunch.

"I should put her in harness, so that we can move off the moment the butcher arrives," shouted Mr. Finchley. Without a murmur of protest Marshall did so, calling for advice on the harnessing at times. Mr. Finchley smiled as he heard him fussing about at the front of the caravan. If

Marshall had seen that smile he would not have been so happy.

Although it was a sultry day, Marshall made no quibble about the lunch which was prepared for him. Mr. Finchley put all his art and instinctive skill into that lunch. It began with a soup. Tinned julienne soup. Then followed lamb cutlets, three for Marshall and two for Mr. Finchley. With the cutlets were new potatoes, succulent and the colour of old ivory, and fried tomatoes. How Mr. Finchley manipulated all the dishes on his one primus he afterwards could not remember. He only knew that he worked like a trojan, warming plates, keeping the dishes hot and manoeuvring things so that it should all come to the table fresh and appetising. With the soup and meat they drank cider, rough cider which he had stopped at the pub to buy, and then, after they had cleared up a tin of peaches and a shillingsworth of raw cream, he brought the meal to a triumphant climax by producing coffee, cigarettes and, the crown of all, a glass of brandy each from the store which his wife had laid in for medicinal purposes.

They both ate heartily. Mr. Finchley took his share so that Marshall should have no suspicions, and when they had finished they lay back against their seats and smiled at one another.

"What a meal, what a meal," breathed Marshall gently as he fingered his second tot of brandy and blew rings of cigarette smoke towards the ceiling. "For three meals a week like that I'd sell my soul to the devil and design him a new and even more macabre and pernicious purgatory."

"It was good, wasn't it?" sighed Mr. Finchley, feeling much as a balloon must feel just before it goes up. "Good is a mild word. There is no word to describe it. I've got a feeling that this meal is an omen. I feel that the next house we look at may be the one we've been looking for. Boy, am I full? Gloriously, happily, sleepily and completely full. I must go out and have a snooze under the hedge. Wake me when that butcher arrives and I'll see that he doesn't cheat us over the price of Ella. Poor Ella, so soon to be ... Oh, no, I mustn't say that ... too much respect for your feelings."

Marshall got up and walked sleepily into the sun. The hot meal, the heady cider, the fiery brandy, the thick, black coffee all played upon his senses. He wanted to lie down and sleep. Mr. Finchley, fighting to keep his own lids from dropping, watched him find a comfortable spot in the shade of the hedge and stretch out.

Five minutes later the sound of gentle snoring proclaimed that Marshall was lost to the world about him. Mr. Finchley gave him ten minutes grace and then, shaking off his own desire to sleep, he set to work. He gathered up the gear around the caravan, packing it all away swiftly and quietly and then he turned to Ella. He untied her from the wheel and led her up the road. She came, unwillingly at first, and then, tempted by half a loaf of bread he held in his hand, willingly. Mr. Finchley knew that he could never have loaded her into the caravan without her squealing waking Marshall. He took her a safe way up the road, tied her to the hedge, and left her with the bread.

A few minutes later he came up to her, driving the caravan. Marshall had not stirred as Churchwarden had drawn the caravan out of the camping-place.

Mr. Finchley got down, grabbed Ella round the neck and hindparts and hoisted her into the caravan, whose floor he had been careful to line with newspapers. She squealed once and then was silent. He slammed the door tight and hurried back to his seat. They jogged off down the road, leaving the well-filled and sleeping Marshall. Mr. Finchley clicked his tongue at Churchwarden, making him hurry his pace. He was a free man again. Marshall, he knew, had no money to buy a bus ticket to hurry after him, and Mr. Finchley felt that he was well rid of him at the cost of a shirt, a pair of socks, one vest and half a pouch of tobacco.

For the next three hours Mr. Finchley kept Church-warden hard at it. He was torn between two desires, to get as far away from Marshall as he could and the craving for sleep which lay heavily upon him. The fight between the two desires tore his body with dissensions. At times he dozed for a second, only to jerk into attention at the passing of a car. Gradually he dropped into a sort of wakeful stupor. He saw the road, he kept Churchwarden to his duty, but his mind soared away into the warm regions of half-sleep so that material objects had a remote, insubstantial appearance. And it was hot. The sun, seeing his plight, had no pity for him. The sultry clouds had gone and the landscape, the hard white road, offered no relief. The hedges and trees danced in the air like objects seen through wavy glass; the paintwork grew red hot to his touch, the flies that tormented Churchwarden sent a squadron to attack him, and the air around him was strong with the smells of dust, horse and pig. He was on a main road now and the passing cars merely moved the warm air in eddies to beat at his face. The houses he passed seemed to leap and dance in the heat, the distant slopes and hills heaved and swung as though the earth was stirring with sea-like unrest.

In the end Mr. Finchley slept. It conquered him before he knew it and before he could draw up in safety at the side of the road. He dropped comfortably in the angle of the driving seat, the reins still in his hands, his face creased with a bland smile of satisfaction, and Churchwarden plodded on.

XIII
The truth about a disgraceful episode and a supplement to a certain regimental history

IT IS unsatisfactory to speculate about the thoughts of animals, unsatisfactory since one can never be sure whether they think or just move to a complicated jig of reflexes. That man is an animal which laughs may be an amiable definition of the difference between humankind and animalkind, but all laughter is not outward and noisy, and laughter itself is sometimes no easier to detect than a thought. We can never be sure whether an animal laughs or thinks. One can only guess, probe empirically and take what comfort there is in the works of Bergson and the neo-Darwinists. And if one wanted a good subject for experiment it is doubtful whether a better subject than Churchwarden could have been found.

A year's study of Churchwarden would have filled a dozen casebooks and posed a thousand questions never to be answered. Looked at materialistically he was a horse, or—as any encyclopaedia would put it—one of the family of the odd-toed group of the zoological order Ungalata. After that he defied any strict classification. He was neither racehorse, carthorse, country horse, cab horse not warhorse. He was just horse, and highly individualistic horse, and his actions were controlled and prompted, twisted and accelerated by a dark, mysterious web of mental processes, peculiarly conditioned reflexes and undefinable cerebric dictates which you can call thoughts, or habits, or whatever you like without insult to yourself or Churchwarden and without, in one jot, approaching the real solution of what went on inside that long and rather clumsy head of his.

As to why Churchwarden did the things he did it is only possible to speculate, and in this world, and especially in the matter of horses, a speculation is the most that any wise man should ever allow himself. Certainty and horses should never be bracketed.

Mr. Finchley had probably struck the easiest compromise by regarding Churchwarden as an individual, as a person, as a horse with attributes which, apart from the inevitable one-toed ungulate zoological business, were as near human as did not matter. Treated as a human being then, and as a not particularly adult human being, it was possible to read some reason into Churchwarden's actions. That was how Mr. Finchley found consolation at times.

It is possible that Churchwarden realised that Mr. Finchley was asleep. If he did not, then it is hard to explain how he rationalised to himself the ease with which he was allowed to enter into and pursue his activities of that afternoon.

Churchwarden was bored. He was bored with caravanning. Pulling the caravan so many miles a day, laying up for the night in the lee of a hedge, even though it was warm and he was well fed, lacked that excitement which his undistinguished form and rare spirit craved. For many days after Mr. Finchley had established his supremacy, Churchwarden fed his soul on the memories of his glorious past. In his time he had played many parts, and those thoughts eased the monotony of the road.

But this afternoon he was even more bored. It was hot and the flies were troublesome, and he disliked with each fresh roar the passage of the motor cars. He plodded forward, his mind way back in the rich fields of the past. If we could have heard his thoughts it is not impossible that they might have been, "What a day, what a life! Slugging at this caravan and smelling nothing but petrol fumes. Not like the old days. Remember the old days in the Marylebone Road, pulling the old coffee stall and the young gents rolling up in their high hats and opera cloaks? Used to make a few funny remarks about me, but youth is youth and always high-spirited. And Madame Angeline from the patisserie, who always used to pass me one of her croutons in the morning. Then there was the circus. Van horse, pulling the old water-carts and sniffed at by the haute-école snobs. Haute-école, indeed; they were high and mighty enough but as ignorant of the real world as a lot of children. I can smell the tan-ring now and hear the blare of the music. And I went from that to delivering bread in Bristol. Ran away down College Green. Lumme, that was a set-out. I was a bit scared at the time, but the bread went rolling all over the place and I took the Bishop of Bristol clean off his bike and ripped his gaiters with the off-side rear …The things I've done, but nothing like the circus life, the music. Must be the Cockney in me, I suppose, that makes me feel ready for a Knees-up-Mother-Brown when I hear the band begin to play … Damn these flies!"

Ahead the road began to be dotted with the new villas and the outer habitations of a town and away in the distance a chimney-stack smoked against the glittering, heat-brazen sky. Churchwarden moved on, avoiding the traffic drawn up on his side of the road with instinctive ease, wondering when he would be unharnessed and given a good feed.

Suddenly, from ahead and to the left, there came, thinly at first like the faint wail of a gnat, the sound of music, of brass instruments.

Churchwarden pricked one ear forward. The music sounded louder. Churchwarden quickened his gait a little. The music now filled the hot air with the rollicky, brassy strain of a march. Cornets shrilled, drums beat like thunder, fife and pipes screamed in an ecstasy of sound and Churchwarden's heart took a quicker beat. The least it could be was a circus, and he hadn't passed a circus for years.

Before him to the left of the road showed up a long, tall iron railing, and in the centre of the railing a gateway round which a few interested spectators were grouped. From beyond the gateway came the maddening, delicious, reminiscent blare of the band, and suddenly between the thick laurels that flanked the inner side of the railings Churchwarden caught a sight of gay uniforms, the yellow glitter of instruments and the movement of men. It was too much for Churchwarden. As he neared the gateway, he swung aside. The little group of spectators about the gate heard the rattle of the caravan behind them and jumped away. From inside the gate a soldier on sentry duty ran forward and shouted at the sleeping Mr. Finchley and tried to hold Churchwarden. Churchwarden snorted in his face and then, as the music soared into brassy, militant heights, he lifted his knees and galloped forward to join the marching panoply and jubilant, music-filled arena. Mr. Finchley woke as Churchwarden began to gallop. He woke to hear the shout of the sentry behind him and the gay lilt of band music before him, and he opened his eyes to be confronted with a sight that was at once unexpected and unnerving.

The caravan was charging at a rattling pace straight across a bare parade ground. Before him was a long column of marching soldiers, swinging along in time to the band, which was quartered at one side of the ground. In front of the soldiers was a little group of officers on horseback and standing out from them another figure on horseback, an upright, martial, medalled, red-faced, white-moustached man, who was taking the salute as the men marched by.

At once Mr. Finchley grabbed the reins and tried to pull Churchwarden in. But the horse would have none of it. He just galloped on. The caravan swirled past the group of officers and their steeds danced and pirouetted aside in alarm. Then Churchwarden thundered between the troops and the saluting colonel, and was away making a grand circle of the ground.

At once the parade ground was in confusion. The band went on playing as though they felt there was virtue in ignoring the unexpected. The colonel's face flushed purple and he turned to the group behind him and hurled an order. An officer galloped away after the caravan. The soldiers kept straight faces and strained their eyes in an effort to look front and yet watch the caravan's swinging, lurching, bumping career around the ground. From the gateway a ribald spectator gave a husky cheer and an ice-cream boy leaned over the top of his box and shouted derisively—"He wants to join the Army. Give him a chance to see the world!"

Mr. Finchley tugged at the reins and shouted furiously at Churchwarden. The horse was beyond his control. He charged back across the ground, forced the men to halt and broke through their ranks and swung about just as the officer in pursuit came abreast of Mr. Finchley.

"What the hell, sir!" he bellowed.

Mr. Finchley raised one hand weakly as though to express his sorrow.

"Get that contraption out of here at once, sir. By Gad, the Colonel'll have you bastinadoed for this." The conversation was not easily maintained because, at that moment, Churchwarden headed for the band. The men stuck to their posts bravely until the last moment. Then they dived aside, still playing, and let the whirlwind through. They re-formed behind the caravan and Mr. Finchley found that the sortie had separated him from the officer.

It was then that Mr. Finchley remembered the switch. In his consternation he had forgotten it. He reached for it. It was the one thing which would tame Churchwarden. But before his hand could take it, the caravan bit a bump with such force that everything inside it shook. The whole affair heaved up like a barge hit by a short sea. The jolt shot through Mr. Finchley's body, nearly sending him flying from the seat, and from the rear he heard the crash as the back door of the caravan flew open.

After that Mr. Finchley had little control over events, nor was he particularly aware of them all.

As the door of the caravan swung open a white-and-black object tumbled from the opening and hit the ground with a terrific squeal. It was Ella. She landed a yard in front of the pursuing officer and, as she landed, she screamed with that peculiar and piercing high velocity, agony and determination which is the prerogative alone of pigs. The shock made the officer's horse rear, and the officer slid gracefully down the animal's rump and landed, in a sitting position, on the ground.

Ella jerked to her feet, saw the close formation of marching men, the flashing hooves of the horse above her—and darted for cover. She headed straight for the line of men, seeking cover in their legs. It was a trying moment for the Territorial branch of the British Army. Only the lumbering impact of the caravan had so far made them break their ranks for a moment, and this had been orderly done. Now Ella scuttled among them, and there was no help for them. You cannot march with eyes front, chin up and arm well swinging, and also contend with a pig underfoot. One man tripped and clutched at his neighbour. A rifle fell with a clang and in a few moments, as Ella threaded her way through them, the march became a rabble, and then someone kicked Ella. The kick was probably accidental, for the British soldier is famous for his kindness to animals, but it was nonetheless painful.

Ella shrilled with pain and anger and charged, curly tail hoisted in anger, head down with panic, straight at the colonel, who was holding in his prancing horse and swearing volubly. The pig flashed under the horse's belly and made for the band.

The crowd at the gate laughed and then one of the soldiers laughed. The laughter spread. They still marched, but they could not hold back their laughter. Around the arena pranced a riderless horse, a runaway caravan and a squealing pig. The colonel's horse bucked and kicked, snorting with indignation, and on her back the colonel hung on with masterful ease, swearing and cursing. His attendants swore and cursed, the men laughed, the band lost tune and filled the air with a dreadful cacophony and Mr. Finchley found his switch. He brought it down on Churchwarden's rump and jerked at the reins. Churchwarden came to his senses and headed, perhaps imbued with a sense of the unpleasantness which must ensue if they remained, for a gate at the other end of the parade-ground.

"Catch that pig!" A savage voice roared above the confusion. "By Victoria! Grab that pig. Stand back!"

As Mr. Finchley galloped through the other gate into the roadway that voice came roaring to him and he recognised its tones. He knew, too, that he must get away as fast as he could. He wanted no second encounter with Colonel Greatorex. He swung the switch again and made Churchwarden keep up his pace. They swayed and clattered down the road and, at the first turning to the left, Mr. Finchley swerved aside from the main road down a narrow lane. He prayed that there would be no pursuit.

Mr. Finchley was saved, though he did not know it, by Ella. Attention had gone from the caravan to her. She was an even more irresponsible element than Churchwarden. Where Churchwarden had acted from joy, she acted from fear. She darted here, there and everywhere with half a dozen mounted officers after her and a company

183

of soldiers, and Colonel Greatorex pranced and careered around directing operations. If you have ever tried to capture a young and active pig in an open field, you will appreciate that it was a good ten minutes before Ella was cornered. She was taken into the canteen and shut in the store cupboard. The colonel reformed the ranks, read them a lecture for laughing and behaving like schoolboys, and then gave them his good wishes for the annual summer camp to which they were going. After that, as no one wanted to go chasing yellow caravans instead of marching off to camp, and the colonel, suddenly aware that publicity would spread the story and make him a joke with his friends, decided, upon consultation with his officers, to ignore the incident and, as a punishment to the now vanished caravan owner, to sell the pig in aid of the canteen funds.

"All the same," said the Colonel, after the parade, "I'd like to have just three minutes with that fellow. I'd tell him! By Victoria!"

But Mr. Finchley knew none of this. He kept Churchwarden going as hard as he could for the next three hours, dreading pursuit all the time. It was very late when they stopped, lost in strange country, both very tired.

As Churchwarden was unharnessed, he muzzled into Mr. Finchley's arm. It was a peace move and Mr. Finchley, his face until now lined with displeasure, suddenly patted his nose and smiled. Then the smile broadened to a grin and he was chuckling to himself.

There was no one he could think of whom he would have wished to be in the colonel's place. It served him right for being such a pompous old stick. He only hoped that they treated Ella well. Poor Ella, she had escaped Marshall's knife only perhaps to meet her end before a firing party! Mr. Finchley would have been happier had he known that, at that moment, Ella, still in the store cupboard, was enjoying a feed of potato crisps from a tin on the floor which she had knocked open.

XIV
Of an old game which has strict rules

THE next morning Mr. Finchley decided not to travel that day. It was well, he thought, not to advertise the presence of the caravan in the district in case he was being looked for.

He had spent the night camped on a small piece of waste ground at the side of an unfrequented road. After breakfast he got out his maps and worked out his position, and he saw that he was not many miles from Faversham, and as his stocks were low and he needed some new handkerchiefs and a shirt to replace those which Marshall had taken, he decided to go into the town and do some shopping.

He carefully locked the caravan and saw that Churchwarden was well tethered before he left. An hour later he was in Faversham, having been lucky enough to catch a bus when he got out on to the main road.

Mr. Finchley wandered around the narrow, crowded streets, filling his carrier bag with purchases. There would, he knew, be no letters for him at the post office, because he had told his wife and Robert to address their letters to him at Canterbury.

When he had bought all his provisions he found an outfitter's shop. It was a long, rather dark shop, a shadowed cavern hung with workmen's dungarees, towelling and displays of ties and scarves. The walls were lined with boxes and shelves.

There were quite a few people in the shop and it was some time before an assistant came to Mr. Finchley. When he did come he was a tall, rather pale-faced youth who seemed to have become rather etiolated by the constant gloom of the shop.

"Handkerchiefs, six? Yes, sir." He swirled round to the stacked boxes and jerked one from its place, flipping it open before Mr. Finchley.

As he served him, Mr. Finchley heard a woman talking at the end of the shop, where she stood at another counter. "Well, you are looking well, Mr. Calthrop. Your holiday certainly seems to have agreed with you. No, I don't think that's quite the shade of blue. Haven't you something a little deeper in colour? Where was it this year—Felixstowe again?"

"What about this one, Mrs. Hart? That's the blue, I think? Yes, Felixstowe again, and a very nice time …"

Something in the voice made Mr. Finchley start. It was like an echo from the past, from the not-so-distant past. His assistant spoke to him about the kind of shirt he wanted and for a moment he was engaged.

"Yes, that's more the colour. I shall want three yards. It's a twenty-seven width, isn't it?"

"That's right, Mrs. Hart." For a moment there was a faint shade of weariness in the voice, as though the speaker were tired of Mrs. Hart and all her chattering kind.

Mr. Finchley glanced round as he handed the assistant the money for his purchases. Standing behind the counter at the far end of the shop was a tall, broadly-built man with pale, sandy hair and a large, red face. Mr. Finchley recognised him at once. When he had last seen him he had been wearing a serge suit which was too small for him and a sailor's jersey. Now he wore a black coat and pinstriped trousers, and his great chest thrust against a white shirt front. It was Bob Trilby.

Mr. Finchley's assistant took his book and scurried towards Mr. Calthrop for him to sign the bill. Mr. Calthrop signed it automatically, with a gesture that bespoke years of such signing.

And as his hand moved over the bill-book, Mr. Finchley knew what it was that had always worried him about Bob Trilby. In his heart he had known always that something was wrong with the seaman. Now he knew. It was his hands. They were no seaman's hands, but the pallid hands of a shopman. They had never hauled on ropes or held the spokes of a ship's wheel. Mr. Finchley went out of the shop carrying his parcel, walking with the unconsciousness of a man who has just learned the news of a friend's passing. Bob Trilby of the *Lady Leaf* was dead, Bob Trilby who had fed on kippers for months on a coral atoll was no more. Instead, there was Mr. Calthrop, outfitter and draper.

Mr. Finchley began to understand. Once, many years ago, there had been a time when young Calthrop had been given a chance to become Bob Trilby, and the chance had passed by unseized. Since that day Calthrop had dreamed of Bob Trilby. In that narrow gullet of a shop, far from the strong winds of the sea and the fierce sun of the tropics, Calthrop had yearned after the ghostly Bob Trilby and, in the short release of his summer vacation, he recreated from that phantom a flesh-and-blood creature who wandered the countryside, loafed about the docks of Gravesend and Tilbury, spinning his yarns, salving his longings with fictions and imposing his new personality on all who showed any interest. It was a harmless deception, it was a legitimate deception so long as it was never discovered. Mr. Finchley had been unlucky to discover his secret. He was sorry for the man, sorry because of this exposure of the romanticism which was pent within him and because he recognised Calthrop's deception as something which was common to all men and women. They were allowed their dreams, they were allowed to play the game of saying, "If only years ago …"; but the first and most important rule of the game was that it must be played alone and never allowed to be more than a game. Calthrop had given Bob Trilby life. He had also killed him for Mr. Finchley.

Mr. Finchley went back to his caravan and spent the rest of the day quietly reading and writing letters. As he was sitting on the backstep after his supper, smoking a last pipe before turning in, a man came clumping up the road towards him. He stopped when he came abreast of Mr. Finchley and nodded affably. He was dressed as a labourer, with corduroy trousers, an old jacket and pullover, and a capon his head. He was smoking a pipe.

"Good evening, sir," he said.

"Good evening," answered Mr. Finchley.

"Do you like peas?" he asked, and Mr. Finchley saw that he was carrying a paper bag.

"I do."

The man smiled. " 'Tain't many that would say no to that question. Here," he handed the bag to Mr. Finchley.

"Here's a pickin' for you from my garden. I live in the cottage down the road. I've got more than I can manage and it's a pity to see 'em left. Not that the birds would grumble. If there's any real way to keep blue-tits from peas, I'd like to know it."

Mr. Finchley took the bag and thanked him. He took them into the caravan and brought back a bottle of beer and two glasses. The man accepted the drink with a natural courtesy.

"Do you live in the caravan all the year round, sir?"

"No, I'm on a sort of holiday."

"You'll be from the town?"

"That's right."

"Maybe that was one of your friends that came along this morning."

"This morning?"

"Yes. Just after you'd gone off down the road. I was working in the field opposite, when I heard the car draw up. A tall gentleman got out and knocked on your door. He didn't see me, but I watched him. Knocked several times, he did, then he tried the door and windows. I was comin' across to tell him that I'd seen you go off, but he went away before I could get here. I had an idea he saw me coming."

"Well, I don't know who that might be. If he wants me he can come back again."

"Maybe he will, but I thought you'd like to know about it in case you'd been expectin' someone."

For a moment Mr. Finchley was silent, wondering who the man might have been, but he could think of no one who might have called upon him—unless it was someone in connection with Churchwarden's last escapade, and the man did not sound as though he were concerned with that.

They drank their beer and chatted a while longer. The man informed Mr. Finchley that he was a farm labourer, a milkman.

"I understand cows," he said, with a faint touch of pride. "Been with 'em all my life. I could never stand a town life. It's like wearin' a collar and tie and your Sunday suit every day of the week, I should think."

Mr. Finchley smiled. "You get used to it."

"That's what my daughter says. She's a schoolteacher in London. I don't disbelieve her but I know what I'm fitted for. I didn't think my children would ever want to be any different from me but children are chancy things. You can never tell what they'll turn out to be." It was not hard to see that he was a man with a great pride in his family. He told Mr. Finchley about them.

His elder daughter had won a scholarship to a secondary school and then obtained a grant from the local authority for the expenses of her training as a teacher. Now she was earning good money in London. His son, nearly fifteen, was also a scholarship boy at a secondary school and determined to win a scholarship to a university.

"No farm labourin' for him, sir. But I tell him that he'll have to pay his own way. Me and the missus have a little saved up, but it won't help him far. I don't stand in his way and I'll help him where I can, but I can't understand the ambition there is in young people. I never had no ambition beyond bein' a good milker, and I'm none the worse for that so far as I can see."

"It wouldn't do for everyone to forsake the land for the towns," said Mr. Finchley.

"That won't happen," said the man confidently. "There's always the ones who must live on the land. You can't do without that. My daughter says that in economics they teach that it is the first source of wealth. Well, if economics is as sound as that all the way through, it can't be such a bad thing to learn. But I could have told her that truth without any economics. And without labour to till the land and look after the cattle that feed on it, there's nothing you can do to bring out the wealth. I know that, too. I reckon there's a good many things men like me know which you'll find put out in fancy language in books. It's a pity most people have to learn things like that from books and not from their own lives. Don't you think so, sir?"

"I certainly do," said Mr. Finchley, impressed by the man's good sense. This was not how he had imagined farm labourers to be. He felt, too, a little abashed by the simplicity and directness of this man.

That night, as he lay in bed, going over the day's twists and turns before he slept, he was struck by the contrast between the two men, Bob Trilby and the labourer. The one harassed by his own longings, by his discontents, his life full of a sense of unfulfilment, and the other, perfectly happy, contented and full of a rich sense of his true importance in the life he had chosen. It was an odd life that could be peopled with such folk, a mixture of injustices and inconsistencies, of happiness for one and discontent for another. The tangle was too much for any one man to unravel. It could only be accepted. It was with a sharp recognition that Mr. Finchley suddenly appreciated that his own existence was not far from that of Calthrop's. Most of his life he had lived a bachelor, wrapped in a small, almost selfish existence, and most of his life he had been, unconsciously perhaps, suffering from a deep longing for a greater freedom and a truer way of expression for all those dreams and ideas which pressed so close to the surface of his thoughts. He had saved himself, practically at the last moment, he mused, by marrying and adopting a boy, by resigning early from the office and setting out to find a country house and enough land to give him a taste of the yeoman joys which had once been the prerogative of his family.

Men could leave the land for the cities, desert their ships for shops and give up the plough for pens. But there was in all men a fine, persistent love of the old way of life, the simple existence of their fathers. With the years the longing might weaken and die, but as yet it was still strong enough to work them into discontents. Underneath their modern aspirations and urban manners was the age-old urge that had filled their forefathers with a sense of the justice and correctness of their way of life. Man belonged to the land; the farther he went from it, the stronger became its call and the more turbulent his discontents. He could drug himself against the yearning with a hundred distractions and small prides but he could not kill it altogether. The earth, the dark soil and the green crops of life. The moment men forgot them and lost themselves in the labyrinths of the cities and the indignities of lives devoted to money-making, they were doomed. There was more true pleasure and satisfaction in a row of beans than in the most resplendent motor car, for one was a miracle which man was graciously allowed to control and the other was an invention which took its life from man alone and obeyed him, and man was not at his noblest when he gave commands, but when he served.

Mr. Finchley finally slept, all thought of the caller who had come to his caravan that morning in a car gone from his head.

XV
How Mr. Finchley crosses the river and finds pleasant company

MR. FINCHLEY came to the sea. He had intended to go through Faversham on his way to Canterbury. But he was late in starting, for his labourer friend of the previous evening had arrived in the morning and had insisted on taking him to the milking sheds of the farm where he worked. He had shown Mr. Finchley the herd he had care of, with childish pride. It was almost lunchtime before Mr. Finchley got away and then, on his way to Faversham, he had taken a wrong turning.

It was not until he saw the sea that he realised it had been a wrong turning. The road sloped through an untidy huddle of houses, met a wide expanse of green riverside fields and there, away to his right, was the sea, a grey, dull waste of water, and the wind came buffeting into his face full of the bright tang of mud and seaweed. He drove the caravan along the road, curious to see where it would go, and finally came out on a small embankment and saw that the road ended in a stone slipway that ran down into the mud of a river which flowed now at half-tide. On the other side of the river was a green hillock and the bare shoreline of what, he soon found from his map, was the Isle of Sheppey. The river before him was the River Swale.

Nestling below the brow of the hillock was a straggling house, a few trees and a tall post on the green before the building bearing a red inn sign. In the river below the inn was moored a variety of craft, small cabin cruisers, trim half-decked yachts, a palatial white-and-chromium motor-cruiser, a black Thames barge and some rowing boats.

He drew the caravan back from the embankment and pulled up on the edge of one of the wide river-fields to have his lunch. As he was eating he heard footsteps outside and a man's head appeared around the doorway.

"Did you want to camp here, mister?" he enquired. For a moment Mr. Finchley had no reply. He had not thought about stopping at the place. He had only done a few miles that day and he was anxious to be on his way.

"I don't know," he answered.

"Well, if you do, you can run into the field and turn your horse loose and it'll be a shilling a night. There's a fresh-water tap at the top of the field. Often get people camping here."

The man disappeared and left him to his lunch, and while he ate, Mr. Finchley decided that he would stay. If he turned back now, he would reach Faversham late in the afternoon and he would not get far beyond it before nightfall. There was a house he wanted to look at just beyond Faversham, and he had hoped to inspect it that afternoon and then get on. But the delay with the farm that morning and then the wrong turning made that impossible. It would be better, he decided, to make a fresh start the next morning. Then he would reach the house just after lunch and be able to get a good way beyond it before drawing up for the night.

After lunch he ran the caravan into the field, turned it so that the doorway commanded the view down river towards the sea and then set Churchwarden loose. He spent the rest of the afternoon walking along the high-water mark of the river, watching the movements of the sea-birds and prodding at the drift wrack with a stick in the hope of finding treasure. It was a pleasant, lazy afternoon that reminded him of his boyhood days when he had scrambled along the sea-line, peering into caves and expecting always to find some bottle with a message in it washed up from the water … Today there was nothing in the wrack; it stretched ahead of him in an unsteady line, an accumulation of straws, tins, bottles, bits of stick and innumerable acorns, little brown husks that had dropped from the parent tree where it overhung some small stream and had made their pilgrimage to the sea, to be stranded on this bare sweep of sand and shingle.

As he returned he saw the ferry boat come chugging out from the island and move across to the slipway. When it went back, Mr. Finchley was in it. The green, smooth line of the island and the white oasis of the inn attracted him.

Later that evening he sat in the little parlour of the inn. It was a very small room, filled with a round apple-wood table and polished windsor chairs. To one side of it there was a little hatchway through which the landlord served the drinks, and opposite the hatchway an iron fireplace filled with crinkled coloured paper. A dartboard hung upon another wall, and there was just enough space in the room to give a proper throw, though if a dart hit the wire of the board and bounced backwards it generally dropped upon the apple-wood table. On the wall hung a picture of the Great Eastern.

There were five men in the room. There was Mr. Rose, the landlord—Mr. Finchley counted him as being in the room, though generally he showed no more than head and shoulders as he leaned through the hatchway—who was a red-faced man with white hair and a white moustache. His white hair seemed to have nothing to do with his age. He spoke vigorously, laughed immoderately and seemed full of a ceaseless energy, for he was continually withdrawing from the hatch into the mysterious recesses of the house and appearing again to make some remark or add some comment to the conversation without once giving the impression that he had missed any of it in his absence. Then there was Joe, a tall, well-built young man with sandy hair. He wore grey flannels and a greasy leather windbreaker and had a habit of spreading his hands out before him at times and staring at them as though they had once acted without his orders and had done something of which he had been ashamed and for which he intended periodically to remind them with a fierce frown of disapprobation. With Joe was Nick, a dark, hook-nosed man with large eyes and a stubby body which he seemed to have difficulty in suppressing into quietude. He always seemed in danger of bounding from his seat at the beginning of each remark. Then there was Mr. Sprockett, one of those scraggy men with drawn necks for whom the finest razor in the world could never achieve a good clean shave. His stubble marked his face like black pepper, and when he rubbed his hand across his chin the sound could almost be felt. Mr.

Sprockett wore a dark suit, neat tie, felt hat and smoked a pipe with an amber stem. After Mr. Sprockett came the Captain. He sat close under the hatchway, where he did not have to reach far for his beer, and he said very little. His veined face had a sort of hard chubbiness, his eyes sheltered behind bays of tired lines and his hair was short and iron grey. He wore a thick blue sweater and tweed trousers half-hidden by long gumboots. He smoked a pipe and stared at the Great Eastern with a faint smile crinkling about his lips.

This company took no unusual notice of Mr. Finchley. They were assembled when he entered the place and they accepted him without comment. Joe and Nick were playing darts. The rest looked on.

"There was a book," said Joe, as he threw a dart and scored a five, "that I picked up in a second-hand shop. Don't know what made me buy it. A shilling. It was by a chap called Thoreau. Boy, did that fellow have his own ideas about how to live."

"Thoreau's *Walden*," said Mr. Sprockett quickly. "One of the early transcendentalists. He, Emerson and others ... Thoreau was a greater man than Emerson."

"Who cares? They're both dead," put in Mr. Rose. "It ain't right to argue about which man was better than another, and I don't like books. They 'arbour dust—you should hear my good lady go on about 'em."

"This fellow," went on Joe, "believed in the simple life. Just a shack in the woods, a row of beans and all that. But that wasn't all. The bit that got me was where he said that it was quite right and natural for a man to sit on the door-step in the sun some mornings and do nothing but sit and stare and let his thoughts wander. He often did it. I tried it once or twice after I'd read him, but always someone came along and busted up my staring. You wouldn't believe how hard it is to find a place where you can sit on the doorstep and waste a whole morning. Five, double nine and three, that's twenty-six. Leaves me thirty-five for game. That's five and double fifteen. Come on, Nick, you'll never catch me!" He pulled out his darts from the board and turned to the Captain with a grin. "How's the hermit tonight?"

The Captain grinned at him. "Well, very well. And how are you still waiting for a war to break out so they'll use some of those torpedoes of yours?"

"Aw, forget it!" Joe waved a hand at him and called to Mr. Rose for more drinks.

"War," said Nick, screwing up his eyes as he threw his darts. "Why is it that men are so wedded to that folly?" Mr. Finchley noticed that he spoke with a foreign accent.

" 'Where bleed the many to enrich the few,' " quoted Mr. Sprockett. "But war is part of man, just as his appendix is part of him—though a useless part."

"Yes, but you can have your appendix taken out, but not war," said Mr. Rose, coming back with more drinks. "I fought in two wars. You can't get rid of war any more than you can get rid of wine or women, god bless 'em! It's horrible, but it's natural. They've tried but they've failed. Look at the League of Nations."

Nick pulled his darts from the board and, as he chalked up his score, he looked over his shoulder and said very seriously to the landlord

"No. The League of Nations has not failed. Not for good. That is only a start. We have tried the thing once and made mistakes. Now we shall try again. I have heard one of your preachers say this of it. At first we had not

200

enough faith to fill so large a church. Next time, the faith will grow."

"If you collect all the voices that cry in the wilderness, you haven't a choir," said Mr. Sprockett, his hand rasped across his chin and he took a drink, very pleased with himself.

"I don't like war, but I like shooting," said Joe. "I don't know. That's a fact. I just don't know. The more you try and think things out these days, the more you get tied up. It was all right for that Thoreau. In his day there was still half a chance left to make something out of ideas. These days we have to be content with the ideas and go on living as we are. I don't get time to do much thinking even. How can I? You get up in the morning and there's the paper to read while you eat. You buzz off to work. You grab a few minutes for lunch and then more work. You come home. Tea. Have a wash and change. There's a programme on the radio you want to hear, or a film you must see, or your lungs ache for a shot of fresh air and you have to get the flying bedstead out and beat it for the country. You come into a pub like this and you play darts and talk and by the time you get home you're ready for sleep. When do I get time to think, let alone do anything about the things that really matter?"

The Captain removed his pipe and said slowly, "You don't want to think, Joe. I've a perfectly good doorstep for you to sit on any time you wish and I'll guarantee you aren't disturbed, but you'll never come and sit on it."

"Non-stop variety—that's what people want from life today," said Mr. Rose, raising his white whiskers preparatory to taking a drink.

"Your own Thoreau said that there were no longer any philosophers, but only doctors of philosophy," announced Mr. Sprockett. "The trouble was as bad then as now. People only imagine they have no time for real thought. The point is they don't know how to think."

"I have thought a great deal about some things," said Nick slowly. "But it did not do any good. It only made me feel how useless it was to try and do anything. The muddle can never be cleared up. I am perhaps a defeatist."

"If that means you think you've already lost this game of darts, you're quite right," chuckled Joe, as he threw the double he wanted to win.

"When I was young," said Mr. Sprockett, blowing a smoke cloud and gazing into it as though it were into the past he looked, "I was full of zeal, full of noble thoughts about my calling. But now I just do my job. That's what's known as growing-up, and that's your trouble, Joe—and yours, Nick—you aren't grown up yet. Youth's skin never fits. Only the years can stretch it into a comfortable fit. Isn't that so, Captain?"

"I wouldn't dream of contradicting you," answered the Captain easily.

"In a pub," said Joe, beginning a fresh game and winking at Mr. Finchley, "conversation hops about like a flea and after a time you begin to take more interest in the hop than on what it lands. If you get my meaning?"

"There are no fleas in this house," said Mr. Rose sternly, from his hatchway, "unless it's dog fleas from the pup and they don't touch humans. And if you know a way to keep fleas from a dog that's got no other idea in its head but rabbit-hunting, I should be obliged to know it."

"Fleece and vorms—all dogs have them," said Nick. "It is interesting, this idea of evolution which is bound up with our talk of war and idealism. Is it progress? Man is moving forward, the scientists say, towards something higher and better. But how do we not know that Man is only moving forward down a blind alley? There are many such blind alleys: the mammoths wandered down one, the great apes another. How should we not know that we are not going down another?"

"We shall know only when we bump our heads against the wall at the head of the cul-de-sac," laughed Joe. "Whoa," he called suddenly as a gust of wind beat against the house. "Listen to that wind."

The Captain took his pipe from his mouth. "It's been backing into the east since late afternoon. There'll be a nice sea now that the tide is running up."

"I looked out just now," said Mr. Rose, putting a match to his pipe. "It's coming up like a mill-race and as troubled as my old lady on quarter day. George brought the ferry boat ashore instead of leaving her at her moorings. He won't want her again tonight. Not that he could get across if he wanted to."

Mr. Finchley heard these words and was troubled. He had been so warm and comfortable in the public house that he had almost forgotten that sometime that night he had to return to his caravan across the river. He looked towards the landlord anxiously.

"Does that mean that I can't get back across the river tonight?" he asked.

Everyone looked at him. They had come to accept him as a silent, interested figure. But they had not expected speech from him.

"Do you want to get back?" questioned Mr. Rose.

"I do. My horse and caravan are across there. That's where I'm sleeping tonight."

Joe laughed. "Not tonight, you won't—unless you walk all the way round by Queen's Bridge and Sittingbourne and then you wouldn't get home till morning—not even if we gave you a lift as far as the main road on our way to Chatham."

"That's right," said Mr. Sprockett, looking through the window.

He jerked the curtain aside and Mr. Finchley looked out. The evening was quite light from a young moon, but it was full of wind and violence. The tall summer grasses bent and waved like a dark layer of smoke pressed close to the earth, the few trees leaned over from the gale and let the wind sing through their tossing branches, and the wide swathe of river was flecked white with high rollers as the tide came swinging in from the open sea, backed by a strong easterly wind. The flotilla of pleasure craft below the inn had turned their noses downstream to meet the gale, but they tossed and strained at their moorings, plunging and dipping as though anxious to shake off their cables and join the wild night.

"George must have forgotten that you came over on the ferry," said Mr. Rose.

"Perhaps you can give me a bed here for the night?" enquired Mr. Finchley. Churchwarden was loose in the field and the caravan was locked so he had no fears about them.

"I've got no proper accommodation, but you're welcome to a bed on the sofa."

"Any man who passes a night on that sofa of yours is a hero," said Joe. "It's got three springs sticking up from it in the middle like power pylons and you'd have to be a tight-rope walker to sleep there."

"That's what I was thinking," said the Captain calmly. "I tried it once. But I shouldn't worry, sir." He smiled at Mr. Finchley. "I've got a spare bunk you can have, if you care to come along with me."

"Take a look."

"That's very kind of you. I don't want to give anyone trouble, but—"

"But what the hell can you do about it?" Joe grinned. "The Captain will be delighted to have you. He's as curious as a monkey and I could see that all the evening he's been wondering who you were. By morning he'll have your life history. You see," said Mr. Sprockett.

"It is bad when you lose your faith in other men," said Nick. "But it is worse when you lose your curiosity about other men. All my life—"

"You'll be a poor darts player," put in Joe.

Later, when the inn closed, Mr. Finchley went home with the Captain. The three other men got into a small car outside the inn and drove off into the night. Mr. Finchley had no idea where he was going. He just followed the Captain, who said nothing, but lowered his head into the wind and moved down the slope to the riverside. They struck a path that led along the river towards the sea. After ten minutes' walking, with the noise of the wind and the sea making all conversation impossible, they came to an indentation of the bank where lay the long, black hulk of an old Thames barge. It was high and dry and a small ladder led from the ground to its deck.

A few moments later Mr. Finchley was inside.

"This is my abode," said the Captain, as he lit the oil-lamp in the main saloon. "Some men prefer a neat villa, others a country cottage, some—like yourself, a caravan—but I choose this. She came up here on a high spring five years ago and she's been here ever since."

Mr. Finchley looked around him and was amazed. The saloon was wide and spacious. Instead of ports there were long, narrow windows. A finely polished Oak table stood in the centre of the saloon and around the walls were fitted seats, padded with cushions of bright colours. One wall was lined with books and another with a low dresser full of blue-and-white china and three low chairs were drawn up around a tiled stove that stood against the forward bulkhead. It was the snuggest retreat Mr. Finchley had ever seen, and the sound of the wind and waves outside emphasised its comfort.

Mr. Finchley was led into a small galley, bright with pots and neat rows of tinned stores. The Captain made coffee and they went back to the main cabin to drink it. In a little while Mr. Finchley was telling about himself and his search for a house.

"You should buy a boat like this, not a house," said the Captain. "All my life in the army I looked forward to the day when I could have a house and settle down quietly, but when the time came I found I didn't want a house. I chose this and it suits me admirably. What did you think of our three friends in the pub? Joe helps make torpedoes or guns or something at Chatham. Sprockett is a schoolmaster and Nick—Nicolai, it is, I think—is something to do with paper manufacture at Sittingbourne. They are close friends and often come out here. Not at the weekends—that's when the inn is busy with the people who come down to their boats. But tonight, it was as it always is—very quiet. Joe's a restless cove. He couldn't sit quietly on a doorstep if he tried. And even if he did I doubt whether it would do him any good. I've been sitting quietly on my doorstep for years, but it hasn't really helped me. Not that I'm particularly in need of help. There's no great sorrow or mystery in my life. I have my pension, this home and the pub to go to when I need company. I find I need very little more."

"You sound as though you're one of those happy men," said Mr. Finchley.

"No, I'm not that. I'm as unhappy as most men at times. Happy men don't exist, not completely happy men. There are men who think they're completely happy, of course. But generally they turn out to be very stupid men. This is the wrong planet and the wrong life for complete happiness. Nature abhors complete happiness more than she abhors a vacuum, and we should be glad of that. Courage is senseless if you haven't known fear, and the man who laughs but never cries is just making a strange sound that has no meaning."

"Nevertheless, you aren't going to argue against Joe's feeling that there is a lot in life which could be made better and happier? That was what he was getting at, wasn't it?"

"It was. Joe, like us all, is conscious of the muddle that makes up our lives. He's a little more conscious of it, perhaps, than some people because he's in an awful muddle himself. How would you feel if your living came from designing instruments of death while you loved life more dearly than anything else? Joe is alive, but all through his working hours death sits on his shoulders. It isn't always so gloomy as that sounds, but it's not far from the truth. And there are many more like him. Men and women live in a welter of paradoxes—and they don't like it, but they find they can do precious little about it. Some of the muddle could be cleared up, but you could never clean the slate entirely, not while men and women are what they are. Take war—it's a subject that Joe and his friends often discuss these days—some people blame wars on politicians, who love to exercise this ultimate weapon of power, others blame it on the private manufacture of armaments, a few—like Mr. Rose—think it will always be because it is man's destiny. There were wars in the Bible, there will be wars always. But the real reason for war lies with none of these. There are wars because man is an imperfect being, because his brain simply isn't developed enough honestly to convince him that war has no victories which do not belong to Death, and that there are no problems in this world which cannot be settled amicably if only men are ready to admit that they have made mistakes. No man likes to admit he has been wrong. His first instinct is to deny, his second to argue and when his arguments fail he often begins to fight, thinking that force can create right out of wrong. The more cultured and civilised the man, the more emphasis does he give to argument, because he believes that words have a magic of their own to change the nature of right and wrong. The savage just begins fighting right away and I think his method is more honest of the two. However … it's an old topic."

"And as men grow wiser? What then?"

"With new wisdom come new evils. We may conquer wars and wipe their existence or causes of their existence from the world. But there will always be evil of a kind with us, I think, because we can never be perfect. War is not the most terrible of evils. It only seems so because it manifests itself so spectacularly and claims its victims en masse. But there are worse and more widespread evils to be fought. There are plenty of children who enter this world never to have enough to eat, to die early from malnutrition. Disease claims more victims than any war ever did or will claim. You can deny a country its rightful boundaries, but it is more terrible to deny a people fresh air and good food."

Mr. Finchley never forgot that evening. The Captain seemed to exercise the uncommon power of making a man reveal himself. Gradually Mr. Finchley began to talk, began to outline the vague forms of his own ideas, and from his host he received encouragement and agreement. They talked as they got ready for bed, they talked as they lay in their bunks in the bow of the stranded barge and they talked until they dropped to sleep, and when they slept the tide, full with the wind behind it, reached up to the side of the barge and lapped against its timbers, giving it the greeting of an old friend.

XVI
In which Mr. Finchley bites a good deal of dust

THE next morning, after a late breakfast, the Captain took Mr. Finchley for a sail in his half-decker. The boat lay in a little slipway cut into the soft bank of the river and Mr. Finchley had not noticed it the previous evening. It was a slim, white boat, beautifully kept.

The wind had gone round to the south overnight and they slipped down the river with the wind on their beam. Slowly the banks widened out and the power of the sea made itself felt. The light ripples moved into the wider waves of the sea, and suddenly the wind was stronger as it gained power from leaving the land behind. The waves rose and swept along their freeboard and fell behind with a swish and stir. Gulls came crying up to them, their yellow eyes watching hungrily. The white sail strained above them, the salt flick touched their lips and their ears were full of the noise of tapping ropes and the seeth of the wake behind them.

Mr. Finchley was surprised at the way the land dropped from them. One moment he turned to see the grey marks of houses and the tree-crested line of hills, and the next time he looked the land had huddled closer to itself, everything dwarfed and compressed so that houses and trees were shadows against a green band, a wavering band that thinned and thickened, gave off patches of smoke from towns and winked at them where the sun caught at windows and factory roofs.

"How do you like this?" asked the Captain, one hand on the rudder bar as the boat heeled before the wind.

"Very pleasant," said Mr. Finchley. He was well aware that he was not a good sailor so he refrained from an over-enthusiastic comment. But he was enjoying it.

"You should buy a boat, not a house," went on the Captain. "Give me the sea every time. They can't muck it up with advertisement hoardings and roadhouses. You won't find any dust out here. You can throw your litter as much as you like but the sea'll swallow it up and a floating tin can is an object of curiosity out here, not an eye-sore as it would be in a country hedge. No noisy traffic, and when there is a crowd it's an interesting crowd, different ships to watch, not different makes of motor cars, and there's always the water. Look at it," he cried enthusiastically. "Every second the colours change, every hour the mood differs. The sea is no woodland glade, meekly suffering the despoiling visits of unthinking townsfolk. Come out here for a holiday, for a blow, and you have to behave yourself. You have to do as the sea says—or it's so much the worse for you. If trees would form the habit of falling on people who cut initials in them, the countryside would be respected … And now," he said a few minutes later, "you really are in the mouth of the Thames."

To Mr. Finchley it seemed as though they were well at sea. The Captain handed him the glasses and to the North he made out the block of Southend and the low East Coast. Behind them stretched the Isle of Sheppey and the Kent coast running away to the North Foreland. Down river, a tiny curl of white at her bows, came a pleasure steamer, and against the blue sky moved the russet sails of a pair of Thames barges. Day and night ships moved up and down: at night guided by beacons and lights, by day following the line of painted buoys. Up the clear swatchways came ships from every part of the globe. For hundreds of years that traffic had never ceased, Roman trireme, Phoenician galley, Viking longboat, Tudor carrack, whaler, slaver, collier, coaster, liner, tender, cruiser, freighter … they all had and some still did nose their way towards London.

While he thought of all those ships, as he watched the rust-red bulk of a cargo boat, its black-and-white funnel trailing a tiny pennant of smoke, come upstream, Mr. Finchley was aware of a quick tingle of pride slipping through his body; for a moment he was closely in touch with the vigour of all that human activity which had passed along this waterway. Not only ships, but men had passed up and down, a line of busy, eager men and women, who had lived their time and died, but in dying lived on in others. It was a ceaseless, timeless flow, so strong, so sure that he could conceive no force that could stop it, so immense that its very power wove into it a faith and belief in its ultimate goodness and sanity. Mr. Finchley had always been an optimist, but out there on the waters, watching the brown sails of the barges, he was confirmed in his faith, that even if he could not see sense in the muddle of life always, even if he was too small to raise himself into a position where he could work some order into the confusion around, there was no need to worry, because above and beyond it all moved a power that was not hindered by the confusion of life, nor cast down by the mistakes of men ... In this tiny boat, rocked and pitched by the sea swell, wetted by the flying tips of the wave crests, he was sharing a real communion, and he began to understand why the Captain seemed so sure of himself and so quietly determined in his views. To men who sail boats, even in quiet waters, there come moments which no landsman can ever have, and this lifting communion was the rarest of such experiences.

They turned and began to work their way home, and as they came into the river Mr. Finchley was glad that he had taken the wrong turning and found himself in the little inn on the island. He would have missed a great deal if he had never known it.

Just before they came abreast of the black barge, the Captain said, "I'll drop you on the other side now and then you can walk up the bank to your caravan. If you're going back through Faversham today, I'll row across in the dinghy and you might be kind enough to give me a lift into the town. I want to do some shopping there."

He ran the boat skilfully into the bank, dropped the sail and held her fast with an oar while Mr. Finchley scrambled ashore. Then he was away, slanting across the river towards his barge. Mr. Finchley watched him go and then climbed up the green embankment that hid the field in which stood his caravan. Near him was the peaceful form of Churchwarden, cropping the green grass. He was about to call to Churchwarden, wondering if the horse would recognise his call and come to him, when he checked himself and frowned. A man had appeared from behind the caravan and, climbing the little steps at the back, was pushing at the doorway. Mr. Finchley saw him try to open the locked door by throwing his weight against it, but it held. Then, in the sunlight, something gleamed quickly as the man drew his hand from his pocket. He half-bent and began to work at the lock of the door. Mr. Finchley did not wait for more.

He charged down the other slope of the embankment, jumped the small ditch, and began to run across the field towards the caravan. Mr. Finchley was not a good runner, his years and his girth were against him, but he surprised himself at the speed with which he covered the ground. He was angry. To him a lock was sacred. It was an indication of ownership and the man who could pick or break a lock was a menace whom society had to restrain. Also, Mr. Finchley was a little tired of the mysterious interest which someone was taking in his caravan. First of all there had been Oliver Watt Anselm and his peculiar client, and then the man in the motor car who had called on him when he was in Faversham. Now, here was someone else, trying to break in. Mr. Finchley fairly flew, his arms working like pistons, his face growing redder with every step, his head slightly lowered, his whole body weighted with a taurine power.

When Mr. Finchley was within twenty yards of the caravan the unknown caravan-breaker was given warning. Churchwarden, who had raised his head as Mr. Finchley had come scurrying across the field, suddenly recognised his master and, with a toss of his heels, he whinnied and galloped away in a circle. The beat of his hooves and the whinny made the man look up. He was a blue-jowled man, with a wide, broad forehead, a heavily marked face and a general air of puzzled amiability, as though he were continually surprising himself by discovering that his good intentions were wrongly construed by people. He wore a check cap, a loud shirt and a suit of rather crumpled grey flannel.

As he saw Mr. Finchley a look of alarm spread over his face and he jumped down from the doorway and turned to run. But he was not quick enough. Mr. Finchley's attack had lost some of its element of surprise, but it had lost none of its swiftness and stored momentum. Mr. Finchley flung himself forward, his hands stretched out towards the man. He crashed into him and the two went rolling into the soft grass.

For a moment the shock of the impact winded them both and they lay on the ground panting and beating at one another feebly with their hands. Mr. Finchley grabbed the other man by his necktie and tried to hoist himself into a sitting position. The man wriggled as the tie tightened about his neck, let out a loud and definite swear word and twisted away like an eel.

There was an ugly ripping sound, and Mr. Finchley fell backwards, holding a torn tie in his hand. The sight of his damaged tie seemed to incense the man. He swore again and, as Mr. Finchley picked himself up and pressed forward to renew the attack, he bent down and grasped a clod of grass. A jerk brought it free from the ground and, before Mr. Finchley could dodge, it flew towards him.

If you have never had a really good mouthful of dirt and grass, you will never be able to appreciate the real essence of Mr. Finchley's feelings at that moment. It is said that before we die we must all eat our peck of dirt, but it has never been said that we should eat it by the mouthful.

The sod caught Mr. Finchley fair and square in the face and for one second he teetered on his short legs, arms waving, his eyes peering from behind a mask of grass and dirt. The sight was so funny that the man before him suddenly burst into a roar of laughter. He slapped his sides and opened his mouth in a bellow of delight.

Mr. Finchley spat dirt and grass from his mouth and, his teeth clogged with grit and mud, dashed towards the laughing man, and this time there was murder in his onslaught—or so the man thought, for he promptly turned and ran. He ran and Mr. Finchley chased him.

The man made for the gate that led from the field to the roadway. He had five yards' start on Mr. Finchley and he increased it to ten by the time the gate was reached, and as Mr. Finchley panted through the gateway after him he saw that he would never catch up. He sprinted up the road to where a motor-cycle stood propped against the fence. He jumped on it, kicked it into life and was away with a ferocious roar of exhaust gases.

Mr. Finchley, heaving with his exertions, watched him go. For a moment there raced through his mind plans for getting to the telephone and letting the police have a description of the man. But he gradually subsided into the calm which realises that to do nothing is the wisest plan. He went back to the caravan. The lock was still intact. He washed out his mouth and went inside and it was then that he remembered the tie. He had dropped it when the turf had struck him. He went out and recovered it. It had been torn clear away from the man's neck. Mr. Finchley saw that it was quite an expensive silk tie in a tartan design of greens, reds and blue, and on a little label sewn into the back of the tie were the words—Tartan Ties Ltd. Macduff.

"Lay on, Macduff," said Mr. Finchley, "and damned be he that cries, 'Hold, enough!' "

If the man was a Macduff he had laid on—with a turf—but he had cried enough by running away.

Mr. Finchley began to put the caravan in order for getting under way. Just as he finished, the Captain appeared and helped him to catch Churchwarden. As Mr. Finchley harnessed the horse, he told the Captain about his visitor. They discussed it as they drove in to Faversham.

"It looks," said the Captain, "as though somebody was taking a very strong interest in you or the caravan."

"But why?" queried Mr. Finchley. "What is there about me or the caravan?"

"Perhaps it is the caravan. You say you bought it in London?" Mr. Finchley had already told him the story of how he had come into possession of the caravan. "Maybe it's something to do with the previous owner."

"How could it be? No one seems to know who he was, and anyway I know nothing about him. Why try to break into my caravan? There's nothing in there. That man just now didn't look like an ordinary sneak-thief. I wonder if I ought to go to the police?"

"You could do, but I don't see how they could help you. They can only help when somebody has done something—stolen something from you. If I were you, I wouldn't worry. Maybe the fellow was just a common thief who thought he might pick up an easy fiver or so from your caravan. It's surprising these days how some apparently respectable people make a living. All you've got to do is to keep your eyes skinned and never leave the caravan unlocked when you go away from it. You can't do more—and I shouldn't spoil your trip by worrying."

"I won't," promised Mr. Finchley. "But I hope I meet the gentleman who threw that turf at me. I shall have something to say to him."

He dropped the Captain in Faversham and went on through the town. It was not until he was some miles the other side of the town that he realised that he had never learned the Captain's name. He had been just the Captain to him. He probably would never know his name, he thought, but that made no difference at all. Most people relied upon their names to keep a place in your memory. You thought of Jones before you recalled the man. But with the Captain you thought of the man and needed no name to jog your memory. He saw a house that afternoon, but he did not like it, and he journeyed on towards Canterbury. It was some time since he had been alone and on the road, and he enjoyed the peace of that day. Churchwarden drew the coloured van up and down the gentle slopes. The white vanes of oast-houses signalled to him from the clustered farmsteads and in the hedges dog roses tipped their pale faces to him in greeting. Mr. Finchley felt very happy. He sat on the driving board, a pipe between his teeth, his shirt-front open, his bald head browning under the sun, his large, cherubic face ready with a smile for all he passed on the road. It was a pity, he thought, that he had not found a house yet, but on the other hand, the sooner he found a house, the sooner would this caravan trip come to an end.

The afternoon of the next day he reached Canterbury. He parked the caravan in the market-place and walked into the town to get his letters from the post office. There were two from his wife and one from Robert.

Mrs. Finchley was leaving her brother at the end of that week and returning to London. Mr. Finchley found his way into the Cathedral gardens and read sitting on a seat in the shade of a laburnum tree. His wife wrote that she was coming home to get some rest. Her brother, a retired engineer, was too restless and vigorous a person for her to endure for long.

"He is," she wrote, "building his own swimming pool in the orchard. It is a pity that most of his engineering work was done in foreign countries where labour was cheap. He treats everyone here like slaves and I have this day completely ruined one dress and a pair of shoes paddling about in mud and concrete. The cook is leaving because she does not consider it part of her duties to mix cement. This—between ourselves—is affectation on her part. If you had tasted some of her cooking, you would know that making cement should come easy to her. However, no woman likes to be regarded as a slave. When the pool is finished he talks of utilising the power from the little mountain stream which feeds it to turn a turbine and make his own electricity. He says it will be a big job and why don't you come up and work off some of your flabbiness instead of gallivanting around in a caravan making yourself a nuisance to motorists. I said I had to go home to be there when Robert returned at the end of term, which is perfectly true, though I had thought of having Robert up here. But that's impossible now—you know what Robert would be like left alone with concrete and a half-built swimming pool! I'm sure you're not making yourself a nuisance to motorists, but I made no retort there and then. I am saving that for the morning I leave. I took a long walk yesterday up the fells and I discovered that the little stream which is to feed the pool receives all the duck and cow pond drainage from a farm about two miles up the valley. I think David should know this and I shall tell him just as I am leaving. I'm not a bit ashamed! I do hope you're having a nice time, dear, and don't worry about not finding a house yet ..."

Mr. Finchley turned to Robert's letter. It began with news of the Caravan Club.

"We have now fifteen members and collected four and eightpence in subscriptions. Rawlinson mi. is in now because he didn't know about blackballing and he says if there is to be any more of it he would like to help. Anstey says we ought to put the four shillings into reserve and spend the eightpence on literature. Every club has literature, he says, and he's glad that Churchwarden means no disrespect. We are hoping, if you get this way, that you will come and give the Club a lecture on caravans. It is an onerous thing to be the treasurer of a club with so much money. I hope it goes into reserve soon because it is near end of term and funds are low with me. Also I want to buy a magic duck from Blithers. It isn't a proper magic duck, but it comes from the egg of one that appeared at the Coliseum and it is about six months old. One quack means yes and two no, but it gets mixed up. Blithers says it is only a matter of training and he will sell it for three shillings because it eats so much and doesn't leave him any over to buy the necessaries he wants. It lives in a wicker cage and is called Dini. I don't know why. If you are still on the road when term ends, can I come and join you? I should look pretty sick as founder of the club to have to tell the others next term that I didn't go with you."

If he did not find a house before term finished, Mr. Finchley knew that it would be very difficult indeed to keep Robert away from the caravan. He was not even sure that he wanted to keep him away. He decided that he had better send Robert some funds, otherwise the subscriptions of the Caravan Club would be in danger. He smiled amiably to himself as he walked out of the Cathedral close into the busy streets towards his caravan. He quite forgot to enter the Cathedral—he had seen it before—and he was quite unaware of its grey, towering beauty so close to him. He held in his hands the letters from his wife and son, and he was thinking about them.

Later, he stocked up with food and then left the town, making for Ashford, following the road that moved along the River Stour. That evening, when he was just beyond the village of Chilham, he pulled into the side of the road to camp. Not far away was the river, and as he prepared his supper he could hear it washing over its gravel bed. He enjoyed a good meal and spent the rest of the time until he retired writing to Robert and Mrs. Finchley. To Robert he sent a careful itinerary of his journey, but he abridged and edited many of his adventures and he promised to consider carefully the question of his joining him later on. For his wife he also did a little editing, but not much, and he asked for her advice about Robert's joining him.

He slept peacefully that night, dreaming of the perfect house which waited for him. He had picked up a fresh batch of particulars from an agent in Canterbury and some of the houses sounded as though they might be what he wanted.

XVII
Of the dignity of labour

THERE are some sounds that once being heard stay for ever in the memory. If you have heard the bittern across the blue-grey water and parchment-coloured reed-beds of the Broads, you do not forget the peculiar loneliness and intensity of that eerie booming. The seething sound made by rain, flung across the racing, chopping crests of waves at sea, as water meets water, lives strongly in the mind, and the snap of an axe-blade cutting into wood on a frosty morning can ring through the imagination and create a picture of a thin ash copse, the hoar-tipped skeletons of wood parsley and the bent tangles of brown bracken stems amongst which the spider spins his net to catch the rare flies of winter. The sound which lives in the hush that follows the last notes of a great singer's song, the happy noise of fat in a frying pan, the thud of snow as it falls from eaves in frayed avalanches to the lawn and the wandering, prying hum of bees over clover, if they have no warm place in your mind, if they bring no train of memories, then you have lived coldly and without friendship and you have missed so much that you deserve shame.

For some people the finest flower is the rose, for others the daisy. Some exalt the splendour of the peacock, some praise the beauty which dwells in the modest wren. And so with sounds; there can be no sound that will find acceptance in the high seat of every memory. But there are some sounds which come near to touching and claiming this universal affection, and one of these is the sound of a mowing machine on a hot summer's morning.

Louder than the hum of bees, more insistent than the call of any bird, the mechanical voice of the cutter calls the hot hours and sings a gay requiem over the falling grasses.

The noise woke Mr. Finchley that morning and it came from across the road, away from the river. It was a hot morning and Churchwarden sought the shade of the trees, shaking his head against the flies. Mr. Finchley had his breakfast and then got out his milk can. Set back from the road he had seen the red-tiled roof of a farm. He walked along a narrow cart track, the noise of the cutter growing louder. He found the cutter in a large field at the side of the farm. It was a fifteen-acre field and half of it had already been cut and dried. The mower, drawn by a horse wearing a straw hat hung with red tassels that gave it a melancholy Spanish air, was plodding round the standing grass, leaving great swathes of neatly laid hay. In another part of the field a tractor drew a hay cart, and hitched behind the cart was a hay loader that fingered up the dried rows of hay and loaded them into the cart. As it moved along two men worked busily with their forks, settling it into the cart and spreading it. In a corner of the field was a rising haystack, a full load of hay on another cart alongside of it and one man unloading it and tossing it up to another, who stood on top of the rick making it.

As Mr. Finchley stood leaning on the gate and watching them, a man came down the track from the farm. He was a tall, rather thin-faced man. His face was burnt a rich red by the sun and he wore an old felt hat, breeches and a brown pullover over a blue shirt. At his heels hung a black-and-white sheepdog. He had a lean, intelligent face.

He looked at Mr. Finchley as he came up to him and, as he put his hand on the gate to go through into the field, he said, "Good morning."

"Good morning," Mr. Finchley replied, and added "You look busy out there." He nodded towards the haycarts.

"That's right," was the answer. "Got to make the most of this fine spell. You from that caravan out on the road there?"

Mr. Finchley nodded.

The man paused. He eyed Mr. Finchley slowly and then said. "We're short-handed. We can give you a job here for a couple of days if you want one. Can you use a hayfork?"

"Well, I ..." Mr. Finchley stammered, not ready for the offer.

"You can soon learn. If you stick it into anyone you buy a pint of beer all round. That makes people careful. What do you say? I could do with help, and I'll pay you fair."

It was obvious to Mr. Finchley that he had been mistaken for a wandering gipsy type, someone on the lookout for a day's labouring. It was not surprising, for he had not shaved that morning and there was a dark line of stubble around his chin and he was wearing a dirty pair of grey trousers and a grey shirt with an open collar. Mr. Finchley had never done any haymaking in his life, but he had often heard the song of the mowing machine reeling through the hot air of summer, and now he found himself eager to join in the activity that moved about that noise.

"I'd like the job," he said. "When do I start?"

"Now," said the farmer. "Stick your pail down in the hedge. You can fill it with milk later on."

He moved off and Mr. Finchley followed. They went to the hayrick and the farmer shouted to the man on top.

"Hey, Harry—here's another hand for you. Better keep out of his way for a time. He's not used to a hayfork." He turned to Mr. Finchley. "Up you go." His head jerked to a ladder at the side of the rack and Mr. Finchley, grasping a fork which the other labourer had handed to him, went up.

That was all the introduction he had to the noble art of rick-making. He was put on top; the farmer joined the man on the cart who was throwing hay up and Mr. Finchley soon found that his job was to fork the hay back to the man behind him who was making the rick. Up came the forks of hay in sweet-smelling clouds, and Mr. Finchley forked them back to his companion. He soon got the knack of getting a good forkful and kept up with the speed with which the hay came to him. Slowly the rick rose, the corners squared and tight, the hay being packed away evenly by the labourer on top with Mr. Finchley. Mr. Finchley smiled to himself, rolled his sleeves in a pause and felt very much like a son of the soil. Here, thigh deep in hay, his nostrils full of the rich smell of grass and summer flowers, he was close to the earth, close to the fine heritage which was his, for had he not, he argued to himself as his fork worked, come from Kent stock, from men such as these who plied their forks with him?

There was little conversation. The cart was unloaded, and the tractor came up dragging the other cart full of hay. The full cart was brought alongside the rick, the tractor swung away, hooked up with the empty cart and was back across the field, and the farmer and his hands turned to unloading the new cart, and high in their ears sang the mower as it cut round and round the standing part of the field.

Two hours later Mr. Finchley would have sold his fine heritage for a glass of water. He would have renounced for ever his Kent ancestors for the pleasure of a cool swim, and he knew that his apprenticeship to the sons of soil and toil could not be served in an hour on top of a hayrick. His arms ached, the handkerchief which he had knotted over his head was wet with perspiration, and there was a great deal of loose grass bits inside his shirt and trousers. The grass tormented him like a hundred furies, and his fork felt like a quant pole in his hands. No one seemed to notice his distress. The two on the cart went on with their unloading in a rhythmic, mechanical way, unflurried by time or hot sun. Their brown arms moved up and down easily and they did not bother to remove either waistcoat or pullover. The labourer who worked behind Mr. Finchley wore a thick pair of dark trousers, tied in at the boots, a shirt, pullover and waistcoat, and about his middle was a wide leather belt, studded with regimental badges. The belt increased Mr. Finchley's feeling of warmth every time he saw it. The man must have been well over sixty, for his neck had that lean, stringy, drawn appearance and his hair was touched with white. He was a friendly soul and grinned affably at Mr. Finchley, but he showed no signs of tiredness. He just went on like a machine and

Mr. Finchley, a younger man, was ashamed of his own weakness, but he could not deny it.

If I don't get a rest soon, thought Mr. Finchley, I shall drop with exhaustion. So great was his distress that he even contemplated quitting, but the thought of the looks he would get deterred him. He had offered to work and work he would. If the old man behind him could keep going then he jolly well could.

He had his reward. He stuck it for another fifteen minutes and then the farmer called a halt.

"Time for a cigarette and a drink, lads," he said, and he dropped to the ground. No summons had ever sounded sweeter in Mr. Finchley's ears. He came down from the rick and flopped in the shade. The farmer, who was not so unobservant as he seemed, tossed him a cigarette and one of the men went to an earthenware jug and poured out four glasses of beer. Mr. Finchley drew his drink back and never tasted beer that was better than that glass.

"Pretty good spell that," said the farmer. "With luck we might get the whole of it in today. Jim'll finish cutting today and we'll get that sometime this week ... Weather looks more settled now. Each year it seems to take longer and longer to get the hay home."

"There'll be a tidy li'l old bit this year, too," said Harry.

Jim left the mower and came across with the two other men who had been picking up hay. Jim was a fair-haired young man with a freckled face, and he seemed on more familiar terms with the farmer than the other men.

They all sat down on the ground and drank their beer and they talked of the other farms around them and how they were getting forward with their haymaking. Mr. Finchley felt a little lost and out of things. He had nothing to add to this conversation. He couldn't give it as his opinion that there would be a nice crop of Bramley's this year, or that some of Reg Binder's ricks would go up in smoke pretty soon if he wasn't careful, gathering it in like that. He knew nothing about the price of sheep.

He just lay back against the tick and rested. In no time, it seemed to him, the spell was over and he was back on top of the rick. For the first five minutes the labour was agonising. He was aware of every muscle in his body and every grass stalk in his shirt. Then it passed, and he settled down to a steady, unthinking rhythm. It was not the rhythm of the practised hands, but the mechanical despair which inhabits the tyro who knows that he must go on. All that morning Mr. Finchley worked like a Hercules. The rick rose and he could see beyond the fields, across the road to the bright twinkle of the river where it flowed through the water meadows. It flashed and glittered tantalisingly. Above him moved a myriad tiny white clouds against a fiery blue blaze, and away across the field stood a line of graceful birches and ash trees, tall, poised and inviting him to their cool shade but he stayed on the rick, little blisters growing on his palms, grunting with each lift of his fork, glad at each little respite in the labour. But he stuck it.

When lunchtime came, the horse was taken out of the mower and given a feed in the shade of the rick. The farmer and Jim went off towards the farm, the labourers settled down in the hedge with their bottles of cold tea and their thick slices of bread and cold rashers.

Mr. Finchley walked back to his caravan. He lunched from bread and cheese and made himself a quick cup of tea, and as he sat on the step of the caravan drinking it, he wondered if he should quietly gather up his traps and steal away, but even as he wondered, he knew that he could not. He was going to finish out the day. If he went away now, he knew what would happen. So far none of the men had said much to him, but he felt that they were watching him. They guessed that he was not a countryman and they were waiting for him to give in. If he did so, he could hear Harry laughing about it in the local inn that evening as he took his glass of beer, laughing about the townsman who hired himself for a day's haying and quit at noon because he was tired out. He might be all right behind a pen, but a hayfork was too much for him. Even the farmer, Mr. Finchley was pretty sure, had soon spotted that he had not hired a real country worker; he must have guessed already that Mr. Finchley was a city man, but he had not said anything. Only once or twice Mr. Finchley had caught a tiny smile curling about the lips of the man and the grey eyes watched him interestedly.

As he turned into the field they were just harnessing up the horse. Jim and the farmer were back. The farmer called to him as he came up.

"Would you like to try the wagon for a spell?"

Mr. Finchley nodded. He was ready for anything. Rolling about the field on the haywagon would be a change from standing on the rick.

He soon found it was a change, not altogether for the better. On the rick he had at least the comfort of stability. It did not heave and jerk under him as he forked hay, but the wagon had no such steadiness. He climbed into it. The tractor started away pulling both wagon and hayloader. The hay started up the long loader and began to drop into the wagon and, as it fell, Mr. Finchley forked it along the wagon to his mate, a round-faced, rather stupid-looking man, who had a villainous appearance because of one eyelid which dropped sinisterly over his right eye. Round the large field the tractor went and, so long as it kept going, the hay rattled up the loader into the wagon and Mr. Finchley had to keep it moving backto his companion. On the rick, when the hay came up too fast he had been able to step back and tread it down. Here, he had no room to step back, no time to tread hay down. He had to keep going or be smothered, and while he kept going he had to keep his balance, for the wagon lurched and swung over the rough field like a ship in a cross sea.

It was not so bad when the hay in the wagon was low because he could cling to the side standards to save himself from a bad lurch, but as the hay rose and he found himself almost level with the mouth of the loader and the standards no more than foot-long stubs protruding through a mass of hay, he felt his position to be even less secure. There were times when he had to fall forward on all fours to save himself, other times when he dropped backwards unexpectedly into a sitting position and others when he staggered about, waving his fork like Neptune flourishing tipsily a trident. On the rick he had felt he needed to be a superman to keep up with the work. On the wagon he knew that besides being a superman he also had to be an acrobat. The tractor shrieked and clattered about the field, the wagon bounced and swayed, the loader spewed up the long winnows of hay and Mr. Finchley sweated and forked like a trojan. All that long, hot afternoon, with a break now and then for a spell, he worked. He worked as he had never before worked in his life: worked with his hands, with his shoulders, with his legs, with his arms and body. He was not required to think or plan. He had only one job, that was to clear the hay as it came to him, to pack it down at his end of the wagon and to keep on top of the growing mound, and all the time he worked there sung in his mind a silly, recurring sentence. *The dignity of labour.* The mowing machine seemed to beat it out as a train wheel beats out a message over the rail joints, the tractor hummed and roared it and it sang through Mr. Finchley's brain like a shibboleth which he had to keep mouthing in order to maintain his strength. *The dignity of labour. The dignity of labour.*

The end came at half-past six. They had picked up and stacked all the hay which was ready. The newly cut swathes lay, drying and waiting another day. As that last forkful went up to the rick, Mr. Finchley breathed a gentle sigh of relief.

The horse and mower rattled away towards the farm, the tractor hauled off the wagon and the men scattered about the various jobs they had to do before their day's work was done. Mr. Finchley went back to his caravan and the farmer went with him. He had to go and look at some of his sheep in a field across the road by the river.

"I made a mistake about you," he said easily. "I didn't realise at first that you were just holidaying. I thought you were one of those coves who bump about the country making a scanty living from one odd job to another. I'll bet this is the first day's haying you've ever done in your life, eh?"

"Well," said Mr. Finchley, smiling, happy that it was over, "as a matter of fact it is."

"And you did it very well. Townsfolk think haymaking is a jolly affair of riding on wagons and tossing forkfuls of hay about lightly. Now you know what it is."

"If you want my honest opinion," answered Mr. Finchley with some feeling, "I think it's damned hard work."

"So it is—but it's good work. Do you think you can manage another day tomorrow? There's another field lying all ready up behind the house. The second day is nothing like as bad as the first," he added, with a smile.

To his surprise, Mr. Finchley heard himself say, "I don't mind it at all."

"Good—and that being so, you'd better draw your van off the side of the road there. You can run into the field by the river and find yourself a pleasant spot. You can turn your horse loose in there, too."

He moved away into a field and Mr. Finchley went on to his caravan. He harnessed up Churchwarden and pulled across the road into one of the river-fields. He found himself a camping spot on a high ledge of grass over the deep channel of the river. He blocked up the wheels of the van and turned Churchwarden loose. Then he looked at the river. Not three feet from the van it ran clear and cool over a gravel bed. Lower down a patch of water buttercups broke its rippled course.

Mr. Finchley slipped into the caravan, took off his clothes and was soon sitting in thirty inches of water, wallowing like a hippopotamus. He lay back and let the stream bathe his strained muscles and the cool water wash over his sun-reddened scalp. When he lay perfectly still, resting on his elbows, a tiny shoal of minnows came back and nibbled at his arms, and downstream a grey wagtail bobbed daintily from one stone to another.

As he lay there a voice called from the bank lower down the stream, and the farmer appeared, driving a cow before him.

"If you care to come up," he shouted, "there'll be some supper at the house in about an hour's time." Mr. Finchley thanked him and then dried himself. He sat on the step in the fresh evening and smoked his pipe. He had worked hard and could appreciate his leisure. He looked at his hands; they were blistered and red and he could feel a stiffness working over his limbs, but he was happy. His pipe had never tasted better. Before him was the prospect of a farmhouse supper and he was camped in a spot which was peaceful and lovely. To his left ran the river, chattering endlessly to its crowded banks and beyond the river, past the meadows, rose the green slopes of the hills, patched with woods and threaded with thin hedges that ran up to the skyline. He sat in a tiny bowl and wherever the eye strayed it mounted by copse or curling cottage smoke to the sky.

When his pipe was done it was time to go up to the farm. It was a low house, its roof red-tiled and its face half-hung with Canterbury tiles. From the centre of its roof rose a fine chimney-stack. It was a typical Kent farmhouse, its floors laid with worn and polished bricks, dining-room and living-room served by large open fireplaces. Before it stood a pleasant garden and lawn, behind it lay a paved yard surrounded by outhouses and a great barn and there was a well to one side of the yard. Beyond the yard was an orchard.

Mr. Thomas Greevey, for that was the name of the farmer, greeted him affably and introduced him to his wife, a quiet, dark-haired woman, who seemed to say little and do less but nevertheless ran her house with a smoothness which was revealed in the course of the evening.

Farmhouses are generally untidy. This is inevitable because a farmer, once he gets indoors, is a naturally untidy person. He likes plenty of space, and farmhouses, though they have more space than modern flats, are not big enough to accommodate tidily the litter of bills, circulars, farming papers, guns, cartridge boxes, gumboots, old coats, hats, dogs, lanthorns, egg baskets, pails and the hundred odds and ends which are found in farm dwellings. When you find a tidy farmhouse, you can be sure that the farmer either does not get his living entirely from farming but has private means or that he has an exceptional wife. Tom Greevey had an exceptional wife.

It was not until he sat down to supper in the oak-raftered dining-room that Mr. Finchley realised how hungry he was. The long table was heavy with food. Nothing was hidden away on side tables or kept back in the kitchen. Everything was on the table so that a hungry man could order his eating with an eye to the correct apportionment of the various foods. There was a gigantic veal and ham pie as large as a paving-stone, which, when cut, was found to be stuck all over with yellow and white egg saturns. There was a bowl of salad, a great, sparkling cut-glass bowl piled high with green lettuces, chopped onions, sliced tomatoes, thin wafers of cucumber and red-and-white radish dices. Mr. Finchley, Tom Greevey, his wife, and Jim—who turned out to be a younger brother of Mr. Greevey's—ate like working people who had earned their food. The food disappeared with an astonishing rapidity. Cold bacon, beetroots, pickles, pie, salad, jam tart, fruit pie, rice pudding, cheese and biscuits ... the four of them made a royal havoc, and with the food went down glasses of cider, water and beer according to taste, and they talked.

"So you come from London," said Tom Greevey, as he helped himself to a great slice of pie. "You wouldn't have believed it, my dear, if you'd seen him in the hay field to-day," he smiled at his wife.

"No, he worked like the best of 'em," said Jim, grinning at him. "Though, Lord, you did look hot for the first hour or so." He laughed and Mr. Finchley laughed, too.

"What I say about London," went on Tom, "is that it's a good place to come from but a bad place to go to. I don't like big towns."

"All people aren't so struck on farming as you are," said his wife. "You want to remember that. It's not the only life—"

"And people do manage to make money in London," said Jim, winking at Mr. Finchley.

"Money!" Tom breathed hard and then he looked at Mr. Finchley. "Don't let them mislead you, Mr. Finchley. They both like farming as much as I do, but they like to pull my leg. Farming isn't supposed to make money for you. It's supposed to be a way of living."

"But farmers do make money, don't they?" asked Mr. Finchley.

"Sometimes, but not often, and when they do it's because they couldn't help making money. Farming is more like a charitable institution which fellows like me run for the benefit of townspeople. We grow your food—or some of it—we raise your meat, we find you with eggs and milk, we work the whole year round, we mortgage our farms and live in debt—all for the benefit of the townspeople. And because it's a healthy fresh-air life, because we have the sense to grow enough vegetables to keep our tables full, and because we can take a morning off to go to market, you think that's compensation for not making a profit. I'd like to see the London businessman who'd sink five thousand pounds in a concern and be content to show a loss every year. That's what many of us do."

"And why is that so?" Mr. Finchley was curious.

"I'll tell you, Mr. Finchley," said Mrs. Greevey. "Because all farmers are either stubborn fools or overgrown schoolboys like my husband, because they're not businessmen. Their job is to grow corn or raise sheep—but when they've done that you'd be surprised how easy it is to cheat them out of their just profit. The Government cheats them, the cattle-food people cheat them, the public and retailers cheat them."

"Yes, they're fair game for every clever businessman or politician," said Jim.

"This country is an industrial country. It's run for the sake of big industries and the votes of townspeople. Farming doesn't get a look in. It's an anachronism. If we want to export heavy goods and industrial products, we have to import foodstuffs. We don't want our own foodstuffs because to encourage them too much would upset the whole system. The only time we worry about producing our own food is when there's a war and then the Government pat the farmer on the back, tell him he's the first line of defence, ask him to plough up his bad fields and produce bumper wheat crops from them all within five minutes. Is that a fair deal? What's the good of having land to let it go derelict except during wartime? Don't you ever become a farmer, Mr. Finchley—not unless you have a constitution which is naturally adapted to deal with worries and anxieties …" Tom Greevey bent over his plate and shook his head with mock sadness.

"Then why," asked Mr. Finchley, who was interested in the conversation, "do you go on being a farmer?"

"I'll tell you," said Jim. "Because farming is the only thing he knows how to do and because he damned well wouldn't do anything else but farm, anyway. I don't blame him."

"You're a couple of fools," said Mrs. Greevey proudly.

The two men laughed and shook their heads.

After supper Jim disappeared and Mr. Finchley sat on the gate by the barn in the yard and smoked and talked with Tom Greevey. Tom was a middle-aged man and lacked nothing in common sense, but he told Mr. Finchley some things that evening which made Mr. Finchley wonder why he had kept on as a farmer. There were very few years in which he had shown any real profit. He had suffered losses and disappointments, bad prices for crops and cattle, heavy tithes, diseases and epidemics amongst his stock. He had seen storm destroy his corn and flood carry away his cows …

"You wouldn't believe what the little old river down there can be when she rises. She's quiet now, but I've seen her come up and spread out over the whole valley so that the roadway was a foot under water …"

But still he had no real grumble against farming. It was his life and it was a special life. For the first time Mr. Finchley understood how different were men who believed in the land from all others. They were not entirely virtuous, but their faith filled them with a fine growth of hope, and they treated their farms and spoke of them as though they were human.

"My family," he went on, watching his smoke go up through a cloud of gnats, "have farmed around here for hundreds of years. The churchyards around here are full of 'em. My father didn't want me to farm. It was a hopeless job in his day—god knows what he'd say if he could see it now. He sent me to a good school and drove the idea into my head that I was to become a schoolteacher or a bank cashier, and I believed him for a while. But here I am with two hundred acres of farmland and here I mean to squat until the end of my days."

As he finished speaking a flurry of sparrows came round the side of the barn and flashed for cover under the wide eaves. The beat of their wings made Mr. Finchley start.

Tom laughed. "Made you jump, didn't it? That's the old kestrel. He generally comes along at this time of the evening to see if he can pick off a sparrow for supper." He looked up at the sky to where a black-winged shape beat away against the pale grey light. "As long as he sticks to sparrows he's my friend, but when he starts on the chickens I reckon I'll have to take a gun to him. Well, I've got some fowls to shut up so I'll say goodnight." He was gone across the yard and Mr. Finchley walked back through the thickening evening gloom to his caravan. The dignity of labour, he was thinking. Tom Greevey had that dignity and it wasn't spoiled or weakened because sharp business men from towns and astute money grabbers found it easy to trick the farmer and his men. Those clever city people weren't even as clever as they thought they were. They were killing the goose which laid the eggs, killing slowly, but the day would come when they would see the real balance of their transactions ruled off in their fat ledgers.

XVIII
How a barber gets a close shave

MR. FINCHLEY did not do any more haymaking for Tom Greevey. When he awoke next morning it was raining, a soft grey drizzle that obscured the sides of the valleys and filled the river-meadows with a faint wash of mist and dampness. The grasses were beaded with it and the mirror of the river was dulled by its touch. After he had had breakfast Tom Greevey came along and told him that there would be no work that day or the next. He paid him off at the rate of ninepence an hour for his work and Mr. Finchley took it, knowing that he had earned it. The farmer left him, saying that he was welcome to stay in the river-meadow as long as he liked.

It was a pleasant berth and Mr. Finchley decided to pass the day there. He spent the morning giving the caravan a general tidying-up. He cleaned the windows, shook the cushions out, dusted his bookshelves and rearranged his food cupboards and then washed the floor and polished the brasswork. It was lunchtime before he had quite finished.

After lunch he put on his raincoat and cap and, leaving the caravan, started off to inspect two houses which were within walking distance. Mr. Finchley enjoyed that walk in the rain. It was far from cold and he walked, pipe in mouth, coat swinging half open and in the pockets his bird and flower books. He made several discoveries that afternoon. He found the flowers of spotted medick, ploughman's spikenard and dyer's greenweed, and he saw a green woodpecker and a bullfinch, and the two houses he saw were, for once, almost up to the agent's description of them. Mr. Finchley liked them but he did not feel that either of them was the place he was looking for. In his mind had grown up a composite picture of the house he wanted. The vision changed a little from day to day as he thought of new aspects, but its general outlines remained the same. He often wondered whether he ever would find the house he wanted, and in moments of dejection he was sure that he would not, yet his hope always flared higher after such moods and he felt confident that somewhere ahead, somewhere in the valleys that he still had to travel, waited the house which should be his and satisfy most of his desires.

He spent that evening reading and the next morning, although it was showery, he set off on the road, moving towards Ashford. He was in no hurry—sometime that afternoon he had planned to reach a house that lay off the road to the left—and Churchwarden jogged along comfortably. Mr. Finchley sat on the driving seat, reins loose in his hands, pipe going and his coat collar turned up against the occasional squalls of light rain.

He was going down a long, straight slope of hill when a car passed him at high speed. Mr. Finchley, who had been deep in his thoughts, started violently as the car passed. It was a long, cream car and its tyres screamed over the wet surface of the road. It swooped by him like an enormous projectile and was gone, leaving a haze of high-flung spray after it. Churchwarden, used to traffic, fidgeted with the shock but soon settled down. Mr. Finchley looked after the car and uttered a few short, pungent remarks about mad motorists. Most motorists treated the horse-drawn caravan with an old-world courtesy and he had no complaint to make against them. There were, however, a few who seemed to be driving fast and madly towards a hell which had been especially created for them.

Mr. Finchley's thoughts about such motorists were interrupted by a noise from behind. He heard a wild halloo and the beat of pounding hooves. He poked his head around the side of the caravan and looked behind him. For a moment or two he could hardly believe his own eyes. Coming down the hill towards him was another caravan. It was a caravan very much like his own in design and it was painted a canary-yellow. But it was not this circumstance which caused Mr. Finchley all his surprise. It was the manner of the other caravan's approach.

It was tearing down upon him like a juggernaut. The horse was stretched out in a wild gallop, a man crouched on the driving seat, one hand grasping at the canopy stay for support, the other tugging futilely at the reins, and the whole caravan swayed and rocked, groaned and creaked, and rattled and bounced alarmingly.

It was a hundred yards away when Mr. Finchley saw it, almost at the top of the long slope down which he was travelling. A wild cry broke again from the man on the driving seat. There was no mistaking the intelligence behind that frantic, incoherent alarm call. It was a plea,

241

a warning to all on the road to draw back and give free passage. The strange caravan rolled down like the Charge of the Light Brigade, it sped forward crazily like an olden-day covered wagon driven at racing pace by settlers fighting to reach and stake the best claim, it rattled and lumbered like Boadicea's war chariot, and the horse stretched itself in a fine frenzy of abandonment.

There was a small dockway on the road ahead of Mr. Finchley, a narrow cut where roadworkers piled their granite chips and gravel, and it was empty. Mr. Finchley swung Churchwarden into the haven and prayed that the runaway would keep its present course.

Almost before he was safely in the cut, the strange caravan flashed by him. It was a magnificent sight. The horse's mane flew free, the harness gleamed and was taut with strain, curtains billowed from an open window, a bucket under the van clanged like a warning gong and through the half-open door at the back issued a fine clatter and jangle of crockery and swinging tins. The caravan seared by Mr. Finchley like a yellow comet and he watched it swoop down the hill, wheels spinning and lifting. Every moment he expected to see the caravan overturn and crash to destruction. Miraculously it survived.

At the bottom of the slope the road ran between flat meadows towards a little hump-backed bridge over the river, and it was the long stretch of straight road and the rise to the bridge which finally slowed the caravan up. It came to a halt on the far side of the bridge.

When Mr. Finchley came up with it, he drew in behind and got down. As he approached the strange caravan, a man jumped out from the back door and shouted happily to him. The man came dancing towards him and Mr. Finchley recognised him. It was Horace Blain. He wore a blue pullover, green corduroy trousers, white canvas shoes and on the top of his head sat a diminutive beret. He came prancing up to Mr. Finchley, his toes flicking the ground like a ballet dancer, his great, fat body filled to bursting with a volatile infusion of joy and soaring emotions.

"Mr. Finchley!" he cried, "Why, it's you. What a surprise!"

"Mr. Blain—"

"Horace. Horace, let it be! Well, I never did. Fancy running into you." Suddenly his face changed, his body swelled with an explosive mixture. "Did you see that swine?" he roared angrily. "Did that swine in a white car pass you?"

"He did," answered Mr. Finchley, "and he was going much too fast."

"Fast!" Horace danced angrily. "He must have been a maniac. Came swooshing under my horse's nose. Swoosh!" His hand cut through the air in imitation of the way the car had swerved by. "And the next thing I know, we're off like Sansovino running in the Derby. I thought my last hour had come. See the headlines—Shocking Caravan Fatality in Kent. I'd like to have just ten minutes alone with that driver. I'm glad you managed to get out of my way. Coming down that hill I thought I was done for. I didn't even have time to pray for myself."

He subsided as he thought of his escape and then smiled at Mr. Finchley.

"And what," said Mr. Finchley, "are you doing with a caravan?"

Horace revived. He turned towards his caravan.

"Isn't she a beauty!" he declared proudly. "You did it," he said, nodding at Mr. Finchley. "It was meeting you that put me on to it. I'd never thought about caravans until I met you that morning. Then when I got back and developed the photographs I'd taken, there you were scrubbing yourself outside your van, and there was the caravan looking like a fairy thing, ready to spirit you away to all sorts of places and adventures—don't mind my poetry, all barbers have a touch of poetry in them, my wife says so. So I decided that I'd have one. Come and look her over—" He tugged Mr. Finchley towards the caravan.

Mr. Finchley saw that it was of a slightly different design from his own, but not so different that a stranger could have told them apart at a quick glance. Its paintwork, however, was almost identical with that of his caravan, canary-yellow, the wheels picked out in red and green, little pictures of lake and castle on the door panels. He looked at Horace and Horace looked at him. Then Horace said:

"I wanted her to look as much like yours as possible. It was a silly sort of feeling, really. You seemed so happy in yours that I felt if I wanted to have the same happiness I should have to have a caravan like yours. This was brown and green when I bought it, but I had it repainted. She was bought, repainted and on the road within two weeks. I had to pay for that speed, but it was worth it. I've hired the horse from a farmer in the village.

"It looks a very fine outfit," said Mr. Finchley, examining the caravan critically. "How do you like caravanning?"

"Fine—except for the cooking. I'm not much of a hand at cooking, but it's wonderful what you can get out of a tin these days, and I stop at a restaurant occasionally. Yes, I like it. And it gives me something to do and plenty of people to talk to. Most days I scarcely do more than ten miles, sometimes not that—and I'm working!" He announced this with a gleeful accent.

"Working? What do you mean? You mean you do odd jobs on the road?"

"In a way. Look!" Horace darted inside the caravan and reappeared lugging a large board. He propped it on the top step and in green letters on a yellow background Mr. Finchley read the inscription—

Horace Blain—Travelling Barber
Moderate Prices

"Any village I come to where there isn't a barber's shop," Horace explained, "I set up on the green or somewhere handy for the day and I get quite a lot of custom. I turn the living-room into a saloon and away I go. All day long I have work and conversation; schoolboys, farmhands, postmen—you'd be surprised. I've taken ten shillings in a day."

"Does your wife know about it?"

"Good Lord, no! She'd have a fit. I kept this part of it secret. She wouldn't approve. But I get a lot of fun out of it—and some of my clients do need haircuts and shaves. My hand"— he waggled a pair of imaginary scissors in his right hand—"is getting quite supple again."

Mr. Finchley laughed. "If your wife gets to know of this, you won't do any more caravan trips."

"She won't find out."

They stopped by the river and had lunch together. Horace invited Mr. Finchley to take it in his caravan and Mr. Finchley, proud of his domestic ability, prepared the lunch. They had a tomato omelette and then cold ham and a salad. Mr. Finchley let himself go over the salad, almost outdoing Mrs. Greevey. He was a little worried at the amount of tinned stuff which Horace had stored and which, apparently, he had been living on. Tinned food was wrong, Mr. Finchley felt, so he gave Horace a healthy salad, and for sweet he made a trifle, decorated with strawberries. The trifle Mr. Finchley looked upon as a flippancy, but he was glad that it came out successfully.

After lunch they sat and smoked and compared their caravan experiences. Mr. Finchley enjoyed that talk. He was able, as an old hand, to give Horace some useful advice, and there is nothing any man enjoys more than a proper excuse to give another man good advice. Not once, however, did either of them make a move to suggest that they join forces and journey together. They both understood that the real joy of caravanning was to be free to go where one wanted, to have no ties and no obligation to study a partner's wishes.

When they got going again after lunch they kept company along the road to Ashford, until they were abreast of the turning to Wye and through the driving, misty rain they could just make out the great chalk crown cut into the downs above the little town. Here Mr. Finchley turned off, for he had a house to visit beyond Wye, and Horace carried on towards Ashford.

They parted amicably and with happy shouts.

"See you again, soon, perhaps!" yelled Horace, shaking his whip.

"Maybe," called back Mr. Finchley. "Goodbye and happy driving."

"Goodbye! Goodbye!" The yellow caravan rolled up the road and Horace was gone and Mr. Finchley, smiling to himself, was driving alone down a twisting side lane towards Wye.

Mr. Finchley found Wye a pleasant little town—apart from the railway. At one time the approach to the town had been by way of a grey stone bridge across the rushing Stour, and the traveller was greeted with the sight of a mill and an inn, the hub of much country activity. Now, Mr. Finchley was greeted by a level-crossing and an ugly station. He drove up the main street and by the dignified buildings of the Agricultural College, wondering why the townspeople had ever let that railway station be dumped across their pleasant doorway. How right, he thought, the Captain had been when he said that the country had no weapon to ward off vandals and only the sea knew how to keep itself free. Because the earth was so patient, men and women thought they could insult and scarify it with impunity. Advertisements to eat somebody's bread stuck on the front of a windmill, reflector signs for petrol and south coast casinos winking on the shoulders of tree-lined hills, the sides of houses plastered with cigarette and liquor slogans, fields whose richest crops were long-legged hoardings commending the amenities of housing estates and laxatives, lovely little cottages cowering beneath an outbreak of tea-signs, and trees stuck over with handbills announcing summer sales … it was as though mankind had entered into a contract to remind itself incessantly of its own bloated and unpleasant body and its drugged demands for stimulation and entertainment. Mr. Finchley was of the school of thought which believed that all advertisement should be made through the newspapers and that any business or concern should be allowed one simple, direct board outside its premises to announce its character. If he were a dictator, he thought, the first thing he would do would be to clean up the countryside so that it could breathe again …

He did not stay in Wye, but climbed out of it by a long rising slope up to the top of the downs. A few miles ahead of him was a village near to which lay a house he wanted to see.

It was late in the afternoon when he came to the house. The agent's sheet announced that it could be seen on application to the caretaker in residence.

A little drive led to the house through a small meadow, which was tall with grasses and powdered with the blue heads of scabious and cornbit. Although it still drizzled, a lark sang somewhere up in the thick rain. The drive stopped at a long white gate on which were the words Wyatt Place. A low stone wall, backed by a wild growth of lilac bushes, the flowers over now and brown, surrounded an unkempt garden. From the middle of the lawn rose a great yew tree, the grass gone from under it. The house itself was long and low, the roof of red tiles had fallen a little with the years, and Mr. Finchley could see the waves in it where it had dropped to rest upon the ribs of the timber rafters, but it was still sound. The face of the building was of red brick, cleverly filled in between the timber framework. It had a solid, good-looking appearance, like a man who has worn well and kept most of his good looks.

Mr. Finchley pulled at the bell and after a long time he heard someone approach from within. The door opened and he was facing an old woman, the caretaker. She was very small, very neat and very old. She had the look of one of those compact, wise women who inhabit Gothic fairytales, the look of someone who had never known youth and never regretted it. It was impossible to imagine her as a young girl. She stood now in a grey dress that billowed from the waist and came low to the ground in stiff folds hiding her feet. A white shawl spread over her shoulders, her face was unwrinkled and had that high colour and smooth texture which some old ladies who do not mind their age are given. Her hair was black and covered partly by the shawl which fell to her shoulders. She saw the agent's sheet in Mr. Finchley's hand and understood his mission before he spoke. She stood aside for him to enter.

"Come in," she said. "You've come to look over the house?"

"If it's not inconvenient to you."

"Not at all, sir. Come along."

She took him in hand. There is no other way of explaining the manner in which the old lady possessed herself of Mr. Finchley. From that tiny, correct body there flowed a great force. Mr. Finchley was helpless against it. She did not appear to move quickly or to talk much, but she manoeuvred him from room to room and left him little to say. It was a pleasant, friendly house and the rooms were light and well-proportioned. It was, in fact, one of the most promising houses which he had seen. Although it was old it had been carefully modernised. There was a radiator system, the kitchen had hot and cold water and each room was fitted with electric light that came from the main outside in the roadway. But it was less these conveniences than the atmosphere of the house which attracted Mr. Finchley. It was one of those houses which do not suffer from being empty. Most houses need furnishing before they can be appreciated. This house was in need of no furniture to demonstrate its true qualities.

"Do you live here all alone?" asked Mr. Finchley, as they came down the oaken stairway to the hall.

"I do, sir. The family keep me on as a caretaker and I have a little bedroom upstairs and live in the kitchen. When you came I was just going to make a cup of tea. Tea is the best drink on a drizzly day like this. Would you like one?"

"Well, thank you, I—"

"Come along then—if you don't mind sitting in my kitchen."

She led him to the kitchen, which was a large room with a long window that looked out to an orchard at the back. A black, well-polished range took up one side of the wall and a fire burned in it now. A table with a green cloth, plush-framed pictures on the wall, a tabby cat, three wicker chairs and a mountainous dresser full of china, marked with a bright design of golden pheasants, these Mr. Finchley remembered a long time afterwards.

The old lady motioned him to a seat in one of the cane armchairs and then busied herself with the kettle and tea-pot. In a few minutes the table was laid—before she did it, Mr. Finchley knew that she was one of those old ladies who would lay the table with a spotless white cloth for tea—and a plateful of tiny cakes put on it. Mr. Finchley, because of his own cooking, now took an interest in food which was quite apart from the pleasure of taste, but he had never come across cakes like Mrs. Maberley's—for that was her name. They had a flavour, a substance, all their own. She watched his face as he ate them and said, smiling:

"You like them, don't you? I could see it on your face. My boys liked them, too. Mab's cakes they called them and they've eaten more than I can remember. You like the house, don't you?"

Mr. Finchley considered this for a moment. Then he answered honestly, "Yes, I do. I've seen an awful lot, but this one seems to be what I'm looking for."

"I know, sir. It's a friendly house. It always was. It's a house you like to come back to ..." She said this quietly, her thoughts away from the room for a while and Mr. Finchley glanced at her, curiously.

"I came here with the family when they first came, long before the Great War. I've been here ever since. I was nurse at first and then housekeeper and now caretaker. Johnson was the family name. He was a scholarly gentleman and he came here after his wife died, that was when the second boy came. Vincent that was. I was mother to those two boys, Vincent and Herbert. They used to spend a lot of their time in here—and they liked those cakes."

"This house must be full of memories for you then, Mrs. Maberley," said Mr. Finchley.

"Yes, sir, it is. They do say that the only thing old people have is their memories."

"And why don't the family live here now?" asked Mr. Finchley. He asked because he could see that her life was woven into the life of the family, and that she loved to talk about them.

"Oh, they haven't been here since the war, sir. But I see some of them often enough. Old Mr. Johnson and Vinny—that was my name for Vincent when he was very young. He was here only last night was Vinny, sitting in the chair you've got now. Herbert's the only one I don't see, but he'll come one day. It's for him the solicitors want to sell the house, but it's been a long time and nobody's

251

taken it. Yes, I'm not so lonely as most would think. There's hardly a night when I don't have company, either old Mr. Johnson or Vinny and sometimes both of them. But when they're both here, Mr. Johnson never speaks much. He just sits in his chair and sleeps while Vinny talks. Vinny's still the same rascal. It does me good to hear him laugh. There was a time when I thought that the afterlife was a very serious affair with no time for fun and jokes. But if you could hear Vinny, you'd know that it wasn't so. He still laughs, the same Vinny. When he was alive it was just the same …"

Mr. Finchley looked at her, not understanding. But she showed no signs of distress or excitement. She talked in her quiet, even voice, putting an edge of reality into the calm fantasy of her speech.

"I don't quite follow you," said Mr. Finchley politely. "How can he visit you?"

The old lady laughed, a quick, almost girlish tinkle of sound that seemed to find an echo amongst the pheasant china. "If Vinny heard you saying that, he would laugh, too. He's always saying that people seemed funny enough to him while he lived, but since he's dead they seem even funnier. And his father agrees with him. He's always say-ing—I told you he was a learned old gentleman—that you can't have a true understanding or philosophy of life until you're dead. I tell them not to tickle an old woman's head with such long words, but I'm beginning to understand what they mean."

A faint chill tiptoed gently along Mr. Finchley's spine. Suddenly the warm kitchen was inimical with unknown forces. Then he saw Mrs. Maberley's old face and her friendly eyes and the feeling passed.

"Do you mean that Mr. Johnson and Vincent are dead, ma'am, but they come and visit you here in this kitchen?" It was an absurd question, but he heard himself asking it, and he heard Mrs. Maberley replying evenly:

"Of course, sir. Vincent was killed in the Great War. Before Hill 60 in 1915. He's always talking about his soldiering days. He came to me two nights after he was killed and before we knew here what had happened. The telegram came from the War Office the next day and when his father read it he dropped down and they put him to bed and he never got up again. He died within a month, and very soon after that he started to come with Vinny. I never know when they're coming—except that it's always at night. I'll come in from going the rounds and there they will be, sitting in their chairs, calling to me to make tea and cakes. Old Mr. Johnson grumbles sometimes about the way the garden's going and blames Herbert, but Vinny always sticks up for his brother and says that Herbert's not to blame. They never visit Herbert. I asked them once why they didn't and they wouldn't answer; they just looked at one another and Vinny laughed and began to tell me a funny story to change the subject. I could tell they didn't like the question and I never asked again. Am I upsetting you with this talk, sir?"

Mr. Finchley stirred his tea and shook his head. Somehow it was impossible to be unsettled by Mrs. Maberley. She related her story with such a precise, cogent faith behind her words that the supernatural went from them. She was talking like a privileged servant of the family, of the young son who enjoyed her kitchen and the old father who found a comfort in her company because it recalled so many things to him.

"It's strange," he admitted, "but it doesn't upset me. Only—"

"Only you're full of questions, sir?" Mrs. Maberley chuckled. "So was I at first. I even began to ask some of them, but I soon found that they didn't like questions of that sort. It made them uncomfortable. I'm not an entirely ignorant old woman, sir. I had a good education when I was young, and I have my own mind, but I came to see that there are some questions which the human mind can ask but for which it isn't strong or big or wide enough to understand the answers. They know that and that's why—out of kindness perhaps—they won't answer."

"It certainly is very queer. I don't disbelieve what you say, Mrs. Maberley. But until a person has actually had such an experience himself, he can't help keeping a little of his doubts. You make it all sound so natural and ..." Mr. Finchley paused for a moment. "Do you tell many people about this?"

Mrs. Maberley put more water into the teapot and poured him another cup of tea. Outside the summer drizzle pressed its soft fingers against the window panes, smearing them with a runnelled haze of water and in a melancholy music a water-pipe dripped into a butt.

"Not everyone, sir. Some people couldn't be told. But there are some, like yourself, who show at once what their nature is. It's people generally who like the house, who have a sympathy for it. As for making it sound natural. It is natural, sir. Death is nothing unnatural and after death is no more mysterious than before birth. Only silly people who never stop to think are afraid of death. It's as stupid to talk of being scared of dying as it is to talk of being scared to be born. I like being alive, sir, and I mean to go on living as long as I can because this body is made to enjoy the things in this life, things like the sunshine on your hands and face and the smell of flowers and the sound of my old tabby cat purring away by the fire, but when I die I shall have another life and a different set of pleasures and pains."

Mr. Finchley drove away from the house full of a quiet brooding. Either, he decided, Mrs. Maberley was honest or astute. And the decision rested not on facts, but upon a man's character. She might be astute, clever enough to pick out the people who were interested in the house and fancied buying it. To them she would tell her story so that they would hesitate against buying the place and so she would retain her comfortable berth there and her pension as caretaker. If that were so she had succeeded with Mr. Finchley. He would not have taken the house now. It would have always been haunted by those figures sitting in the cane chairs by the kitchen fire. It would never have been his house.

Again, it would have been simple, and a comforting dismissal of the odd story, to have written her down as an old woman gone unhinged in the loneliness of the house, her head full of fancies. Mr. Finchley felt that she was far from mad. She seemed the essence of common sense and sanity.

Yet Mr. Finchley felt that she was neither mad nor scheming. There were so many things in life which eluded the grasp of man's intellect that he could accept her story. He could not understand it, but he could believe it because she was so sure of its reality. So Mr. Finchley accepted Mrs. Maberley, and so, according to their own natures, other people who visited the house had to make their decisions.

XIX
The effect of cider upon social conscience

SOMEWHERE in Kent, not more than ten miles from Ashford, and halfway up the scarp-side of a finger of the downs, is a village which has a public-house, a Women's Institute wooden hut, a church with a great ivy growth up one side of the tower and about two dozen old cottages and houses grouped around the church and the inn. The village looks across a plain ribbed with dykes and patterned with fields, orchards and patches of wild marshland. Along the foot of the hill runs a main road, and a shoot from the road twists laboriously up the hill to the village. You should know the village when you come to it because jackdaws nest each year in the church ivy and the inn carries the name of the Quart Pot. Outside its doorway stands a large besom, fixed to the ground, on which customers wipe their muddy feet before entering.

Mr. Finchley came to the village the day after his talk with Mrs. Maberley. It was noon and he was thirsty, for the weather was fine and he had spent a great deal of the morning walking by Churchwarden's head up hills. While he had walked he had set his mind on cider and cheese. The green-and-red swinging sign of the inn promised him both. He went in and found himself in a large room with a sanded floor, a curved bar of scrubbed white wood in one corner, a fireplace with an inglenook in another and three or four circular tables of fruit wood placed over the floor. Mr. Finchley went to the bar and asked for a pint of cider. The landlord, a thin man with a wispy moustache and an air of sorrow, drew him his drink and then watched with a half-mournful expression as Mr. Finchley slaked his thirst.

"Ha," said Mr. Finchley, as he put his glass down with very little left in it, "that was good. It's hot this morning!"

"Ay," said the landlord.

As he spoke there came a shuffle of feet from the shadows by the fireplace and a voice broke out cheerfully:

"Ay, ay, ay! That's the extent and limit, the top and bottom, the *fons et origo* of his vocabulary. For the last ten minutes I've tried him on politics, religion, cricket and women, and all I get from him is—Ay! What would you do with a man like that?"

A young man, rather short and tubby, wearing a grey flannel suit and a cloth cap, his eyes winking behind thick-lensed spectacles, his reddish face shining, came up to the bar and put down his glass. "Fill it again, please, and"—he turned to Mr. Finchley—"would you care to join me? You would? Fill them both."

"Ay," said the landlord, and he filled the glasses. The young man drank, smiled at Mr. Finchley and said:

"Harbottle's the name, journalist by profession, never-do-well by inclination, British by birth and, at this moment, loaded just a wee bit below the plimsoll line."

"I'm glad to know you," said Mr. Finchley, not sure of this young man.

"Glad to know you, too. Glad to know everybody. Journalist's job—get around among people. Circulate, that's the idea."

There was no stopping Mr. Harbottle. He was a very ebullient young man with little regard for the more polite forms of social conduct. In a short while Mr. Finchley knew that he was a reporter on one of the local county newspapers, that he really wanted to be a poet, only times were hard for poets, but meanwhile he was a journalist. And in a little while he knew something about Mr. Finchley, knew that he was on a caravan trip and that he had retired from a solicitor's office. Mr. Finchley gave the information with a certain reserve, for he could not entirely feel that he liked this young man.

"And you wandered in here today, touching the Quart Pot on your peregrinations, just by chance? Chance, the blind and fickle goddess. Well, well, and just by chance you wandered into this village on the day which is going to be writ large in its parochial history. Hasn't he, landlord?"

"Maybe," said the landlord, proving that his vocabulary was a little more extensive than had appeared.

"Why, what's happening here today?" asked Mr. Finchley.

"You should ask! After today this village may have a right to be mentioned with Wat the Tyler—he was from Kent—and Tolpuddle. It may not be as big as Magna Charta, but it's in direct descent. Ay—to quote the landlord—today the yeomen, the village folk, may declare their independence and strike a blow against private interests which shall ring around the world, or a good way round about here."

"What is he talking about?" Mr. Finchley looked at the landlord. The landlord, busy cutting the bread and cheese which Mr. Finchley had ordered, had no time to answer.

Harbottle cried, "This—this is what I'm talking about. Look." He dipped his finger in what was left of his beer and began to draw on the counter. "See this, this is a hill. Here's the village, halfway up the hill. At the bottom the main road, and coming up here in loops and twists the side road to the village. But here, going in a straight line down the hill from the village to the main road is a footpath. It goes straight. That's the significant thing, and if you live in this village and want to get to the main road to catch the bus or walk to the next village, you never walk down by the road. You go by the footpath. But you see this box of matches." He put a box of matches on the hill, athwart the footpath almost and below the village. "Do you know what that is?"

"No, I don't," said Mr. Finchley. "And I don't know that I care what it is." He drained his cider and, out of politeness, had the landlord fill his and the young man's glass.

"You don't care! Impossible. You're an Englishman, you believe in your ancestral rights, so you must care. This matchbox is the house of Sir Simon Penickle. O, Sir Simon, great is thy name in the ears of all financiers and strong thy arm as ticker machine tape. The slug!" Harbottle spat accurately towards the fireplace and then said soberly, "Mind you, I'm not taking sides. Journalist has to be impartial. But there it is. Six months ago Sir Simon, hell claim him, bought that house, and today the right-of-way down the hill is threatened because it goes through one of his fields which he plans to turn into an orchard. He doesn't want the villagers to go through his orchard. He thinks they'll pinch his fruit just as any good financier among his associates would pinch another money-grubber's fruit, and, anyway, he doesn't like the idea of a right-of-way across his land."

"But surely that is a bit high-handed of him," exclaimed Mr. Finchley.

"It is, but that's how he made his name and fortune. He's had that path blocked up where it enters his property and confused everybody with a fine lot of legal talk about easements. You'd be surprised how easy it is sometimes to rob the common folk of their rights. A good many of the men in this village work for him, so they don't feel any too comfortable about making a fuss. But there are others, thank the Lord, who are free men."

"Why, I've never heard such nonsense," said Mr. Finchley indignantly. "A right-of-way is a right-of-way, and if the village has enjoyed it for years he has no right."

"You'd be surprised what a man like Sir Simon Catchevery-Nickel can do. That path is blocked up already. It was done yesterday. The next move is with the villagers, and that's why I'm here today. There's only one person who may really do any good, and that's Miss Slater—she's a retired schoolteacher sort of creature and lives in the village. She's holding a protest meeting today at two o'clock—isn't that right, landlord?"

"Ay, every word."

"See—even the landlord is touched. He's beginning to speak. Fill 'em up again and let me have some of that bread and cheese, too."

"Well, at any rate, I'm glad to hear that the village folk are not going to let him get away with it. Men like that are no less than pirates."

"They're pirates all right," said Harbottle. "But successful pirates, and I don't know that he won't get away with it."

Mr. Finchley was stirred to irritation almost at the suggestion, and maybe the two large glasses of cider he had taken so quickly on top of a hot morning's travel had something to do with his quickly roused ire.

"Nonsense, Harbottle—no decent villager is going to put up with that kind of thing. They're very ready to defend their rights."

"Are they? I wonder. They used to be, but the spunk's all gone from them these days. Do you know what's really troubling most of the lads about the blocking of that path? It's this. It will make going to the pictures a little more difficult for them. They'll have to walk down the road."

"That's an exaggeration of a semi-truth."

"You can't blame me for that. I'm a journalist. I'm wondering whether they will do anything beyond having a protest meeting. Sir Simon put a hurdle across that path yesterday and it's still standing. In my opinion, if the villagers meant business, it would have been kicked down ten minutes after it was put up. I went and looked at it this morning and felt tempted to kick it down myself. But it's not my quarrel, nor my village, and I have to be impartial."

"I think what you're trying to suggest is that the Kentish stock is degenerate and that the men of this county are unwilling any longer to uphold their just rights!" Mr. Finchley frowned severely at Harbottle, and went on before the other could reply. "It may interest you to know that I, myself, come from Kentish stock and I resent your inference. Kent men have always been fighters. They've always been in the first line of every battle. First the

Romans, then the Angles and Jutes, and after them the Normans, and so on. A thin red line of heroes. No damned London financier can block up a Kent right-of-way and not expect opposition of the severest kind. Of the severest kind!" Mr. Finchley reiterated his warning, accompanying it with a quick waggle of a finger.

Harbottle chuckled at this outburst and said, in almost a kindly voice, "It's funny how few people really have the right kind of head for cider. The only folk who can really drink cider are marshmen, Somerset men whose blood is mixed with the damp of the rhines and sedgelands. Cider can't touch you if you've got mist and rain in your blood."

"And you needn't think," cut in Mr. Finchley sharply, "that I don't also understand the inference in that statement. Let me tell you what I think of journalists."

"Don't—I've heard it all before. And I apologise if I've annoyed you. But I still think the whole question is open to doubt. I don't say the country folk are degenerate, but they are changed. People hesitate to raise a fist for their rights, and that hesitation gives shyster lawyers and greedy Sir Simons just the chance they're looking for."

"And what manner of man," said Mr. Finchley, "is this Sir Simon Penickle?"

"Well, he's the sort of fellow who wears a hard collar and a bow tie with tweed plus-fours and he talks like the clack of an adding machine. I interviewed him at ten this morning, and I've had to drink quite a lot since then to remind myself that there are human beings in the world. If you've ever seen a nice, tidy bank statement, full of beautiful figures and a fat credit balance, wearing a hard hat—that's Sir Simon. His blood is red ink, his veins blue ruling lines and his skin legal vellum."

"I don't like the sound of him," Mr. Finchley announced, draining his glass and tapping for another.

"Nobody who appreciates cider, cheese and pickles ever would like the sound of him," said Harbottle, and he tapped for his glass to be filled. "He's the kind of man who secretly wishes he could clip the wings of the pheasants on his land so that he could get better sport. But I won't say any more. A journalist has to be impartial. What about this meeting? Are you going to come along with me?"

"Of course, I'm coming. This is an important matter. I shall, of course, only be an interested spectator, but it will give me pleasure to see the men of this village refute your base suggestions that they are not ready to fight for their rights."

So Mr. Finchley and Harbottle went to the meeting. They got there a little late because Mr. Finchley, on coming out of the Quart Pot, had insisted on feeding Churchwarden and driving the van round to the back of the inn where it would be safe. There were not so many people in the institute but as they had expected. It was Saturday afternoon and many of the villagers were busy haymaking, and most of the young men had gone off to play cricket. Cricket and haymaking were important things which could not be interrupted by quibbles about rights-of-way. And, besides, the absentees argued to themselves, there would bound to be someone at the meeting and, with a lazy English indifference, they felt sure that something would get done without them. They honestly believed that they could leave any affair of public interest to the other man while they reserved the right to come back from haymaking, cricket or a shopping visit to Ashford and criticise what might have been done in their absence. For them, if they ever thought about it, that was the beauty of a democratic State. It never compelled you to give up what you wanted to do in order to mind your own business and interests.

In fact, Mr. Finchley felt that there were far fewer people in the hall than there should have been. To be exact there were twenty. A handful of older villagers, a preponderance of women, since women are sometimes readier to defend their men's rights than the men are, a few middle-class people who lived in and around the village at weekends, a spattering of young men and girls and, on the platform, Miss Slater.

The Miss Slaters of this world are many and seldom appreciated. Nature, denying them good looks or charm and so closing the door to marriage for most of them, does not stint them of an instinct for love, a wide, maternal love which they are forced to lavish on small causes and quick enthusiasms.

Miss Slater was forty, wore brown tweeds and an ugly little felt hat over her flat hair. She had a squarish, very prim face, the lips as precise and unattractive as a letterbox slit, and her nose, which was inclined to be red, hung above the slit like a heavy knocker.

She was talking as Mr. Finchley and Harbottle entered, and her voice slopped around the hut like the sound of water slapping against the sides of a tank.

"We all appreciate Sir Simon's many generosities towards this village. The village hall fund, the Boy Scouts, the cricket team … He has made generous contributions towards these. But he is a man of wealth and, while I do not wish to belittle his kindnesses, we all know that he can afford to be charitable. Because he employs some of the village people on his estate and in his house, and because he acts as a fairy godfather to the various organisations in this village, it does not mean that he can take liberties with our rights. We—and I say it with disrespect to no one—are not to be bought! And a man in Sir Simon's position should know that!"

"Hear, hear!" an old man called, and a rustle of approval raced round the hut.

"The vicar himself has protested to Sir Simon. Unfortunately the vicar cannot be with us today because he has been called away to a diocesan meeting. But I feel sure that I have his support, when I say that we have a right to object most strongly to Sir Simon's attitude. We have enjoyed that right-of-way for years, and before us the people of the village enjoyed it longer ago than any of us can remember. I do not understand the technicalities of the law, but of this I am sure. If Sir Simon thinks that the right-of-way is not valid, or capable of being disputed, we will meet his argument in a court. But until then, and until a decision is reached, he has not the flimsiest excuse for blocking up the right-of-way. In doing that he acts without authority and contrary to every principle of English law. Maybe he thinks if he blocks the way now we shall submit tamely and save him the expense of a lawsuit. Is that what you want to do?" She paused, breathing heavily. Thus, thought Mr. Finchley, Boadicea paused in the lull of battle.

An old man got up quite close to Mr. Finchley. He was very old, his face rough with a white stubble, his scraggy neck protected with a twisted green handkerchief and his body clothed in a large jacket with bulging pockets.

"Of course, it ain't what we want, missus. I know l'il ole Sir Simon. I bin trapping 'e's rabbits for un and trimmin' 'e's 'edges for the last three month and 'e come to me this mornin' while I was diggin' out a ferret in Long Acre and 'e says 'e hoped 'e wouldn't hear of me goin' to the meetin' this afternoon. See what I mean, missus?" The old man laughed and looked round the hut. "And do 'ee knaw what I said to un? I said this were a free country—leastways I ain't 'eard to the contrary yet—and that if I wanted to go to the meedn' I should go, and if 'e didn't like it—well, I said 'e mustn't think that all the rabbits to be caught and 'edges to be trimmed and ditches to be cleared out around these parts was on 'e's place. You should 'uv sin 'e's face. Why, for a minut I thought 'e was going off like a ginger-beer bottle. I've lived around 'ere for seventy year and seen a few different people come to the Manor, but that be the first one I ever 'ad words with …"

He sat down and received the handshakes of some of his cronies sitting with him. It was a great speech and would no doubt be celebrated in the Quart Pot that evening.

"Anyone else?" cried Miss Slater.

At once a cottage woman jumped up and began to speak, but in such a quiet, nervous voice that Mr. Finchley heard nothing except the phrase "somethin' oughter be done about it."

A few other people rose and voiced their opinions. All of them thought that Sir Simon had done the wrong thing.

"The whole thing," whispered Harbottle to Mr. Finchley, "lacks the militant spirit."

"Very well then," called Miss Slater. "We will do something. We'll go down now and remove that hurdle. We've as much right to pull it down as Sir Simon has to put it up. Come along and the more the merrier!"

She was off and, to Harbottle's evident surprise and Mr. Finchley's joy, the hutful of people went with her. They raised a cheer and poured through the door.

"Come on," cried Mr. Finchley, tugging at Harbottle's arm. "We must follow them." He was excited and felt as though he, too, were one of the villagers and it was his privilege to pass along the path which was being questioned.

They went out of the hall and through the village in quite an orderly crowd. They might almost have been a party of sightseers going to visit the church, all a little exhilarated from a long ride and a picnic lunch on the downs, an excited handful of holidaymakers come from one of the south coast towns for a day in the country.

In front strode Miss Slater, at her side village folk, and behind in a thinning tail the rest of her audience, and bringing up the rear were Mr. Finchley and Harbottle, both a little burdened by the effort of keeping up a quick pace after their lunch at the Quart Pot. Mr. Finchley was finding it to be quite true that some people have not got the right kind of head for cider. To his eyes the crowd was a mob, an inflamed mob, rushing with pitchforks and raised axes upon the barricade which had been thrown across the ancient right-of-way. It was a crusade. He was so much impressed with this thought that he communicated it to Harbottle.

"It's a crusade," he said, laughing, "a crusade against meanness and evil!"

"You're tight," said Harbottle cruelly. "And they won't do anything. You can lead a horse to the water but—gosh, it's hot, isn't it? Anyway, don't try to drag me into this. I'm an impartial witness. Got to be. Professional etiquette."

Mr. Finchley laughed again, the happy, irresponsible laugh of a man who has drunk too much cider on a hot day and now feels the earth spin violently under his feet and sees the landscape as a tantalising blur of blues, greens and yellows. Houses, fields, smooth shoulders of the downs, the white patches of cloud … he saw them all, moving in a distorted dance as though they were mirrored in an uneven film of oil.

"The land belongs to the people," he called. "Liberty!"

"Liberty!" echoed Harbottle faintly and plunged forward, pulling out his notebook and pencil. "My shield and buckler," he explained, waving them in the air. "When I return let it be either with my shield or on it."

"You've drunk too much cider," said Mr. Finchley sternly. He did not approve of tipsiness at such an important moment in the history of the village.

No one in the crowd took any notice of the two trotting and bouncing along behind them. Their minds were full of what lay ahead. By the church they went, across the road, and through a little wicket gate, and on to the footpath that led down to the green hillside. Wild apple trees bordered it on one side and thick brambles reached out to clasp the legs of passers. At the bottom of the field was a gap in a hedge through which the path went. Across the gap, shining whitely in the fierce sun, showed the lines of a new hurdle. It grimaced upwards like a set of teeth at the villagers. The sight made their hearts beat fast with a queer trepidation.

"The ivory gates of Babylon!" shouted Harbottle, giving way to an esoteric emotion, and he was rewarded with a cold glance from Miss Slater, who had marked him down as a reporter and as usual, such was her opinion of reporters, an inebriated one.

"Now is the time for all good men to come to the aid of the party!" cried Mr. Finchley, and he waved his cap in the air and followed behind the mob. He felt young and carefree, and full of a wide irresponsibility.

The party came to a halt at the hurdle and there, on the other side of it, stood Sir Simon Penickle and his bailiff. The bailiff wore breeches, a yellow stock and carried a sporting gun and he looked very red and embarrassed, but Sir Simon was not at all embarrassed. He was a smallish man, dressed in a brown suit, panama hat and cream waistcoat, and his face was pale like old paper, an unhealthy colour. He stood looking at the little crowd and sucking at his teeth with quick clicking sounds that twisted his face into tiny grimaces that seemed to express a derisive scorn for this exhibition of mob law. Between mob and bailiff stood the new chestnut hurdle.

"Well," said Sir Simon, "what do you want?"

Miss Slater spoke, and she spoke firmly. "We want that hurdle taken down, Sir Simon. This is a public right-of-way. If you prefer to think that it is not, you have the right to take the matter to court for a decision, but until then you have no authority to block up the path."

At this, Sir Simon smiled. It was a discomforting little smile that revealed a set of perfect false teeth and rather pinky artificial gums.

"I'm sorry you should feel like that, Miss Slater. Very sorry. But I have a perfect right to do what I like on my own property. The hurdle was put up by my orders and it stays up. I don't wish to cause any unpleasantness, but if you are so sure there is good legal authority for a right-of-way here, I suggest that you take the matter to the courts and, in the meantime, refrain from using a path to which you will ultimately find you have no claim."

It was very clear what he was thinking. Almost everyone in the small crowd understood him. He was saying that he stood on the other side of the fence and with him was his bailiff with a gun. Guns often went off in scrimmages. He was telling them that the initiative now lay with them. The next step was to pull the hurdle down.

At the back of the crowd Mr. Finchley and Harbottle looked first at the composed little financier, sucking his teeth and smiling easily, and then at one another.

"You can almost hear the courage and determination running out of these people," whispered Harbottle. "What did I tell you? Degenerate. No leader, no militant spirit! Old Catchpenny's got them where he wants them."

Mr. Finchley was distressed to find that the reporter spoke so true. Even Miss Slater was a little set back. She could talk, she could stir her people, but she could not start them into action because there was no violence in her nature to catch and cherish the proper response from them.

"But you've no right ... no authority," cried Miss Slater, her voice angry but hesitant.

Sir Simon shook his head gently. He seemed to know that he had won and he contemplated his victory with a sad, almost disappointed spirit, as though he could have wished for a harder fight so that his true powers might have been tested.

But Sir Simon had not won. Mr. Finchley almost danced with fury as he witnessed the deflation of the mob's militant fervour. Here were solid English folk meekly giving over their rights to a grasping little financier, to a man who was out of place in the country. The thought made Mr. Finchley angry and want to do something about it. Mr. Finchley had walked a lot that morning, so that his tired body was offering little resistance to the physical onslaught made by his lunch cider. He was full of strong sympathies towards the soil and the rights of the village people, so that he had little room for stable considerations of just conduct. He was, in fact, overcome with a mounting passion of distaste for Sir Simon and all that he stood for and he became the willing vehicle of expression for that passion. His subliminal mind took a hand in the immediate movements of his body.

He bent quickly to the ground and, before anyone observed the movement, had plucked from out of the grass a large and well-balanced sod of turf. It came away easily in his hand, ripe with long, soil-clad roots.

"Forward!" Mr. Finchley cried heroically, pressing upon the people in front of him as he threw the turf.

It drew a graceful parabola through the air, trailing meteor-wise a tail of dirt, and landed with almost mathematical precision and accuracy square in Sir Simon's face, knocking him backwards like a ninepin at the end of a bowling alley.

"Forward, men!" roared another, equally tipsy voice, and another sod circled the bright afternoon air and struck against the bailiff's chest, exploding in a fine spout of dry soil.

The effect of those two blows was magical. They released the spring which controlled the mob.

"Down with the hurdle!" cried Miss Slater, and she pressed forward, her people with her. The crowd cheered and rushed at the hurdle. The bailiff, stubbornly trying to do his duty, set his shoulder against it, but he was pushed aside. The hurdle was swept from its place and borne forward, high in the air, like a battle honour.

Sir Simon, with commendable agility, rolled away from the juggernaut and got to his feet, rubbing his eyes and shouting with incoherent rage. But no one took any notice of him or the bailiff. The crowd surged along the path, laughing and slapping itself on the back, towards another hurdle which stood at the other side of the field. This went down before the splendid onslaught and the path was free. Then the crowd turned and moved back to the first gap, but Sir Simon and his man had taken themselves off. They could be seen climbing the hill towards the Manor House, the bailiff trotting behind like an embarrassed hound.

Miss Slater beamed about her. "That's shown them," she cried. "And now, if he wants to keep up the fight, we're ready for him!"

There was no mistaking the temper of the crowd now. Their blood was up and they would want no more urging. By evening the village would know the news and share their feelings.

They moved back towards the village again in a wild, happy rabble and behind them came Mr. Finchley and Harbottle, slapping one another on the back, laughing and shaking their heads and crying, "Long live the people! Hurrah for us!"

"And it was you," shouted Mr. Finchley, "who threw the other turf."

"Not at all," denied Harbottle indignantly, "I'm an impartial witness, got to be. Hurrah for the people!" As they came through the little wicket gate on to the road Miss Slater stood, watching her flock emerge. Her eye fell on the two and for a moment her face moved to a wide, expansive smile and she nodded to them as though there was a secret understanding between them. Then it slipped back into a quiet look of disapproval for their cider-excited condition. But neither of them minded.

"A turf," expounded Mr. Finchley as he drove away from the village with Harbottle beside him, for he was giving the reporter a lift to the bus stop on the main road, "is a useful projectile. If it strikes the face it fills the mouth with dirt, the eyes with dust, the hair with grass stems and so damps the whole spirit, producing a feeling of complete consternation and dejection. I know because I have both received and thrown turfs."

"You should write a monograph on it," said Harbottle, smiling happily at the blue sky and the fluffy white clouds that chased one another across the bright bowl.

XX
Of a magical duck and a mistaken identity

ROBERT Finchley had run away from school. There were various reasons why he had done this, reasons all perfectly adequate to anyone eleven years old or to anyone who remembers what it was like to be eleven years old. To purely adult minds the reasons might not have sounded very convincing.

There was first of all his father's letter to him. It had enclosed a five-shilling postal order and a carefully worded approach to the question of his joining him at the end of term. As the end of term was only a few days off, Robert felt that the wording was too cautious. Parents seemed incapable of answering yes or no. They always had to think it over. Anyhow the money had secured Dini, the calculating duck, to him, and the funds of the Caravan Club were still intact.

Then there was the letter from Rawlinson's father saying that he was taking his son caravanning that summer down to Cornwall. Of course, it was only a motor-trailer, but as Rawlinson had been, at first, an unwilling member of the club it would never do—if anything should happen to prevent him from joining his father and Churchwarden— to let Rawlinson come back after the holidays and brag about his caravan experiences. Rawlinson was an unpleasant little beast even when he had nothing to brag about. He would be insufferable if he found out he was the only one to have lived in a caravan. Some of the other members of the club felt this and Robert had been asked anxiously whether he was joining his father and had replied, with complete conviction, that he was. That had been burning his boats, or at least piling the brushwood about them as they lay on the beach. The actual brand to start the fire had been handed to him by Sohard, the pantry boy.

Sohard was eighteen and no good as a pantry boy: He was also a little weak in the head and his place was any-where but in a preparatory school where he was known to the boys as Sodumb Bicarb, Nohead and many other names not very funny but which struck Robert and his friends as being uproariously amusing. However, in the mysterious way of small boys, Sohard was well-liked and even respected for some things. He had one claim to es-teem and that was his ability as a cricketer. Although he was not, nor ever would be, a batsman, Sohard was the shin-ing star of his village cricket team. He bowled left-handed googlies and other pernicious bedevilments and was loud-ly acclaimed whenever he took the ball. It was Sohard who had travelled on the back of a friend's motor-cycle that Saturday afternoon to a small village near Ashford to play cricket. He arrived back late, to the butler's annoyance, at eight o'clock and he had a conversation with Robert at nine o'clock.

It was that conversation which set the boats burning and brought out the Napoleon touch in Robert. Robert did not look a bit like Napoleon. He was a small boy, rather thin in the face, but with a healthy, brown complexion, rather dirty fingernails and a nose that flipped up at the end in a gesture of charming surprise and camaraderie. His hair was dark and curly enough to avoid the frequent combings demanded by less fortunate heads.

"I see this caravan," said Sohard, who, because he was supposed to have gipsy blood in his veins, had been made a member of the club at a reduced fee, "just t'other side of High Halden. Yellow and green and red and the horse an' all—just like you've described. I didn't see anyone about it because we were speeding by, but there wasn't no mistake. It was your father's caravan all right. If the last time you heard from him he was at Canterbury, then he could have got there easily by now."

"How could I find it—supposin' I wanted to?"

"Easy. Go from here to High Halden—you know that road. When you get through High Halden you look out for the first field on the left what 'as a pond with bulrushes in it. It's the next field after that, under a big tree. But you wouldn't be going to see your father? I only told you because I thought he might be coming here to give that talk you was mentioning the other day. It's time the club did something for my money. I haven't got no money to waste."

"I hope you're not criticising the club, Sodumb? After all the other members paid full subscriptions, you only paid half, and they're not grumbling."

A ringing bell called Sohard away before he could answer this and it left Robert thinking. He went to bed thinking and at eight o'clock the next morning he was on the road to High Halden.

Running away from school had been easy. He just rose at six and walked out, taking Dini in her wicker cage, and rode off on his bicycle. He wore his black-and-yellow school blazer, lost his cap going down a long hill and was deterred from trudging back to look for it in the hedge because his brakes did not pull him up until he was a good half-mile beyond the spot where it had been blown off.

He had no qualms about leaving the school. He knew he would not be missed until chapel and by then he would be a good ten miles away. He was happy because he would see his father and maybe manage to persuade him to let him stay with him. After all, the term was nearly over and it was hardly worthwhile bothering about a few days. It never occurred to him that High Halden was thirty miles from the school, and that the caravan might have moved off in any direction long before he reached the field with the large tree.

Occasionally, Dini squawked as the bicycle rode over a bump in the road and for a time, because she might be feeling upset, Robert sang to her. He tried her with "Rock of Ages," "Jerusalem the Golden," "Little Old Lady" and "I'll be Comin' Round the Mountain." But although it was Sunday, Dini did not care for hymns and the most success came with the last song, words for which Robert had none but a monotonous repetition of the title, but this seemed to soothe Dini and she weathered a particularly shaking bump without murmuring while he sang.

For lunch he had two packets of potato crisps bought at a little shop he found open in a village he passed, and then, when he resumed his journey after lunch, he had a puncture in the back wheel. He had no outfit with him and he rode the bicycle on its rim, Dini squawking desperately all the way, to the next village, where he found a garage and a sleeping mechanic who slowly set about mending it for him. The crisps and the mending of the puncture cost him one shilling of the eighteen pence he had set out with, and by the time the puncture was mended he had only twopence left because there was a sweet shop open next door to the garage and he had to do something to while away the time.

"What," said the mechanic as he came back for the bicycle, "you doing with that duck?" He cast a drowsy eye at Dini in her cage.

"It's a pet," explained Robert. "She's not an ordinary duck. She's a calculating duck."

"Yes, does she lay golden eggs as well?"

Robert was offended. He proceeded to vindicate Dini by giving an exhibition. "It's one quack for no and two for yes," he said. "Now watch." He addressed himself to the duck:

"Dini, do five and four make ten?"

Dini raised a yellow bill, ruffled her tail feathers and quacked once protestingly.

"Dini, do five and four make nine?"

Dini, perhaps annoyed at the repetition of her name, scratched at the nape of her neck with a webbed claw and quacked twice.

"See!" Robert straightened up triumphantly. He was met with a wondering look on the face of the mechanic. It was all the applause he wanted. This was Dini's first venture in the world and she had come out with flying colours. At school she had proved a variable performer, but apparently the wider horizons of the world stirred her to her best.

Robert rode on and the afternoon drew in to that warm, hushed close which is peculiar to Sunday afternoons in summer, an afternoon when the wind stirred lazily for a moment like a giant moving restlessly in a warm bed. In the cottage gardens the borders of catmint and lavender poured out a rich fragrance on the hot air and tall lines of mallow and hollyhocks turned pretty enquiring faces towards the road. There were all sorts of things to delay Robert. First of all a fisherman on a stream bank, whom he plagued with a lengthy stare and then a conversation on the eating merits of tench and barbel. Then he came across a red sports car overturned in a ditch and a speculating crowd watching a breakdown van trying to haul it out. Robert joined the crowd, learned that no one had been hurt and spent a delightful half-hour discussing accidents with an old man who spat between every other sentence.

He spent his last twopence on an ice-cream for tea and, thinking that Dini might be hungry, he found a pond off the roadside and took her to it. Here, he tied a long length of cord to her leg and set her free to forage on the waters while he held the string. Dini, used to similar treatment on the pond at the bottom of the school cricket ground, quacked and shovelled her bill in the rich mud and made a good meal, disregarding Robert's frequent advice to try other and more promising parts of the pond.

Robert deliberately let himself be drawn aside by all the attractions the road had to offer. He knew that if he reached his father early in the afternoon, there would be time to put him on a bus and send him back to school. If he timed his arrival for the evening, there would be no bus and he would—whatever else happened—have at least one evening to his credit in the caravan.

When Dini had supped he drew her ashore and pushed her, quacking hard, into her cage.

High Halden drew nearer, and with every mile that dropped from the signposts Robert's legs moved more slowly round the pedals, and he began to frame his opening speech to his father. It was going to be difficult.

The evening dropped in a faint blue mantle over the fields, and the swallows which had been hawking high all day came down and skimmed the meadows, shaking the pollen from the moon daisies with the passage of their wings. A clump of dark trees framed against the egg-grey sky heralded High Halden and Robert cycled through the village, conscious that his heart was beginning to bump unpleasantly, as it often did before the door of the headmaster's study.

He was past the village and searching diligently to the left for the pond with the bulrushes. He found it, a reedy, wide pond tucked away under the lee of the hedge and studded along its brink with tall mace reeds, great grenadiers of stiff bearing. The field was large and its companion field hidden by a hedge grown tall with a wind break of slender ash trees. Robert cycled down the slight slope towards the far hedge. Over the top of the hedge he could see the spreading crown of a massive oak tree. Under that oak tree when he had gone another hundred yards would be—.

His heart leaped as the field came into view and there, snuggled close to the base of the tree, was a caravan, its coloured shape dulled by the slight mist which came up from the meadow. Close by a tethered horse grazed complacently. Robert had no doubt that it was Churchwarden. He cycled furiously down the last few yards of the slope to the field gate. Excited at the prospect of seeing his father and entering the caravan, he dropped his bicycle into the hedge at the roadside and climbed over the gate. He scarcely noticed a black saloon car which was also drawn up by the gateway.

Robert raced across the soft turf towards the caravan. He had forgotten all about his opening speech of explanation to his father. All he wanted to do was to burst through the doorway on to him.

When Robert was only a few yards from the caravan a surprising thing happened. The rear door suddenly flew open and through it came a succession of objects. Robert pulled up with a jerk as a voice cried, in high protest: "Stop it, you're hurting me!"

From inside the caravan came a loud laugh, the laugh of a tormentor, and through the door came another string of cushions, rugs, books and clothes, and the voice of the laugh said: "I know it's here and I'm going to find it if I have to pull the whole place to pieces. You might as well tell us where it is! Twist his ear, Duffy, that'll make him find his memory!"

A loud wail of pain followed this, and Robert, standing trembling alongside the caravan, knew that Duffy had twisted the ear. His father's ear!

From inside the van came a bumping and rattling and the angry expostulations of men. Outside Robert stood, halted by fear. It was obvious to him what had happened. Thieves had set upon his father and were searching for his money, and his father, suffering torture rather than tell them, was helpless to protect himself. For a moment an heroic vision of himself leaping in to his father's rescue filled Robert's mind, but almost at once he discarded the colourful project. He was no match for two, possibly armed, desperadoes. There might even be more than two, a third, silent, with one eye filmed over and his mouth a thin switch of hate ... Robert abandoned his thriller reminiscences as someone thudded on the caravan floor and a voice said: "Get outside, Duffy, and have a look in the locker under the driving seat, and keep your eyes peeled for busybodies. And you keep your mouth shut, mister, or I'll have to quiet you in a way your doctor wouldn't approve of!"

At this Robert fled. These men were dangerous and his father needed help. He panted back to the gate, flung himself over and grabbed his bicycle. He was pedalling away down the slope as he saw the dim figure of a man come out of the caravan. In the fading evening light that figure, glimpsed as he fleeted away down the road, had a looming, evil suggestiveness which coiled tendrils of delicious fear around Robert's heart. It was just like the feeling he had in the last chapters of *The Talking Corpse Takes a Bow* that Anstey had brought back from the last hols. after finding it folded inside his father's, the bishop's, copy of the Greek Testament. The holiday before that he had brought back *Bloodstains on Velvet*, which he had found inside a copy of Warburton's *The Divine Legation of Moses*. Anstey said that his father probably read them to give himself a truer insight into the criminal mind so that it would help him in his Christian mission.

In his excitement and confusion Robert was quite unaware that he was pedalling away from High Halden. But when he was a safe distance from the caravan he began to shout: "Help! Help! Thieves!" and Dini, roused to anger at the violent motion and the awful noise, began to quack as quickly and as bad-temperedly as a swinging wicker cage would allow.

"Help! Murder! Thieves! Robbers! Fire! Police!"

Robert added to the list of offences in order to heighten the effect of his wild tocsin, and so great was his excitement that he swept past two cyclists, who might have given help, without seeing them. They stared after him, smiled and went on.

Along the road raced Robert, down a small dip towards a stone bridge over a little stream. Beyond the bridge was a quick turn, and on that turn Robert's war-alarm, his rousing call, came to an end. As he bumped over the little hump of the bridge a grey shape, two tiny lights winking on either side of it, loomed up before him. He swerved aside, and his front wheel found a patch of loose road gravel and he went over, spilling neatly from the bicycle into the soft lap of a turfy bank.

He rolled over, and before he could sit up, felt a strong hand on the collar of his blazer. He was jerked to his feet as an angry voice said:

"You fool of a boy! Haven't you any more sense than to come round a corner like that! You'll be killed if you don't mend your ways. Are you hurt?" The question was asked without anger and with a certain anxiety.

Robert looked up and stared, unable to believe his eyes. He knew that voice, he knew that face. And through the blue light the face looked down at him and stared, filled with the same wonderment.

"Robert!"

"Dad!"

On the roadway, waiting obediently between the shafts of the caravan, Churchwarden swung a long head round and viewed this crepuscular meeting with a solemn gentility of feeling.

"But what on earth are you doing here, Robert?"

"I've just come from—" Robert for a moment felt himself unequal to the problem. "You were up the road. I was coming for help. They were twisting your ear and I had to get someone—"

"Wait, wait," cried Mr. Finchley. "What is this all about, Robert?"

"There was a caravan up the road. And they were doing the most horrible things to the man in it. I thought it was you, so I came away to get help. Oh, dad, if it wasn't you it must be someone else, and they were twisting his ear and doing the most dreadful torture. Oh, sir, we must go back and help him. Quickly, we may be in time!"

Robert leaped towards his bicycle and righted it, quieting Dini, who had been loudly protesting.

Mr. Finchley could see that Robert was excited and, although he by no means understood him, he saw that something was wrong.

"Robert—"

It was too late. Robert was already cycling back along the road, shouting, "This way, dad!"

Mr. Finchley could do nothing but follow. He got up into the driving seat and shook the reins. Churchwarden, scenting adventure, broke into a gentle trot which he maintained for a hundred yards and then dropped back, good sense getting the better of his enthusiasm, into a smart walk. Ahead, Robert wobbled and called from his bicycle.

In ten minutes they were at the entrance to the field. Mr. Finchley got down. There was a caravan under an oak tree in the field.

"Their car's gone!" exclaimed Robert. "This way." He climbed over the gate and ran across to the caravan and, after him, went Mr. Finchley.

Robert stopped at the door of the caravan until his father caught him up. "In there," he said.

Mr. Finchley climbed the steps to the door and entered.

Inside—for he had recognised the caravan as he crossed the field—he was not surprised to see Horace Blain, but he was very much surprised to see what had happened to Horace Blain and to his caravan. The interior was in an awful confusion. Drawers had been jerked open and their contents spilled, curtains and rugs had been ripped away and, in three places, at the back of the berth, on the ceiling and behind the lounge seat, the panelling of thin plywood had been ripped out. The caravan was in a wreck. In the midst of the confusion, lighted by a tiny, swinging oil-lamp which was turned up too high and gently belching forth a cloud of soot that settled like blight over the waste, sat Horace Blain. His hands and legs were tied with thick cords and a red bandana handkerchief was stretched tightly over his mouth and tied in a large bow at the back of his head.

"What on earth's happened?" cried Mr. Finchley, and he turned the lamp down and began to release Horace. The moment the handkerchief came away from the barber's mouth he was not long in explaining.

"Thank goodness you've come. I was beginning to think I might have to sit here all night and possibly burn or choke to death from that light. An outrage! A positive outrage!

That's what I've been the victim of! Never in all my life have I ever suffered physical violence from any man until tonight. He tweaked my ear as though I were a schoolboy and then - but …" He spluttered into incoherence for a moment as his eyes went round the caravan.

"Sit down and explain things calmly," ordered Mr. Finchley.

"Did they kick you in the stomach, sir, and then hit you across your face with the butt of a gat? That's what gangsters always do?" enquired Robert eagerly.

"Gat? What's that boy doing here?" snorted Horace. "Go away, boy. Go away!"

"He's my son," explained Mr. Finchley. "Tell me what happened."

"I don't know, really I don't know. I once had an assistant who robbed my till. But the police got him easily with a marked half-crown. That's all the experience I've had of criminals until tonight. A ferocious type they were. What I've been through, Finchley! I wouldn't ask it for any man, not even my worst enemy."

"Yes, yes, I know. But tell us what happened."

"That's what I'm trying to do, but you keep interrupting."

"Perhaps he's suffering from shock, dad? You often do after such experiences. In *Bloodstains on Velvet* the millionaire—"

"I'm not suffering from shock. If that's your son, Finchley, I wish—"

"Robert!" Mr. Finchley turned to his son and spoke the word with an emphasis which carried a rich meaning. Robert was silent, but his dark eyes never left Horace Blain's face. It was not often that a boy of his age came into such naked contact with life in the raw, and he did not mean to jeopardise his chance of knowing all.

"Well, as I've been trying to say, I was here about an hour ago, just thinking of getting some supper. I'd lit the lamp and was trying to make up my mind between a few slices of cold bacon and a salad or a tin of salmon and tomatoes when in they walked. Just like that." He snapped his fingers. "As cool as you please. Just came into the caravan and sat down. Two of them. One a tall, dark fellow— got just a touch of wave in his hair, artificial, or I'm not a barber, and the other a square, ugly sort of man. The blue-chinned type that never gets properly shaved. Not even a good barber can do anything for them. Well, they came in and sat down and they told me to sit quiet and behave myself. Of course, I did nothing of the sort. I wasn't going to be ordered about in my own caravan. But that didn't worry them. The ugly one just pushed me down and the other began to search the caravan. I couldn't understand it at all. He fiddled about with the roof and then with the lockers, and kept on asking me where it was. It was like a nightmare, you know how you live in a dream where things go on and you haven't the faintest idea what it's all about and yet at the back of your mind you feel you ought to know. Anyway, I said if they'd tell me their business perhaps I could help them. I wanted to get rid of them. But they laughed, and said as if I didn't know. But after a bit they began to get angry and the tall one told the other—he called him Duffy—"

"Yes, that's the name I heard," cried Robert, unable to hold himself back from the interruption. "And I saw him, too, come out of the caravan. Golly, he was as big as a barn-door and looked terrible. Just like Mick the Masher in *The Talking Corpse Takes a Bow*. Gosh, Anstey would like to know about this. He's got a theory about criminals and he's measuring the head of every boy in the school so that he can tell which will be a crook when they leave. Did you notice Duffy's head much, sir?"

Robert found himself looking at Mr. Blain and his father, and they were regarding him with cold stares.

"What does he know about this?" asked Horace suspiciously.

"He came along while the men were here and heard them. He thought this was my caravan and he was riding off for the police when he met me."

"Oh," the note was a shade warmer. "Well, Duffy did the strong-arm stuff on me. I didn't know what that meant at first. But I do now. I must be a mass of bruises. But how could I tell them where what it was they wanted was if I didn't know what it was they wanted? They began to tear the place to pieces. Just look at it!" wailed Horace.

"We'll soon tidy up," Mr. Finchley soothed him, "and that plywood can be easily replaced."

"Then when I thought they'd pull the caravan apart a funny thing happened. The tall man came across to me and gave me a most villainous stare. It sent a cold shiver all through me and he said, 'Now come on, Mr. Finchley, you'd better give us a little co-operation or I'll fix you up so that the morgue won't take you on account of your not being a complete corpse!' He called me by your name!"

"Good Lord!" Mr. Finchley was at once disturbed. Whoever these men were they had mistaken Blain's caravan for his.

Horace smiled, a weak but brave smile. "Don't worry, Finchley. I fooled them completely. I must have shown my surprise, because they could see that something was wrong. And then I did a very clever thing. Maybe I'm only a barber but there's a streak of heroism in me. Barbers have never really been given all the credit they should get. I said, 'But I'm not Mr. Finchley, Blain's my name. But I know Mr. Finchley.' They jumped on that and Duffy said I was to come across at once or he'd land me a sock that would raise a dust in Paradise as I made my landing. So I told them I was a retired man and that, a few days ago, you'd camped on my ground and that you'd grown tired of caravanning and wanted to sell the outfit, so I bought it because I liked the idea of going around the country. You should have seen their faces. They were full of questions. You see, I knew that if I told them that they'd made a mistake in the caravans, they might begin to search for you, thinking that you had whatever it was they wanted. Do you know what it is, by the way?"

"I haven't the faintest idea, but I'm beginning to think that these gentlemen have been interested in me for some time. But go on."

"Maybe it's something to do with Tong warfare, like in *Bloodstains on Velvet*, and there's a clue in one of the cara—" Robert subsided like a pricked balloon at a scowl from Horace.

"They asked me if you seemed anxious to sell. So I said yes you did and you'd asked a very small price. And then they wanted to know if I knew where you'd gone, and if you seemed in a hurry to go there. So I said you'd been saying that you were tired of caravanning and thought of going abroad, and you seemed in a hurry to go. I'm afraid I said a few other things about you, but they seemed to expect them. That you looked nervous at times. They asked that, and that you didn't like anyone poking around your caravan and that you seemed to have something on your mind. You haven't, have you?"

"No, of course not."

"I thought not, but it seemed to satisfy them, and then the man Duffy took a good look at me and turned to the other man and said that he was pretty sure I wasn't the man, only he hadn't bothered to look closely before because it didn't seem necessary. So at that, the other—they really were a pair of brutes—gave him a good hard kick, so that he shot out of the door on to the grass with my cushions, and said it was a pity he hadn't thought of that and how hard it was for a smart man to get anywhere when he was cluttered up with eggs like him. But I must say, he was polite enough to me after that. He tied me up like this and left me saying he was sorry to have caused me so much trouble and hoped I would forget the annoying little incident. It had all been a mistake. And then you came along and found me. I was hoping that you could tell me what it's all about?"

But Mr. Finchley could not tell him because he did not know. The only thing he could do was to help Horace tidy up his caravan and to thank him for protecting his own caravan from such a visitation by lying nobly. At heart he was a little nervous at the thought that Duffy—he was undoubtedly the man who had thrown a turf at him—and his companion might come to visit him. But Horace's story seemed to have satisfied them and they were probably gone off to hunt for him abroad.

While Horace and Robert finished making the caravan shipshape, Mr. Finchley went back to the roadway and drove his caravan into the field. He had been late on the road, looking for a suitable place to draw up, when Robert had met him.

"I didn't know," said Horace, when Mr. Finchley returned, "that you had your son travelling with you?" Mr. Finchley looked at Robert, and Robert steeled himself for the effort he felt was to come.

"Neither did I," said Mr. Finchley. "I didn't know it until he came pelting into me down the road. Perhaps Robert can explain?"

"Oh, sir, don't you think we ought to get the caravan tidy first and make everything ready for the night?"

"This caravan is tidy enough," said Horace. "How did you get here, Robert?"

Robert told them about Sohard seeing the caravan in the field and how, being Sunday, he thought he would cycle over and see his father and bring Dini.

"Dini?" questioned Horace.

"Yes, sir—she's a magical calculating duck. Would you like to see her perform? I'll go and get her—"

"No, you won't, Robert," put in Mr. Finchley. "Did you have permission from the school to come over?"

"Well, sir …"

"I see you did not."

"But if I hadn't come, dad—think what might have happened to Mr. Blain. It's just like the detective in *Bloodstains on Velvet*. He had an impulse to go to the Crystal Palace to see the firework display. He didn't like fireworks, but he felt he wanted to go and when he got there he quite by chance saw Hi-fu Wang—"

"Hi-fu Wang?" Horace's brows crinkled in a puzzled frown.

"He was leader of the Red Box Tong and the firework display was a kind of code message to all the Tong members in London—"

"You must go back to school!" said Mr. Finchley abruptly.

"But, dad!"

It was then that Horace Blain earned Robert's undying friendship. Horace was a barber and a great student of human nature. He had, in his less prosperous days, clipped many youthful heads on Saturday mornings at threepence a time and he still enjoyed a fourpenny blood. Robert's tortuous plans were open to him.

"He can't go back tonight, Finchley. It's too far. The boy couldn't cycle through the dark and there's no bus. He'll have to sleep here. You can telephone the headmaster in the morning."

Mr. Finchley grunted and then gave in. Actually, he was quite glad to see Robert, but he knew that it was fatal to encourage the boy. Back to school he went in the morning.

Ten minutes later, Robert was examining his father's caravan, talking away and bubbling over with excitement. His pleasure soon eased Mr. Finchley of his parental strictness and, later, they all three sat down to a late supper.

When Mr. Finchley turned in that night, Robert had the opposite bunk and was soon asleep, his steady breathing sighing happily through the darkness. But Mr. Finchley did not sleep for some time. He was thinking of the two men who had visited Horace. He was sure they had something to do with the man who had called upon the caravan when he was near Faversham, with the man who had tried to break in when he had been sailing and perhaps with the client of the eccentric Oliver Watt Anselm. Why so much interest should be taken in him or his caravan he could not imagine. In the morning, he decided, he would examine the caravan carefully. Perhaps it did - a suggestion of Robert's flew across his tired mind - contain a clue to something or conceal hidden treasure. He dropped off to sleep to dream of Mick the Masher and a bevy of yellow-faced, pig-tailed Duffys who went about stuffing enormous turfs down their victims' throats until they choked to death, while from a safe eminence in the background of fantasy an amorphous, sinister figure, now with the face of Sir Simon Penickle and now with the robust visage of Tom Marshall, looked on and chuckled evilly.

XXI
How Mr. Finchley ships a new hand

IT RAINED during the night and it was raining hard in the morning. Robert lay in his bunk and thought how much better bunks were for sleeping in than beds. He lay and listened to the sound of the water chuckling along the roof gutter and splashing with a flat, angry sound on to the grass, and then he thought of going back to school and his face clouded.

"I should think, dad," he suggested as Mr. Finchley busied himself with breakfast, "that you would feel nervous about those two men. They might come back, mightn't they? It would be better for you if you had someone with you."

Mr. Finchley flipped an egg over adroitly and said, "They won't come back. Mr. Blain sent them off."

"Oh!" Robert said no more for the time, but later, when they were having breakfast and Mr. Blain joined them, scurrying across through the rain, he said, "I wonder what it was they were looking for? Those two men, I mean? What do you think, sir?" Robert looked at Horace.

"I haven't the faintest idea," confessed Horace. "But they were looking for something all right."

"I wonder," mused Mr. Finchley, "whether I ought to go to the police—"

"Oh, don't do that." Horace jumped up in alarm. "You'd have to tell them about me and it might get into the papers, and then my wife would come along. Lumme, Mr. Finchley, you can't go to the police. Those men aren't going to come back. And anyway," he calmed down a bit as a more reasonable argument presented itself, "what could you tell the police? That you thought two men might come and search in your caravan for you didn't know what?"

"Why don't we search the caravan ourselves?" suggested Robert, and added brightly, "Of course, we might not find whatever it was right away. But I'm quite sure that if I was given a couple of days to examine the caravan I could find it—if it was anything. Like Operator 7 in the *Talking Corpse Takes a Bow*. It took him four visits to the mortuary before he really spotted the clue he guessed must be there, and what do you think it—"

"We'll search, but it won't take two days. We can do it in half an hour," said Mr. Finchley bluntly. "And then I'll go into the village and ring up your headmaster."

They did search. They shook out all the cushions and books, flapped all the curtains and turned all the saucepans and crockery upside down. The only unexpected thing they found was a tiny lizard which had taken up its quarters behind the paraffin tins and which escaped into the rain, much to Robert's sorrow. They tapped all the walls and roof for the sound of a secret cavity, but as everything they tapped gave forth a hollow ring and none of the carved projections of the woodwork released any secret drawer they decided to refrain from tearing the caravan to pieces in the hope of discovering some hidden recess which contained clue, treasure or whatever it was the men might want.

"There's nothing here," said Mr. Finchley at last. "I can't understand it. Whatever could they have been after?"

"Perhaps there isn't anything. Perhaps they only thought there was something but they weren't sure," suggested Horace. "Anyway, I don't think they'll trouble either of us again. They're catching the boat-train now—going after you." He chuckled as he thought of the way he had fooled them.

An hour later Mr. Finchley, wrapped tightly in a rain-coat, was on the driving seat of the caravan, directing Churchwarden towards High Halden. Behind, looking out over the half-door, was Robert, watching the wet road tail away. His bicycle was tied to the back of the caravan and Dini squawked occasionally from the cage at his feet. Horace Blain was not with them. He was going to wait for the rain to stop before he moved and then he was to set up his barber's saloon near the village. He had not completely recovered from his adventure and he felt that the soothing snip of scissors and the rasp of a keen razor would restore his nerve and old spirits.

As Mr. Finchley drove he was thinking about Robert. Although his meeting with his son had been overshadowed by Mr. Blain's affair, he had been glad to see the boy. Before he had adopted him, Robert had lived in France and he had never seen England. He had come to England full of quaint gallicisms, but a few terms at a preparatory school had driven all those traits from him. Now he was—

except in moments of extreme excitement—as English as any of the other boys.

It was pleasing to think that he had run away from school for the purpose of coming to see him, and, he had no doubt of it, Robert had hoped that he would be allowed to stay. It was a pity, of course, that he could not stay. Mr. Finchley would have liked him. After all there were only a few more days to the end of term so what did it matter? But it did matter. He could hear his wife scolding him for encouraging Robert in his transgression, and then there were the school authorities. Lord knew what they might not already be up to because of the boy's disappearance, and for them there was the important matter of discipline. The end of term was the end of term and not five days before the end of term, and Mr. Finchley knew his duty. So he gave Robert no encouragement, spoke a little sternly to him and asked the first native he met for a direction to the village post office.

Mr. Finchley pulled up outside the little shop, called to Robert to come and take the reins through the front half-door of the caravan, and then got down. Robert watched his father cross the road and enter the shop. In a few minutes he would be talking to his headmaster and his fate would be sealed. Back to school and a certain amount of unpleasantness, which would not altogether be offset by the admiration he would reap from Anstey and company from having slept in the caravan. Robert stared at the wet flanks of Churchwarden and hoped for a miracle. It was the only thing he could do.

The rain slanted down into the village, the gutters foamed with a brown spate and the colours on an advertisement bill outside the shop dribbled into one another.

It was not a good day for miracles. If Robert had been a professional thief he could have invoked Mercury's sympathetic aid, had he been a soldier facing the dawn of a day of battle he could have called upon Mars, but he was only a schoolboy and the gods have no time for schoolboys.

Mr. Finchley was a long time. Robert could not think why he was so long. It seemed ages that he waited, holding the thick reins and watching the door of the post office. Behind him Dini quacked once or twice in a doleful way as though she resented this imprisonment on such a fine duck's day and Robert, feeling the shadow of his own particular prison closing about him, felt a great sympathy for her.

Ping! The shop bell rang clearly and Mr. Finchley came out. He paused for a moment on the doorstep, turning up his collar against the rain, and then darted across the road.

Robert watched him climb into the driving seat and he handed him the reins. He dared not say anything, but waited for his father to speak. But his father did not speak and the suspense was too much for Robert.

"Did you speak to the Head, dad?"

Mr. Finchley shook the reins and stirred Churchwarden into a walk.

"Yes, Robert," came the answer. "He was very annoyed at your behaviour."

"Yes, sir. And are you driving me back to school?"

"No, Robert, I am not." Mr. Finchley turned and looked up into the face of his son. The dark hair was damp with the driving rain and the small brown face was clouded with an appealing look of anxiety. Mr. Finchley suddenly grinned and reached up a hand. He caught Robert by the hair and pulled his head gently.

"You're a rogue, Robert, and what is more you're a lucky rogue. You can't go back to school. Yesterday evening ten of the boys went down with measles or mumps or something infectious and the poor Head was worried so much that he scarcely knew he was talking to me. He says that as you're away from the school and apparently in good health you'd better stay away since there are only five more days to go to the end of term. You don't feel ill, at all, do you?" he questioned sharply.

But Robert did not answer. Instead he let out a shrill shriek of delight and began to turn somersaults in quick succession on his bunk until he fell off and bumped his elbow against the floor.

"I'm to stay!" he cried at last. "Oh, dad, won't it be fun! Golly, what will the other chaps say now when I go back—"

Mr. Finchley chuckled at his son's excitement, and then sobered it a little by saying, "I should add that the Head has said that he means to have a little talk with you when you return next term."

But that could not dampen Robert. Next term was far away. There was the rainy, splendid present to think about. The miracle had happened.

He came back to the door, his face solemn with a serious determination. "You are the captain of the caravan, dad, and I am under your orders. You must give me duties to do and I will do them. I shall cook, I shall feed Churchwarden and at night I shall sleep in a bunk. Oh, sir, it is nice sleeping in a bunk, isn't it? And I shall keep a diary—then next term I shall read it to the Caravan Club. Oh, dad, can we stop at the next village so that I may buy a pencil and a book for my diary?" It was the first of Robert's demands, but it was far from being the last.

They had their lunch that day just outside the little town of Tenterden and, after they had eaten, drove into the town and made several purchases for Robert's benefit, pyjamas, washing gear and a raincoat, which were immediate necessities, and then they left the town, going south towards the coast, for there was a house along the road which Mr. Finchley wished to see.

The sun came out in the afternoon and a wispy trail of vapour rose up from the road as the heat beat upon the wet surface. The sky cleared and tall fortresses of cloud pinnacled themselves against the blue. They went over the house together and agreed that they did not like it. It was a tall, ugly house, Victorian in shape with wide, sash-framed windows and cold rooms. The only thing of interest about it was the large cellar which the last owner had left full of a jumble of rubbish. Robert had to be torn away from this treasure-house and left bearing a large chocolate-box with a picture of a brigantine in full sail on the cover. The box, he declared, was just the thing for keeping his diary in. The diary book had been purchased in Tenterden and already it bore across its first page the title

LOG BOOK OF THE CRUISE OF THE YELLOW CARAVAN

Master .	.	Dad.
1st Mate	.	Myself.
1st Hand	.	Dini, calculating duck.
Horse .	.	Churchwarden.
Course .	.	Out of London under sealed orders with general cargo.

"I think you have to treat it like a ship, don't you, dad?" Robert enquired seriously.

"Of course—after all, it's a kind of landship."

"That's what I think. It's a pity we haven't a compass, isn't it, sir? Don't you think that the next place we come to we might buy a compass?"

"No, I don't, Robert. There are several perfectly good maps on the shelf behind you."

"But we might get off our course one night and then a compass—"

"Would be no earthly good. There are always signposts, and, anyway, we don't travel at night."

"But we could travel at night, if we had a compass, dad."

"We do not want a compass!" said Mr. Finchley firmly, and Robert knew that they were not going to have a compass—though he still was not convinced of its uselessness.

That night, when Robert was asleep, Mr. Finchley came into the sleeping compartment from writing letters and he looked down at the quiet face. Even in repose it had an eager look and the soft lips, half-parted, seemed framed about a question. What a bundle of energies, questions and surprises a boy was, thought Mr. Finchley, and he pulled the blanket closer about Robert's shoulder with a gentle movement.

XXII
Of realism and romance

FOR the next two days the canary-coloured caravan headed south and her progress was faithfully recorded by Robert in his log. They finally reached the sea, not because Mr. Finchley wanted to reach it or because there was a house near the coast he wished to view, but simply because Robert, when they were five miles off the coast, conceived the idea that it would be unthinkable to come so near salt water and not actually see it. The result was that they spent a day on a crowded, sandy beach at a bungalow-infested resort which was untidy, crowded and hot with that sticky, sandy heat which comes from any aggregation of half-naked bodies, ice-cream carts, mineral water stalls and cheap cafés.

But Robert enjoyed himself and that was enough for Mr. Finchley. Dini and Robert went swimming and were watched by a small crowd. Anyone could take a dog in swimming with them and there would have been no comment, but because a boy went in with a duck which, after all, was a much better swimmer than a dog and looked more at home in the water, a crowd collected. Human beings, Mr. Finchley decided, were queer.

From the coast they went inland, moving across the marshland towards the Weald. They took their time and the weather favoured them. They had a succession of warm days and still nights. They camped beside the wide drains, reed-fringed and stirring with moorfowl, and at night a thin slip of a moon lay on her back in the sky and threw a pale, tender light over the wide fields and the grey sheep which cropped the rich grass. When Robert was asleep of an evening, Mr. Finchley would sit on the back step of the caravan with his pipe, eyeing the peaceful country and thinking. He never knew what his thoughts were, for his mind ranged wide in the quiet regions of the night. He just sat and wondered at his own contentment, a contentment that arose from simple things. Occasionally the white, soft-winged shape of an owl would come floating across the fields, a rat would splash heavily in the water and, far away, on the rising hills before him, a car's headlights would send out a long finger of light, probing for a moment, then lost. From the shadows of the tall sorrel clumps a rabbit would come into the moonlight and sit up, its long ears trembling, the dark eyes full of reflected light.

In the daytime they sometimes never moved at all. They forgot about the houses which had to be visited and just stayed in one place, bathing in the wide streams and wandering over the fields collecting flowers and trying to identify the birds they saw. A fragile runner of water pimpernel or the quick flight of sedge warbler gave them all the pleasure for which many men and women hope but never find in expensive amusements. And Mr. Finchley was glad Robert was with him. He began to appreciate that new interests are best shared with someone. Caravanning with Robert was quite a different affair from travelling alone.

But they had to leave the marshes. There were other houses to be seen and, lying awake one night, Mr. Finchley was suddenly seized with the fear that unless he began to take his mission more seriously he never would find a house. Caravanning was all right in the summer, but winter was coming and by that time he wanted at least the prospect of inhabiting a country house. A London winter had no joys for him. He ran over in his mind the houses he had seen. There were about four which might be worth taking his wife to see, but he could not feel that any of them was the house. Perhaps, somewhere ahead … He went to sleep with that hope spreading through his imagination. Always, a little farther ahead there was something better. Just around the corner it waited, the house of his dreams; around the corner, that wide, curving corner which takes so much rounding and beyond which lie so many good things, a store of bright visions.

It was a fine windy morning when they came up off the marshes. Great pads of white cloud streamed across the sky, twisting and fretting into a hundred shapes within the minute. Little scuds of white detached themselves from the main clouds and, like frisky lambs, gambolled away into the blue for a spree, sometimes to be lost for ever. The full-leaved trees curtsied and spread their billowing skirts into the wind and their heads swayed together in a whispering, gossiping crowd so that they seemed to need only a patch on their cheeks and powder over their tall heads to turn them into Regency ladies. The waterways were burnished with ripples and against the royal, boisterous wind handfuls of rooks scattered up and down, and twisted and swung like a bunch of black acrobats.

Churchwarden, who did not like wind, plodded along, and the two Finchleys sat on the driving seat. Robert was reading his father the entries in the log for the previous day.

"In a ship, dad, it's really much easier, because you don't often sight another ship, and then you can put it down. Like 'passed a top-sail schooner well battened down and making heavy weather, holding a southerly course. Hailed her. *Elizabeth Harvey* from Seattle. Two men gone from scurvy, must call at one of the islands for fresh vegetables and water.' But in a caravan you pass so many other vehicles. I couldn't be expected to put them all down, could I?"

"No, I suppose not. But you might put down the more notable ones. That red charabanc we saw, for instance—"

"Oh, but I have done that. I was just coming to it. 'Sighted derelict charabanc. Happy Day Coach out of New Eltham bound for Rye. Ditched fifteen miles north of Rye and crew obviously under influence of strong liquors and singing *Lambeth Walk*.' I suppose, dad, after we've finished with the caravan and you've found a house, we couldn't have a boat and go sailing? Anstey's father has a boat with four bunks at Falmouth. It's got a compass, too. Would you like to hear me box the compass?" Robert, without waiting, went into an unintelligible sing-song which he held in one long sustained breath until his face was almost purple.

"You'll burst yourself," chuckled Mr. Finchley. "Then you'll have to enter, 'First Mate a total loss owing to bursting himself while boxing the compass. Committed his body to a duck pond with full naval honours and a salute of three motor horns.' "

Robert, the boxing over, thought this so funny that he was in danger of falling off the seat.

They were well up on to the Weald by lunchtime and they stopped in the lee of a tall thorn-hedge that made a windbreak for a hop garden. To be out of the wind, they sat inside the caravan and ate cheese and pickles. They looked back along the road from whence they had come, watching the wind lick at the tall summer growths and the crabbed skirl of little birds being blown across the road.

"What's that?" Mr. Finchley put his fork down and listened.

"Music," said Robert, swivelling towards the door. From down the road came the sound of music. It had a martial, vaguely challenging air, and the wind brought it to them, now loud, now muted, now wild, now sweet. Gradually it came closer and they recognised the air *Marching Thro' Georgia*. The drums thumped, the cymbals clashed, pipes squealed and a concertina panted and wailed. Suddenly the tune changed and they were having *Alexander's Ragtime Band*. On it came, jaunty, catching, filling the windy day with a merry, abandoned jumble of music. And then, around the far corner, came a man.

He was a little, fat droll of a man with a red, dewlapped face, bright blue eyes and wiry, thin appendages for arms and legs that oddly recalled a spider. He seemed nothing else but arms and legs, a whirling, dancing mass of energy that drew upon the vast stores of the round, settled body. He wore a faded grey suit and a bowler hat.

Mr. Finchley and Robert watched him with amazement as he came up the road, for it was from him alone that all the band music came. It poured, beat and thudded from him in waves as he jerked and twitched in a St. Vitus dance. Around his neck hung a concertina which he squeezed briskly. To each elbow was clipped a drumstick and, as he marched, he swung his elbows and beat the sticks against the skin of a drum which was slung upon his back. In his mouth was a tin whistle, and fastened to the inside of his trouser legs were cymbals which he clashed together when the tune demanded it by giving a pert, frog-like hop. Arms, legs, and elbows going, he came up the road. He seemed to be aware of nothing outside his own frantic, hopping, harmonious microcosm. As he neared the caravan he executed a few fancy steps, slammed the drum, clashed the cymbals, and broke into a popular number *Come Back, My Fair-haired Swede*.

It was a difficult number and the fat fellow fairly hummed and whirred like a dynamo, the perspiration rolled down his plump cheeks, his dewlaps shook, and he skipped, hopped and waggled like a man tormented by a thousand devils.

He was within five yards of the caravan before he noticed it. He looked up, saw the canary yellow and the bright pictures on the back panels, and, instantly, the music died away from him like air seething from a punctured ball. He stopped, took the whistle from his mouth and came over to the open door, crying cheerfully:

"Micky Jonston! Hey! Come out, Micky, and greet an old pal."

The sunlight cast the interior of the caravan in shadow and he could not see Mr. Finchley and Robert.

He came towards the door, bellowing happily, "Micky, you old thief. Come out! Music hath charms, by golly, and so has beer, and you'd better have some in there for me!"

He hoisted himself up the steps with a beat or two on the drums as he worked his arms, and then thrust his red face into the caravan like a seal coming to the surface.

"Micky!" he yelled. His mouth stayed open as he saw Mr. Finchley and Robert. For a second or two they stared at one another. Then the man shook his head and blinked. "You're not Micky," he said, puzzled. He popped his head outside the door, took a look at the pictures on the back panels and popped his head back and said, still puzzled: "But this is Micky's van, ain't it? The pictures on the back. I was here when Micky painted the one with the castle and the cows. I know I was, because if you look closely you'll see that the farthest cow is a bull. That was my idea. No artist like Micky, but a realist I am. Where's Micky?"

Mr. Finchley nodded a pleasant greeting and said: "I don't know this Micky of yours. This is my caravan. I bought it a little while ago in London."

The fat man took some time to assimilate this and, as he stood in thought, he slipped off his instruments and piled them on the grass outside the caravan. Then he sat down on the top step and looked at the two.

"Did you buy it from Micky?"

"I bought it from a Mr. Harricot. He's a publican in London. The previous owner had left it with him for a long time in his stable and he sold it to cover the stable dues. Perhaps that was Micky."

"Maybe, maybe—it would be like Micky. Hard up one moment, rich the next. Well, well! Three years since I saw Micky. Met him in Devon last. Hard up then. Always hard up when he took the old van out. Nice bit of cheese you've got there." He looked at the table.

"Perhaps the gentleman would join us, dad," suggested Robert, who was staring at the man with eyes full of admiration. A new world had swung into his ken.

"Jenks is the name. Jumping Jenks, the one-man band, and I'd be glad to."

Mr. Finchley made room at the table, and Robert got another plate and a knife and fork. Mr. Finchley reached under the bunk and fetched out a bottle of beer.

"Ha," said Jenks, eyeing the bottle with a discerning eye. "Beer. Thirsty work mine." He filled his glass and drank their health.

"Did it take you long, Mr. Jenks, to learn to play all those instruments at the same time?" asked Robert breathlessly.

Mr. Jenks looked up and winked over a mouthful of bread and cheese.

"One week," he exclaimed exultantly, "seven days, one hundred and sixty-eight hours, and you can work it out in minutes for yourself. Adaptability—you've got to have that these days to keep out of the poor-house. Was just working out some new routine. *Come Back, My Fair-haired Swede*—they write some tripe these days, I'll say, and then make the bell ring. Turnip-headed songs for turnip-headed people. But you've got to give 'em modern stuff or they won't flash so much as a shine at you. So you've bought the caravan, eh? Well, well, keep the home fires burning if I know what must have come over Micky to let the old van go. Must have been very hard up. It's his van all right. Couldn't miss it among a million—"

"Who was this Mr. Jonston?" asked Mr. Finchley curiously. He had often wondered about the real owner of the caravan.

"Micky?" Jenks looked across at him, a pickled onion perched on the end of his fork like the dome of a mosque. "Artistic type, Micky. Affable and moody, unprincipled

309

and friendly. Give you his last penny one minute, pinch your sock-suspenders the next. Nice fellow, though, but he was weak, something wrong with the chest. Never knew much about him. Sometimes knocked into him on the road. Never seemed to do anything. Last time I saw him he was painting them panels. Touch of the master about them. Castle might be Warwick if it weren't Windsor. Come to think of it, he was a romantic, all for cows but no time for bulls. When he did the lake on the other panel he had to have a swan on it. I says, clip the old bird's wings, Micky, and send it back to the Serpentine, or else paint in a few floating bus tickets and cigarette packets. Never seen a lake yet without it didn't look like a dustbin." Jenks belched politely and sang, with a wrinkled, comic look at Robert, "Come back, my Pickled Onion," and then with another wink at Mr. Finchley said: "Excuse my vulgarity. Goes 'and in 'and with realism. Can't help meself. What did you think of the show?"

"It was jolly good," cried Robert. "I thought it was a regimental band at least. You must be awfully clever, Mr. Jenks."

"Sure thing, son. All the Jenkses is clever. Runs in the family like German measles. We can't escape it." He drained his beer and wiped the back of his hand across his brow.

"Could I try?" asked Robert, ignoring Mr. Finchley's restraining frown.

"Go ahead, son. Start in on the '1812'. Plenty of room for noise there."

"You be careful of Mr. Jenks's instruments," warned Mr. Finchley.

"They won't hurt," cried that gentleman, helping Robert on with the harness. "Come rain, come shine, they still play fine. Poetry, not of the best. Always could recognise me own deficiencies. Now then, boy. Waggle your knees and flip them elbows like a duck going to market and away we go!"

Robert went off, clashing the cymbals and beating the drum awkwardly while he blew a high, appealing squeal on the whistle. The noise was awful and Mr. Finchley grinned at the small figure cumbered almost to the ground with the weight of the drum and the concertina.

"He's a spark, ain't he," chuckled Mr. Jenks, as Robert marched down the road.

"He's certainly a handful," Mr. Finchley said, not without some pride.

"Small boys always is. Remember what I was like. Time flies and we get fat. What's your line, chum?"

Mr. Finchley told him and Mr. Jenks seemed to be very pleased.

"Buy a caravan, take a holiday and look for a house. Original. Wish I could do the same, but I just keep going from one place to another. Rolvenden tomorrow. Sheep fair there, and maybe a few of the lads and lassies will want music. Blimey, there are days when I wonder if I won't turn right into a bleedin' kangaroo. Still, lavee est der, lavee est long, a pew damer et puee—the gong. French. Educated sort of cuss I am. Here comes the young hopeful."

Robert came clanging and thumping back, his face flushed, his thin arms flapping. He collapsed at the foot of the steps.

"Golly, Mr. Jenks," he panted. "You must be very strong."

"Strong?" laughed Mr. Jenks. "Son, give me two glasses of beer and the right song and I can make King Kong look like a bed bug with influenza. Well, must be gettin' along. Thanks for the meal. Perhaps I'd better finish that bottle or you'll think I'm being imperlite and don't appreciate your beer." He raised the bottle and drained it with a vast surging and throbbing of his adam's apple.

He buckled on his harness. "Nice to 'ave met you both. So long, and I'll be seein' you at Cinderella's Ball if they still sell glass slippers. Here we go, son!"

Whang! Whang! The drum sticks beat home and with a magnificent flourish he was down the road playing himself away with a rousing *Hullo, Hullo, and Who's Your Lady Friend?*

They watched him out of sight, and then Robert turned wistfully to Mr. Finchley.

"Do you think, dad, that they sell one-man outfits like that in the shops? If they did, perhaps next term I could take a one-man band back to school. Mr. Jenks said that in a week—"

"I doubt whether they do sell such outfits," said Mr. Finchley firmly, "and anyway, I'm sure your Head wouldn't approve."

"The difficult part," said Robert reflectively, "is remembering to knock your knees together as you jerk your elbows back. Golly, though, that's one thing about not being on a ship. You wouldn't meet a Mr. Jenks in mid-ocean, would you, papa?"

Mr. Finchley grinned as he put away the lunch things. From what he had seen of Mr. Jenks's optimism and bounce he would not be surprised to meet him anywhere.

XXIII
The eclipse of a star

FOR the next few days Mr. Finchley and Robert, like a pair of bumble bees, flew from one house to another, humming with excitement, only to find that there was no honey for them. As each new prospect drew near they told one another that this was the place. They even pointed out things on the road which in time they felt they would come to know very well, a Douglas fir with a fantastic kink in its upper trunk, a culvert under the road where water-rats could be hunted and a green-and-yellow baker's van which would one day bring their bread.

Always they were disappointed. It was surprising how difficult it was to find the right house. There was always something wrong. It was too big or too small, too ugly or too fanciful, or the garden was inadequate. No orchard, too much orchard, too isolated or too closely surrounded by other houses ... there was no end to their objections and gradually their hopes began to pine and wilt like spring flowers brought into a hot room.

They were going along one morning, after visiting a house near the little town of Cranbrook, feeling very depressed because the house they had just visited had a barn fitted up as a gymnasium, but apart from this glory the place was quite unsuitable. Robert was very depressed that they could not take it for the sake of the gymnasium alone.

"What we shall have to do, dad," he said, taking the end of a long grass stalk from his mouth, "is to buy a piece of land and build our own house. Then we could have a gym attached to the house."

"But building a place takes a long time, Robert, and we don't want a modern house. Don't you want to live in one of these Kent houses?"

"Yes, but we may never find one. All the nice ones seem to be taken."

"We shall find one. There's plenty of time yet. Perhaps we'll write to your mother and ask her to join us. Maybe she'll change our luck."

At this moment a terrific roar burst out behind them. For a second or two Mr. Finchley imagined they were about to be struck by the epicentre of a cyclone. The air bent and quivered with a vicious series of crepitations and past them shot a gleaming black-and-white motorcycle, a man huddled close to the saddle tank. It seared by them like a comet, swerved violently round the corner ahead, throwing up a tail of smoke and dust, and then was gone. Mr. Finchley was left with an agitated Churchwarden to calm. It took some time to settle the horse and then Mr. Finchley muttered fiercely:

"The fool! What on earth was it?"

Robert, who had been staring after the motor-cycle with a trance-like smile on his face, answered for him. "Did you see how he took that corner, papa? Just like a T.T. driver. That was a Blackburn-Simplex, 350 c.c. shaft-driven, overhead camshaft model. They cost ninety-five pounds. Parkinson's brother has one—Parkinson's pater has a factory at Coventry—and it'll do over ninety an hour with special tuning. Gosh, how I'd like to be on the back of that. Brrrrrrh!" Robert bent low over a pair of imaginary handlebars and made a fierce noise. "Look out! Look out! I'm coming round the hairpin bend at sixty! Whee!" He lurched and swayed.

Mr. Finchley regarded his son with an amazement which was faintly touched with horror. For a moment he felt that he must at once stamp out any admiration the boy could have for such a noisy, dangerous machine. But a second's reflection convinced him that he would be doing no good. The dreams and desires of a boy don't evaporate before the heat of any cautionary tale. For Robert a Blackburn-Simplex was a magic charger—any knight who preferred a horse to its stirring horse-powered vigour was a back number.

"When I grow up"—Robert came out of a long skid—"I shall have a motor-bike. By that time they'll have improved no end, dad. Maybe it'll be super-charged, have four cylinders, rear wheel springing and do over a hundred. I wonder you didn't buy a motor-cycle and side-car, really, instead of a caravan. Churchwarden's awfully slow, isn't he?"

"He may be slow, Robert, but he gets there and at a speed which I find very comfortable."

"That's because you're a different generation, dad. The stinks master was telling us about that. Old people, he said, were conditioned by their environment in their early days and they can't alter themselves now. But today we don't have any fixed environment—it's always changing—so we never get old-fashioned. That's all evolution is, he said. If you don't change with the times, then you become a kind of human brontosaurus and die out."

"So you think I'm a human brontosaurus?" Mr. Finchley smiled.

Robert looked up at him with a quick twinkle of affection in his eyes. "Not really, but you are a little bit old-fashioned. That's why you don't like motor-cycles."

"Well, maybe the time will come when you won't like rocket trains and an inter-planetary air-service," said Mr. Finchley. "We all get old-fashioned. That's the privilege of the elderly and it's a very good thing, too. If it weren't for the old-fashioned people, this world would topple over from top-heaviness. We're the ballast."

Robert considered this aspect seriously, his brows wrinkled, one thin hand pulling at his under-lip. And as he cogitated, the caravan drew round a sharp corner and there, at the left-hand side of the road, a black-and-white confusion of metal winked at them from the depths of a ditch. Long spikes of hogweed surrounded the wreck and a drift of pollen from the tall grasses had settled over the saddle in a greyish powder. On the roadway was a long, black skid mark and standing at the side of the ditch was a young man nearing his thirties.

He looked up as the caravan came round the corner and waved one hand in airy greeting. Mr. Finchley and Robert jumped down and went anxiously towards him.

"Are you hurt?" enquired Mr. Finchley.

"No, no, not at all. Came off and landed like an angel on a cloud bank. Softest ditch for miles around." The man smiled. He had a tanned, knobbly face that twisted into a mass of contours as he grinned and his eyes were lost in deep folds above his cheeks. He was bare-headed and dressed in a pair of green trousers and an open cardigan that showed a checked shirt of yellow and black. He lit himself a cigarette and his eyes reappeared and went beyond the two to the caravan.

"What happened?" asked Robert, looking at the machine, whose front wheel was buckled hopelessly.

"Rabbit. Just a damn fool of a rabbit, sitting there in the middle of the road giving itself a wash and brush up. Had to do that this morning in that particular spot when there's the rest of the country to pick on. Humane sort of person. Never could bring myself to run down animals, so I swerved. Gee, what a skid that brought on." He pointed to the mark across the road. "Wish it could have been photographed, make a swell shot. Bang—hit the ditch and went flying, just like the man on the trapeze, and I landed soft twelve yards away. Been into Cranbrook to do some telephoning, too much of a hurry to get back. Got to grab this weather while it's going. Like to give me a lift? It's only just down the road, then off to the left."

"What about your machine?"

"We'll leave it there and one of the trucks can pick it up later."

They went to the caravan and he climbed up on to the driving seat. Robert went inside and hung out over the half-door.

Mr. Finchley shook the reins and Churchwarden started off.

"Awfully nice of you," said the young man. He was quiet for a moment, then went on, "Say, is this your caravan or did you hire it?"

"It's mine," answered Mr. Finchley, and he added a trifle maliciously, "It's slower than a motor-cycle, but it never skids."

"Got me there, pal." The man's laugh was so friendly and infectious that it could not be resisted. "You two in any hurry to get anywhere? Seeing you has given me an idea. I could use you for a day. What do you say? Five pounds for a day's work and easy work at that."

"What kind of work?"

"Oh, easy work. You'll see when we get there. This is the very thing." He screwed round and looked at the caravan. "I knew there was some touch missing from that sequence and this is it. Give it just the right atmosphere—that is if I can persuade Grimes, and I can."

Mr. Finchley tried to get from him what the work was, but the young man, who gave his name as Popper, Jim Popper, refused to say.

"You'll like it—and don't think I'm having you on a string. Know plenty of people would give a lot for the job. Say, son—" He turned to Robert. "Did you ever think of going on the films? Ever fancy yourself as little Freddie Bartholomew? Can you dance, sing or swing from bough to bough like Tarzan?"

Robert shook his head. "I can swim under water the length of the school bath, sir. But I want to be a T.T. driver when I'm old enough for a licence. Or maybe go to sea."

Jim Popper smiled with relief and gave Robert a grin that raised a chain of alps across his forehead.

"Nice, human, sensible boy you've got. We go down to the left here."

Mr. Finchley turned down a side road, which twisted laboriously for about five hundred yards. Then they came to a little lodge house and a pair of wrought-iron gates. The gates were open and outside stood a tall policeman and a little knot of local people. As the caravan approached there was a stir in the crowd, a gentle movement that grew quickly into a wriggling, excited shuffle and the people began to run towards the caravan.

Mr. Finchley looked at Jim Popper and Jim Popper shook his head wearily. "Take no notice of 'em," he said, "but if it's not too much of a strain just fix your face in a silly grin. That's good business."

The crowd surged around the caravan, shouting excitedly at Jim Popper and waving autograph books in the air. Most of them were young girls.

Jim waved a hand airily to them and then the policeman came up and drove them back, making a way for the caravan through the gates. The crowd stayed outside, gazing hungrily after them.

From the gates a long drive curled away into a belt to tall beech trees and far away, on a little mound, Mr. Finchley could make out the grey shape of a large house.

"Private grounds, been lent to us," explained Jim. "Explain it all in a minute."

Halfway down the drive, in a hollow out of sight of the house and the road, they came upon an interesting little colony.

There were two or three trucks drawn up on the grass, loaded with complicated mechanisms which Mr. Finchley vaguely recognised as cinema cameras. Two tents were pitched by the trucks and, lying around on the ground, smoking and chatting, were about fifty people. They were an odd collection. Some were in shirt sleeves, some wore eyeshades, some carried megaphones, others stood rather stiffly in the costume of policemen, their faces taut with make-up, and there was a young girl in a flowing summer dress who sat on a small camp-stool, smoking a cigarette and holding an enormous glass of beer from which she drank thirstily. From inside one of the two tents came a furious murmur as though it were a beehive.

Jim Popper's arrival was greeted with a hail of shouts, and he jumped down, told Finchley to wait, and darted into the tent from which the noise came. No one took any notice of the caravan. It was hot and there seemed an air of disinterest everywhere, as though the heat had driven out all curiosity from the minds of the people in the hollow.

Mr. Finchley looked at Robert.

"They must be making a film," said Robert. "I've seen pictures like this in a magazine at school."

"That's what I think. I suppose that Mr. Popper is something to do with them. Good Lord!" Mr. Finchley's heart suddenly broke into a brief tap-dance. Do you suppose he wants us to act?"

Robert looked around at the people in the hollow.

"Why should he, dad? He's got plenty of people here already. Yes, it's a film all right. Look—you see that lady sitting down over there. The one with the glass of beer. She must be a film star. Golly, if old Parkinson was here he'd go crazy. He's a terrible film fan. He's got a signed photograph of Charlie Chaplin and he collects autographs."

"But maybe he does want us to act," insisted Mr. Finchley. "It would only be a small part …" He lapsed into silence as his thoughts went back to the past, the far past when he had been a member of the local amateur dramatic society. They had put on some very good shows and it was only sheer bad luck over parts which had prevented him from letting everyone see what a good actor he was. For an amateur he had been very good, there was no doubt of that. Mr. Finchley searched his soul for those glimpses of the past and found, as any middle-aged, elderly man or woman will find, that here was lurking a faded, but still colourful ambition which had never come to anything.

While he was still way back in the old days, Jim Popper reappeared, bringing with him a short, sturdy man with the brows and face of an ape. He walked with a slight roll, held a half-smoked cigar tightly between his teeth and scratched his chest through the open vee of a blue silk shirt. His plus-four trousers were kept up by a length of bright blue pyjama cord.

Jim Popper introduced him.

"Hyah," said Mr. Grimes.

"It's all fixed," said Jim. "You get five pounds for a day's work. It's the caravan really we want, but you go with it."

"Are you making a film?" enquired Mr. Finchley.

At this Mr. Grimes gave a snort, puffed hard at his cigar and expelled from between his teeth the harsh comment, "It started that way, but it's gonna finish up an almanack. Give him the layout, Jimmy, and let's get started."

Jimmy gave Mr. Finchley the layout. Mr. Finchley understood that the film was about a young boy who, harshly treated at a home into which he has been adopted from an orphanage, runs away with the intention of going to sea as a cabin-boy. On the way to the nearest port he gets hungry and breaks into a house for food. At the same time the house is broken into by burglars who steal Lady De Vere Watson's jewels. The thieves make off and the boy is discovered, as he leaves the grounds, holding a piece of pie in his hand. There is a chase by the local constabulary, and it was to this chase that Jim Popper had wanted to give atmosphere. The caravan was to give that atmosphere. The boy would come out of the hedge as Mr. Finchley drove along and beg a lift. He would ride with Mr. Finchley until the scream of the police whistles were heard behind and then he would dart away into the fields again.

"And what happens after that?" asked Mr. Finchley, interested.

"We go back to the studio and finish the shooting where there ain't no midges and a finicky sun to pop in and out of the clouds," said Mr. Grimes, scratching himself.

"The rest is complicated but touching," said Jim apologetically. "Lady De Vere Watson—that's her with the pint of old-and-mild over there," he nodded towards the pretty young girl—"meets the boy while she's taking a walk through the woodland. Gee, and it goes on. You know—the boy is really the rightful heir to Marbury Towers, and there's a young hunting squire who falls for Lady De Vere. And the jewellery is got back because the burglars—"

"Can it, Jimmy," grunted Mr. Grimes.

"Sure—anyway, you get the main idea." He nodded at Mr. Finchley. "It took four men to write the story and two more for the extra dialogue. I don't know how they did it."

"What about the boy?" Mr. Finchley began to get down from the caravan.

"I was saving that until last," said Jim, with a look at Mr. Grimes. A furious puff of acrimonious smoke was Mr. Grimes's only comment. "He's Clarence Armitage, star of *Heartbreak Abbey, Hullo, Mr. Fortune!* and *Convict's Son*, and the most unpleasant piece of biochemistry that ever left the mint. Come and meet him. He's got a way of trembling his under-lip as though he's going to break into tears and that's a surefire for filling the ninepennies. He's got nice crinkly hair and a pleasant face, but don't trust him. He's concentrated evil."

Jim Popper led the way to the other tent, while Mr. Grimes began to shout and stir things up in the hollow. Inside the tent Mr. Finchley found Clarence and his mother. Mrs. Armitage was a large woman with a high bosom like a mountain cairn and a face which was hard and suspicious, except when she gazed upon her Clarence, and then it softened to an emotional thaw and her eyes went misty with affection and wonder.

Clarence was a nice-looking boy, frank-faced, curly-headed, and dressed in a crumpled suit of Etons. The end of his collar had sprung free—apparently from the stress of escaping from Lady De Vere's house.

Jim introduced Mr. Finchley. Mrs. Armitage nodded distantly to him and Clarence held out his hand in a very gentlemanly manner. Mr. Finchley was convinced that Jim had exaggerated about Clarence, but he lost that conviction almost immediately as he withdrew his hand from Clarence's and found that a sticky wad of chewing gum had been pressed into his palm.

"Clarence, darling." Mrs. Armitage ruffled the curly hair affectionately. "That was naughty. So high-spirited," she explained to Mr. Finchley. "Like all great artists." Her smile changed to a glare which defied Mr. Finchley to be unpleasant about a boyish prank.

Jim explained the new sequence to them and a few minutes later Mr. Finchley was on his way to becoming a film actor. His face was touched up a little and Mr. Grimes had decided at which point on the drive Clarence was to break through the bushes and ask for a lift.

Robert was nowhere to be seen.

It did not take Mr. Finchley long to master his part. He said practically nothing, except when the police came up in chase of Clarence and then he pointed into the bushes with his whip and said, "That's the way he went!"

The first rehearsal was held up for a while because Clarence suddenly decided that it might be better if, after getting the lift, he should drive the caravan for a little way. Mr. Finchley, remembering the gum, was adamant.

"Nobody drives this caravan but me, Mr. Grimes," he said, as that individual appeared to weaken under the barrage put up by Clarence and his mother.

"But it would be such a good touch," persisted Mrs. Armitage. "The unhappy child, snatching a moment of pleasure in the midst of his terror, by driving the horse."

"Yeah, there's something there," said Jim. "What do you say, Mr. Finchley? He can't do any harm."

Mr. Finchley shook his head. "This is a peculiar horse and I'm not risking it. Nobody but me drives this caravan, and if you don't like it, I'll take the van off now and finish with the whole affair. I'm not in need of your money, I'm just doing it to oblige you."

A gleam of pleasure wakened in Jim's eyes. "You mean that? Good ... I mean, what a pity. You see, Mrs. Armitage," he turned to the woman, "we can't do a thing. Little Clarence will have to sit on the seat beside the driver. It's just as good."

"But I want to drive!" cried Clarence.

"You can't!" bellowed Mr. Grimes. "Come on or I shall go nuts!"

"Now, now, Mr. Grimes, there's no need to shout at the lad," said Mrs. Armitage, a she-wolf protecting her pup. "You'll upset Clarence."

"Upset him! He's been putting everyone on edge for the last two days. Gee, after this I'll keep to animal pictures. You can get more co-operation from dumb beasts."

It was half an hour before everything was smoothed out again and they were ready for shooting.

The cameras were hauled into position. Everyone was set and the scene was begun. Mr. Finchley drove slowly down the drive until he came to the fringe of bushes. Clarence broke through and asked for a lift, was given permission by a nod of the head and he climbed up. The caravan started away and before it went a travelling camera running along an ingenious track at the side of the road. The caravan had not gone two yards before Mr. Finchley spoilt the whole shot by leaping violently out of his seat, shouting agonisedly and turning furiously towards the angelic-faced Clarence.

"What's the matter now?" wailed Mr. Grimes, rushing forward after the cameras had stopped.

"He pinched me!" said Mr. Finchley, rubbing his flank.

"I did not!" declared Clarence.

"You did!"

"I did not. Why should I?"

"Clarence," his mother came bridling forward, "did you pinch him?"

"No, mother, of course not."

"I believe you. There must be a nail in the seat or perhaps it was a wasp," explained Mrs. Armitage.

"Nail, wasp or just the devil trying to goad me into insanity, what do I care!" shouted Mr. Grimes. "Come on back to your places and let's have it again."

Mr. Finchley turned the caravan and drove back, Clarence still with him.

Clarence looked up at him, his blue eyes shining, his face dimpled with a smile. "I did pinch you, you old turtle. And serves you right for not letting me drive."

Mr. Finchley, a pacific man and full of natural kindness, was never nearer striking a child than at that moment. He began to appreciate the quality of hot, dull misery which seemed to have settled over the film people. If they had to put up with Clarence for long, apathy was their only guard.

They started again and this time everything seemed to go all right. Clarence came out and asked for his lift and got it and they drove off down the road until the shout to cut came. But Mr. Grimes was not satisfied. He came up to Mr. Finchley.

"Whadya want to edge away from him as if he smelled bad for?" he asked sternly.

"I don't want to be pinched again," Mr. Finchley defended himself.

"Oh, forget it. He never strikes in the same place twice. Clarence, you behave yourself or I'll twist your neck. Now—let's have it again, and this time sit up a bit closer and give him a smile or two. You know, just as though you were remembering your own boyhood days."

They did it again and this time it seemed to please Mr. Grimes. He looked at Jim Popper and nodded, a faint flush of satisfaction touching his dark face. They called Mr. Finchley to them and, as he came across the grass, something stung him sharply on the back of the neck. He swung round. Behind him was Clarence sauntering along with his hands in his pockets, his eyes fixed on a fleecy speck of cloud, a faint whistle pursing his lips. Mr. Finchley scowled. He knew what it was like to be hit by a pea from a tin shooter.

Jim Popper took his arm and breathed hoarsely, "Take no notice. He'll only get you mad. He's been acting like a gadfly around here for the last two days. If it wasn't for his box-office draw, I'd have kicked him in the pants long ago. And you'd better keep an eye on your own boy. He's going around plaguing everybody for autographs and this company ain't exactly in the mood to give autographs to small boys. They don't like small boys of any kind at the moment."

Robert came towards them from the lee of the tents, his eyebrows screwed into a frown, an open exercise book in his hand. Mr. Finchley recognised the log of the caravan and wondered that Robert, who was little interested in films or actors, should be anxious to get autographs. He put the book away as he came up to his father and Mr. Finchley said:

"I hope you've not worrying the people for autographs, Robert? I didn't know you collected them."

"If I did I shouldn't get any. Everyone seems in a frightful temper about something. Have you finished yet, dad?"

"It won't be long now," said Jim.

In a few moments the policemen were taking up their positions for the chase and Mr. Finchley went back to his caravan.

Mrs. Armitage and her son came out of their tent and as Clarence passed Robert, who had his back to him, he smartly cut Robert across the back of his knees with the side of his hand. It was expertly done, as any boy could do it, and Robert dropped backwards with a thump on to his stern. He sat looking after Clarence, his eyes narrow with thought, and back to him floated a mimicking voice, "Have you finished yet, dad!"

A handsome young man, dressed in riding breeches and carrying a crop—the young squire who provided the love interest—jerked Robert to his feet and said casually:

"If a fellow did that to me, he wouldn't get away with it."

"Who is that?" asked Robert.

The actor explained who Clarence was, and added, "Why don't you ask him for his autograph?" He strolled away chuckling to himself to talk to Lady De Vere Watson.

Robert wandered along the drive towards the spot where the shot was being taken and was promptly cursed by an eyeshaded cameraman for getting under his feet. He slid away.

This time Mr. Finchley had less trouble with Clarence but more trouble with Mr. Grimes. Time and again the police came bustling up, Clarence dodged away into the cover of a tall shrubbery and Mr. Finchley said, "That's the way he went!" pointing with his whip. Until that moment it had never occurred to Mr. Finchley that there could be many variations of tone in such a simple sentence. To judge by Mr. Grimes's rising frenzy of encouragement, it was possible to say, "That's the way he went," in a manner and voice which would give the banal words the essence of a sonnet and the music of the spheres, and the flourish of a simple whip by a simple countryman had to have the braggadocio, the Bergerac swagger and Quixotic humour of the sword flourish from an Elizabethan knight. And when Mr. Grimes was finally satisfied and Clarence slipped away into the bushes for good, Mr. Finchley was privately convinced that his words had less true tone and meaning than they had the first time he mouthed them.

The cameras stopped rolling, everyone breathed a sigh of relief, and the policemen who had plunged off the road into the bushes after Clarence came back.

"Half an hour break and then we'll do the woodland De Vere scene with the squire, and then we can all go home," shouted Jim Popper, and he grinned at Mr. Finchley. "You were a great help, great help, and you did well. Grimes'll see you about your cash. If you care to stop and watch the rest of the shots, you're welcome."

Mrs. Armitage came sailing up, holding a glass of milk and a plate of sandwiches in her hand.

"Clarence, where's Clarence? He must be exhausted after all that trouble. It's a pity you didn't get a professional to do the caravan scene, Mr. Popper. So tiring for my boy to hang about while you dragoon people without talent into their parts. Where is Clarence?"

"Last I saw of him he went into the bushes with the police after him. Maybe he's three miles away raiding someone's hen coop by now," said Jim wearily.

"Clarence!" Mrs. Armitage ignored him. "Clarence! Find Clarence, someone."

"Perhaps he's gone and had a stroke and died," said Mr. Grimes quietly and hopefully to his cameraman. At that moment there came from the depths of the shrubbery a long and anguished wail. Then there was silence, followed by a series of grunts and scuffles. Everyone looked towards the bushes, and then, drawn by some force greater than themselves, they converged upon the shrubbery. In every heart but that of Mrs. Armitage, a tiny joy began to work because that yell of pain had come in a tone which was unmistakeably that of the darling of the screen. Little, curly-headed Clarence had cried out in pain. Suddenly to extras, technicians and the more important actors the day grew bright and full of promise.

Mr. Finchley followed Jim and Mr. Grimes through a bank of laurel bushes, round a clump of rhododendrons rich with green seed-pods into a little open circle of grass. With them went the rest of the film crowd.

In the circle were two small boys, Clarence and Robert, grappling and wrestling with one another. As they watched, and before Mrs. Armitage could interfere, Robert jerked a short-arm jab into Clarence's chest and toppled him over. He jumped astride of his victim, and with complete disregard for rules or English usage, sat on him and began to punch his head with a swift, methodical succession of crisp blows. Clarence yelled, Clarence howled, Clarence wriggled and Clarence heaved, but Clarence was quite helpless.

Mrs. Armitage gave a wail of angry rage and pushed forward, and it was amazing how much she found her way impeded by film people, who seemed clumsily to be getting between her and her son. Mr. Finchley reached Robert before Mrs. Armitage. He caught his son by the collar and hoisted him off Clarence.

"Robert, what on earth is all this?"

"Clarence, my darling! What have they done to you?" cried Mrs. Armitage, rushing up and helping her son to his feet. From her tone one would have imagined that Clarence had been set upon by a band of Cherokees. He did look as though he had been badly treated. His Eton suit was torn, he had no collar at all, his nose was the fount of a thick line of red blood and one eye was puffed and darkening rapidly to a thundercloud hue, wrongly known as black. It was an unwholesome mixture of brown and purple. He sniffed and blubbed as he stood up.

Robert, lips firm, one cheek scratched and his shirt ripped at the front, regarded him defiantly.

Mrs. Armitage rounded on Mr. Finchley and Robert. "I'll sue you for this! You and your bad-tempered boy! Look what you've done to Clarence. You've spoilt his looks!" For a moment she seemed about to advance on Mr. Finchley and attack him, but Mr. Grimes came up and took her arm.

"Easy, easy, Mrs. Armitage," he called soothingly, but his face was bright with a smile. "You can't go on like that. You can't sue boys because they have a fight occasionally, and there isn't anything wrong with Clarence's face that the make-up man and a day's rest can't cure. What was the fight all about, son?" He looked across at Robert happily.

Robert sniffed and said quietly: "I was sitting in here and he came in and pulled my ear from behind. So I jumped up and twisted his nose. Then he punched me in the chest. So I hit him in the eye and it went on like that."

"And you did very well for yourself," laughed Jim, as Clarence was led away to the tent by his mother. "Gee, don't be angry with him, Mr. Finchley. Remember when you were a lad. Boy, what an eye that Clarence is going to have! And he could give you half a stone and two inches on the arm to look at him."

Mr. Finchley frowned. It was wrong to encourage Robert. Fighting was bad manners, and the boy should have known better. Then he remembered the chewing gum, the pinch and the pea-shooter and he felt less angry. He led

Robert away through a crowd of film people who laughed and called out cheering remarks. The atmosphere of the little dell seemed to have changed completely. Only from Clarence's tent came a demoralised blubbing and the raised voice of Mr. Grimes trying to soothe the angry Mrs. Armitage.

"Get into the caravan, Robert," said Mr. Finchley.

Robert climbed in obediently. Mr. Finchley walked round and took off Churchwarden's nosebag, and then climbed on to the driving seat and turned the van. He was a little apprehensive that Mrs. Armitage might come rushing out at him at any moment and he wanted to get away. He had no wish for an angry scene.

He drove the caravan down the drive towards the lodge gates, but before he reached them there came a shout behind him and Jim Popper came flying after him.

"Hey! Hold hard for a moment!" He came up, panting, and flourished some papers at Mr. Finchley.

"What's the matter?"

"Your cheque. You can't go without that. And here's a sheet of autographs from all the bunch on the set for Robert. There's one missing, of course. You can guess which that is. Gee, everyone's grateful to your kid for pasting that Clarence. Yes, sir! Sure feels like summer is here again!"

He laughed, thrust the papers into Mr. Finchley's hand, and then watched the canary-coloured caravan turn out of the lodge gates, shake off the tiny crowd and make along the road.

Mr. Finchley held the reins and a tiny smile wreathed his lips as he heard the top half of the door behind him swing back.

A contrite voice said, hesitatingly, "Dad …"

Mr. Finchley did not answer for a moment. Then he said very slowly, "Yes, Robert."

"Dad, it wasn't true what I told you ... about Clarence, I mean. He didn't pull my ear when he came into the shrubberies; I pulled his ear first, and then we started to fight."

Mr. Finchley breathed a little heavily and was glad that Robert could not see his face. "I think we'd better forget the whole incident, don't you?"

"Yes, dad," said Robert, but there was a lingering note of rising optimism in his voice, a conviction that it would be impossible to forget the bliss of those moments in the shrubbery so easily.

"Here's the sheet of autographs," said Mr. Finchley, handing the paper back to Robert. "I can't think why you wanted them. You never said you collected them before."

"I don't collect them. But Parkinson does. I can trade these for his pack of trick cards. Now I've got a calculating duck I ought to have some conjuring tricks. With this pack you can make someone take a card and put it back and then by just flipping your thumb along the pack the card springs out. Nobody but Parkinson knows how it's done, but he'll trade for these autographs, he's so mad about films ..."

Robert rambled on happily, forgetting the momentary displeasure which had clouded the day, and Mr. Finchley lit his pipe and felt very happy. He had earned five pounds, become a film actor and seen a particularly unpleasant child overtaken by Nemesis. It had been a good day.

XXIV
In which, since the end is in sight, there is much to explain

MRS. FINCHLEY was reading a letter from Mr. Finchley. She sat with her back to the window to catch the last of the evening light.

"With some of the money we bought Churchwarden a new nosebag and one of those straw hats with holes for the ears. It makes him look ridiculous. And a new whip. Robert wanted a compass, but I squashed that. We came here the day before yesterday and think we shall be here for another three days at least, because the swimming is so good and Robert doesn't want to move. To tell you the truth, my dear, I'm not keen to move, either. It seems that I shall never find the house I want. I can see myself at the age of a hundred wandering around England with a grey beard looking for the house of my dreams. Why don't you come down and join us? You know what pleasure it would give us and you might change our luck. You could easily join us here. Get the train to Bartenden station and at the village enquire for Burton's Pitts—that's the name of this quarry—anyone will direct you, and it's not more than half a mile's walk. If you'll write when you get this to the village P.O., I'll get your letter the next morning and come in and meet you. But, anyway, I'll be here until Friday, and I'll enquire at the P.O. for letters until Friday morning. Do come. I'm sure you'll enjoy caravanning even if we don't find a house ..."

Mrs. Finchley twisted her head slightly and stared out of the window. In the little garden at the front of the house a grey cat was carefully stalking a young and foolish sparrow which was pecking at the lobelia flowers in the bed. She rapped her ringed finger against the window sharply and scared off the bird. The cat gave her a slow, offended look and then moved leisurely away to fresh hunting-grounds.

Although the letter said no more about the quest for a house, Mrs. Finchley knew that her husband's despair was much stronger than showed in his words. She had looked for houses herself and she had been suspicious of the high spirits in which Edgar had set out on his search. Such optimism could come only from great innocence of the ways of house-agents and the trials of disappointments.

She got to her feet and walked slowly from the room up to her bedroom. She didn't feel that by going to him she would change his luck, but it would cheer him up and, for her, at the moment, that was very important. She liked the people she knew to be happy. And, also, she could not prevent the suspicion forming in her mind that Edgar was not really looking for a house so earnestly as he could. He was a little inclined, she felt, to be drawn aside by the attractions of the road and the people he met. He needed a woman to keep before him the main purpose of the caravan trip.

And while Mrs. Finchley looked out of the bedroom window thinking of her husband, Mr. Finchley sat on the back steps of the caravan thinking about her and wondering whether she would join him.

The camping-place at Burton's Pitts was an ideal spot. The side of the hill had been quarried out for local building stone more than a century before, and now the quarry was an overgrown tangle of briars and birch and great pads of gorse and wild sage. At the foot of the quarry was a wide pond, almost a lake, very clear and fringed on one side by a strip of green turf and a row of tall ash trees. It was in the shadow of these trees that the caravan had been pulled up. Behind the trees ran the road, going one way down to Bartenden village and the other way winding up a narrow, wood-banked valley.

Mr. Finchley sat on the top step, Robert lay on his bunk inside the caravan and was supposed to be asleep and Mr. Joe Turnbull sat on the lowest step talking.

Joe Turnbull was a retired sergeant of the Metropolitan Police Force. He had an enormous head, cropped close, and a body which had a slow, powerful vigour. He was a lazy, sluggish giant with small, very brown, bright eyes and a mouth which yawned like a cavern when he laughed, and when Joe laughed it was like a mountain rocked in the grip of a landslide. His shoulders, arms, chest muscles and thick neck bulged and stirred from a tremendous agitation. He was a bachelor and lived in a little bungalow on the village road not far from the quarry, and he spent a great deal of his time fishing in the quarry pond. When Mr. Finchley and Robert arrived he had not been long in making their acquaintance.

From the first moment of that acquaintance he had talked of many things, his personal reminiscences of his days in the police force and the habits and peculiarities of the fish in the pond and a host of other topics.

"I'm a man of action," he was saying, "a man built for exercise, for doing things. Even now, when I'm retired, I'm as spry and quick on my pins as many a youngster. And what do I do all day? I fish. I sit on my tail and watch a float. And very nice, too. Because do you know why?" He leaned forward closely to Mr. Finchley and eyed him confidentially through the evening gloom. "If I stare at that float long enough I get a release from this body of mine. It's a psychic experience. I go clean off, go clean wandering off, half over the globe, leaving my body sitting over there a-staring at a float. Many's the time a pal has come along and spoken to me or touched me on the shoulder and I've had to come back from Java or South Africa. The times I've had, fighting and fair busting myself with adventures. And it's all a matter of concentration on the float. There've been times when I've just been on the point of going off when I've had a bite and the float's gone under and spoilt the whole thing. But I never mind so long as it's a good bite. Day before you came I pulled out a roach three pounds if it was an ounce, lovely fellow, all red and silver underneath …"

A faint whisper of breath from inside the caravan told them that Robert had dropped to sleep. Joe Turnbull cocked an eye towards the open doorway and grinned.

"Wish I had a kid," he said softly. "One like yours. By golly, I didn't know I could spin such lies as I did to him this afternoon about dope fiends and criminals. Hope you don't mind, but it was a treat to see his face. No good telling youngsters the truth about crime. Wouldn't believe

337

it. Got to make it high-coloured and full of vim. Must be good to have a child and see yourself beginning all over again." He stared into the purple plume of darkness which had settled over the quarry top, a darkness cut by faraway stencil points of starlight.

Mr. Finchley made no answer because there was none he could make that would touch the man's longing. He had known that same emptiness of spirit before he had adopted Robert.

Sometime later Joe wandered off and Mr. Finchley turned in quietly for fear of waking Robert. As he lay in his blankets before he dropped off, he could hear Church-warden munching away at the sweet grass and the splash of a rat by the water and across the black frame of the open doorway a shooting star suddenly trailed, its milky, melting tail lighting the whole of the caravan for a second.

The next morning Mr. Finchley walked into Bartenden to see if there was a letter from his wife. But there was no letter. He came back to find that Robert had prepared the breakfast, bacon and eggs and black coffee.

"Is she coming?" enquired Robert eagerly, as his father came into the caravan.

"There's no letter, but maybe she didn't catch the post in time. There's sure to be one tomorrow morning." Mr. Finchley sat down to his eggs and bacon. He was hungry after his walk. Robert sat on the steps and fed maize to Dini, who was so accustomed to the caravan now that she seldom strayed far from it.

Outside a string of swallows dipped and swung across the pond and a dragonfly hovered with a blur of blue-green wings over a patch of reeds. It was going to be a hot day.

"If she comes will she be second-mate or just crew?" asked Robert.

"I don't know," answered Mr. Finchley idly, watching the boy's face. "If we don't treat her properly we shall have a mutiny and maybe she'll set herself up as captain and make us be just crew. I think we ought to make her cook with privileges."

"Perhaps she'll bring a chocolate sponge cake with her and my air gun. I wish I'd asked you to mention my gun in your letter, dad."

Mr. Finchley was glad that he had not been asked.

After breakfast they bathed. Mr. Finchley enjoyed his bathes with Robert. They chased one another across the pond, dived and rolled, and made a great deal of noise with their shouts and laughter.

"Look! Look, I'm a submarine," cried Robert and began to swim on his back with one leg in the air like a periscope.

"And I'm a battle cruiser ramming you," roared his father, and he surged towards Robert, rolling him over and ducking him. From the shade of the trees Churchwarden eyed them curiously and Dini fussed about the edge of the pool, quacking vague disapproval from time to time.

They came out and went back to the caravan to dry and dress. Dini followed them and Robert lifted her into the caravan on to his bunk where she was accustomed to taking her morning nap.

It was as they were dressing at the far end of the caravan that a shadow fell across the bright panel of the doorway and a man coughed gently. They turned. Mr. Finchley, caught in the act of hoisting his shirt over his shoulders, stood for a moment like a scarecrow, two hands flapping from the loose sleeves, while Robert, balancing on one leg like a heron, struggled with a rubber shoe.

A tall, rather elegant man was standing on the top step. He wore a well-cut flannel suit, a light trilby and his face had a lean, rather amused expression. When you first looked at him you thought he was young, but a moment's examination showed that he was not so young. The eyes were lined with crow's-feet, the skin of his cheeks sagged above the jaw just enough to give that shadow of age which makes a young face interesting before it increases to the point of making any face old. In one hand he held a thick malacca cane and the back of the hand which fingered the cane head was marked with a large star-shaped scar.

"Good morning," he said affably, and he took off his hat to show dark, faintly waved hair. "Don't let me interrupt your dressing. Carry on!" He flourished the stick jauntily and sat down on the seat under the row of books by the doorway.

"Who are you and what do you want?" asked Mr. Finchley, a little peeked by the man's calm manner. He jerked his shirt straight and tucked it into his trouser top.

The man did not answer but from outside came the clink of harness and a sudden long snort from Churchwarden.

Both Mr. Finchley and Robert jumped to the window and looked out. What they saw surprised them. Two men were backing Churchwarden into the shafts and, as they looked, proceeded to harness him.

"Hey! What is this? What are those men doing with my horse?" Mr. Finchley came forward angrily, but the man raised the end of his stick and pushed him back with a sudden show of force.

"Sit down!" he said firmly, and then more affably he went on. "There's no cause for you to worry, Mr. Finchley. None at all. If you avoid making a nuisance of yourself, I will promise you that no harm will come to you. Now sit down and be quiet. Above all be quiet—or I may have to enforce quiet. And that goes for you, too, son." He gave Robert a swift, cold glance. Then his eyes swept round the interior of the caravan in a quick, appraising look.

"Good Lord!" said Mr. Finchley with a sudden resurgence of memory. "You're the man who wrecked Horace Blain's caravan, and that short fat man out there is—"

"Is Duffy who tried to break into this caravan some time ago and had to throw a turf at you to get away. Yes, you're quite correct, Mr. Finchley," said the man smoothly.

"It was his voice speaking that night," said Robert suddenly. "What are you going to do? We haven't done anything, have we, dad?"

"Of course not, and I've had enough of this nonsense!" Mr. Finchley got to his feet, brindling with a swift anger. He was not going to be played about with. Unfortunately as he rose, the caravan jerked forward and he was knocked off his feet to fall back on to his bunk.

"And that's where you'd better stay, if you don't want to be hurt," said the man.

"You must be a criminal," said Robert.

The man blinked and then smiled. "Son, I'm no criminal. I just earn my bread and butter. I try to get along."

"We're going up the valley road, not back to the village," said Mr. Finchley. "Where are you taking us—and why?"

The man laughed. "As if you don't know why? Or I wonder? Maybe you don't. No, maybe you don't, and so much the better. As for where we're going. Don't worry about that. It isn't far."

Robert's hand found his father's. He was not frightened but he was anxious for some touch he understood.

"What do you think he wants, dad?" he whispered.

"It's probably all a mistake on his part," said Mr. Finchley quietly.

From the driving seat of the caravan came a mumble of voices and then a gruff, rather harsh voice began to sing *A Life on the Ocean Wave* rather dolefully.

"That's Duffy," said the man, lighting himself a cigarette. "He's no singer. And don't keep looking at me, son, as though you expected me to produce a knife from behind my ear or an automatic from my pocket at any moment."

"I'm sorry, sir."

"That's all right. Don't you go getting exalted ideas about crime. I don't admit I'm a criminal, but I do know about crime and believe me there's no glamour about it. Just as boring and uninteresting as going to an office every day."

Mr. Finchley listened to the man. Although he seemed to practise a flippant manner, there was no missing the serious intent which lay beneath his words and manners. He was in earnest about his mission, whatever it was, and Mr. Finchley had the good sense to realise that he could do nothing against the three men. He had Robert to think about as well.

After about twenty minutes the caravan swung off the road on to a rutted farm track and from the window Mr. Finchley had a glimpse of an orchard, the red and brown bulk of a barn and a house, and then a dark shadow fell across the caravan and the wheels were suddenly muted as they rolled across soft straw.

The caravan stopped and someone came round behind and opened the door.

"Did you find them yet, boss?" enquired a thick voice and the large, blue-chinned face of Duffy appeared. It was a broad, amiable face, thick and cheerful. Underneath the chin showed a tartan tie. His short, spreading body was clothed in a suit of brown-and-green checked plus-fours. Behind Duffy stood another man, a thin, hollow-checked man who said nothing, perhaps for fear of disturbing the dirty stub of cigarette which hung from his lower lip.

"Shut your mouth, Duffy," said his boss. "Let's get these two into the house. Come on—get out," he called to Mr. Finchley and Robert.

The two climbed out of the caravan and found themselves standing in the brown-shadowed interior of a great barn. Above them stretched cobwebbed rafters and in the tiled roof showed chinks of sunlight. As the men talked, sparrows and other birds stirred. The great doors of the barn were closed behind them.

The boss led the way down the barn to a small door in its end. This opened on to a small yard, walled with a high brick wall and, facing the barn, was the back of an old house. Mr. Finchley was given little time to look around before he was hustled across the yard and into the house through a side door.

They went down a long passage and into a large room, dark with beams and half-panelled walls. One end of the room was taken up by a magnificent open fireplace, a coat-of-arms carved upon the supporting crossbeam, and a wide, latticed window in another wall gave a momentary glimpse of a bowl-shaped garden. The room was empty save for a few packing-cases, and Mr. Finchley and Robert were ordered to sit by the empty fireplace while Duffy screwed himself up on to the wide window ledge.

"Now you keep them here while we go and have a look around that caravan," said his boss.

Duffy nodded, and the boss left the room with the other dark man.

Duffy stared at the two for a moment, a tiny frown rippling about his eyes. Then he shook his head.

"You've given us an awful lot of trouble," he said sternly.

"And you're going to get into an awful lot of trouble over this, if I have anything to do with it," replied Mr. Finchley tensely, and he made to rise.

"Sit where you are, uncle," said Duffy, and he pulled a little black object from his pocket and tossed it about in his hand. "Ever seen a blackjack? Nasty little things. And don't worry about the trouble. The boss looks after that. There won't be no trouble. Gee, we was nearly over to France to look for you when the boss got to thinking that maybe we'd made a mistake over the caravans. It was the horse that give him the clue. He's a one for spotting things. Horses was different colour. See? Give him a suspicion that we was being led away from the truth."

"Are you a criminal?" asked Robert, eyeing the blackjack with interest.

"I am, son. One of the worst criminals in the country. Eat you as soon as look at you and nothing safe from me. Got an awful record. But I ain't aimin' to touch you or your pa. Duffy's the name."

"You threw a turf at me," said Mr. Finchley angrily.

Duffy laughed. "You tore my tie. That makes us quits."

"What's the other man's name?" asked Robert.

"The boss? Call him Turk. Don't ask me why. The other—Hardy. But don't you go thinking I like crime. Just couldn't help it. Guess my environment must have been all against me going honest."

"What are they looking for in my caravan?"

"You'll see, and very nice, too. It's a pity you two had to get mixed up in this. I like you. Still, it ain't no good mixing sentiment with business. Don't suppose you've ever come in contact with the criminal classes before this?"

"Only in books, sir. I read a book, the *Talking Corpse Takes a Bow*—"

"Say, did you read that as well?" cried Duffy excitedly. "Gee, I got that, pinched it out of the sixpenny box in Charing Cross Road. Now there was a book with some real characters. Not whimsy-whamsy Cyrils and Harriets talking about what a pain they've got in their bellies, but real honest guys with a purpose. Mick the Masher. The way he murdered that old judge was neat—"

"But Operator 7 got him in the end—"

"Yeah—but that was bunk. Just a sop to the readin' public because most of 'em happen to be law-abiding and they insist on having it that way round. In real life that Number 7 would have finished floating face upwards in the Surrey Docks."

Mr. Finchley, conservative, age tightening his mind against the elasticity which characterises youth, listened in amazement as Robert and Duffy plunged into an animated discussion of murder stories. Duffy was no longer their warder, no longer an unexplained menace, but just a fattish man sitting on a window ledge.

"Ha, but take a real crime. That guy in *Diamond Cut Diamond* was too smart. Too fanciful to be real.

Didn't enjoy that a bit. Remember how he hauled Lady Do-Something's jewels? Know a guy—ain't seen him for a long time on account he's taken a holiday—that done a similar job, but he didn't go in for any fancy fal-lahs like burrowing under the house and connecting with the air shaft and all that ghost business to clear the people out. No, know what One-Arm did? Big fellow he was. Waits until he knows there's only four people in the house. Butler, footman, maid and the old girl herself. Goes up to the door at night and rings. Footman comes along. He slugs him at once and drops him behind a cupboard in the hall. Goes out and rings again. Butler comes along. Slugs him ditto and drops him behind cupboard. Then he tears the phone wires out by the roots and goes up to Lady Dohickey's boudoir and makes her hand over the keys. She screams, but he's firm, and she hands over, and he takes the jewels and hops it and the maid sits down in the basement scared out of her wits, and afterwards none of 'em can remember what he looks like, because they ain't got no control over their imagination. Footman and butler swear he ain't got only one arm because it would look bad if they admitted a one-armed man could knock them into shuteye. That's how it goes in real life, and that's how it ought to go in the best books. Take Turk, for instance Well, perhaps we'd better not. Here he comes."

He slid off the seat as Turk came into the room with the man Hardy. One look at Turk's face showed Mr. Finchley that whatever he had been searching for in the caravan he had found. Under his arm he carried a flat package wrapped about with a green cloth.

"You got it, boss?" said Duffy hoarsely.

"Almost first time off. It wasn't in the roof like he said, but in the panel at the side of the window. He must have been wandering a bit when he told me." He laid the package on a case and turned with a warm smile towards Mr. Finchley.

"Well—"

He was interrupted by Hardy.

"There's a woman coming to the front door, boss," said the man sharply.

Turk swung round, the lines of his face deepening.

He spoke quickly. "Duffy, stand over these two, and at the first sign of a peep from them, let 'em have it. We can't take risks now. You stay here, Hardy."

He slipped out of the room and closed the door behind him. Mr. Finchley heard him hurry along the hallway and a few seconds later the knocker on the door banged twice. From a distance they heard the faint murmur of voices.

Duffy stood over Mr. Finchley and Robert, his hand ready on the blackjack. Hardy stood at the window. He turned slowly. "She's going," he said.

Turk came back into the room and whistled gently. "That was a sharp one. Some old girl wanted to look over the house. Told her it was no longer for sale as I'd bought it yesterday and was having the boards taken down today. Don't think she relished her wasted journey, but what the hell."

"I'm hungry," said Duffy suddenly. "Hellish hungry. Don't seem to remember having any breakfast."

"There's no food here," said Turk. "And anyway, we've got what we wanted. We can go."

"What about these two?" questioned Hardy.

"If you're going to leave 'em here for a while," suggested Duffy, "so we can get a good start, it wouldn't be a bad idea to stake 'em to some grub. We could have some, too. Plenty in that caravan, I'll bet, tinned stuff and pickles. Boy, I'm hungry."

Turk considered this for a moment. Then he nodded. He was in a jubilant mood. "Go and get the stuff, Duffy," he said, and he crossed to Mr. Finchley.

"I'm still waiting for an explanation," said Mr. Finchley.

Turk fingered his chin and said slowly, "I don't know that you aren't entitled to one. Maybe quixotic of me, but it's fair. Don't suppose it can affect anyone if you know. Yes, you shall know. I'll tell you in return for your food."

Turk paused for a moment and lit himself a cigarette. Mr. Finchley heard Robert breathing behind him.

"You enjoy a mystery, don't you?" said Mr. Finchley, longing to know what the package was and the reason for Turk's actions.

"We all do," the man laughed. "Listen. A good time ago I spent quite a while in one of the Government's institutions for men who have peculiar ideas about property— other people's property. You get me?"

"I don't see why you can't say prison. It's shorter," grunted Mr. Finchley.

"Prison. And because I was a good boy I was given work in the hospital ward, and while I was there a man was brought in dying of pneumonia. I looked after him and, in one of his more lucid moments towards the end, he gave me an interesting piece of news. This man's name was Micky Jonston, and he was a queer sort of fellow, bit of an artist. He told me that he used to travel around the countryside in a caravan and, by putting on a bit of a show, get the local knobs to take an interest in him. Then he'd leave 'em and a few nights later, or maybe a month later, he'd come back and lift from their houses anything which had caught his eye. Well, the police caught him at last after he'd done a job at the house of Sir Wrekin Maleby in Hertfordshire. He lifted a couple of paintings from the house. He never got rid of the paintings, although he had a customer lined up for them. Surprising what kind of a market there is for stolen paintings."

"And are those the paintings?" asked Mr. Finchley, a little overwhelmed.

"They are. Micky wouldn't part with them when he'd got them. I said he was a bit of an artist. He kept them in his caravan in a secret panel. You've been carting them around for weeks. Micky grew quite fond of them. But he was hard up and, after he'd parked his van in London, he went out on another job and got caught. And when he was dying he gave me the tip about these paintings. Told me all about them. Look." Turk took the wrappings from the package and showed them two canvases stretched over wooden frames. One showed a group of peasants outside a village church and a half-filled grave under the shade of a wide-spreading tree. The other was of two soldiers in tattered accoutrements accepting a drink from an earthenware jug which was held out to them by a country girl. Both paintings had a sombre, rather inflexible quality as though there was a spirit behind the composition which refused to be held by paint and canvas and sought to stand forth stubbornly. Yet, despite this suggestion, all the figures had a quiet resignation, a depth and steadiness which gave them a bold, tangible quality.

"Good, aren't they? Quite a history attached to them, too. The man who's going to buy these from me at a good price told me about them. Seems there were three French brothers—Le Nain—who painted under the same name, and seems it was difficult to tell which did which, and that makes the collectors keen about their stuff. Bit too dark and sad-feeling for my taste, but there you are. I'm no artist, like Micky. But when he told me his story I didn't miss any chances. But I was a bit late. You'd bought the caravan. So I had to do something. I found out about you and tried to get a quiet snoop around your caravan. But something always happened, and then you took to locking it, and as I was pretty sure you wouldn't know or find out about the paintings, I didn't want to disturb you if I could help it. Well, after that fool episode with the other caravan and the shock I got from thinking you might have found the paintings, I decided you would have to be disturbed. And here we are. You—preparing to spend a few hours here while we get away, and me—with the two pictures! The Brothers Le Nain. Know the names of those pictures? I got them from my collector pal. *Les Soldats Buvants* and *Enterrement d'un Paysan*."

Mr. Finchley said nothing. He looked at Turk and understood a great many things. His meeting with Oliver Watt Anselm, the private detective, the attack on Horace Blain and the attempt of Duffy to enter the caravan. And the caravan had never been claimed from Mr. Harricot, because its owner had died in prison, and when Turk had come out he had got on the trail of the pictures at once. What kind of man could possibly give a high price for paintings which he knew were stolen? Mr. Finchley knew that there were such men, but he could have little feeling for them.

"I can't think," said Robert, who had listened overawed, "why we never discovered the secret panel? We even looked after you attacked Mr. Blain."

"It's very ingenious. I'll show it to you before we go, if I remember. Trouble was Micky had said it was in the roof, but his mind was going and he meant the wall. If I'd known exactly where it was, you might never have known you'd carried such treasure. Hullo, here are the boys with the food. And I'm hungry."

Duffy and Hardy entered laden with tins and provisions from the caravan.

Mr. Finchley and Robert discovered that they were hungry, too.

XXV
Of peaches and punches

AT ten-thirty exactly by the post office clock Mrs. Finchley got off the long-distance coach in Bartenden. She had caught it in London at nine o'clock. She stood for a moment, her large suitcase at her feet, wondering what she should do, her mind a little confused by the excitement which was rising within her at the surprise she would be giving Robert and his father. She stood, a trim, brown-suited, competent figure, her bright eyes taking in the curve and colour of the village street, the cream wash over the plaster, the pink flutter of larkspurs and the flurry of dust where sparrows bathed in the gutter.

After a moment's thought she took her case into the post office and left it there. She enquired the way to Burton's Pitts and set off. Not long later she arrived at Burton's Pitts. She came up the little rise from the road and ran towards the belt of trees. She reached it to find the green sward bare. There was no sign of a caravan. Nothing moved, except the birds and the insects and a faint plume of smoke from behind a patch of briars overlooking the pool.

Mrs. Finchley walked towards the smoke and, reaching the briars, found herself looking down upon the top of a very square, close-cropped head. Joe Turnbull was sitting comfortably by the water with his float out. At regular intervals puffs of smoke went up from his pipe and his eyes had a dreamy, placid air as he stared at the red-and-white float.

"Good morning," said Mrs. Finchley, fingering the brooch in her blouse. Mr. Finchley must have moved that morning and, if this man had been fishing long, he might have seen the caravan go away and be able to help her.

Joe Turnbull appeared not to hear her.

"Good morning," Mrs. Finchley repeated, a little louder. No reply, only a quicker succession of smoke puffs.

"Good morning. Have you seen a caravan about here?"

Joe stared glassily at the float and Mrs. Finchley, after a decent interval, stamped her foot angrily and decided that the man must be deaf.

She stooped and picked a hard lump of mud from the ground. She threw it at the float and said very loudly, "Good morning."

The mud splashed alongside of the float and Joe jumped nervously. He turned and saw Mrs. Finchley standing above him and at once a look of deep reproach flooded his face.

"Pardon me, ma'am, but you ought not to do that. You brought me back from Arizona, and that's a long way to travel in a hurry. I was fighting single-handed ..." His words trailed away.

"Arizona?" Mrs. Finchley was puzzled.

"That's all right, ma'am. Just a dream," explained Joe, as though he did not care to go into the real situation.

"I'm sorry to disturb you, but I'm looking for my son and husband. They wrote to me that they were here. They've got a caravan."

"Oh, them." Joe stood up and grinned. "Yes, I know them."

"But where are they?"

"Not far off. Though it's a bit odd, I thought. However, as I came up this morning I saw them moving off. They went up the valley road. I guess they've gone up to see the old house at the top of the valley. The road doesn't go any farther than that. Then they'll be back. But it was a bit odd that they should take the caravan for such a short trip. You can walk it in ten minutes—well, maybe fifteen."

"Thank you. You're sure they'll be up there?"

"Positive. You'll be Mrs. Finchley, of course? That's a fine boy of yours. Swims like an otter."

"Thank you."

"Not at all. You'll find them up there."

He watched her set off up the valley road and then sat down and took up his rod again. A few moments later and he was stirring up trouble single-handed in Tibet against a faction which wanted to put a false Dalai Lama into power. The float bobbed and nodded in the sunlight and Joe struggled across snowy passes and knife-edged traverses dealing out death and sudden justice. And Mrs. Finchley walked up the valley road, listening to the pleasant burble of a small stream that ran alongside the road and her eyes watched a cloud of wood-pigeons flocking above the comb crests of pines on the skyline.

Three quarters of an hour later Mrs. Finchley came back. This time she used a lump of mud and a loud shout as her first manoeuvre and brought Joe back from a thrilling fight with forty Shirpahs all armed with knives against his stout bamboo stick.

"Hullo, it's you again," said Joe affably. Mrs. Finchley was a pleasanter sight than any Shirpahs and Joe liked the bright glitter in her eyes.

"I'm worried," said Mrs. Finchley, and she was pursing her lips seriously.

"What about?"

"They're not up there."

"They must be. I saw them go and they certainly haven't come back. I may go a-travelling out of the body when I'm sitting here, but I wouldn't miss that caravan coming back."

"You're sure they went that way and sure they haven't come back?"

"Positive."

"That's what I think. But I couldn't see them. I went as far as the house. I even called at the house—"

"But it's empty."

"It says it's for sale. But a man, a tall fellow, answered the door and, when I said I wanted to look around, seemed anxious to get rid of me. He said that he'd bought the house and he was sorry. He walked with me to the garden gate and saw me out on the road. I didn't get a chance to look around. But there's a big barn and various other outhouses where a caravan …"

"You mean you didn't see a sign of them? That's rummy. And I'm sure no one's bought that house. The village would know about it. It's been for sale for ages. We must look into this. Don't worry, ma'am. I'm an ex-sergeant of the Metropolitan Police. I can handle this."

"Something about that man made me very uncomfortable," said Mrs. Finchley.

"If he's up to any hanky-panky, I'll make him feel uncomfortable all right. Come along, we'll have a look into this."

"Don't you want any help? I mean, shall we go to the village and get the local constable?"

"The local constable is a prize fool," snorted Joe. "And all the help I want is contained here." He flexed his right arm and set off. Mrs. Finchley followed, considerably heartened by Joe's confidence in himself.

All the way up the valley Joe kept her entertained with accounts of his adventures and, if he forgot to make the distinction between those which occurred during his life as a policeman and those that took place during his psychic flights, it was probably because his real interest was focused on what might lie ahead.

When the house came in sight, Mrs. Finchley suggested that they should avoid attention and creep up. Joe scouted the idea.

"Frontal attack. No deception. We're on their only line of retreat. You say they had a motor car."

"There was a motor car outside the house, but I didn't say 'they', I only saw one man."

"Bound to be more than one."

They walked up the road to the barn which fronted it. Joe put his eyes to the crack between the barn doors and gave a happy exclamation.

"There's the horse and van, all right," he cried. Mrs. Finchley looked through the crack and saw the end of the caravan.

"Perhaps they're there, inside it."

"We'll see."

Joe pulled aside the doors, which were not bolted, and they entered the barn. The caravan was empty. Only Dini lay curled asleep on Robert's bunk.

"Must be in the house. We'll go out and around to the front entrance." Joe, anxious to get to grips with the mystery, stalked ahead.

Inside the house Mr. Finchley, Robert and the three men were eating. They had made a table from the packing-cases and they were all tucking into the food appreciatively. There was corned beef, pickles, vegetable salad, new bread, cheese and a large bowl of tinned peaches. Cutlery, china and food came from the caravan.

Turk poured thick tinned milk over his peaches and raised his head.

"It's nice," he said, "to meet folks like you, Mr. Finchley. You're appreciative of the difficulties under which different sections work. Any other guy might have made an awful row at being treated the way I've had to treat you. But you understand. No point in standing in front of the way another fellow has to make a living.

"But if you had tried to get in our way—it would have been just too bad for you!" There was undisguised menace in his last words.

"That's right," said Duffy, and he winked at Robert, who was watching his trencher work with genuine admiration.

"We'll have to leave 'em here, roped up while we get clear," said Hardy shortly.

"Naturally, but they understand that. Twelve hours at the most they'll be here. That gives us plenty of time to cover our tracks. And we've given them a good meal so they can last out."

"Thoughtful of us," said Duffy, and he cast a hungry eye over the bowl of peaches.

At that moment there came a knock on the door. Turk was on his feet at once. He swung round towards the window, barking over his shoulder: "Keep an eye on them, Duffy! I'll see who it is."

He looked out of the window.

"Who is it?" asked Hardy.

"That dame again and a man. What the hell do they want? I'll go and see. You keep these two in order."

Turk went out of the room, leaving the door ajar.

Duffy grinned across the table at Robert. "Be a good boy and pass them peaches. My favourite dish. Californian peaches, full of sunshine."

Robert stood up to pass the bowl of peaches. Duffy took them with a grunt. But Robert, instead of sitting down, dodged quickly round the table, and made for the door.

"Hey ! Stop him!" shouted Hardy and flung out a leg to trip Robert. The boy cleared the obstacle before Duffy could move. The next moment he was through the doorway. He went down the long hallway towards the open front door. In the doorway stood Turk, Joe Turnbull and Mrs. Finchley.

Turk was saying, "Yes, the man and the boy you describe asked my permission to leave their van in the barn and they've gone for a walk through the woods."

"Joe! Mother! Help!" Robert came sliding across the wooden floor and there was an edge of fear and panic in his voice which set Joe moving.

"That for a tale!" he shouted, and his fist cracked against Turk's jaw just as that gentleman started to turn for Robert.

Turk dropped to the floor with log-like precision and he stayed there, breathing noisily through his mouth.

Robert, who had never seen a man given a knock-out before, stared fascinated.

"Where's your father?" cried Joe.

"In there!" Robert pointed to the room door. Joe sprang forward and threw open the door.

Inside, Mr. Finchley was struggling with an enraged Duffy and a bitter, cursing Hardy, holding high above his head the packet of paintings, which Hardy had tried to snatch and make off with at the alarm.

"Dad, I'm coming!" Robert, concerned at the plight of his father, dashed forward. As he went he grabbed the bowl of peaches from the packing-case and flung bowl and contents at the two men. The bowl cracked against Duffy's head and spilt syrup and peaches over all three.

"Hell!" Duffy roared, his face a sticky mask.

"Stand by!" shouted Joe and rushed forward. It was like an avalanche moving down on a pair of flimsy chalets. He bowled Duffy and Hardy to the floor, grabbed them by the collar, lifted them, banged their heads, flung them to the ground and laughed savagely. His laugh was terminated rather sharply by a kick which Duffy dealt him as he lay on the floor. Duffy rose, his hair in rat's tails from peach syrup, and charged at Joe, and Joe, seeing that kindness would get him nowhere, stepped aside and applied more ruthless tactics. He hit Duffy on the side of the head with a swing that sent him crashing against the panelled wall to collapse into the same noisy stupor that had taken his master. Hardy sat up, removed a crushed peach from his neck-band and signified that he accepted defeat.

"Short but very sweet while it lasted," said Joe, turning to Mr. Finchley. "And now what is it all about?"

"Yes, I'd like to know that," said a voice from the doorway, and Mrs. Finchley came in accompanied by Robert, who eyed Duffy's prostrate body with wonder that shone more strongly as he looked at the magnificent Joe, ripe with the bloom of righteous battle.

Mr. Finchley went to his wife and kissed her. She grimaced. "You taste of peaches," she said.

XXVI
Which, like the end of most things, is the beginning of something else

MR. FINCHLEY, his wife and Robert sat on a grassy bank on the valley side looking down at the house in which his last adventure had taken place. The grass on which they sat was studded with tall mulleins, patches of pink centaury and bright, flaming spots of rock roses and yellow wort, and the air was thick with the scent of marjoram and thyme. Behind them the hillside was tipped with a dark fir wood from which came the rich note of pigeons.

Below them was the house. It was an Elizabethan house, its face pleasantly marked with timbers and worked plaster, the barge boards of the one gable carved into a pleasant line. Around it was clustered the barn, a few outhouses and at its side stood an enormous walnut-tree that rose high above the fine brick chimney stack. In front of its wide and pleasant windows stretched a lawn that was grown long from disuse and through whose tangle the colour of flowers marking old beds still showed. Beyond the house was an orchard, and through the orchard meandered a tiny stream that widened into a pool big enough for bathing.

As they looked down at it different thoughts filled their minds. Mr. Finchley's eye was on the barn. At very little expense it could be turned into a fine gymnasium. There might even be a reward for the recovery of the Le Nain pictures. He would know about that when Joe got back from delivering the criminals up to justice. He had taken them off, securely roped, in their own car.

Mrs. Finchley was seeing the cool, raftered rooms with warm rugs across the rich brown boards, with flowers standing on the wide window-shelves. And there was a central heating plant already installed. Electricity could be brought up the road. There were not too many rooms. Bartenden seemed a nice village from what she had seen and they were not far from Maidstone and other centres.

Robert's eye was watching the thin slip of stream. That pool, he thought, would have to be deepened and widened more so that there could be a diving board and enough room to race. Joe would help. Golly, what a man!

They got up and walked down the hill to the wide white gate which protected the short drive up to the house. On it was a red-and-white notice which read, "This house for Sale. Immediate Possession. Apply Windridge and Thrush."

"Well," said Mr. Finchley, "what do you think?"

"If it hadn't been for Turk and his pictures we should have missed it," said Robert.

"No, it wasn't that. I think it was really me who turned your luck," said Mrs. Finchley. She caught Mr. Finchley's elbow affectionately.

"Let's call it just one of those happy things," he said. "It's a house. The house, and it's going to be ours!"

He put up a hand and pulled the loose board from the gate. Then he pushed the gate open and went inside to have another look at the house—which they were soon to know so well.

THE END

Also Available

Also Available

An ebullient Mr Finchley is about to propose marriage to the lady he rescued from mishap in Book 1, when he is sent to Paris by his firm.

There he manages to upset a boat, adopt a stray orphan and get himself kidnapped. The fine tangle he gets into takes some unravelling! Only when eventually back in London does he complete his proposal of marriage.

Mr Finchley, Book 2

OUT NOW

About the Mr Finchley Series

Mr Finchley is a middle-aged solicitor's clerk who takes
a holiday for the first time in his life and finds himself in
all kinds of unexpected situations across the length and
breadth of England.

These gentle comedy adventures were a runaway success
on first publication before the Second World War, and retain a
timeless appeal today. They were serialised and dramatised for
BBC Radio, with the 1990 dramatisation regularly repeated.

Titles in the series, and further humorous works by
Victor Canning –

Mr Finchley Discovers His England

Mr Finchley Goes to Paris

Mr Finchley Takes the Road

Polycarp's Progress

Fly Away Paul

Matthew Silverman

Fountain Inn

About the Author

Victor Canning was a prolific writer throughout his career, which began young: he had sold several short stories by the age of nineteen and his first novel, *Mr Finchley Discovers His England* (1934), was published when he was twenty-three. It proved to be a runaway bestseller. Canning also wrote for children: his trilogy The Runaways was adapted for US children's television. Canning's later thrillers were darker and more complex than his earlier work and received further critical acclaim.

Note from the Publisher

To receive background material and updates on further humorous titles by Victor Canning, sign up at farragobooks.com/canning-signup